S0-BRR-531

Eyes
in the Fishbowl

Eyes
in the Fishbowl

Zilpha Keatley Snyder

Drawings by ALTON RAIBLE

AN ALADDIN BOOK
Atheneum

PUBLISHED BY ATHENEUM
COPYRIGHT © 1968 BY ZILPHA KEATLEY SNYDER
ALL RIGHTS RESERVED
PUBLISHED SIMULTANEOUSLY IN CANADA BY
MCCLELLAND & STEWART LTD.
MANUFACTURED IN THE UNITED STATES OF AMERICA BY
THE MURRAY PRINTING COMPANY,
FORGE VILLAGE, MASSACHUSETTS
ISBN 0-689-70410-0
FIRST ALADDIN EDITION

To Mother and Mom, with love

Eyes
in the Fishbowl

Chapter 1

LAST NIGHT I GOT THE IDEA TO PUT THE WHOLE THING into a song. I've been writing songs again lately, but this wasn't like the others. What I had in mind was a kind of ballad, a song story like the ancient troubadors used to make up about an important event so it would never be forgotten. I wrote the chorus first and it went like this—

The Fishbowl Song
by Dion James

Nobody's shopping at Alcott-Simpson's
The very best store in town.
Nobody's dropping by Alcott-Simpson's
Since the rumors started going around.
Strange things have been heard there,
And stranger things are seen,
And a customer fainted dead away—
In the French Room
On the Mezzanine.

3

I did that much in about fifteen minutes and it, like they say, almost wrote itself. I worked out a melody and some chords and it sounded so good that I would have called up Jerry or Brett to tell them about it right then except it was pretty late already, and a school day today.

So instead I started in on the first verse, but that's where I bogged down. It was hard to know where to start—what to put in and what to leave out. Obviously you couldn't put the whole thing into two or three verses. I started going over it, trying to get some ideas —and the first thing I knew I'd gone back to the very beginning.

The real beginning—at least for the store and the people in it—must have been a little less than a year ago, around the time I first saw Sara. But for me the beginning went back to a long time before that. In a way, my part in the whole thing started about six years ago on the day I first discovered Alcott-Simpson's. I was eight or nine years old at the time, and had just started to shine shoes on the corner of Palm and Eighth Avenue. Of course, it was only natural that it made a big impression on me when I first saw it. When I was eight years old—for various reasons having to do with my health and family situation—I'd hardly ever been outside my own neighborhood. Up until the day when José, who runs the flower stand on the corner of Palm and Eighth, found me being chased up an alley by some other shoeshine boys whose territory I'd wandered into, I'd never really been uptown; and my idea of a department store was Barney's Bargain Center two blocks from our house. But then José said I could set up shop right outside his flower stand where he could look out for me, so I went with him to Palm and Eighth and there it was—a whole block of marble pillars, crystal chandeliers and gilded wood. I mean, it was like I was Aladdin and the genii had just plopped me down in the middle of an enchanted palace.

I was only in the store a few minutes that first time, but I can still remember how it was. For one thing, it was right then, that first time, that I got that feeling of walking into a separate world. After the ordinary winter world outside, dirty gray with a cold wet wind, inside Alcott-Simpson's was like being on a different planet. The warmth was clean and smooth and loaded with something that was too high class to be called a smell. As a matter of fact, I was still standing just inside the door trying to sort out the smell—I'd gotten about as far as new cloth and leather and perfume and dollar bills—when somebody came along and invited me out. From then on, I was always prowling around Alcott-Simpson's—and being invited out from time to time.

My main enemy was Mr. Priestly, who was in charge of the store detectives. It's easy to see why he didn't appreciate me hanging around Alcott-Simpson's looking the way I used to until a couple of years ago.

If you can picture a bundle from the Good-Will's trash bin, with a mop of curly hair, a bad limp and dragging a big shoeshine kit, you'll know what I must have looked like. It couldn't have been good for the Alcott-Simpson image. But even after I changed a lot, and started dressing better, Priestly and his henchmen didn't much like having me around, because by then they were convinced that I was a shoplifter.

They were dead wrong about that, because I never took anything from Alcott-Simpson's that I didn't pay for. I'm not sure why exactly. It was no big moral thing with me, and I certainly had chances. Maybe it was just that I've never liked taking risks—or maybe it had something to do with the way I felt about the store. It would almost have been like stealing from myself. Anyway, I didn't. But Priestly was hard to convince, and two or three times he had me taken upstairs and searched. He always seemed puzzled when he didn't find anything on me, and he probably thought I'd very cleverly gotten rid of the loot somehow. I guess he just couldn't figure out why else a kid like me would hang around a big department store so much. I had my reasons, but I couldn't have explained them, even if I'd wanted to.

Of course, one reason was probably just that it was so handy. For a few years I shined shoes right outside the big glass and bronze doors of the east entrance, and from time to time I'd just stroll in—to get warm in bad weather, to see what was new, or just to catch up on the latest store gossip with a few friends I'd made among the clerks. Then when I began to outgrow the shoeshine business a couple of years ago, most of the new jobs I found were pretty much in the same area. Usually in the city a guy is pretty much out of luck from the time he outgrows the shoeshine and paperboy businesses, until he's sixteen and can be put on a payroll. But I'd made a lot of contacts while I was shining shoes, and I managed to do all right. Most of my jobs were pickup things that I'd developed into a regular schedule. I ran errands, washed display cases, cleaned up and did occasional stock room jobs—mostly in the smaller shops on Palm Street. Also, I still kept my shoeshine stuff at the flower stand, and even though I didn't shine shoes on the street anymore, I kept a few old well-paying customers who liked to have me come up to their offices to give them a shine. That whole area, around Eighth and Palm was kind of my territory and Alcott-Simpson's was right in the middle of it—in a lot of ways. I guess that's why, when all the trouble started at the store, I was right in the middle of that, too.

I think the trouble probably started early in January, and it was around the middle of the month that I first saw Sara. Before that time I *had* heard a rumor or two, but nothing definite; and I don't think the rumors were on my mind at all on that particular afternoon. If I had any special reason for walking through Alcott-Simpson's that day, it must have been partly that I wanted to see what the decorating theme was for the after Christmas sales. Alcott-Simpson's was practically famous for its display themes. But mostly I just wanted to get in out of the cold for a minute. Outside it was doing the Winter-Wonderland bit for real, and my jacket wasn't exactly mink, if you know what I mean.

The first thing I did was to drift over to a bench I knew about near the east entrance and sit down. The bench was in a little alcove behind Ladies Gloves where customers were supposed to get out of raincoats and boots and stuff in bad weather. Mrs. Bell, who worked in Ladies Gloves, knew me. She was a typical Alcott-Simpson clerk, a shell of perfect dignity hiding a heart of pure nothing, but she was friendly enough to warn me if Priestly or one of his boys were heading my way; so I used the bench behind Ladies Gloves quite a bit. Quite a few times I'd even curled up there and gone to sleep—when I'd been particularly tired and cold. But it was late that day and I only meant to stay there until I got warm and then go on home. I'd only been sitting there for about a minute though when I began to notice something.

I don't know exactly what it was I noticed. I don't remember seeing anything the least bit unusual. I didn't hear anything either, at least nothing definite— but maybe it did have something to do with hearing. It was as if the low hum of movement and conversation that you can always hear in a big place like that was on

8

a different key, higher and faster, like the tuning was a little bit off. I was beginning to get the feeling that something was up, so instead of going on home I dropped in behind two fat ladies with a lot of packages and strolled down the aisle towards Cosmetics. I had a good friend in Cosmetics.

Madame Stregovitch lived near us in the Cathedral Street district, and she had worked at Alcott-Simpson's for years and years. I don't know why everybody called her Madame instead of Mrs., except that you just couldn't imagine calling her anything else. It went with her accent, and her personality, which was very positive. She'd been at Alcott-Simpson's so long that a lot of the important customers were convinced they couldn't get along without her, and for that reason she could do just about as she pleased. But she was the only one. Most of the clerks at Alcott-Simpson's wouldn't have sneezed without asking permission.

It's a funny thing, but when I first started hanging around, I used to think the Alcott clerks were something special. The way they dressed and acted, you got the feeling that they were all a bunch of eccentric aristocrats who were just working for the fun of it. You had to be around for a long time to find out what most of them were really like. Basically, most of them were a scared bunch of underpaid apple-polishers, who put up with all sorts of bullying just so they could go on associating with all that mink and money. At least, I guess that's the reason they did it. You'd have to have some sort of hang-up to make you go on putting up with a lot of those A-S big shots and all the rules and regulations, the way the clerks at Alcott's did.

All except Madame Stregovitch. If there was any bullying going on around her, she was right in there doing her share of it. She even ordered her Rolls-Royce-type customers around, and nobody ever complained. They wouldn't dare. She affected everybody that way. It was just something about her that you couldn't exactly put your finger on.

When I got to Cosmetics that day, Madame was busy with a customer; but she saw me and arched an eyebrow in my direction. Madame's face was dark and sharp and full of bony edges. She almost never smiled, and her mouth hardly seemed to move even when she talked; but her eyes and eyebrows had a large vocabulary all by themselves. Right at the moment she was busy rubbing a drop of something on the cheek of a great big woman with a long nose, saggy eyes and a short brown fur—probably a beaver. (The coat I mean, anyone who hangs around Alcott-Simpson's can't help getting to know a lot about furs.)

"You see, my dear," Madame was saying in the soothing hum that she always used on customers, "how it brings out your delicate coloring." Madame doesn't have much of a foreign accent, but she clips off her words and arranges them a little differently than most people.

In a few minutes the big woman went away with a

dazed smile and a whole box of make-up stuff, and Madame came over to where I was waiting.

"Dion," she said, "I have missed you. You have not been to see me since Christmas. You have not been sick?"

"No," I said. "I've been around. I just haven't been coming in much. Not enough business the first of January. Nobody to hide behind when old Priestly makes his rounds."

"Mr. Priestly, pah!" Madame Stregovitch said, shrugging her shoulders and tilting her eyebrows to a disgusted angle. "He has greater things to worry about these days than one harmless boy. You must come and see me, as always. In the midst of so much falseness, one's eyes are gladdened by the sight of such glorious youth."

Actually, Madame Stregovitch wasn't as weird as she sounded sometimes. It's just that she got started raving about how good-looking I was, way back when I first used to visit her, when I was a skinny little crippled kid. Of course, I really knew, even then, that she was only trying to make me feel good, but I got a kick out of it anyway. Eventually it was just a routine we went through.

"Sure," I said, "me and Mr. America. As a matter of fact, I'm thinking of going into business. Like— EYES GLADDENED. TWO FOR THE PRICE OF ONE! It ought to beat shining shoes." I usually do all right wising-off around adults. It's only around kids my own

11

age that I get tongue-tied.

Madame Stregovitch just narrowed her eyes and nodded slowly. She always appreciated a joke that way. We talked for a few minutes more about various things and, when I started saying I'd better go, she got something out from under the counter and gave it to me.

When I first knew Madame, she used to work in Alcott's Sweet Shop, and we got in the habit of her always keeping something for me under the counter. In those days it was usually a piece of fudge or a gumdrop. But this time it looked like a few pages from a newspaper. "It is for your collection," she said. "I've been saving it for you since before Christmas."

I thanked her and started to unfold the paper, but just about then I caught a glimpse of a familiar face. It was one of the store detectives, a musclebound character named Rogers. He was always cruising around the store looking as neat and chummy as a penguin, but I'd discovered a long time before that he could lose his Alcott-Simpson manner in a hurry, when he was sure nobody important was looking. A couple of times when I was younger he'd escorted me out through one of the storerooms and sort of bounced me off a few walls along the way. I wasn't really afraid of him. I had learned not to allow myself to be taken out through a storeroom, without putting up a fuss—a fuss is something that all of Priestly's henchmen were trained to avoid at all costs. But Rogers was looking particularly determined, and I wasn't in the mood for an argument. So I nodded to Madame, tucked the paper into my pocket and started for the door.

But Rogers had a head start on me and he was coming as fast as humanly possible for someone who was supposed to pretend to be just another shopper. He was already past the escalator and shopping up a storm right through the middle of the Knit Shop. I saw right away that he was going to cut me off unless I broke into a run, and of course I wasn't about to do that. Alcott-Simpson's is the kind of place where no one would think of running unless his life depended on it; and personally, I probably wouldn't run if it did —because of my crummy limp. I'd just about resigned myself to an unpleasant discussion—at the very least— with old Rogers, when all of a sudden I realized he was after somebody else.

It was a girl. When I first saw her, she was looking back over her shoulder at Rogers and I couldn't see her face; but from what I could see, she was a typical Alcott customer. At least she was dressed like one. She was wearing high narrow boots, a kind of sleeveless thing of orangish suede and a cashmere sweater; all very latest fashion and expensive-looking. Her hair was long and straight and very black.

I'd hardly had time to wonder why on earth Rogers should be after her when she brushed past me in the aisle, so close I could have reached out and touched her—and I noticed something that really gave me a jolt. She was wearing the sweater just hanging over her shoulders, and on the empty sleeve there was a cardboard tag. It was an Alcott-Simpson price tag!

That could only mean one thing—and it was right then that I remembered the rumor I'd heard a few days before. José, at the flower stand, had told me that he'd heard from one of the Alcott janitors that there was a bunch of plainclothesmen hanging around the store, and that there was talk about some kind of gang of thieves and vandals.

As the girl turned the corner at the end of the next counter, she looked back at Rogers again, and I got my first real look at her face. It wasn't at all what I expected. I can't exactly explain why it was a shock, but it was. Actually, I don't know what kind of face I expected on a shoplifter, but I knew right away that this wasn't it.

She was quite young, for one thing. Maybe about my age, or even younger. And her skin was dark—not darker than a beach tan, maybe, but with a different shade to it, like a shadow of purple under the brown. But most of all I noticed her eyes. They were very big and dark—black, but clear and deep—like the night must be to a cat. For just a second she looked right at me and smiled like she thought the whole thing was a joke, and then she hurried on.

On the other side of Hosiery she turned quickly to the left, and I almost yelled at her to go the other way. If she had turned to the right, she just might have made it to the Palm Street entrance in time; but the way she was headed, she was walking right into a trap. Behind the hosiery counter there was only a short corridor that led to some storerooms, and the doors were always kept locked.

But I didn't yell, and the girl disappeared into the corridor and a few seconds later Rogers followed. I knew he had her then, and I could just imagine the smug look on his slick face. But the girl was obviously a thief all right, and that was her problem. There was no reason for me to get involved. I had plenty of troubles of my own. I told myself that the thing for me to do was to turn around and cut out, while Rogers was occupied. But I didn't, and when I reached the end of the hosiery counter, I met the great detective on his way back—all by himself. Behind him the short corridor was empty. The girl seemed to have completely disappeared.

It occurred to me that maybe one of the storeroom doors had been unlocked after all. But that didn't explain why Rogers came back so quickly, or the look on his face. I got a good look at him as he came back past me, without even glancing my way. His eyes were wide open but without any focus, like a sleepwalker looking at his dream.

Out on the sidewalk the wind was colder than ever and full of freezing mist. As soon as I picked up my stuff from José, I turned up the collar of my jacket and headed south towards Cathedral Street. I kept thinking about the girl on the way home.

Chapter 2

OUR HOUSE IS AN OLD VICTORIAN BROWNSHINGLE IN the Cathedral Street district. Matt Ralston, who studies sociology and lives in our attic, says the whole district is in what is called a "changing neighborhood," but I don't know what that means, because what neighborhood isn't? I mean, as long as there's people in it? But as far as our street is concerned, the change seems to be towards more kids on the sidewalks and less paint on the houses. And our house is no exception.

It must have been quite the thing when my dad's family built it, but it's pretty beat up now, and getting worse all the time. It has so many missing or crooked shingles that it looks like a moulting chicken, and the yard is bare except for clumps of mangy grass and broken toys and an iron pole with a sign that says James Music School—Second Floor. The toys belong to the Grovers who live on the first floor, and James is my father.

My dad is Arnold Valentine James, music teacher and neighborhood philosopher, known as Val to his many friends and students. He is also sometimes known as Prince Val. The "Prince" is as in "he's a Prince of a guy." He is also the world's worst business man and the most famous soft touch in this part of town. He really is a great music teacher, but he doesn't charge enough to make people think he's any good, and half the time he doesn't collect even what he does charge. He's always letting people give him some worthless piece of junk instead of money. As a matter of fact, when I was younger, I used to wonder sometimes if that was how he got me. I couldn't remember my mother and I'd never heard much about her, so it occurred to me that maybe somebody with kids to spare got a little behind on his lesson payments and talked my dad into a trade. It wouldn't be the first time he got the worst of a deal.

Anyway, Dad and I live on only the second floor of the old house, now. The downstairs is rented to this family with three noisy little kids, and three university students live in the attic. The Grovers pay their rent most of the time, but the college guys only paid for four months last year; and so far this year they're still working on November—on the installment plan. Anybody but my dad would have kicked them all out a long time ago.

And besides not paying their rent, the whole bunch of them, at least the students and the kids, spend half their time in our apartment. The students come down to get away from the cold—there's not much heat in the attic; and the kids come up to get away from their mother who is the nervous type.

That day, the first day I saw Sara, was typical. When I got home, there were seven people, two cats and a dog cluttering up our apartment. My dad and Matt, the sociology student, were playing chess on the kitchen table. Phil and Duncan, the other two so-called collegians, were sitting in front of the fireplace playing a banjo and a guitar; two of the Grover kids were tearing around shooting each other with cap pistols; and in the studio somebody was trying to play a march on the piano. Tiger, the Grover's mutt, was leaning against the kitchen door and whining because somebody had just fed our cats, Prudence and Charity, and they wouldn't let him have any. Everybody was suspiciously glad to see me.

"Dion! Welcome home."

"Here's Dion."

"It's Dion."

"Hey look. It's the teen-age tycoon of Palm Street."

I looked around and just as I thought—even though it was almost six o'clock, there wasn't a sign of anything to eat around the place; unless you wanted to count the cat food. That probably meant it was up to me if there was going to be any dinner.

"Look Dad," I said, "I thought you were going

to collect from the Clements for sure, today."

"I tried, Dion. I went over there. But they've had a lot of illness——"

I slammed out of the room without waiting to hear the rest. It was a very old story. Every now and then towards the end of the month, I had to chip in with some of my money to buy stuff for dinner—or else go hungry. I didn't mind so much for Dad and me, but when it included everybody in the neighborhood who happened to be broke, it burned me up. Strictly speaking, it was usually just one or more of the guys from upstairs—but not always. My Dad would invite a perfect stranger with six inch fangs and three eyes up for dinner if he found him on the corner looking like he needed a square meal.

Out in the hall I let off a little steam by chasing the Grover kids and Tiger downstairs. The noise level went down several decibels right away. The kid in the studio kept forgetting to flat the same note. It was enough to drive you out of your skull, so I went in and chased him home, too. He wasn't there for a lesson anyway. My dad lets several neighborhood kids who don't have their own pianos at home come over to practice whenever they feel like it. Prudence and Charity weren't making any noise, but they'd finished their cat food so I threw them out, too—just for a finishing touch. By then I was feeling better so I went back into the kitchen.

"Look, Di," Matt said. (If you can picture Abraham Lincoln with a curly blond beard, you've got Matt to a T.) "We have some spaghetti and a fairly youthful head of lettuce upstairs. If you could chip in enough for some odds and ends for a meat sauce, et-cetera, we'd be in business. And I'll finance a real feast next week when my check comes."

"Sure you will," I said. "If you don't find some girl to spend it on first."

"Not a chance. I've reformed." He grinned at me coaxingly. "I'll shop, and we'll make Phil and Dunc do the dirty work."

I weakened. I was tired and hungry, and Phil really was a good cook. So I handed over a couple of dollars and went in my room to rest and wait for dinner. I kicked off my shoes and flopped down on the bed. My room is way at the back of our floor. It's little and dark, but I keep it sort of neat and peaceful looking, and no one ever goes in there but me. I'd been saving money for over a year to buy a Danish modern desk like one I saw at Alcott-Simpson's, but I still needed about thirty dollars. It was an executive type desk, big and solid looking, and long enough to fill up all one end of my room. I'd spent a lot of time lying there picturing how great it would look, right at the end of my bed—big and smooth and shiny; and I couldn't help thinking that it might already be there if I didn't have to feed so many scrounging renters.

But thinking of Alcott-Simpson's reminded me of Rogers and the girl, and I went over that whole thing

21

again. But no matter how I looked at it, it just didn't make much sense. About the only explanation I could come up with was that the girl had unlocked the storeroom door earlier, or else someone did it for her. But even that didn't explain why Rogers didn't go on into the storeroom after her. Finally, I'd gone over it so much that I was beginning to think in circles, so I decided to think about something else. That was when I remembered about the papers that Madame Stregovitch had given me.

It was a few pages from the magazine section of the Sunday *Times*, with an article about Alcott-Simpson's. A long time ago I'd started a scrapbook about the store, and of course I'd told Madame about it. Actually it had been quite a while since I'd added anything to the book, but since Madame had gone to the trouble to save it for me, I decided to tape it in. So I got the book out of my closet and opened it to the first empty page.

It was one of those five-and-dime store scrapbooks with the picture of a collie dog's head stamped on the front. Inside, there were no pictures on the first page —only some big careful printing that said: ALCOTT-SIMPSON'S THE GREATEST STORE ON EARTH—by Dion James. It was pretty stupid and childish, but I'd started it when I was only eight. After the fancy title page there were dozens of pages of pictures—some with corny comments written under them in green ink. They were mostly newspaper pictures, like a spread the *Times* did when Alcott's opened the remodeled mezzanine; plus some advertisements that I happened to think were particularly interesting. There was a magazine story that came out when the store had a big fiftieth anniversary and some nice slicks of display windows that Madame got for me from the art department. It was all put together very carefully and neatly and I could remember how much time I used to spend working on it or just looking over the pictures.

Actually, a lot of kids make scrapbooks—particularly a certain type of kid, like I was, who gets a kick out of saving and organizing stuff. The only difference is that most kids make books about airplanes or sports heroes or that kind of thing; I just happened to make one about a store. It's not as if Alcott-Simpson's was just any big city department store. I've been around quite a bit in the last few years and I've seen a lot more than I had when I was eight years old; and there just wasn't anything anywhere quite like it. It seems the original Alcott and Simpson were a couple of old millionaires who decided to build the world's most beautiful and luxurious commercial palace. The ground floor was divided into a lot of fancy little shops connected by a walk called The Mall. Then in the center there was a kind of indoor garden with a fountain and statues. The building covered an entire block and I used to think there wasn't anything in the world, worth having, that you couldn't buy there. After I'd been around for a while and looked at everything, I think

that impressed me even more than the building itself
—how many things you could buy there. Just about
anything you could possibly want from diamond rings
to motorcycles. Everybody who saw it for the first time
was kind of overwhelmed, so you can imagine what it
did for a kid who'd never had anything that cost more
than five bucks—except for operations. As a matter of
fact, I even used to dream about it.

It wasn't a dream, exactly. That is, I wasn't exactly
asleep. It was that half-awake kind of dream—awake
enough to start it on purpose, but near enough asleep
not to know where it's going. It usually started out
about how eight-year-old Dion James, shoeshine boy,
had inherited the fabulous Alcott-Simpson department
store from some kind old gentleman. Sometimes I
thought it all out, how I'd done this old gentleman a
favor, like pushing him out from in front of a bus, so
he put it all down in his will about the whole store and
everything in it going to me when he died. In my
dream I never operated the store. I mean, I never sold
anything. I just owned it and sort of lived in it. Sometimes, I brought in all my special friends and gave
them stuff, like a new seven-foot Steinway grand for
my father; but other times I was just there in the store
all by myself, looking around and playing with the toys
and stuff like that.

Of course, that was all in the past. I'd pretty much
outgrown the daydreams along with scrapbooks. But I
couldn't help being interested in the article that Ma-

dame Stregovitch had been saving for me. It really belonged in my scrapbook—it was so—kind of typical of Alcott-Simpson's. It was a feature article on some special luxury gifts that the store had been selling for the Christmas season.

The article started off humorously about how Alcott-Simpson's had opened a special department for people who wanted to buy a gift for the "Friend Who Has Everything" or even for the "Friend You Want to Flatter by Pretending to Think He Has Everything." There was a list of very expensive, very kookie gifts, and colored photographs of a few of the most spectacular. There were things like a diamond studded thimble, a solid gold toothbrush and a silver-mink bathmat. The last page had a big picture of the craziest of all, a mink-lined fishbowl.

That's what they called it, but of course, it wasn't meant for real fish. Some little golden fish and some imitation water plants were imbedded right in the glass walls of the bowl, and because the glass was thick and wavy, they were supposed to seem to be moving. You couldn't tell it from the outside at all; but if you looked in the top, you could see that the inside of the bowl really was lined with fur. The blurb under the picture called it a conversation piece and said that it cost seventy-five dollars.

I was starting to cut out the picture and thinking you'd have to be pretty desperate for something to talk about to buy a thing like that, when suddenly I saw this weird thing. Right in the center of the fishbowl there was a pair of eyes. The eyes were shadowy—but clear enough so I knew I couldn't be imagining them. I stared for a minute, and the eyes seemed to stare right back, vague and dim and sad-looking. And then suddenly I realized what I was seeing. The eyes were part of something on the other side of the paper.

I turned the page over and, sure enough, right on the back was a picture of a girl with great big eyes and stringy dark hair. When I had started to cut out the picture, I'd held it up so that the light from my lamp was right behind it and it made the eyes seem to come right through. I'd just had time to notice that it was a part of an article about some foreign country, when I heard Phil yelling at me that the spaghetti was ready.

I taped it into the scrapbook in a hurry—and that was that.

I don't think I thought much more about it then, but I do remember feeling more relieved than seemed to make sense under the circumstances. I mean, what other reason could there be for a pair of eyes in the midst of a mink-lined fish bowl?

Chapter 3

I STARTED OUT DINNER THAT NIGHT NOT SPEAKING TO my father. I was pretty burned up at him, not that there was anything particularly unusual about that. It seemed like I spent half the time not speaking to him, not that it ever did any good. As a matter of fact, I doubt if he even noticed most of the time. At least, if he did he was careful not to make an issue of it. That's one of his peculiarities. I doubt if he has ever made an issue out of anything in his life.

My dad is tall and blond, and if he weren't so un-warlike he'd look a lot like an old Viking warrior—and not a whole lot better groomed either. He's been kind of a neighborhood landmark in the Cathedral Street district for years and years. As a matter of fact, he was born right here in this house way back when this was a fashionable part of town; and he's always lived right here, except for some years he spent in Europe, study-ing music and drifting around, when he was young. His father was a professor at the university, and Dad still has some friends on the faculty. Actually, he has friends all over everywhere, but most of his students come from our neighborhood—and that's part of the problem. Nobody in our neighborhood has much money.

Just that morning before I left for school Dad and I had had a talk about finances; and he'd absolutely promised that he was going to collect some of the money that his students owed him. It was obvious what had happened. As usual, he'd listened to some sob stories and let himself be talked out of collecting. There was almost nothing he did that frustrated me more.

So, for a while I just stared at my plate and shoveled up the spaghetti, but before too long I had to thaw a little. For one thing the spaghetti sauce was really good, and for another our kitchen is a great place to eat dinner on a cold January night. It used to be the master bedroom once, when the house was a one family affair, so it has a big fireplace and a nice comfortable atmosphere. Besides, Phil and Duncan were clowning around as usual, and keeping a straight face got to be too much of an effort. Those two could make a corpse laugh.

Phil and Dunc came from the same little town somewhere out in the boondocks, and I guess they've been friends since they were practically babies. Their families don't have much money, so they're working their way through college by scholarships and odd jobs, and scrounging—like they do off my father. They're both nineteen years old and in their second year at the university; but they're not studying the same things. Dunc is taking art courses, and I'm not sure what Phil is doing. I asked him once, and he said he was studying to be rich. But as far as I can see, they both spend most of their time thinking up things to laugh at. That night they were doing something they called nationalistic spaghetti eating.

The way it worked, they took turns acting out how someone from a particular country would eat spaghetti and the rest of us were supposed to guess what nationality. First, Phil was a super-polite Englishman, whose monocle kept falling out and getting lost in the spaghetti. Then Dunc did a Chinese trying to eat spaghetti with chopsticks. Next Phil chopped up some spaghetti, mashed it all to pieces and finally put his plate on the floor and pretended to march back and forth across it. That was supposed to be a German. Another one was the efficient American trying to tie all the pieces of spaghetti together end to end so he could suck up the whole plate without stopping. It was all pretty corny, but the way Phil and Dunc throw themselves into a thing like that—you just can't help laughing. I had forgotten all about being mad, until Dad brought out the doughnuts.

When the spaghetti was all gone, my father got up and went over to this great big bread box we have and opened it up, and it was absolutely packed full of doughnuts. There must have been six or eight dozen—a lot more than we could possibly eat before they spoiled. All of a sudden I knew exactly where they came from.

Mr. Clements, who just happens to have two kids who take piano from Dad, and who just happens to owe us more money than anybody else, just happens to work at a big doughnut factory. And Joannie Clements just happened to tell me once that her father gets to take home any doughnuts that get a little old before anyone buys them.

Dad put about a dozen doughnuts on a plate and passed it around the table. I could tell that he was trying to keep from catching my eye, so at last I said, "How much did you knock off for this junk?"

Dad smiled in that vague way of his. "Just a little," he said. "But I did tell Dan that we might be able to use a few more from time to time."

That did it. I stood up and threw my half-eaten doughnut at Prudence, who was sitting in front of the fireplace washing her feet. I missed, but it was close enough to make her jump. She gave me a dirty look and then she sniffed at the doughnut, looked disgusted, and went back to washing her feet. Even the cat wouldn't eat them. "Good Lord, Dad," I said. "You don't even *like* doughnuts!" And I stormed out of the kitchen and back to my room.

That was the way it had been between my father and me for a year or two. Before that we got along pretty well. As a matter of fact, when I was a real little kid I used to think he was just about perfect. Of course, he was as easygoing with me as he is with everybody, and at that age you don't notice much else. He almost never got mad or ordered me around, but I wasn't so awfully spoiled, either. I think I sort of had the feeling that he expected me to act like some kind of small-sized adult and I just couldn't bear to let him down. He seems to have that effect on the little kids he teaches, too. It's only older people who take advantage of people like him.

Anyway, when I was little we used to have a lot of good times. I was only four when I had polio, and after that there were three operations a year or two apart, so I never did go to elementary school very regularly. I was home in bed or in a wheel chair a lot, and having the house always full of people seemed like a great thing to me, then. There were my Dad's students and his musician friends and his neighborhood friends and his chess friends and his political-enemy friends—not to mention the ones who showed up regularly just for a square meal or for someone to listen to their troubles. People were always drifting in for an hour or a day—or even a month or two if they happened to feel like it. Not many of them were kids, but in those days that didn't matter very much. There was always a lot of music going on, and I was right in the middle of it all the time. Dad had started me on the violin when I was almost a baby, and I took up the guitar, too, a few years later. When I was about six, I started thinking up lyrics and tunes to go with them, and Dad would write them down. All his friends were always carrying on about what a lot of talent I had.

That part of my life was okay in those days—school was the bad part. During the spells, in between operations, when I was well enough to go to Lincoln Elementary, I began to realize that I didn't exactly fit in. I couldn't play any sports, which was terribly important at Lincoln, and I didn't know how to make the right kind of conversation. And besides that I didn't dress right. A lot of the time Dad wouldn't even notice my clothes, and I'd go for days in outgrown, worn-out stuff. Then he'd decide to dress me all up in some out-of-date sissy suit that some old family friend had donated, and that was even worse. It got so I hated to go to school; and the more I hated it, the worse it got. But I never blamed anyone. Little kids are apt to be pretty fatalistic. You just take what comes, and it doesn't even occur to you to wonder if things are the way they ought to be or if you could do anything to make them better. It was in between my second and third operation that I started shining shoes and hanging around Alcott-Simpson's, and not too long after that I began to quit just accepting things and started making plans for the future—all sort of plans.

That night, after the doughnut episode, I shut myself in my room again and started in on my homework. I'd nearly finished my English assignment when there

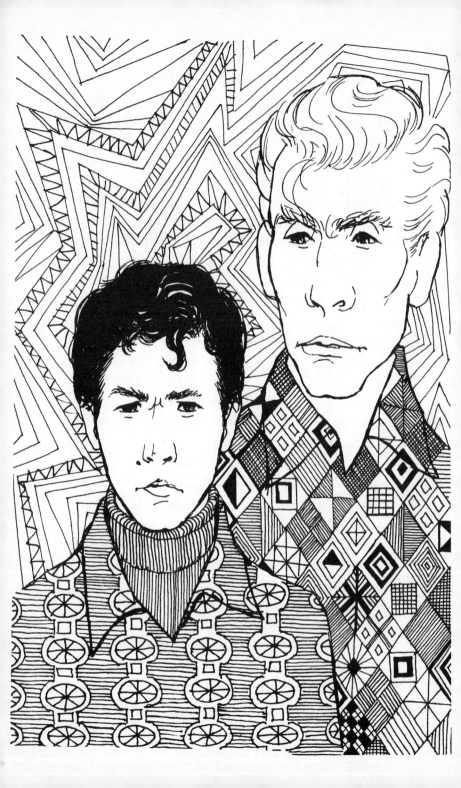

was a knock on the door. I didn't even answer at first, but then I heard Matt's voice saying, "Di, it's Matt. Let me in."

Matt is a graduate student and he's older than Phil and Dunc—around twenty-three or four. He's been staying with us off and on for years. But being around for a few years doesn't really make him part of the family—even though he acts like he thinks he is at times. When I opened the door that night, he came on real casual-like, but I knew him too well to be fooled. I could tell he had something on his mind. He stretched out on my bed with his heels up on the footboard and started out like he'd just come to chat.

"How's it going?" he asked, nodding at my homework.

"Okay," I said. "It's just English. I got my algebra done in study hall." Sometimes Matt helped me out with my algebra when I hit a snag. I'm not too good at that sort of thing, and Dad's not much better.

Matt asked some more questions about the English assignment and we kicked that around for a while, but I had the feeling that he was looking for an opening for something in particular. Finally he looked around my room and said, "Very cozy. Sure is a nice pad, you've got here."

"Nothing special," I said. "It just looks good in contrast to the rest of the house."

Matt didn't say anything for a minute. Then he asked, "What's the matter with the rest of the house?"

"Oh, not a thing," I said. "If you like living in a disaster area."

Matt just raised one of his curly blond eyebrows at me and said, "Hmmm."

"Hmmm?" I asked. "Like, hmmm—as in what?" The way I said it was kind of sharp and sarcastic, because I was thinking to myself, "Here we go again with the 'big-brother' bit." Matt seems to think that just because he's known Dad and me for such a long time it gives him the right to tell me what to do. It always makes me angry, but at the same time I think I kind of like it—maybe because nobody else ever tries to tell me what to do very much and it sort of makes you feel somebody cares. Anyway, whenever Matt starts preaching I always get this, "Oh boy! Am I going to get mad this time." feeling.

Matt just grinned. "Hmmm as in—so that's it. So that's what's behind all this not-so-happily-ever-after-bit. You may not have noticed it, but lately you've been operating as if you were trying to set the whole togetherness program back by about one hundred years."

"I don't know what you're talking about," I said very coldly. And I didn't either, at least not entirely.

Matt stopped grinning. "All right," he said. "I'll draw you a picture. I happen to think you have a very nice old man, and I don't think much of the way you've been treating him."

"You're sure someone to talk," I said, and I was so

mad I couldn't keep my voice from wobbling. "At least I don't owe him three hundred dollars rent."

Matt nodded. "Right you are," he said, "you don't, and I do. However, there's nothing I can do about that right now except move out, and I don't think that would make matters any better for anybody. And, believe me Di, I *am* going to pay him back, and with interest. Money's a lot easier to pay back than some other things."

I walked over to the window and stood looking out at the brick wall two feet away across the air vent. "You can leave anytime," I said.

But he just sat there on the edge of my bed. He sat there and I stood there and looked out the window and waited, and finally he started talking again. "Look Di. I know how you feel."

That really burned me. I knew enough about Matt to know that he couldn't have a clue about how I felt. His father was a rich doctor and he'd been brought up with servants and everything. His folks were mad at him right at the moment because he wouldn't live like they wanted him to and study to be a doctor like his father. But he sure as hell *didn't* know what it was like to grow up in a sort of neighborhood soup kitchen and have to shine shoes so that you could have the kind of things most kids have handed to them on a silver platter.

"A lot of people want the kinds of things you're wanting." Matt went on. "As a matter of fact, a whole

37

lot of people never discover there's anything else in life to want. So I'm sure not going to knock you for it. It's just that I don't think you're appreciating what a rare bird your father really is."

Suddenly I wasn't so mad anymore. I came over and sat down. "I know it," I said. "I know what he's like. But you can't count on him for anything. And it isn't as if he couldn't. He could get a steady job teaching at a high school or even a college if he wanted to. But he just likes it here. He likes it where he can go around looking as if he's slept in his suit all the time and nobody cares. I don't know what's wrong with him. Why isn't he more like—other people?"

Matt rubbed his beard. "I don't know, Di. I don't know why he's the way he is. I suppose it's probably some ignoble human reason, just like the ones that bug all the rest of us. It's just that his kind of reaction is in considerably shorter supply than most." He grinned at me. "Let's just say he's a natural born lame-duck hunter, and Cathedral Street just happens to be one of the best lame-duck covers in this part of the country."

Matt's crooked sorrowful grin can cool just about anybody. I didn't really mean to, but I smiled, too. "Yeah," I said. "That's for sure."

"And personally," Matt said, getting ready to go out the door, "personally, I feel pretty lucky to be one of your father's walking wounded."

I laughed. "I know what you mean. But you and Phil and Dunc aren't walking wounded."

"Sure I am. The lamest of the lame. I don't know about Phil and Dunc, though. They have their problems all right, but as far as I can see most of them are spelled Y O U T H."

"You're always talking like that—like you were about a hundred years older than Phil and Dunc."

"I am," Matt said. "I am. That's another myth this country believes in—that chronological age has anything to do with how old you are. Phil and Dunc aren't just young, they are young-young. I was older than that before I started kindergarten." Matt went out the door and stuck his head back in. "And so were you," he said.

I knocked off the rest of the English assignment and sat there for a while staring at nothing. I kept thinking about what Matt had said. It was true all right, particularly about the lame-ducks. People with serious problems just seemed to take one look at my father and say, "This is it!"

It hadn't occurred to me before, but I suddenly realized that that was what my mother must have been. I really didn't know too much about her or what her problems were, because Dad never seemed to want to talk about it; but from the little he had told me, I could imagine the whole story. She had been just another one of his lame-ducks, only she had married him; but when she found out he couldn't really help her very much, she walked out. And she left me behind, and I turned out to be the biggest lame-duck of all.

All of a sudden I was mad again, for some reason. All the time I was getting ready for bed I was fuming, throwing things around and slamming them down. In the bathroom, I kicked some dirty towels that were lying on the floor clear out into the hall. Then I clumped back to my room limping hard—I really don't *have* to limp at all anymore, except when I run. And after I was in bed I stared into the darkness, waiting angrily, as if sleep were somebody who had promised to be on time and then wasn't.

Chapter 4

EVEN THOUGH I LAY AWAKE FUMING FOR A LONG time, I got up very early the next morning. As a matter of fact I got up early nearly every week day so I could spend an hour or so on my various jobs before I went to school. I had certain places I was expected on certain mornings, and I always showed up. I had to. Most of my jobs were the kinds of things that the people who hired me could have done themselves or gotten along without, if they'd wanted to. So all I had to do was miss a few times and they'd get out of the habit of leaving it for me. Like, for instance, every Monday and Thursday mornings I swept out the workroom at Jayne Anne's Hat Shop and carried all the trash out to the alley. The Hat Shop was too small to hire a janitor, and Jayne Anne hated sweeping out—and I was always handy, so she left it for me. But she really had plenty of time to do it herself if she'd felt like it.

Anyway, it was three, four days later, the next Monday after I first saw Sara, when I was on my way to Jayne Anne's Hat Shop, that I saw the police dogs. I was walking up Eighth Avenue on my way to the corner, and as I was passing the alley where the trucks unload into Alcott-Simpson's storerooms, I noticed a commotion at one of the alley exits. I stopped and watched while two guys with big German Shepherds on leashes came out and got into a police car. When I got to the flower stand, I told José about it.

"Sure," he said. "Cop-dogs every night. Tree, four nights, now. Big store got big trouble." José grinned happily. The big shots at Alcott-Simpson's had tried to make him move his flower stand once, and he'd had it in for the whole store ever since. But I couldn't get much more out of him about what was going on, so that afternoon I paid another visit to Madame Stregovitch to find out what she knew.

But even before I talked to Madame, as a matter of fact almost as soon as I got inside the big brass and glass doors of the east entrance, I began to get that feeling of something strange again. There was a difference in pitch, like before—but there was something else, too. Right at first I couldn't put my finger on exactly what it was.

Everything looked just the same as always. There was a pretty fair sized crowd of shoppers for a Monday afternoon, the floors gleamed, the fountain sparkled, and the air was full of that special Alcott-Simpson perfume—Essence of New-and-Expensive. The clerks stood around like always, looking neat and dressy and superior, except— It was just about then that I noticed that there was something different about them—they were noticing me. Except for a few friends, and now and then someone who'd been told to keep an eye on me, most of the clerks never seemed to notice that I was around at all. I didn't take it personally. Nearly everyone who just walked in cold got the old invisible treatment, unless they were dripping with mink or some other kind of wearable bank statement. It wasn't anything to get touchy about. The clerks just didn't want to get tied up with some sightseer and maybe miss a live one. Actually, you couldn't blame them.

But that day things were different. As I walked down the Mall towards Cosmetics, every clerk I passed who wasn't busy with a customer gave me her full attention until I got by. And not just me, either. That day the clerks were noticing everybody—and the way they were doing it sort of gave you the feeling that someone had just told them that Jack the Ripper was coming in disguise.

When Madame Stregovitch saw me, her eyebrows flared up and she went off into one of her fancy greetings. "Ahhh! The shadows are lifting. It is the Golden One, the Adonis of Eighth Avenue."

"Hey, I like it," I said. I got out my little notebook that I kept track of my job money in and pretended to write it down. "Let's see. How did that go? Adonis, A—D——" But as soon as we got through kidding around, I got right down to what I'd come to ask. "By

43

the way, how about letting me in on the big mystery. I mean, what's going on around here anyway?"

Madame had been looking down at a tray of lipsticks she was arranging, but when I said that her eyes whipped around to me so hard and fast that for a minute I started to stammer. It happened to me all the time with kids, particularly girls, but hardly ever with adults—especially Madame. But when she wanted to, she had a look that could really nail you—like a bug on a pin.

"I—I mean, the police and dogs and everything. José's been saying the store has some kind of big trouble. I just wondered if you'd heard anything."

After a minute Madame nodded and went back to fixing the lipsticks. "Yes," she said." I have heard a little. There have been extra detectives hired and more guards at night. There is always some trouble in a big store like this. Perhaps it is the guards themselves. They say most of the damage has been done at night."

"You mean stuff has been stolen more than once at night, and no one can find out how anyone's getting in? Sounds like it *must* be the guards, or someone who's working with them. What are they taking? And how come it hasn't all been in the paper?"

Madame shrugged. When Madame shrugged, everything got in on the act—her eyebrows, her chin, her hands and even her nose; and her shrugs said a lot more than other people's. This one said that the store officials were idiots, that the whole thing was a big joke, that there was nothing to worry about—but then right at the end her eyes came back to me and sharpened, and the shrug ended up saying something like, "Too many questions can get you in trouble." It felt almost like a threat. But out loud all she said was, "I think, actually, very little has been stolen." She reached under the counter and brought out some fudge. "See, your favorite from the Sweet Shop. Just like old times."

It was obvious that for some reason Madame didn't want to talk about it any more, but I was still curious; so when she went back to her customers, I decided to cruise around a bit just to get the feel of things. I happened to be wearing some of my best stuff, so I didn't figure I'd attract any special attention, unless I ran into Rogers or Priestly or one or two of the others who knew me.

I toured the main floor first. I walked all the way around the Mall, which was just a wide aisle lined with potted plants. On the inside was the indoor garden and fountain and some lounging areas where shoppers could sit down to rest their feet. And all around the outside were the different departments—some of them fixed up like separate little shops. There were dozens of them—Gifts and Notions and Cosmetics and Books and Jewelry and Silver and Stationery and Hobbies and Hosiery and the Travel Shop and the Gourmet Shop and the Import Shop and the Music Shop and the Art Shop and the Sweet Shop and the Flower

Shop, and a lot of others. Then all along the south side there was the Alcott Tea Room, which was indoors like everything else, but was designed to look like some kind of lawn party, with umbrella tables and potted trees.

I went all the way around the floor without seeing anything out of the ordinary, except for the way the clerks were acting. There did seem to be a few more men shoppers than usual; they may or may not have been extra store detectives.

Next I got on the elevator and went to the second floor. I didn't get off at the mezzanine because it was absolutely impossible not to be conspicuous there. It was where they had the best ladies' clothing and there was nothing on the whole floor but some chairs and couches sitting around on a practically knee-deep rug, plus a few artistic objects like pictures and statues. The idea was, you were supposed to tell the clerks—a bunch of dowager types in black dresses—what you had in mind and they trotted out some models wearing things you might like. I never could see just how it worked because the models were all nearly skin and bones and most of the customers weren't, but that wasn't my problem.

The second floor was clothing, too, only not quite so exclusive, and the third floor was one of my favorites —boys' and mens' clothing and the sporting goods department. I strolled around for a while on each floor, but I didn't see anything else that looked fishy. So I went up to the toy department on the fourth floor.

At one time I used to think that Alcott's toy department was just one step below Paradise—but that was when I was a kid. I hadn't even been there for several weeks, but right away I got the feeling that something was different. It hit me as soon as I stepped off the escalator. For one thing, there didn't seem to be nearly as many clerks as usual, and for another there was a new detective staked out between dolls and stuffed animals. He was all dressed up in an expensive tweed suit and he was kind of half-heartedly pretending to be shopping, but it was pretty much wasted effort. There are some cops who have COP written all over them so loud and clear that you couldn't mistake them if they were wearing lace negligees.

But, at least, since the guy was new he wouldn't recognize me, so I just got into the act and pretended to shop, too. First I looked into a junior planetarium that cost around two hundred dollars, and then I checked out a practically life-sized plush tiger that was a bargain for eighty-five. I was still putting on an act for the benefit of the tweedy cop—like I was some rich kid trying to decide what to buy for my little brother's birthday—when I saw Mrs. Jensen coming out of the toy department office. The office was in the storage area behind the children's book department, and the door was camouflaged with a book shelf to keep customers from strolling in by mistake. Mrs. Jensen is quite an old lady and she'd been the head buyer for the toy department for years and years—so of course, I knew her pretty well. She wasn't the kind of person you could kid around with, but she'd been patient with me all those years when I used to visit Alcott's toy department almost every day. I hadn't seen her for quite a while, though, so I decided to step over and say hello, and maybe get her version of what was going on.

When I came around the corner of the display case where I'd seen Mrs. Jensen go, she was squatting down counting something in the storage bins under the case. I came up behind her, but she didn't seem to hear me and I didn't want to interrupt her counting so I just picked up a model car that was on top of the case to look at while I waited for her to finish. It was one of those beautifully-made intricate miniature models, all real steel and chrome with real rubber tires. I was crazy about them when I was a kid, but I got pretty well bored with the thing that day while I waited. Mrs. Jensen finally seemed to have finished her counting, and she was just staring straight ahead as if she was thinking or trying to figure something out. At last I got impatient and gave a little cough to get her attention.

I *was* standing pretty close to her, but it wasn't a loud cough and I certainly didn't expect a reaction like the one I got. Like I said, Mrs. Jensen is an old lady, but she shot to her feet like a five-year-old and whirled around with her hand up to her throat. A funny little scream, more like a strangled squeak, came out of her mouth and her eyes behind the rimless glasses looked faded with fright.

She saw me then, and in the next few seconds her expression went from blind terror—to recognition—to relief—to embarrassment—to anger. It would have been funny except that she'd scared me almost as much as I'd scared her. I mean, it's kind of nerve-racking to be screamed at for nothing at all, and besides it occurred to me that maybe she was going to clutch her heart and topple over—and it would all be my fault.

But she didn't have a heart attack, after all. Instead she started bawling me out. "Dion," she said when she finally got her voice back, "what do you mean sneaking up behind people! What do you mean—" She noticed the model car in my hands then and she reached out and snatched it away. "What do you mean handling things? Wearing things out? No wonder things are getting broken. No wonder things are scuffed and shopworn before they've been on the shelves a day. No wonder—"

She was still sputtering along like that when a deep voice interrupted, "Is something the matter, Mrs. Jensen?" And there stood the tweedy cop who had stopped pretending to be a customer and was standing over me, kind of twitching the way a cat does just before he pounces.

Seeing the cop standing there seemed to bring Mrs. Jensen back to her senses a little. "Why—why—no," she stuttered. "It's only that Dion here came up

49

behind me and startled me. I know the boy. It's all right." She managed a very wobbly smile. "It's perfectly all right, Mr. Crane." She took me by the elbow and started steering me out of the department. "I'm sorry, Dion," she said on the way out. "I don't know what came over me to make me act that way. It's just that I'm tired—and nervous. Things haven't been—that is, things haven't been going well in the department lately. I'm just not myself. I'm sorry I scolded you so." We'd gotten to the beautiful handcarved archway of elves and animals that led into the toy department. Mrs. Jensen turned loose of my elbow, and I started off.

"Well, good-by, Mrs. Jensen," I said.

"Good-by, Dion," she said. "Oh, by the way. I almost forgot in all the—" she smiled kind of sheepishly, "—excitement. Did you want something? Could I help you with something?"

"No," I said. "Not really. I was just going to say hello. I haven't been around for quite a while, so I thought I'd just say—hello."

"Oh," Mrs. Jensen said, and her smile was finally back to normal. "How nice of you, Dion. Hello to you, too."

"Yeah," I said, "Hello." And I left.

I went on up through Housewares without noticing anything else strange, but I kept thinking about Mrs. Jenson and wondering what had gotten into her to make her act so jumpy. She'd always seemed like a pretty calm person before.

I was about to get on the escalator to go up to the sixth floor, Furniture and Antiques, when I heard the closing bell ring. That meant it was five-thirty and time I stopped playing Sherlock Holmes and went home to dinner. But just a few minutes later, right at the very moment that I stepped on the down escalator on the second floor, suddenly all hell broke loose somewhere below me on the mezzanine.

The escalator was crowded with a closing time rush of downward bound customers, and the first scream seemed to freeze everyone still. But at the second scream, everyone suddenly decided that the escalator was moving too slow and started to run up or down. Probably the curious ones were trying to get to where the scream came from to see what had happened, and the scarier ones were trying to go in the opposite direction. But since it was hard to tell where the sound had come from, both types seemed to be heading both ways. Whatever they had in mind, what they actually accomplished was a kind of mass wrestling match, on a moving escalator. But the escalator kept going down, so eventually we all got dumped on the mezzanine landing.

The mezzanine was full of people running in all directions. As soon as I got untangled from the crowd, I got behind a statue of a Grecian lady and surveyed the scene. Fur-coated customers, black-dressed sales ladies and plain-clothed detectives were whizzing by like

crazy. But it was so noisy I couldn't hear what anyone was saying, and I couldn't make any sense at all out of what was going on. There were a couple more screams, not quite so loud, in the direction of the dressing rooms and then a janitor came running by carrying something that looked like a big butterfly net.

The whole thing was so interesting that it never occurred to me I might get myself in trouble by hanging around, until I saw Mr. Priestly getting off the elevator. I'd only gotten behind the Venus, or whatever it was, to keep out of the flight pattern; but all of a sudden I realized how it would look. There I was, a guy who was already suspected of being a troublemaker, if not a shoplifter, hiding behind a statue on a floor where goodness knows what had just happened. And to make matters worse, I suddenly remembered the tweedy cop in the toy department. He'd probably be only too glad to testify that I'd just been scaring the buyer in the toy department half to death—even if she was too nice to press charges. It didn't sound good. In fact, it even sounded suspicious to me, and I *knew* I was innocent.

Priestly was pretty close to me when I saw him, but he was looking the other way, towards the dressing rooms. I wasn't positive, but I didn't think he'd seen me—not yet, anyway. I eased out from behind the statue and started to stroll back towards the escalator. I couldn't get to the down one without going right past him, so I took the up one, thinking that I'd go up a few floors and then catch the elevator straight down to the street floor.

I don't know why I went clear up to the sixth floor before I crossed over to the elevators, except I was thinking that if I got on up there I'd be clear at the back of the elevator and all the people who got on at the floors in between would hide me from view when we stopped at the mezzanine.

No one else in the whole store seemed to be going up, so I kept on going up all by myself: third, fourth, fifth. And when I got off at the sixth floor, everything seemed to be deserted there, too.

As I walked across to the elevators, I didn't see a single person on the whole floor. Either the salesmen had gone home already, or else they had been called down to help with the emergency on the mezzanine. I pushed the *down* button and waited.

I was thinking hard about something—the scream, I guess. I was trying to figure out what had caused it. It didn't seem like something being stolen could cause that sort of scream, not even if it had been the Hope Diamond. It hadn't been an angry scream, or even outraged, that scream had been *fear*. I'd gotten about that far in figuring it out, when I realized that I'd been waiting quite a while. I checked the little pointer above the door and all of a sudden it dawned on me that the elevators had quit running.

My watch said six o'clock. I'd known that it was a little past closing time, but I hadn't thought it was that much. That meant I'd have to risk the escalator, and I was on my way back to it when I heard men's voices—it sounded like two or three of them on their way up. I whirled around and hurried in the opposite direction. It had occurred to me that there was one more way downstairs. So I dashed off across the huge floor, ducking around highboys and love seats, thinking to myself that it was a good thing I knew about the emergency staircase.

The emergency staircase was clear across the building from the escalators, and on the sixth floor it was in a little hall right between two of the furniture display rooms. There were a lot of display rooms fixed up to look like different rooms in houses—living rooms, dining rooms and so forth—but I knew just which two to look for. I ducked in between a red and white bedroom and an orange and yellow dining room, and there it was—the door to the stairway. The only thing was—it was locked.

I'd been scared before, but there was something about jerking on that locked door that made me push the panic button. I could hear the voices coming closer across the floor, and the word TRAPPED kept flashing across my mind like one of those blinking billboards. I had a crazy urge to do something, anything, in a hurry —and what I did was pretty stupid. I ducked into the red and white bedroom and slid under the bed.

Chapter 5

I'VE HEARD THAT YOUR WHOLE LIFE CAN PASS BEFORE your eyes in a few minutes when you're about to die, and I can believe it. I know for a fact that an amazing amount of insignificant stuff can shoot through your mind when you're only trapped under a bed on the sixth floor of a closed department store. As I lay there and listened to the voices of the men coming closer and closer, all sorts of useless thoughts popped into my mind. I don't remember most of it, but I do remember realizing that if I had to spend the night there, under that bed, my dad wouldn't even miss me until way after midnight. This little chamber orchestra that he plays with had a date to play for some women's club way out in the suburbs, and he wouldn't be home until late. Of course, the guys from upstairs would probably be down, particularly if it turned out to be a cold night. They came down to study by our fireplace whenever they felt like it, even when we weren't there; but they wouldn't worry about me. For all they knew,

I might be at the movies or spending the night with a friend.

I don't know why, but realizing that no one would be worrying about me made me feel worse than ever. It didn't make sense. If my dad was home and worried, all he could do would be to call the police. And the kind of mess I was in wasn't the kind of thing you wanted to be rescued from by the cops.

I could hear the two men doing something not far away. They were moving around from place to place as if they were checking to see if everything was ready for the night. Now and then I caught bits and pieces of their conversation—enough to know they were just salesmen, not detectives with dogs—and enough to tell that they were discussing what had happened on the mezzanine.

Once I heard one of them say something about "—nothing to get excited about. Whether she admits it or not, that girl in the Pet Shop must have let it get out." The other voice came from farther away and it sounded fast and jittery, as if he were pretty excited. I couldn't hear much of what he was saying, but when he finally stopped the closer voice answered, "That's a lot of nonsense. The old gal must have been hysterical or off her rocker. It must have been in there all the time and she just didn't notice it. It couldn't have been flying."

The jittery voice had moved closer. "Well," it said, "she seemed so positive. But I suppose it might have climbed up the wall and she saw it falling off and imagined it was flying."

"Sure," the first voice said, "there's bound to be a logical explanation."

They both moved away then, and after a while it got very quiet and most of the lights went off. As I began to calm down a little, I began to notice that I was very uncomfortable. The bed was so low that I had to stay flat on my face. I couldn't raise my head more than an inch, and some kind of a metal cross bar was pressing into my back. The air was stuffy; the dust in the thick rug choked me so that every few minutes I had to fight back a sneeze.

But in spite of the discomfort, I knew that getting up my nerve to crawl out into the huge open emptiness of the store was not going to be easy. And crawling out would be only the beginning. After that would come getting down six flights. The escalator would be stopped, but I might be able to walk down it. Then, there would be goodness knows how many watchmen and cleaning crews and policemen with dogs—not to mention getting out of the building through doors that would probably be locked from the inside as well as from the out. With all that to worry about, it wasn't any wonder that it seemed easier just to lie there, at least for the moment.

I told myself that I had to start planning—deciding what I was going to do—but for a long time all I seemed to be able to do was torture myself with "if only" possibilities. "If only" I hadn't waited so long for the elevator before I realized it had stopped running; "if only" I'd risked being seen by Mr. Priestly and taken the down escalator in the first place; "if only" I'd tried to bluff it out with the two salesmen instead of hiding, like telling them I'd been in the men's room and hadn't realized the store was closing.

But the chance to do any of those things was gone, and when I came right down to it there were only two things left that I might do. One was to stay there under the bed all night and hope to go out in the morning with the early shoppers. And the other was to crawl out now and start trying to find a way out without being seen. The only problem was that knowing about the extra watchmen and the dogs made me pretty sure I wouldn't be able to make it either way.

There was one other possibility that came to mind, but I didn't consider it even for a minute. That was to go looking for the nearest guard and turn myself in, explain as well as I could, and face the music. Of course, there wasn't a chance that they would believe all of my story, but they might believe part of it, and because I was a first offender they might let me off pretty easy. However, I'd never be able to set foot inside Alcott-Simpson's again. Like I say, I didn't consider it for a minute. Somehow I was going to have to find a way to get out without being caught.

I don't know how long I lay there trying to get up my nerve to make a move, but it seemed like half a lifetime. I thought about the dogs a lot—what it would be like to be found by one—a huge shaggy head with long gleaming fangs lunging in towards me from the side of the bed. I pictured it coming in from different spots around me and each time the part of me closest seemed to shrivel in expectation. But for a long time I didn't hear anything that sounded at all like a dog, and after a while I began to worry about other things.

As time went by it got quieter and quieter, and as it did I began to listen harder and harder. The faint sounds of the city seemed a thousand miles away, and I could almost feel all the dark floors of the store stretching out around me like a huge deserted city. Then I began to think again about the screams on the mezzanine and what I'd overheard the salesmen say. I thought about what it could have been that could "crawl up a wall" and frighten someone enough to cause a scream like that. I even began to imagine things crawling in towards me under the edge of the bedspread—horrible vague things that crawled up walls and maybe flew——

Then I began to hear things. First I heard foot-steps. Not like a watchman's feet, firm and heavy, but a light quick brush of sound that seemed very near and yet so soft that I couldn't be absolutely positive. Then there were voices that were the same way—whispers so soft that I never quite got to the point where I said, "There, that time I know I heard it." But once, with-out hearing anything, something made me turn my head and I saw the fringe on the bedspread swaying as if it had just been touched.

After that I lay there absolutely frozen for several minutes, but nothing more happened and the soft sounds seemed to have gone away. I was just beginning to tell myself that it had all been caused by the strain of waiting and that I had to pull myself together and crawl out, when suddenly very close to me a soft but very distinct voice said, "Hello."

I jumped so hard that my head bounced off a metal mattress support and my face ricocheted off the floor. For a minute I was blinded by the pain in my nose and the dust in my eyes, but I could hear all right and what I heard was the same soft voice saying, "Oh, did you hurt yourself? Are you all right?"

When I managed to get my sight back, I saw what looked like a girl's face, upside down in a pool of dark hair. As a rule I don't even have the nerve to be nice to girls, but I guess a hard bump on the nose can really affect your personality, at least temporarily.

"Oh sure," I growled. "Except for a concussion and a broken nose. What do you think you're doing anyway?"

The face disappeared for a minute. In the meantime the pain began to fade, and I began to get back to normal. When the face came back, I kind of quavered, "What do you want?"

That's the kind of stupid remark that's my usual speed around people my own age, but at least this girl didn't make things any worse by laughing or making a crack. She didn't try to answer my stupid question, either. What she said was, "I'm Sara." Actually, she didn't say Sara, exactly. At least not the way it's usually pronounced. The "*r*" was softer and sort of swallowed. But Sara is as close as I can get to it.

After a minute I said, "Hi" or "Hello" or some such remark.

"Who are you?" she asked.

"I'm Dion. Uh—Dion James. What are you doing here? Did you get shut in, too?"

She just went on looking at me for a while without answering, and then she said, "You'd better come out from under there. They always look under the beds."

"Yeah," I said, "I was afraid they would. But I didn't have much time to pick a place." I remember that right about then I was getting a surprised and hopeful feeling that maybe she wasn't going to turn me over to the guards—that maybe she even meant to help me.

62

"Can you get out?" she asked.

I began to try to scoot out, but the bed was awfully low. It's really amazing what you can do if you're scared enough. I couldn't remember having any trouble getting under the bed at all. I wiggled and puffed for a minute without making much progress until the girl reached under and got hold of my foot. She pulled and I pushed and before too long I was out.

It wasn't until then, when I saw her face right side up, that I realized who she was and where I'd seen her before. The light was dim where we were, but it was bright enough for me to be pretty sure it was the same girl I'd seen Rogers chasing a few days before on the main floor. She was dressed differently, but I was sure I remembered the eyes and the smile and the long black hair. Instead of the suede jumper, she had on a short shiny skirt with a low belt and a matching blouse with long tight sleeves. She looked very expensive and stylish, except that around her shoulders there was something white and pink and frilly that didn't seem to go with the rest of it. The frilly thing had slid around while she was helping me, and when she noticed that I was looking at it she started straightening it out. She had very small hands—very brown—and there was something about the careful way she touched the lacy stuff that made it obvious she really liked the way it looked. When she got it straightened out, I could see it was one of those little jackets that women wear in the hospital or when they're having breakfast in bed—I'd seen them in the movies and places like that. This one was one big mass of ribbons and lace and little pink flowers.

She said, "Isn't it beautiful?" The way she said it wasn't the way most girls would talk about something they were wearing. It was more the way you'd talk about a sunset or something.

"Yeah, nice," I said. "But look. Hadn't we better be getting out of here before we get caught?" But then all of a sudden it occurred to me that maybe she belonged there in some way. She looked too young to be an employee, but maybe she was the daughter of one of the big shots who was working late or something like that. She certainly didn't seem as worried as you'd think a young girl trapped in a closed department store would be. As a matter of fact, she didn't seem anywhere near as worried as I was.

She finished fixing the jacket and smoothed her hair down before she answered. Her hair was very thick and almost to her waist, and when she moved her head it slid around on her shoulders—soft and heavy like black silk. Her face was smooth and even, the kind that looks best with straight plain hair. In the half-light it seemed to have a kind of patterned perfection that was almost weird, like a planned design or a face seen through crystal. After a minute she said, "We'll have to find you a place to hide."

She looked all around and then she nodded and said, "Stay there a minute." She ran out of the display room and disappeared around the corner. She was back before I even had a chance to start worrying; and she was carrying a comforter, one of those fluffy satin quilts stuffed with feathers. She turned back the top of the bedspread and took out the pillows and told me to lie down across the bed where the pillows had been. It was a king-size bed so I just about reached across it from side to side without hanging over. She folded the quilt into a long fat roll and tucked it over me and patted it into the same shape the pillows had made. Then she pulled the spread back where it had been. "It looks just the same," she said. "Lie still."

"Hey," I said, but I heard her running again, out of the room.

For a minute or two I lay there in an absolute panic. It had all happened so fast and the girl had seemed so sure of what she was doing that I just went along with her, but suddenly I began to see the loopholes. It was a good hiding place, all right, if it weren't for the dogs, but they wouldn't be fooled for a minute. And what was going to happen to the girl? I was about to jump up and make a run for it when all at once she was back.

"Shhh," I heard her whisper. "I'm back. I had to put the pillows with the others so they wouldn't be noticed. Are you all right? Can you breathe?"

"Pretty well," I said. "But what about the dogs? And what are you going to do?"

"I have another hiding place. I'll go there in a

minute. Don't worry about the dogs. They won't find you. There are ways of making them go other places. They'll come soon with the men, and then they'll go back downstairs. When it's safe, I'll come back and show you how to get out of the store. Just remember not to move until I come back."

She was quiet then and I wasn't sure whether she was still there. I whispered, "Sara."

She said, "yes," from very nearby. I decided she must be sitting on the floor near the head of the bed.

"You'd better go. They'll find you there."

"I'll go soon, when it's time. The others will tell me."

I was thinking about that, wondering if she'd said what I thought she said and what it meant, when suddenly I felt her touch the spread over my head. "I'm going now. Don't move."

I lay there, trying to listen through the thick quilt and stuff over me. It seemed like years but it probably was only a few minutes before I heard voices. There were two or maybe three men, and they were going back and forth across the floor. They came closer and I heard another noise—a sharp whining bark. It was quiet for a while, and then there was more whining and voices giving commands. The dogs went on whining and whining, but they didn't seem to be getting any closer—and then I heard someone walk right into the room where I was hidden.

I held my breath and hoped that the quilt would

muffle the sound of my heart pounding. I could hear a man moving around, but no dogs' sounds, up close at least. In fact, the dogs were still whining now and then someplace quite a ways off on the other side of the floor. Finally the bed moved a little as if the man had put his hand on it as he got down to look underneath. "No sign of anything here!" he called a minute later, and then I heard him go on to the next display room.

Things had been quiet again for quite a while when I heard Sara's voice saying, "All right, you can come out now."

After we'd fixed the pillows back the way they'd been before, I said, "Okay, how do we get out?"

"Do you want to go right now?" Sara asked.

I guess I stared at her. The way she said it, it was like she thought I might want to sit down and play a hand of cards first or something.

"Well, I'm not exactly looking forward to the trip downstairs," I said. "But waiting around isn't going to make it any better. No telling when they'll be back with the dogs."

Sara thought a minute. "They'll go to the employees' room now and drink coffee. In an hour they'll take the dogs around again. But you're right. Now is the best time. Come on, we'll go this way."

She started towards the emergency staircase, so I told her that it was locked. She only said, "I think it will be open now." And it was.

At the top of the stairs we stopped and stood for a while listening. All of a sudden she said, "Now—hurry."

We ran all the way, and when we got to the ground floor we stopped and listened again, and then she led the way through a storage room that I recognized as one Rogers had dragged me through once. At the door that led out into the alley, she stopped.

"Aren't you coming, too?" I asked.

She shook her head. "I can't," she said, "because of the others."

Chapter 6

IT WASN'T EXACTLY THE KIND OF THING THAT HAP-
pens to just everybody, and for several days I thought
about it a lot. I went over it and over it in my mind—
the scream, getting locked in, the dogs and why they
hadn't found me, and the girl.

Sara was a real puzzle. Who she was and how she
happened to be in the store after closing were the biggest questions; but I also wondered about why she
bothered to help me, and how old she was, and if I'd
ever see her again. The way I remembered her, she
was really beautiful—dark and foreign looking, with
perfect skin and teeth and eyes like something from
outer space. She had that way of moving some girls
have, soft and bendy, like their bones have some rubber in them. But, she *did* look awfully young at times,
as if she might be only twelve or so—more of a little
kid than a girl.

The next few days I dropped by the store every
afternoon and took a quick look around; but I didn't

see anything new. And I didn't see Sara, either. And meanwhile, something turned up at home that gave me something else to think about for a while.

The thing that happened at home had to do with a letter, a letter about a job that my dad could have had if he'd wanted it. Well, actually it wasn't entirely a sure thing. Nobody gets handed a job they haven't even applied for. That was what really burned me up, Dad didn't even intend to apply. In fact, I wouldn't even have found out about it if I hadn't just happened to run across the letter. But I did find the letter and I read it and I made a scene about it; not that it did any good. Afterwards I wished I'd never even seen the letter, and I wouldn't have if it hadn't been for Mrs. Grover's nervous headaches.

When the Grovers moved into our downstairs flat, they made an arrangement with Dad for Mrs. Grover to clean our apartment once a week, and in exchange they got a big hunk taken off the rent. Well, the Grovers still pay the low rent, but recently Mrs. Grover's headaches have gotten worse, especially on Tuesdays when she's supposed to be cleaning our apartment. Oh, she usually makes it up, all right, but she's discovered what a good listener my dad is. I'm not there on Tuesdays, but the guys upstairs are in and out and they say that any minute Dad isn't busy with a student, Mrs. Grover corners him and starts crying into her dust cloth about her headaches and life in general. Anyway, the result is the house isn't much cleaner at the end of the day, so once in a while I try to straighten things up.

That's what I was doing that Sunday morning when I ran across the letter from the Wentworth School. It was lying there wide open, on top of the usual pile of debris that covers my dad's desk: unpaid bills, unsharpened pencils and unfinished symphonies. So I read it, and at first I was all excited.

Wentworth is a private high school out in the suburbs on the north side, and John Hubell, who is one of Dad's oldest friends, has taught music there for years and years. There was going to be an opening in the music department, so John had recommended Dad. And the headmaster was willing to consider him. The salary wasn't terrific, but it would be steady and a lot better than promises and stale doughnuts; best of all, we'd have to move. At least that's the way I looked at it. I charged into the kitchen where Dad was making a pot of lentil soup, waving the letter over my head.

"Hey," I babbled, "why didn't you tell me? Did you get it? When do you start?"

Dad looked at the letter and then he looked at me and then he went over to the table and sat down and started lighting his pipe. Lighting his pipe slowly and thoughtfully while you wait for an answer is one of the most maddening things he does. Finally he got it lit and took a deep puff and let it out slowly before he said, "You'd like for me to teach at Wentworth?"

It occurred to me just about then that John was

always complaining about what a lousy place it was to teach. It's a private school for girls, and according to John the girls are mostly spoiled brats and the administrators are a bunch of two-bit tyrants.

"Well, it's a steady salary," I said. "And if it's as bad as John makes out, why doesn't he quit?"

"John has a family, and he doesn't have his degree," Dad said. "It would be hard for him to find a job anywhere else. Besides, the time for John to break away has passed. He's been at Wentworth too many years. . . ." Dad took the pipe out of his mouth and put it down on the table, where he'd probably forget it and let it go out. "I have a great deal of sympathy for John's situation, but not enough to make me want to share it, I'm afraid. And the salary is really not a consideration. By the time I paid for transportation, it would be very little more than I'm making now. But I certainly didn't realize that you'd be so enthusiastic. It didn't occur to me—"

There were a lot of things that didn't occur to Dad where I was concerned. I shrugged and mumbled something about thinking maybe we could move to the north side. But I didn't wait for an answer. It was pretty plain that Dad had already turned down the chance to teach at Wentworth, so that was that. He was starting in on some of his reasons for not wanting to sell the house as I left the kitchen. I'd heard them all before.

Out in the hall I stumbled over Charity, so I

picked her up to put her out. The window at the end of the hall opens on the fire-escape, and the cats always use that route to get to our floor. When I opened the window and dumped Charity out, I decided to climb out, too. I hadn't done that for a long time, but when I was younger I had used the fire escape landing a lot. It was one of my favorite places to sit with my guitar and make up songs and sing them. It's on the south side of the house, sheltered from the wind, and on sunny days it can be warm there even in the midst of winter. The trapped sunlight warms your skin, but the thin air stays as cold as ever in your lungs. If you stay too long the air wins out, but for a little while it feels wonderful.

Charity had started down the fire escape, but when she looked back and saw me, she came right back up and climbed into my lap. I'm not crazy about cats in general and Charity in particular, but she made a good hand warmer so I let her stay. Prudence and Charity are Dad's cats. At least he was the one who brought them home because somebody was about to drown them. They're real nothings, as cats go, scrawny black-striped alley cats, both of them; but at least Prudence has enough originality not have kittens two or three times a year.

Charity was so surprised to have me hold her that she started purring up a storm, and it felt good on my hands, warm and vibrating. I leaned back against the sunwarmed shingles and vegetated. I tried not to think

74

about anything, but in a couple of minutes I was thinking about the job at Wentworth and what it would have been like if Dad had taken it.

First of all, if we had moved it would have meant no more Randolph High. There were a lot of reasons why I would have been glad to see the last of Randolph. I felt then that it was really a lousy place to go to school—unless you happened to be part of the "in" group that ran everything. And if you weren't a part of it, there was nothing much you could do about it. I knew because I'd tried.

A year and a half before, when I had started in at Randolph I'd had high hopes. I'd never felt like I really belonged to a school before—I'd always been a real outcast at Lincoln—but I'd decided that things were going to be different at Randolph. All the time at Lincoln I'd had this vague idea that everybody else, all the other kids, had some kind of secret that I wasn't in on—something that made them able to talk and laugh and kid around together. And I was so sure that I couldn't find out what the secret was I didn't even try. I just did my work and left. But then in the eighth grade I began to see things differently.

I was noticing a lot of things along about then. I began to watch people—I mean, really watch them— and I decided that nearly everyone was afraid, at least a little, and there wasn't any big secret. Only a lot of little ones. One of the little secrets was to dress like everyone else, or just a little bit better. And another was to talk like everyone else and about the same kinds of things. Another one, for a boy, was to be a good athlete. Of course, that was out for me, but I decided there wasn't any reason why I couldn't work on the other things. I knew I was smart—everyone said so and my grades were always good—so why couldn't I learn how to be just like everyone else? Only at Lincoln it was too late to start.

So I concentrated on getting ready for Randolph. I saved money for clothes and practiced remarks and wisecracks that might come in handy. I even dropped out of orchestra because the violin didn't fit my new image. Dad didn't like my quitting, though he didn't try to make me change my mind, but Mr. Cooper, the orchestra teacher, almost had a fit. It was too bad, I guess. But it couldn't be helped.

Then I'd started high school and things weren't anything like I'd planned. Oh, it was better than Lincoln and I made a few friends, but not anything like I'd been counting on. I did get to know this one kid in my English class right away. His name was Jerry Davidson and he was almost as quiet as I was, but he had a good sense of humor when you got to know him. He lived up in Hill Groves and he asked me up to his house a few times. His family had this terrific place with a swimming pool and a rumpus room and the whole bit and they were all very nice and friendly.

I also began to find out that girls thought I was good-looking, but the ones who seemed to like me usually weren't the ones I was interested in—and most of the time I couldn't get up my nerve to talk to any of them, anyway. I still panicked and got tongue-tied at times, particularly around kids I used to know at Lincoln before I started work on the new me. So I'd finally decided that what I needed was a new start. A new start in a school where nobody remembered how I'd been at Lincoln.

For quite a while I'd been thinking that if Dad would just get a job, or even a new batch of students in a part of town where people had enough money to pay a decent fee for their lessons, we could sell the old house and move into a house or apartment in another part of the city. It didn't have to be anything fancy. Just a normal place, instead of a kind of perpetual open house for all the kids and bums and college students and animals in the neighborhood.

So Wentworth would have been the answer. But Dad had turned it down already so that was that. I knew from past experience there was no use discussing it with him any further. It all had to do with a difference in the way we looked at things that was absolutely basic.

My dad's life is the kind of life he picked out for himself a long time ago, and it suits him fine. His mother's family had a lot of money at one time and Dad was brought up in a very strict and proper home with all sorts of rules and regulations. So, when he was still pretty young he ran away from home and lived in

Paris for several years with a lot of artists and writers and types like that. Then when his money was gone and he had to come back home, he just brought his Paris way of living back to Cathedral Street. By renting part of the house and teaching a little, he made enough money to get by and the rest of the time he spends "living" as he calls it. He composes some and plays a little—accompanying and with chamber orchestras—and he goes to all the cheap musical events at the university and to standing room at the opera and symphony. Besides that he reads a lot and spends time with his thousand and one friends—and then there's the mountains. He has this thing about the wilderness, and every few months he takes off with a friend or two and they back-pack into the mountains for a week or so. I've gone with him a time or two, but I'm not much of a hiker because of my leg, so usually I stay home with whoever happens to be living here at the time.

It's a great life I suppose—a lot of people say so. Phil and Dunc and their friends are always raving about how Dad is one guy who dropped out of the rat-race and made it stick. I don't argue with them. I can't even explain to myself exactly how I feel about it. But I know that day on the fire escape I decided it must be a lot bigger kick to drop out of something than not to be *in* in the first place.

Chapter 7

THE NEXT DAY ON MY WAY HOME FROM SCHOOL I
stopped by Alcott-Simpson's again. I was planning on
walking right through from the east entrance to the
west—just to have a quick look around. At least that's
what I had in mind when I went in. Everything
seemed quiet, and there was a fairly good-sized crowd
of shoppers. If there still seemed to be something not
quite normal—well, I thought maybe it was only my
imagination. I was almost to the west entrance when
somebody touched my arm.

I glanced around, and there was this fantastically
sophisticated-looking woman. Since I couldn't imagine
what she wanted of me, I decided I must have been in
her way, so I said, "Excuse me" and stepped to one
side. But then this dame, instead of breezing on by,
put her arm through mine and smiled at me. I nearly
passed out.

She looked like a model who had just stepped out
of one of those really far-out fashion magazines. Her

hat was an egg-shaped helmet that completely covered her hair and sloped down to a little slanted brim over her eyes. Her suit was kind of egg-shaped too, and made out of some very heavy material with a thick stand-out collar. She was wearing very short black boots with high heels and some huge wrap-around dark glasses that covered more than half her face. Everything she was wearing positively reeked of money, but like most of those high-style things, the whole effect was just a small—but important—inch away from being ugly. But there was one thing you could really say about it, it made a great disguise. Until she started to talk, I hadn't the slightest idea who she was.

"Don't you know who I am?" was the first thing she said.

I started to laugh. The minute she opened her mouth, it ruined the whole effect. All of a sudden it was like some little girl dressed up in her mother's clothes.

"I didn't even know you," I said.

"Do you like it?" she asked. She tugged at the helmet where it came down tight and flat against her cheeks. She sounded worried.

"Like it? You look like something from another planet."

She turned around and looked at herself in a mirror on the counter. "Another planet?" she said thoughtfully. "I saw a model wearing it, and I thought it would make me look different. So no one would know me. But you don't like it?"

"It's fantastic," I said. "You look better than most people would in it."

She smiled again and took hold of my arm. "Let's go to the Tea Room and eat something."

That shook me a little. I'd never taken a girl anywhere to eat anything before, for one thing. And for another, I didn't have a whole lot of money along. At the Alcott-Simpson Tea Room, even a milk shake isn't exactly cheap. I didn't have the slightest idea what I'd do if she ordered a whole lot of stuff. And she certainly might. A teen-age girl who could afford to buy an outfit that probably cost several hundred dollars, just because she wanted to look different, probably wouldn't think anything of ordering everything on the Tea Room menu. Of course, there was the other possibility—that the outfit was stolen, and Sara was a thief, a shoplifter. But that didn't make my problem any better. It wouldn't be any easier to predict what a girl who could *steal* an outfit like that would do.

But when we got to the Tea Room, Sara didn't even look at the menu. She just said, "What can we have? I don't have any money. Do you have any?"

I was right in the middle of making feverish plans to keep her from knowing that I wasn't carrying a bank roll, but the way she asked—straight out—surprised me into answering the same way. "Not much," I said. "But we could have a shake or something."

"Could I have one of those?" Sara asked, pointing

81

to a soda that a waitress was serving. I checked the menu and told her it was okay. I had enough for two sodas.

We didn't talk much at first while we drank our sodas, but I did get a chance to really look at Sara. Of course, I couldn't see her eyes because of the dark glasses, but I could see enough to tell that I had been right about her face, it was really fantastic. Every time she looked up and caught me looking at her she smiled —not a come-on smile or a wise one, at least not as far as I could tell. Just a quick straight unconditional sort of smile, like you might get from a friendly four-year-old. I couldn't begin to figure her out.

After a while I got around to asking some of the questions that I'd been thinking about. For instance, I started out by asking how old she was.

"By the way," I said. "I've been wondering how old you are. It's sort of hard to tell. Sometimes you look lots older than others."

She gave a little laugh. "How old are you?" she asked.

"Almost fifteen," I said.

She just nodded, so I said, "Well?"

"Oh," she said. "I'm—almost the same."

"You mean you're fourteen?"

She puckered her forehead for a minute, and then she smiled and said, "Almost?" But it sounded more like a question than an answer. It wasn't until later that I realized I still wouldn't want to bet on how old she was. That's the way most of the things I asked her seemed to turn out. Like, I mentioned that I'd seen her at Alcott-Simpson's three times lately and asked how come she spent so much time there.

"Oh, it's all right," she said. "I'm supposed to be here."

That made me think maybe I was right when I'd guessed that she was the daughter of some store big shot. That would explain a lot of things. "Do you have relatives here in the store?" I asked.

Sara just looked at me for a minute and then she nodded and said, "Yes. You're here a lot, too. Do you have relatives here, too?"

So I got started trying to explain why I hung around the store so much. It took quite a bit of explaining. I even went into how I had plans to maybe work there someday, after I'd had business training of course, so I could be something besides just a clerk. Then I asked her if she knew anything about the mysterious stuff that had been going on lately, the dogs and special detectives and everything.

Right away she bit her lip and looked away. I couldn't see her eyes behind the dark glasses, but I had the feeling that she didn't want to answer. She poked at her soda with her straw, and then she sighed and shook her head. "Things have happened—accidents. Most of the time it was just an accident."

"What kind of things?"

"Oh, things get broken. And noises. There have

been noises."

"What do you mean noises?"

"Oh, just laughing and talking. Some of the clerks say they've heard laughing and talking." Sara shook her head and pulled her lips down as if she were disapproving.

"Laughing and talking?" I said. "Why would that bother anyone? I'm talking about whatever it is that made them hire all the extra detectives and dogs. That scream for instance, the other day. Do you know what the screaming was about?"

Sara started playing with her straw again, and I could tell she didn't want to answer, but after I'd asked her again about the scream she finally said, "Yes, I know. There was a lizard in the dressing room. Just a lizard from the Pet Shop. A big green one."

I started to laugh. It hit me all of a sudden—the picture of some old dame suddenly noticing she was sharing her dressing room with a big green iguana. That would explain the scream all right. "But how did it get there?" I asked. "The Pet Shop is clear down on the first floor."

"Someone forgot to put it away. I don't think they meant to frighten anyone." Sara was leaning towards me and she sounded very serious and kind of apologetic, as if she were worried about what I would think. I wished I could see her eyes. I couldn't help wondering if the whole thing was some kind of a put-on. She sounded so sincere and on the level, but the whole thing didn't quite make sense. The whole conversation seemed to have holes in it, like when you tune in late to a mystery program and miss a bunch of important clues.

"Look," I said, "I'm not sure I know what we're talking about. It doesn't matter to me who put the iguana in the dressing room, and I really don't care whether it was done on purpose or not. But what I would like to know is exactly who you are and what you have to do with the whole thing—and where you get your information. I'm around this store pretty much myself, and usually I hear a lot about what's going on but—"

Just about then Sara stood up suddenly and looked around. "I have to go now," she said; and without even waiting for me to answer, she walked out of the Tea Shop. By the time I'd paid for the sodas, she had disappeared. I looked all over the store but I couldn't find her anywhere.

While I was looking around, it occurred to me that Madame Stregovitch might know something about Sara. In the past I'd found that if there was any interesting gossip going around the store, Madame would be sure to know all about it. I was almost back to Cosmetics before I remembered that it was Madame's day off. There wasn't much else I could do right then, so I started down the Mall towards the west entrance. But somewhere along the way, I drifted into the indoor garden. There was still a quarter of an hour until closing time, and I guess I was thinking that if I waited around there was a chance I might see Sara again.

The indoor garden, or the Garden Court as it was called, was one of the most unusual things about Alcott-Simpson's. It was a large area in the middle of the street floor that looked so much like a real garden you could almost believe it was, unless you looked up and saw the ceiling instead of the sky. The walks were made of something that looked like stone. There were stretches of green carpeting that looked a lot like grass, and dozens of potted shrubs and bushes and even small trees. Here and there there were singing birds in cages and hanging baskets full of fancy flowers like orchids and begonias. The smaller plantings were always being changed to fit the seasons, and at Christmas time it was always made into a winter garden with artificial ice and snow. All through the garden there were little alcoves with benches for shoppers to sit down for a few minutes and catch their breath. Right in the middle of the garden there was a big fountain.

The center part of the fountain was a pyramid of stone cupids and dolphins. The water came out of the dolphins' mouths and arched down into a large pool. Around the pool was a stone wall about two feet high and wide enough to make a comfortable place to sit. It was always a good place to kill a few extra minutes.

I sat down on the stone wall and wiggled my fingers in the water to make the goldfish curious. I hadn't seen anyone near the fountain as I came up, but I'd only

been sitting there for a few minutes when a toy ship came bobbing into sight from the other side of the pyramid. It was a typical Alcott-Simpson toy, a beautiful scale model of an old Spanish galleon, with three masts full of tiny sails, and ropes and rigging in all the right places. For a second I wondered if someone had left it there, but then I realized that it was moving too fast to be only drifting. Someone on the other side of the stone pyramid had given it a push or else blown into its sails, probably some little kid whose mother had just bought it for him on the fourth floor and who couldn't wait until he got home to try it out. I started listening then, and sure enough, in a minute I heard something—little kids' voices whispering right on the other side of the fountain. Because of the noise of the splashing water, I couldn't make out what they were saying; but I thought I could tell that they were giggling a little, as if they thought they were playing a trick on me—maybe making me think the ship was sailing around under its own power. I decided to go along with the gag, so when the ship got clear around to my side I leaned way out, caught it, turned it around and blew it back the way it had come. It went bobbing back around the fountain, and in a minute I heard giggling again, and in another minute it came sailing back. I was waiting for it to come alongside, and thinking that this time I'd pick it up and carry it back to them just to keep the game from getting monotonous, when I heard the closing bell begin to ring. So I left the game unfinished and hurried off to take a last look through the homeward bound crowds. I didn't even think much more about it at the time.

Chapter 8

THAT NIGHT WHILE I WAS TRYING TO TRANSLATE SOME
French sentences, I kept thinking about Sara. I'd translate a few words and then just sit there for several minutes staring into space. After a while I began to realize
that I was thinking about Sara all the time, even when
I was looking up words and practicing pronouncia-
tions. I could be right in the middle of some word,
with all the old brain cells clicking away normally, but
in some strange sort of way, Sara was there, too, like a
shadow hovering right there in the back of my mind.
I remember that once, right out loud, I said, "Dion,
old pal, you've got it bad. You are really *haunted*."

That is the exact word I used—*haunted*. I had a
feeling even then that it wasn't just the ordinary boy-
girl thing. Of course I wasn't any great authority on
the subject, but I'd spent some time thinking about
girls before. Who hasn't? I mean, nobody gets to be
almost 15 without giving quite a bit of thought to people of the opposite sex. And even though I hadn't had

much experience with girls, because of being out of things all those years, I'd had plenty of chances to make observations and get a lot of general information. Among the people who hung around the Val James Combination Music School—Group Therapy Center—and Soup Kitchen, there had always been a certain percentage of females: friends of Dad's, or of our renters, or just friends of friends. And I'd had lots of opportunities to observe the kind of hang-ups that people can get into over a person of the opposite sex. But this was different. I didn't know how or in what way, but I knew this was not the ordinary kind of thing.

When I finally finished my homework, I went into the kitchen for a bedtime snack. Dad was out at one of his musical evenings somewhere, but the college crowd was there as usual. Matt was reading, or trying to, and Phil and Dunc and a friend of theirs named Josh were practicing on their guitars.

Josh was one of the characters who hung around our place a lot, and he and I had never particularly appreciated each other. We get some far-out types around our place, and Josh is one of the farthest. He's supposed to be some sort of expert on the guitar, and that night he was teaching Phil and Dunc some new picks and strums.

Nobody paid any attention to me, which was fine as far as I was concerned, even if it was my kitchen. I looked around for something to eat, but I couldn't find much except dirty dishes. Finally I put some butter and brown sugar on a piece of stale bread and poured myself a glass of milk. I sat down to listen to the guitar lesson while I ate.

Josh was trying to show Phil how to do something that looked a lot like the Travis pick, but it seemed to me that neither one of them really knew what he was doing.

I was thinking of saying something about it when Matt, who had quit trying to read and was listening too said, "Di used to do a pick something like that. Didn't you, Di?"

I nodded. "Something," I said.

Josh rolled his eyes up at me from under his wad of hair without uncurling from around the guitar. "Yeah?" he said. "Like what?"

"Oh, I just had a melody and a rhythm beat going at the same time. But it wasn't quite like that."

"So show us," Josh said, unwrapping himself and sticking his guitar out in my direction, like he thought I was going to drop my bread and leap across the room to take it.

"No thanks," I said. "I gave it up."

"Gave what up?" he said, still holding the guitar out sort of limply.

"The guitar habit. I quit. It takes too much time."

Josh went on looking at me, and then he looked at Phil and Dunc, and then he shrugged and pulled in his arm. He hunched over and began to strum. "Man," he muttered into his beard, "this kid has a problem. What is he—about twelve? And already he's running out of time."

Phil laughed. "Oh, Di's all right. It's just that he's a throwback. A typical member of the younger generation of 1910."

I wasn't sure exactly what he was driving at, but I didn't want to give him the satisfaction of asking; so I went back to my bread and sugar, and in a little while Phil and Dunc and their crummy friend straggled out to go to some coffee shop where a lot of their other friends hung out. So Matt and I were left alone in the kitchen.

It was getting cold and Matt got up and rummaged through the wood box for some more stuff to throw on the fire. There wasn't much left but he managed to stir up a little heat and we both moved closer.

"Is that the straight scoop?" Matt asked. "Have you really quit playing the guitar for good?"

I shrugged. "I don't know. I think so."

"Why?"

"Why not? As far as I can see, this whole music thing is for suckers. There's almost nothing you can do that takes so much time and work, and what do you get out of it? Maybe one guy in a couple of million gets to where he can make any real money with it. Besides, I've got my future all planned and there just isn't going to be much time for music."

"I see," Matt said. Then he just sat there for a long

time fooling with his beard and looking at me in a funny way, like he was half amused and half disgusted. I was already beginning to get mad when he started out. "Well, there's just one thought I'd like to offer. You might very well get to be the one in a couple of million who makes it with music. I'll bet the odds against being born with the kind of musical talent you have are almost that extreme."

I laughed. "Thanks," I said. "But I've been through that stage. Daydreaming about being some big star or concert artist. Fat chance. And besides, I don't have the personality for it. To be a big star, more than half of it is personality—the way you come on. And I just don't have it."

"How do you know you don't?"

"I know. When I went to Lincoln, I used to have to play violin solos with the orchestra." All of a sudden I was remembering those solos—in the bottom of my stomach. Me limping on stage in my outgrown suit and frozen smile, and the guys from my class giggling in the front row. "It made me sick," I said. "I mean sick!"

"Okay. Okay," Matt said. "So you don't want to be a professional musician. You still wouldn't have to quit music all together. You used to play and sing for hours at a time, with nobody ever twisting your arm or even telling you to practice. And now—nothing. I don't get it."

"I told you. I don't have time anymore," I said. "I

have plans, other things to do."

"Yeah, I know," Matt grinned. "Phil was right when he called you a throwback. With half the kids in the country rebelling against the whole scene, here you are knocking yourself out to be a part of it. How come?"

I got up and slammed the milk into the refrigerator and started out of the room. "Di! Di, wait a minute," Matt said.

So I stopped halfway out the door, without turning around. "I'm sorry," Matt said. "I wasn't trying to put you down. I really just want to know. How come?"

"How come!" I said. "How do I know how come? I haven't figured it out. I don't have time. And I can't help it if I'm not rebelling in the right direction. Everybody has to rebel against what he has to rebel against. Not what somebody else has."

Chapter 9

WHEN I GOT TO MY ROOM, I SLAMMED THE DOOR AND threw myself down on my bed. I lay there for about thirty seconds and then I sat up and punched my pillow, took off my shoes, turned off the light and lay back down. In about thirty seconds more, I got up again, turned on the light and put my shoes back on. I found a book I'd been reading, took it over to my desk and got out a pencil and ruler to mark important passages. After I'd read about two sentences, I put the book down, grabbed my jacket, and left the house.

I didn't have any idea where I was going. I just felt I had to get out. I hunched my head down inside my turned-up collar, stuck my hands in my pockets and started to walk. But I'd only gone a few blocks when I realized I was heading toward Alcott-Simpson's. I knew it would be closed, but I told myself that as long as I was walking, there wasn't any reason why I shouldn't walk in that direction if I felt like it.

It was a strange night. There was a low misty overcast, so thick that in spots it was almost like walking through drifting clouds. There wasn't any wind, though, so after a few fast blocks I didn't feel the cold at all. In what seemed like only a few minutes, I'd reached the corner of Palm and Eighth.

I looked around. The cold mist was thicker than it had been down in our part of town. The street lights were only small fuzzy glares, and José's shuttered-up flower stand was draped in a floating white veil. There was a stillness, as if the city sounds were deadened, drowned in the fog. Except for a car or a scurrying pedestrian appearing and quickly disappearing into the gloom, the city looked deserted, like a land of the dead. I decided to walk around the block once quickly and then go right on home.

All around Alcott-Simpson's the fog was almost like a living thing, clammy cold and dripping; but inside the display windows, the lighting had a golden tone, warm and rich. More than ever it was like looking into a separate world. I walked by windows set up as rooms beautifully furnished, windows full of haughty manikins dressed in the latest styles, and one that was an elaborate ski lodge scene with a bunch of manikins in ski clothes standing around a fireplace with lots of skiing equipment carefully scattered around. When I came to the west entrance, I stopped and peered into the ground floor.

The huge stretch of the main floor of Alcott-Simpson's was almost dark. Dim lights were on in just a few

places, and here and there a pale glow lit a length of gilded pillar or reflected in a mirror or counter top. In between and back behind, the rest of the floor seemed to go on forever, dim and shadowy. It made me think of a huge cave, maybe the treasure cavern in the Arabian Nights with endless riches making golden sparkles in the gloom. I leaned against the fog-wet glass and whispered "Open Sesame" but nothing happened. I went on around the block, and it wasn't until I had stopped again at the east entrance that I saw something moving way back in the shadows.

It was a long way off at first among the potted trees at the edge of the Garden Court and it appeared and then disappeared among the deeper shadows. Two or three times I told myself that I was only imagining it; but then suddenly it was close enough so that I knew I wasn't. I wasn't imagining it, and when she turned into the main aisle that led to the east entrance I could see that it was a girl—a girl wearing a long white dress with dark hair hanging down over her shoulders. Even before she was near enough for me to see her face, I knew it was Sara. When she was quite close, she began to run and in a second she was unlocking the door; I was inside before I had time to think.

The minute I heard the door locking behind me, I wasn't sure I wanted to be inside Alcott-Simpson's again after closing time. The first time had been bad enough. "Hey," I whispered, "what's going on. What are you doing in here? I mean, what are we doing in here?"

For a second she didn't say anything; she just looked at me and smiled that all-out smile, like a little kid on Christmas morning. Then suddenly she looked behind me at the door and said, "Hurry. This way." We ducked back into a side aisle as some people walked by on the sidewalk outside.

We stood there in the shadows waiting for them to get out of sight, and I said, "Look, this is crazy. I don't want to go through this again."

"It's all right," Sara said. "The dogs are gone now. And the guards are all in the watchman's room. I know all about when they come and where they look. They won't see us. If we go upstairs, no one will see us."

I don't know why, but I believed her absolutely. I was sure that she knew what she was talking about; I was sure that the police dogs were gone and that the watchman would only be where she expected them to be and that she was right about us being safe upstairs. But there was one thing I wasn't sure about, and I was thinking about that all the time as Sara led the way through the shadowy aisles and up the escalator. I was wondering *how* she knew and *why* she knew and what part she played in the whole big mystery that had been going on at Alcott-Simpson's.

When we got to the mezzanine, she stopped and waited for me.

"I didn't believe it," she said in a breathless rush.

"When they said you were right outside, I didn't believe it."

For a second I thought I mustn't have heard her right. "When who said?" I gasped. "Who said I was right outside?"

Sara looked startled for a split second, but then she laughed. "Oh just some friends of mine," she said. "I have some other friends in the store."

I looked around. "But who—and where are they? I haven't seen anyone except you—and the guards that time. Is that it? Are the guards your friends?"

She laughed. "Oh no. The guards aren't my friends. My friends are—they're here someplace, in the store. It's a very big store."

"It's a very big store," I said in a sarcastic tone of voice. "Well, thanks for the news. Now look. You've said something about other people, other people in the store, before. I want to know what you're talking about. I want to know what I'm getting into. These friends of yours, are they people who work here or are they—the ones the guards have been hired to catch? The ones who've been stealing things. I'm not going to rat on anybody, but I don't want to get mixed up in——"

I faded out about then because all of a sudden I noticed that Sara was—well, not crying exactly, but her eyes had an underwater look and her chin was moving. It shook me up. I'd never seen a girl cry before, except a few real little ones, and I'd sure as hell never *made* a girl cry before. I don't remember exactly what I said next, but I do know I stopped asking questions. I just began talking and I kept on until she smiled again, and when I was through I knew I'd said things I hadn't meant, or at least I hadn't meant them until I said them. I'd said that it didn't matter to me who the others were and it didn't matter what they were doing in Alcott-Simpson's and that I wouldn't ask her about them any more. She looked up at me then and smiled, and her eyes were fantastic. For just a minute I felt my skin prickle all over the way it does when music is beautiful beyond any sort of reason or expectation.

"Let's go up to the second floor," she said, and her voice sounded normal and cheerful. "I left some things up there, and I have to put some dresses away."

So we went on up to the second floor and walked way back through the women's clothing departments to where evening dresses and coats were sold. Near some tall three-sided mirrors there was a chair piled high with evening dresses. Sara began putting the dresses on hangers and putting them away. "I was looking at them," she explained. "But I always put things away when I've finished." One of the dresses she put away was very much like the one she was wearing, long and white and floaty. I wondered if she'd just borrowed it off the rack, too.

On another chair near the mirrors was a bouquet of flowers, some kind of very small orchids—golden tan flecked with brown. When Sara finished putting away the dresses, she picked up the flowers. "I got these downstairs," she said. "Would you like one?" She gave me an orchid, and I put it in the buttonhole of my jacket. Sara stood in front of the mirror and put the others in her hair—crisp dark gold against soft black.

"What do you want to see?" she asked then.

"I don't care," I said.

"All right," she said, "I think I'd like a necklace. Shall we go find me a necklace?" I guess I looked worried at that because she added, "It's all right. I'll put it back after a while."

I was afraid she meant to go back down to the Gem Shop on the first floor where there were real diamonds and other jewelry that cost an awful lot of money. I didn't much like the idea of fooling around with that sort of thing, even if she did mean to put it back. But it turned out that she was only heading for a costume jewelry counter on the second floor. When we got there, she took all kinds of things out of the cases and tried them on—earrings, necklaces, bracelets. She kept asking me what I thought about each one, but they all looked okay to me and I said so. At last she put everything back except a long string of green beads and a heavy medallion of some kind of metal. After she put them on she said, "Where shall we go now?"

"I don't know," I said, but then I had an idea. "I always used to have dreams about having the Alcott-Simpson's toy department all to myself. It might be fun to see what it's like—just for old time's sake."

Sara paused for a minute, and I thought she looked uncertain, maybe even worried, but then she nodded. "All right, let's go to the toy department."

So we started on up to the fourth floor, but not very directly. Walking with Sara was not like walking with anyone else. We moved in the same direction but not in the same way or at the same rate of speed. I walked slowly, trying hard not to make any noise, straining my ears and eyes against the unaccustomed silence and shadows. And all the time Sara came and went around me so that it was almost like walking with an unleashed puppy. She kept going and coming—skipping ahead and running back—telling me to come see something or else bringing something back to me. Once she was gone for a second and came back with a big hat made of pink ostrich feathers. "Isn't it beautiful—so beautiful," she said, holding it out for me to touch. She put it on her head and pulled the feathery brim down around her face and laughed and ran back to put it away. We made detours to look at some golden slippers, a manikin in a wedding dress, and some home gym equipment. Sara wanted to touch everything, try it out, and she kept saying that everything was beautiful. After a while I felt a little less nervous, and I tried out a few things, too. I rowed on the rowing machine and rode the stationery bicycle in the gym display, while Sara sat on a balancing horse and watched and laughed. I laughed, too, but I couldn't hold on to the feeling of having a good time. There was a kind of frustration in the strangeness of the situation that kept bothering me, when Sara was out of sight, and other times, too. The other times were now and then when Sara would stop and a shadow would pass over her face, like a memory of something terrible and hopeless.

We had just gotten to the top of the escalator at the fourth floor when Sara stopped and stood for a second as if she were listening. "Wait," she said. "Wait here a minute. I'll be right back."

"Why?" I asked. "Where are you going?"

Sara motioned to the left where you could see the top of the arch that led to the toy department. "There," she said. "To see if everything is all right. I'll be right back. Stay here until I come back. Please stay here."

"But—but," I said, and I was still protesting when she ran away. I hadn't really promised, and I had almost decided to follow her anyway when she came running back.

"No," she said. "Let's not go there now. We'll go there later. Let's go back downstairs now."

She started back down the escalator, and I followed after her feeling stranger than ever. Like having the kind of dream where crazy unexplainable things keep happening and you realize it's crazy but you can't wake up and make it stop.

When we got back to the ground floor, we went to

the left around the Mall. I tried to question Sara about the toy department and why we couldn't go there, but she only shook her head. Except for that, she seemed the same as before, laughing and talking and rushing around. We stopped for a while in the Music Shop. There were a lot of guitars in some big glass cabinets and I mentioned to Sara that I played. Right away she wanted me to play one. "Sure," I said. "That's all we need to bring every guard in the place down on our necks."

"Oh no," Sara said. "It's all right. The guards don't go on their rounds very often anymore. They have a place down in the basement where they all stay together. They won't hear."

If I'd really stopped to think about it, I would have realized that that didn't make much sense, but at that point I was ready to believe just about anything Sara said. I was starting to see if I could get a guitar out of the cabinet when all of a sudden I heard voices. I froze on the spot, listening. In a minute I could tell that I wasn't hearing loud voices still a long way off, but very soft voices coming from someplace very near. My heart went limp for a second and then caught up with a huge thudding rush. I reached for Sara's hand to pull her away, but she dodged away from me and stood still, listening.

"Come on," I barely breathed. "Let's get out of here."

She shook her head. "Stay here," she said. "I have

to find out. I'll be right back."

She moved in the direction of the voices, and after a minute I followed. By the time she got to the arch that led into the next department, I was only a few steps behind. We went around the corner—and then I started to laugh. We were in the TV shop and all it was was a big color TV set that had been left on by some careless clerk.

I began laughing like crazy; it really wasn't that funny but I was feeling dizzy with relief. Then all at once I noticed Sara's face. She wasn't laughing, and she looked hard at the TV and then very quickly all around the shop as if she were looking for something. She was frowning a little and pressing her lips together hard.

"What's the matter?" I said. "It's nothing to worry about. Some dumb clerk just forgot to turn it off." Sara nodded, but she didn't say anything, and she looked back over her shoulder again uneasily.

I remember that it was some old movie that was showing on the TV, one of those old musicals with mobs of dancers in fancy costumes. I walked over to it and gave the knob a big whack and shut it off. "There!" I said, with a big phony self-confident grin. "That takes care of that. I press the magic button and —Presto! No more mysterious voices."

Sara smiled back, only it wasn't a real smile; actually the way she looked at me was almost like an apology. It made me feel confused and stupid and helpless. I had an urge to yell or hit something, but all I did was whisper, "For cripes sake will you tell me what's going on?"

But she didn't. I mean she didn't tell me anything. Instead she walked on slowly, and I followed. We went back around to the east entrance, and Sara opened the door and I went out. The fog was even thicker, and the city seemed, more than ever, like the end of the world.

I was outside before either of us said anything at all. Then Sara said, "Will you come back again?" I nodded and she closed the door and locked it. I watched her walking back towards the escalators with the night lights gleaming and then fading on her white dress until she disappeared in the darkness.

It wasn't until I was home in bed going over everything in my mind that I realized the voices hadn't come from the TV set at all. We'd stood right there in front of the set for at least a minute before I turned it off, and it hadn't made the slightest noise. The sound must have been turned off the whole time.

Chapter 10

Maybe alone on the elevator
A chattering gasp was heard,
Or a pattering rush on the escalator,
Or perhaps it first occurred
As a brush of fingers against the cages,
Of the pet shop's golden birds,
They heard, they sensed, they almost faced it,
And they said it was absurd.

IT WAS THINKING ABOUT THE VOICES AND THE SILENT TV set that gave me the idea for the first verse, because that's the way it was with me. I sensed something that night that I didn't let myself even think about for a long time afterwards because it seemed so crazy. Oh, I thought about what had happened all right, but mostly to figure out some logical explanation.

I lay awake for a long time after I finally got home that night going over and over the whole thing in my mind. It occurred to me that there was a chance something had gone wrong with the sound part of the reception just as we came up—right after I heard the voices. But I knew it wasn't too likely because the sound is usually the last part to go out when there is reception trouble; and if something does go wrong with it, it's more apt to turn into static than into complete silence. Besides, there was the strange way Sara had acted. Finally there didn't seem to be any other explanation: there really were people who were able to get into the store at night—and Sara *did* have something to do with them.

The way I figured it out, Sara must have had some connection with somebody important in the store. Like maybe, her father was one of the owners or executives. That way she would have been able to hang around enough to get hold of some keys and a lot of information about schedules and things like that. And then maybe, she just got started letting other people into the store. Maybe just other kids now and then, like she let me in, or maybe there was a regular gang of some sort. If there was a gang, I was pretty sure it was made up of kids. I don't know why exactly, except that Sara was so young, and also because of things I'd heard. Like, Madame Stregovitch had said that there had only been a little stealing, and Sara herself had said something about accidents and tricks being played. It all sounded like kid stuff.

So I made up a theory, a long complicated one,

about how Sara was a lonely rich kid who didn't have many friends, and who thought up the Alcott-Simpson business as a way to meet people and have something exciting to do. It occurred to me that if she met somebody she really liked, maybe she'd lose interest in letting all the others in before they all got caught and got into serious trouble. I remembered that Sara had said that the dogs weren't being used anymore and that the guards didn't go on their rounds so often, so maybe she'd already stopped letting most of the others in, probably the ones who'd caused the trouble. Only I wasn't just one of the others, because Sara had asked me if I would come back, and I had said yes.

After a while I got too sleepy for long complicated theories, but I went on thinking about Sara clear up until I went to sleep; and even afterward—because I dreamed a lot of crazy stuff that night, and Sara kept drifting in and out of the dream. It was one of those long mixed-up dreams where all sorts of crazy things keep happening, and when I woke up I could only remember bits and pieces of it here and there. But there was one part about me riding this fantastic black horse with a silver mane and tail. I was riding it right down the middle of the street and all the cars were stopping and honking, and then I was riding it up the stairs in the main building at Randolph High. The stairs kept getting longer and longer and wider and wider, and a lot of the kids I know at Randolph were running up the stairs trying to keep up with me on the black horse, and I was laughing and waving back at them. And then all of a sudden the horse started to grow, and he got bigger and bigger until I was like some little monkey clinging to his back, and he began to kick and jump and plunge around. Then I was lying on the ground, and the horse was standing over me as big as a house; and way up on his back I saw Sara, and she was leaning over and reaching down as if she were trying to help me. I could see her as plain as day. She had on the same white dress she'd worn that night at the store, and the wind was whipping her hair across her face so that all I could see was her eyes and they were full of tears the way they'd been when I'd tried to make her explain everything.

When I woke up the next morning, the fog was all gone and it was a bright, sunny day. Everything seemed different. All the things that had happened at Alcott-Simpson's, particularly all the strange unexplainable things, seemed faded and indistinct and sort of a part of the dream I had just been having. During the next few days it all blended and mixed together until at times I wasn't really sure which things had actually happened and which had been part of the dream. I went to school and to work, but for a day or two I didn't go into Alcott-Simpson's at all. I wanted to see Sara again very much, but I didn't want to be in Alcott-Simpson's again at night, and I had a feeling that if I saw Sara again I wouldn't have much choice. Two or three times I walked all around the Alcott-

Simpson block, but I didn't go inside. Not even to get warm, in spite of the fact that it had turned foggy again and very cold.

Once I stopped for a while to talk to José. "Hi, José," I said. "What's new? Seen any more police dogs lately?"

"No, no dogs," José said. "Them dog men geeve up and go away long time ago."

"Gave up?" I asked.

"Sure. Dogs don' do no good. Them dogs go in there and they jus' lie down and cry."

"Lie down and cry?" I said. "What makes them do that? I thought those dogs were supposed to be great at patrolling stores and places like that."

José just shrugged and rolled up his eyes in a way that meant it was too much for him to explain. I stepped inside his booth to get warm by the little foot-warmer stove that he kept there. I bent over it and warmed my hands. "This is the coldest fog I've ever seen," I said.

José nodded. "Spirit-fog," he said.

"What?" I said.

"You know my friend Luke?" José asked.

I nodded. Luke was an old man who had been a janitor at Alcott-Simpson's for years and years. He was a good friend of José's, and he used to come over to the stand during his breaks, just to pass the time of day.

"Luke tell me about theese spirit-fog," José said.

"Back where Luke come from in the big hill country, they have theese theengs."

"What things?"

"Theese fog, that comes white and cold in the place where the spirit leeves, een a low and lonely place between the tall hills. And Luke say that sometimes a man go into theese fog—and he not come out."

"Yeah," I said. "I've heard some of Luke's ghost stories before. He has a million of them. It's just superstition. I'll bet he doesn't really believe all that stuff he tells himself."

"Maybe not," José said. "Maybe not."

I had heard Lukes's stories before, and I'd never paid much attention to them; but that night I was glad when the fog began to thin a few blocks from Alcott-Simpson's. By the time I got home it was practically gone.

Right about then if anyone had asked me if I'd ever go back in Alcott-Simpson's again after hours— that is, if I ever had the chance, and it wasn't likely I ever would—I'd have told them that wild horses couldn't drag me. But that very night I did a funny thing. After I'd finished my homework, I got my guitar down off the wall and began to practice. I didn't decide to do it, I just did it. And while I was practicing I caught myself several times thinking of something to play in terms of what Sara might like to hear. I told myself I was really stupid, but the thought kept coming back. Anyway, regardless of what I was practicing for, I had to admit that it felt great to play again. It had been months since I'd even touched the guitar and I was very rusty, but actually I was surprised how quickly my fingers loosened up and it all began to come back.

The next Saturday was a calm clear day with a softness in the air that almost felt like spring. On my way to Palm Avenue to do my regular Saturday morning jobs, I walked past Alcott-Simpson's and everything looked bright and normal. The morning sun sparkled off its hundreds of windows and lightened the gray of its stone walls. I decided that as soon as I'd finished my work, I'd drop by for a quick visit. If Sara was still hanging around the store, she'd probably be wondering where I'd been. While I swept out at the travel bureau and washed display cases at the stationers store, I was thinking over my "poor little rich kid" theory about Sara, wondering where she lived and what her life had been like to make her so—well, strange really, or at least different.

But when I stopped by Alcott-Simpson's on my way home, I couldn't find Sara anywhere. The store wasn't at all crowded, so it shouldn't have been difficult to find someone; but I didn't see Sara anywhere. As a matter of fact, for a nice warm Saturday, Alcott-Simpson's was amazingly empty; but then, I told myself, maybe it was only because a lot of the customers had taken advantage of the good weather to get out of town for the weekend. Anyway, I looked around pretty thoroughly and I didn't see anyone I knew very well. I even dropped by Madame Stregovitch's counter, but there was a different clerk on duty—someone I'd never seen before. I tried asking her some questions, but she seemed nervous and snappy. She said she didn't know anything at all. She didn't know for sure, but she thought that Madame Stregovitch had been ill. "But I'm not sure," she said. "I haven't been sure about anything at all, lately."

That night right after dinner I went to my room. I knew what I had in mind when I changed my clothes and put my guitar in its plastic case, but I didn't stop to think about it very much. I moved quickly, as if I had an appointment to keep. When I was all ready, I dropped by the kitchen to tell Dad I was going out.

Dad wasn't in the kitchen, but nearly everyone else in the neighborhood was. Phil and Dunc and a couple of their girl friends were sitting around the fireplace arguing about where they ought to go to spend the evening. As usual the problem seemed to be that no-body had any money. The youngest Grover kid was crawling along on the floor, dragging a dishtowel and watching Charity, who was hiding behind a chair leg and getting ready to pounce out as the dishtowel went by. Matt and Mr. Rosen, an old chess friend of Dad's from up the street, had the chess board out on the kitchen table.

I took the dishtowel away from the kid and made a werewolf snarl at him; he rolled over on his back like a puppy coaxing to be played with. Charity must have thought I wanted to play, too, because she danced out sideways from under the chair and grabbed me by the ankle. But I didn't have any time to play. I shook Charity loose and asked loudly if anyone happened to know where my dad was. Everybody looked up blankly, like they couldn't remember who I was for a minute. "My Dad?" I repeated, "you know, the guy who lives here?"

"Oh yeah, him," Phil said. "He retired to his studio just a minute ago—" he stopped and fluttered his eyebrows "—with a charmer from the P.T.A."

It might have taken me a minute to figure out what he was talking about, except that just then I heard the piano and, a second later, a horrible screeching soprano with a vibrato like an excited turkey. "Ohhh-say can you seeeeee?" the voice warbled. I knew, then, what was going on. Dad had told me about this dame who'd been over a couple of times to practice her singing. She was the mother of one of his piano students, and she imagined herself to be a singer. Somehow she'd talked the P.T.A. she belonged to into asking her to lead the National Anthem at their next meeting. Of course she wasn't paying Dad anything for coaching her. She was just "dropping by a couple of times to warm up with a piano." Dad told me about it as if it were kind of a joke on him, but I had an idea that it was one charity he regretted. That kind of a voice would be like scraping chalk on a blackboard as far as

Dad was concerned.

When I opened the door to the studio, the P. T. A. prima donna unclasped her hands and drifted to a stop in the midst of "the perilous night." Dad turned around from the piano looking so grateful for the interruption that for a minute I felt sorry for him, even if he had brought it on himself.

"Uh, excuse me," I said. "Dad, Jerry Davidson wants me to give him a lesson on the guitar. I won't be back until late." It didn't happen to be a lie. Both statements were true. They just didn't have anything to do with each other. Dad looked at the guitar case and for a second his eyes crinkled up with pleasure. Then suddenly he cooled it and said, "I see. Well, I guess that will be all right," in a carefully indifferent tone of voice. It was easy to see that he was trying not to show that he was happy to see me doing something with music again. It was a perfectly obvious put-on; he never was any good at pretending.

I was on my way down the stairs before it occurred to me what his problem was. He was probably thinking that if he approved of something, I'd quit wanting to do it. I had to admit to myself that it had worked that way at times lately. But I didn't know he knew it.

Chapter 11

IT WAS DARK WHEN I GOT TO ALCOTT-SIMPSON'S, BUT it wasn't foggy and there were a lot more people on the streets than there had been the last time I'd been there at night. I walked around the block, stopping for a few minutes at each entrance. Inside everything looked the same as it had before, dim lights and white-draped counters. I went back around and stopped again at each entrance, but all it got me was some suspicious stares from passers-by. Finally I admitted to myself that it was pretty stupid to think that I could get in that way again—at least, not unless I let Sara know I was coming. She might not be there; she might be there but not know I was outside; or she might even know and be afraid to open the door because of there being so many people on the sidewalks. It had just been a coincidence the time before.

I knew it would look strange if I went home so early, and it occurred to me that I might do what I'd pretended I was going to do. So I called Jerry from a pay phone, and luckily he was at home. When he heard that I was on my way over with my guitar, he got very enthusiastic. I'd given him a couple of lessons when I first got to know him, before I decided to quit music for good, and he'd been after me for a long time to teach him some more.

So instead of seeing Sara that night, I sat around and played the guitar at Jerry's house. Actually it turned out to be not a bad evening. We ate a lot of food that Jerry's mother fixed for us, and Jerry called up another friend of his who wanted to start on the guitar. This guy, whose name is Brett Atwood, came over and I showed them some chords and strums, and the three of us worked out a couple of new arrangements for some old songs. It turned out that Brett had a great voice and he even knew something about music, so together we came up with some pretty good ideas.

After we'd been fooling around for quite a while, I decided to play some of the things I'd written. It was the first time I'd done any of my own stuff for anyone except my dad and some of the people around home; but everything seemed to be going so well that I decided to try it. I was really surprised at the reaction I got. Actually, they made such a fuss I was a little embarrassed. I mean, they really knocked themselves out. Like for instance, Brett—who is a much more swinging type than either Jerry or me—said, "Jerry, Baby, you have really been holding out on me. You said he was good, but you didn't tell me the cat had a bad case of genius."

Afterwards I took the bus home, and when I got off downtown to transfer I walked by Alcott-Simpson's again. It was late by then, and everything in the area was closed up tight. Almost all the pedestrian traffic had stopped and the fog was rolling in, drifting down into the canyons between the tall buildings. Inside Alcott-Simpson's, everything seemed just the same as before. But I waited for a while, and all at once I thought I saw something move way back near the escalator. It was so dark back there it was hard to be sure, but then I thought I saw it again on the same spot. It wasn't coming closer or going away; it was as if someone was just standing there watching. I waited, straining my eyes to see, and whatever it was waited, too. Then a police car drove by slowly, and the cop stared at me so I had to move on. A bus was rolling up to the corner, so I hurried and caught it and went on home. By the time the bus had arrived at our stop I'd figured it out, and gone back to thinking about the evening at Jerry's. What I'd decided was that I'd only been watching a dust sheet draped over something way back in shadows. I'd only imagined I'd seen it move.

That was on Saturday. It was the next Monday morning at the hat shop that I talked to the clerk named Myrna. Myrna had been a clerk in the Pet Shop at Alcott-Simpson's for a year or so. She was a good friend of Jayne Anne, who owned the hat shop where

I worked every Monday morning. She was fairly young and very pale and nervous looking, so that she always made me think of the white mice that were sold in the department where she worked. Now and then, on her way to work in the mornings, Myrna would drop by the hat shop for a quick cup of coffee and a little gossip with Jayne Anne. At the hat shop she was always friendly to me, but if I saw her in Alcott-Simpson's she was very formal because she was afraid of the man who was the department manager. That morning when I got to the hat shop, Jayne Anne was late; the shop was still locked, and Myrna was having hysterics in the alcove outside the front door.

"Dion," she sobbed when I came up, "I'm so glad to see you." She rubbed her eyes with a handkerchief that looked sopping wet already. "Where on earth is Jayne Anne?"

"I don't know. I guess she's a little late. She's this late lots of times on Monday mornings. She'll probably be here any minute."

Myrna wiped her eyes again and looked at her watch. "Oh, I guess it isn't so very late. It just seems like I've been waiting here for—ee—ev—ver." And she broke down and started to cry again.

I felt very uncomfortable. It seemed as if I ought to do something, but I couldn't think what. Finally I said, "Is there anything I could do?" It occurred to me that maybe someone had been chasing her, but there didn't seem to be anyone around. Besides she wasn't

the kind of girl that anyone would want to chase, unless it was just to see her run. "Could I call the police,
or something?" I said.

"Oh, no-o-o," Myrna said, pulling herself together
a little, "no thank you. I'll just wait here and talk to
Jayne Anne when she comes. Not that she can help me
either, but I just have to talk to someone or I'm going
to go crazy." And then she added in a kind of a wail,
"if I haven't already."

It occurred to me that if what she needed was
someone to talk to, I'd be glad to oblige. I didn't want
to see her go crazy and, besides, I was curious. To start
things out I ventured a guess. "Did you get fired, or
something like that?" I'd heard that the manager of
the Pet Shop was a real tyrant.

"Fired?" she said. "Oh, no. Oh, my no. I'm almost
the only full time clerk Mr. Braunstetter has left. He
couldn't fire me, though I suppose he'll try to blame it
on me. He always tries to blame it on one of us. But he
couldn't fire me." She stopped and looked at me, and I
could tell she was trying to decide how much she should
say. I tried to look mature and helpful. She took a deep
breath and started out, and once she began it was like
a break in the dam. She never even stopped to take a
real breath.

"It was this morning—I don't mean that what happened this morning is all of it, because it's been going
on for weeks and weeks, but this morning was the last
straw. It was my turn to get to work early to clean the

cages and do the feeding, so I got there just as the morning janitorial crew was going in. And when we got in, the canaries and parakeets and mynas were loose and flying all over the store. They're catching them now—running all over the store with nets and ladders—but I just couldn't stand it. I couldn't stand it anymore—I just had to get out of there. I didn't even stop to check out."

Myrna had been looking scared to death all along, but when she said that she looked horrified. She was the type who wouldn't be caught dead breaking even the littlest rule, and checking in and out was almost sacred at Alcott-Simpson's. "*I didn't even stop to check out,*" she said again, "*I am going crazy—I'm sure of it.*"

"You said it had been going on for weeks and weeks," I said. "What has? Have the birds been out before?"

"No, not the birds, but other things. Some of the mice, and the kittens—the kittens so many times that we had to stop stocking them. And the chipmunks—and, oh yes, once an iguana. But that's not all. They feed things, too. Right in the middle of the afternoon They feed things. So that you look in the feed trays one minute and they're empty, and the next minute they're full. And They put things in places they shouldn't be—spools of thread in the kittens' cages—wind up toy submarines in the fish tanks—"

"They?" I asked.

"Yes. They!" she said angrily, as if I'd meant I didn't believe her. "Don't take my word for it. It's not just me. It's not just in the Pet Shop either." Her voice got higher and more hysterical. "Oh, a lot of them won't talk about it, because they're afraid of what you'll think, or because they're afraid they'll think it themselves. But if you pick the right ones, the ones who *have* to talk to someone and who can see that you're as scared as they are, they'll tell you. They'll tell you about the sounds They make—feet running and laughter, and voices—and the things that move by themselves—toys, balls that bounce by themselves—and things you see—in dark corners——" She pressed her hands over her mouth as if she were trying to make herself stop.

I felt paralyzed. I opened my mouth to say something, but nothing came out. Just then Jayne Anne came around the corner. "Hello, Di," she said, "sorry to be so late. Myrna! What is it? What on earth is wrong?" She unlocked the door and led Myrna inside, patting her and making sympathetic noises. She stuck her head back out long enough to say, "Di, run along, won't you please. We'll skip the sweeping up for today. Catch me later in the week if you have time." She nodded towards Myrna and made a face that said, "You see how it is."

"Sure," I said. "See you later." And I started off down the sidewalk toward my next job in the Mc-Adam building.

I finished the rest of my Monday morning work in a kind of daze. My mind was just treading water, doing the same things over and over without getting anywhere. The only positive conclusion that I came up with was that I was going to have to see Sara again right away. I was going to have to break my promise about not asking any questions. For my sake, and maybe for her own too, Sara was going to *have* to tell me what she knew about whatever it was that was going on at Alcott-Simpson's.

Chapter 12

Maybe they've heard in the toy department
The endless whispered sighs,
Or have they seen on the goosedown couches,
Where each night something lies?
Could they be learning to shun the shadows
For fear of great dark eyes?
They know, they fear, they're almost certain
But they tell each other lies.

REMEMBERING ABOUT POOR MYRNA GAVE ME THE idea for the second verse.

I finished my work in a hurry on that Monday morning, and on my way to catch the bus to school I walked back past Alcott-Simpson's. Through the doors I could see that a few more clerks had arrived. The birds must have all been caught, because I didn't see any ladders or butterfly nets. That is, if there had been any birds; I'd almost decided that poor Myrna was right about going crazy.

But whether there was anything to Myrna's story or not, I was getting more and more frantic about seeing Sara. I almost decided to wait around until nine-thirty so I could take a quick look for Sara before I went to school. I would have, too, even though I hated being late, but I was almost positive she wouldn't be there. No matter what kind of weird home life she had, she probably had to be in school on Monday mornings like everyone else. So I went on to school and tried to keep my mind off the whole thing until I'd had a chance to get some more information. But that afternoon I was back at Alcott-Simpson's as quickly as I could get there after school.

Sara wasn't in the store that afternoon either. I hung around until the closing bell rang, and she just wasn't there. The crowds were very light again, so I was fairly sure that I'd have seen her if she were anywhere around. There weren't many customers, and there didn't seem to be as many clerks as usual. I glanced in the pet shop and it seemed quiet and normal enough. Except that Mr. Braunstetter, the department manager, was waiting on customers himself, which was something I'd never seen him do before.

I was on my way home, just a couple of blocks from Cathedral Street, when I passed a bus stop and there was Madame Stregovitch getting off the bus. She was carrying a couple of big packages, so I hurried and caught up with her and asked if I could help her carry something.

"Dion," she said. "How nice to see you. You appear like magic and in the nick of time. My arms are very tired." She gave me the biggest package, and we started off down Willow Street. I'd been wanting another chance to question Madame about the trouble at Alcott-Simpson's, and this seemed like a made-to-order opportunity. But I remembered that the last time I'd tried, she'd seemed pretty reluctant to give any answers. So I thought I'd ease into the subject as carefully as I could. I began by saying that I'd heard she'd been sick and I hoped she was okay now. She said yes, she had been and that she was better. Then, just as I'd gotten around to asking if she thought the store was still having as much trouble, she turned into a driveway.

I had known for years that Madame Stregovitch lived somewhere in the Cathedral Street neighborhood, because I used to see her around now and then, but I'd never known exactly where. The driveway we were walking down led back behind an old Victorian town house that had been turned into apartments years and years before. It was a mess of peeling paint, cracked windows and crumbling ornaments—the kind of thing that artists and tourists love, but nobody in their right mind would want to live in. But Madame didn't go into the big house. We went around back and behind the garage we came to a gate that led into a tangled overgrown mess of trees and bushes that had probably once been a garden. Almost hidden in the bushes was a small house. The little house was probably built at the same time as the big one in front of it, maybe for servants to live in; but now it was fenced off into what looked like a little world of its own. It was old and a little shabby, but not rundown and uncared for like the big house; and sitting there almost hidden in the undergrowth, it gave you a funny feeling. Like you'd stumbled onto a place where time had stopped a long time ago.

Madame Stregovitch unlocked a heavy front door with a small oval window, and we went inside.

"I'll just put these things away," she said taking the packages. "And in the meantime you can get the fire going in the fireplace. Then we'll have a nice cup of tea."

I don't spend much time having tea with old ladies as a rule, but I was curious, and besides I hadn't had a chance yet to ask the questions I'd been planning. The logs were all arranged in the fireplace, so I found some matches on the mantle and got the fire started. Somewhere not far away I could hear Madame bustling around running water and clinking dishes.

When I was putting the matches back, I noticed a bunch of pictures on the mantle—mostly big framed photographs of foreign-looking people. There was one picture I noticed especially. It was larger than the others and in a very fancy frame. It was just a photograph, an old dim photograph of a woman, but there was something about it that made me keep staring at it. She had a kind of shawl draped over her head, and her face looked a little like Madame Stregovitch, dark and bony. But it was mostly the eyes I kept looking at. I've seen pictures before that had eyes that seemed to follow you, but these did more than that. They made you feel like squirming.

The fire was going pretty well and Madame S. still hadn't come back, so I turned away from the picture and walked around the room. It was a small darkish room, stuffed with lots of big old-fashioned furniture and smothered with heavy drapes and curtains. The few places the walls did show, they were covered with pictures, some of them painted or sewn on heavy cloth. In two corners of the room there were little cupboards full of weird looking what-nots. All the time I was wandering around I kept glancing back at that one picture on the mantle, and finally I went back to look at it again. I was standing in front of it when Madame finally came back into the room. She was carrying a tray with a teapot and cups and a plate of little cakes and pastries. She came and stood beside me and looked at the picture, too.

"Who is she?" I asked.

Madame turned away without answering and put the tray on a little table. After a minute she said, "She was my mother."

"I thought she might be," I said. "She looks a little like you."

"Do you think so?" She motioned for me to come

132

and sit down. "Yes, I suppose it is quite evident. I am quite like her in many ways. It is a likeness I've spent most of a lifetime trying to escape."

"Trying to escape?" I said. I guess I sounded a little surprised. Kids are always running their parents down and nobody pays any attention. But you just don't expect people as old as Madame Stregovitch to do that sort of thing.

"You are shocked," Madame said. "You are thinking perhaps that such an attitude is unsuitable for one of my generation?" I knew she was kind of teasing me, and I got the point. But then she shrugged and said, "Well, perhaps. However, in this case I think you did not understand my meaning. I did not intend to suggest that I disapproved of my mother in the usual manner of younger generations. She was an extraordinary woman, and I did not wish to be like her for an extraordinary reason—I was afraid."

"Afraid?" I said. "Afraid of what?"

But Madame just began pouring tea and saying things like, "Do you take sugar?" and I got the feeling she was wishing she hadn't let the whole conversation get started. I was curious, but I had some other important questions to ask and I didn't want to wear out my welcome before I got around to them. So I went back to the question I had started to ask when we were just getting to the house.

"Well, what do you hear about the trouble at Alcott-Simpson's?" I asked. "Do you think there's been as much—er—excitement lately?"

"Why do you ask? Have you been hearing more rumors?"

"Well, I heard that they weren't using the dogs anymore and not so many extra guards. I was wondering if they've already arrested somebody. Do you know if they've arrested the ones who were causing the trouble?"

Instead of answering me, Madame went off into a long string of the silent chuckles that were her way of laughing. "Hah!" she said finally, "Arrested them. I am afraid not. And as for there being less excitement lately, I had not heard that such was the case. If they are no longer using the dogs, perhaps it is because they proved to be useless. And as for the situation improving—just today one department was closed, perhaps permanently. And there may be others soon."

"Closed?" I said. "I haven't heard anything about that. What did they close?"

Madame looked at me for a moment with a strange expression on her face. "The toy department," she said finally. "Today the toy department was closed. Oh, there was no official announcement, but there are rumors that tomorrow it will be roped off and no clerks will be on duty."

The way Madame was acting puzzled me. I knew that she made fun of Alcott-Simpson's lots of times, particularly the executives and some of the customers. But I didn't think she really hated it or anything.

After all, she'd been making her living there for a long time. But I kept getting the feeling that she was pleased, or at least a little amused by all the trouble.

"But why?" I asked. "Why the toy department?" It gave me a kind of empty feeling. Even though I wasn't hung-up on the Alcott-Simpson toy department the way I once had been, I felt a loss, like when an old dream finally fades away for good. "I mean, the Alcott-Simpson toy department is famous all over the country. It's kind of a symbol for little kids. Even the ones who can't afford to buy anything there."

"Well," Madame said, "the reason being given is that there were economic difficulties—the department was not able to make a profit. But in the past the profits have always been high; for a symbol, the public expects to pay dearly. The real problem seems to have been that the store was no longer able to keep a staff. The clerks in the toy department have been quitting almost as quickly as they have been hired."

"But why?"

Madame shrugged. "Who knows? Many reasons have been given. Who knows which reasons are true ones? Perhaps the real reasons have not yet been given at all. But then, reasons rarely have much to do with reality. Won't you have another pastry, Dion?"

Up to that point I hadn't intended to do much talking myself. I'd only planned to find out what I could from Madame Stregovitch, without going into the rumors I'd heard or any of the things that had happened to me. But something about the way Madame was taking it, making a joke out of it, made me want to force her to admit the seriousness of the whole thing. I guess I was feeling a lot like poor Myrna was when she wanted me to admit that it was more than just a crazy dream.

"Look," I said, "you seem to think this is all very amusing, that there's really nothing to worry about. Well, I know some things—some things I haven't told you. Maybe you'll just laugh them off too, and maybe I hope you do, in a way, but anyway—"

So I started out and told her everything. I began with the rumors I'd heard and the strange little things that had happened: the things José had told me; the way Mrs. Jensen had acted in the toy department; and all about Myrna and the things she had said.

Madame was interested. She watched me closely as I talked, and there was a sharpness to her eyes. But at times her lips still twitched, and her shoulders jerked with amusement. I took a deep breath then and started to tell about Sara. I began at the very beginning—how I'd seen her being chased by Mr. Rogers—and I told it all. How I'd gotten shut in the store the first time. How Sara had let me in again. What Sara had told me about herself, and how she talked about someone she called the Others. About the strange things that had happened when we were together. Long before I was finished, I could see that Madame was finally impressed. Her face had turned as still as stone, but her eyes blazed with interest.

When I had said all that I had to say, Madame leaned towards me. Her voice was harsh and tense, "This child, this Sara, describe her."

"She's not a child," I said, "although, I guess she's not far from it. She's small and dark with huge dark eyes and long black hair."

Madame stood up slowly. She had a strange distant look, as if her eyes were focusing on something far beyond my range of vision. "There is something I must attend to," she said. "Wait here. I won't be long." And she disappeared into the next room.

I waited, wondering uneasily what I'd gotten into. Now that it was done, I wished that I hadn't said so much about Sara. It seemed to me that Madame Stregovitch wasn't at all the kind of person who'd tell on anyone, but you never could be sure. And I knew that, more than anything, I didn't want to be the one to get Sara in trouble. That is, in more trouble than she was already in.

Madame must have been gone for ten or fifteen minutes. When she came back into the room, I hardly knew her. Her face was pale and tired, and her eyes seemed to be set in black holes. She sat down and pulled her chair close to mine.

"Dion," she said, "you must listen carefully and do exactly as I say. You must not go back to Alcott-Simpson's again for a while. Most particularly you must not go back again at night. Perhaps in a few days I may need your help there, at the store, and if I do I will let you know. But until that time, you must *not* go to Alcott-Simpson's again."

"Now wait a minute," I said. "You can't just tell me to do that without explaining why or anything. I have to go back right away. If there is some kind of danger——"

Madame held up her hand to make me stop. "Yes, you are right. You should be told enough to make you understand the importance of what I ask of you." She covered her eyes with her hand and sat perfectly still for so long I was beginning to wonder if she'd gone into some kind of trance. When she finally uncovered her face and began to speak, her voice was high and humming, almost as if she were chanting or reciting from memory. "There are times and places when the usual barriers can be overcome and certain individuals are able to experience the overlapping of divergent forms of existence. This overlapping can take place through many different thresholds and can take many forms. One such form—one such overlapping of worlds —takes place only through a particular threshold, the sleeping or unconscious mind of a child. The mind of a child who is himself at a threshold between two forms of his existence, his childhood and his adult life."

Madame's voice stopped, and her eyes came back from looking somewhere through and beyond and focused again on me. "Dion," she said in a more normal tone, "perhaps you have heard that there are per-

sons with unusual psychic powers that enable them to establish contact with beings in other forms of existence. I am such a person, and I am responsible for what has happened at Alcott-Simpson's. But I want you to understand that I meant no evil. There should be no danger to anyone, and there *is* no danger to those whose experiences are limited in the usual way by their imperfect senses. But there can be danger to the individual whose experience is broadened too suddenly and too far. The danger is to the one who becomes involved beyond barriers he is not meant to cross. There are thresholds, Dion, that are meant to be crossed by the patient crawl of discipline and dedication, and to cross them by any short cut, even the short cut of love, can bring great danger." Madame stood up suddenly and motioned for me to do the same. "I know you are greatly confused and you have many questions. But I cannot say more. If you think carefully about what I have said, you will experience the truth more completely than if I tried to make you understand with many narrow words. It is only necessary that you remember that danger exists for you now at Alcott-Simpson's." .

Chapter 13

I RAN. I RAN ALL THE WAY HOME AND WENT RIGHT TO my room. Dad was out somewhere. He'd left some dinner for me on the stove but I didn't feel much like eating. I must have stayed in my room for about an hour, going over everything in my mind and deciding what to do.

In a way, the things I'd learned at Madame Stregovitch's hadn't shocked me as much as you might expect. Perhaps I'd already known some of it before in a wordless part of my mind. And it was almost a relief to have it put into words so that I could take it out and face it.

Part of it was very clear. Madame Stregovitch had made it possible for whomever or whatever it was—the ones Sara called the Others and Myrna called They— to invade Alcott-Simpson's. Some of the rest of it was harder to understand. Somehow a person in-between was needed to do what Madame had done, a person who was in between childhood and maturity. I was pretty sure that Sara had been that person.

There was one other thing that I didn't understand completely, though I got it enough to make me feel scared to death every time I thought about it. These invaders—these Others—were not dangerous *except* to someone who had become too closely involved with them. And that Sara was terribly involved was only too clear.

First, there was the fact that she was almost certainly the inbetween person Madame had used to summon them. And besides, even though I'd tried to fool myself with my "store executive's daughter" theory, it was pretty plain that without the help of the Others, Sara could not have known all the things she knew or done all the things she did. The Others had been protecting Sara from the guards and dogs, helping her to open doors and unlock locks, and maybe even telling her when I was looking for her. And in exchange what? What kind of hold over Sara's life had They taken in exchange?

I was sure that the things I had told Madame had made her realize how much danger Sara was in, and I knew that she was going to do whatever she could to help. But it worried me that Madame had said she might need my help at Alcott-Simpson's in a few days. It sounded as if she wasn't sure she could help Sara by herself. And I thought perhaps I knew why. It occurred to me that maybe Madame was afraid she was too late. That the Others would not let her find Sara and warn her. The last few times I had looked for Sara, I hadn't been able to find her. Maybe the Others had already hidden her or taken her away.

I knew that Madame meant well in telling me to stay away. I'd been kind of a pet of Madame's for years and years. It was natural that she wouldn't want me to get involved, too. What she didn't know was that in a way I already was involved. She didn't know how I felt about Sara. And how Sara felt about me, too—I was pretty sure of that. And that was why I felt that if she could still be helped—if she would really try to break away for anyone, maybe it would be for me. That was the reason I decided I couldn't obey Madame's warning and stay away.

The next day I didn't go to school. I went to my morning jobs because I had nothing else to do with the time; but as soon as Alcott-Simpson's opened for the day, I went inside. I went over the entire store, except for the area near the cosmetic counter. I got close enough once or twice to catch a glimpse of Madame, but I was very careful not to let her see me. It was all wasted effort, though. Sara just wasn't there.

Everything inside the store was pretty much the way it had been the day before. There were very few customers and fewer clerks than usual. Most of the clerks who were there were new, people I'd never seen before. The only real difference was that the toy department had been roped off, just as Madame had said it would be. After I had looked all the way through the store, I went out and wandered around town. In an hour or so I came back and looked again. And that's the way I spent the whole day. By closing time I knew what I had to do.

A few minutes after five o'clock, I went up to the sixth floor. I had noticed that there seemed to be only two clerks on the whole huge floor, so what I had in mind would not be hard to do. There was a scattering of customers, and I walked around looking at people as if I were looking for someone. When a clerk came up to me and asked me what I wanted, I said my mother was shopping somewhere in the store and I thought maybe she'd come up there. He left me alone then, and I wandered around until I saw my chance. I slipped into the same display room I had hidden in before and slid back under the same bed.

I lay there for what seemed a very long time, listening to the distant voices of the clerks and customers. Then the closing bell rang and almost immediately all the voices stopped. The clerks must have gone downstairs almost on the heels of the last customer. Apparently they didn't want to be left alone way up there on the sixth floor when the elevators stopped running and the lights went down.

I waited, lying there in the dust under the low bed. After a while the big lights went off and the silence widened around me. I waited a while longer to be sure that all the clerks had had time to leave the store. Then, just as the silence seemed complete, the other noises began.

They were the same noises I had heard before. There were faint whispering voices and muffled footsteps, always so soft and indistinct I could never quite rule out the possibility that perhaps I was imagining it all. I had been planning to climb out from under the bed and start looking for Sara as soon as I was sure the clerks had all gone home, but the noises kept me where I was. Somehow I felt I had to stay there until I could decide if I was really hearing something or not, as if deciding what I had to face when I came out would make it easier to face it.

But the noises went on and on, and I went on lying there, getting stiffer and stiffer from fright and from not moving, until I wondered if I would ever be able to get out at all. And then suddenly I heard someone saying my name. "Dion," the voice said, and there was a pause and everything was very quiet. The noises were all gone. "Dion, I'm here. Please come out."

It was Sara. I struggled out from under the bed and there she was, standing in the edge of the shadow on the other side of the room. I sat down on the side of the bed because my knees felt unhinged and my voice wouldn't start working. As soon as I could, I said, "Am I ever glad to see you."

Sara looked down and away so I couldn't see her eyes. "I'm glad to see you, too," she said. She was wearing a long dress again, but this one was pale blue with a scarf that was attached to one shoulder and went up over her head. "You shouldn't be here. You shouldn't have come, but I'm glad you're here."

I was so relieved to see her looking just the same as ever, as if nothing was really wrong, that for a second I almost forgot what I'd come to do. But then I remembered. "Sara, I've got to tell you something," I said, "but not here. Could we go somewhere else?"

"Somewhere else?" she asked. "What do you mean?"

"I mean outside. Could we get downstairs and outside without—I mean would you come some place outside the store with me?"

She stared at me, and her fantastic eyes seemed to get wider and wider and she made a sound like a gasp. "No, no I can't." She stepped back away from me as if she meant to turn and run.

"All right," I said quickly. "All right. Not outside. But isn't there a better place we could go—to talk. A better place than *this*." I rolled my eyes in a way that I hoped would tell her what I really meant.

"The garden?" Sara asked. "We could go down to the garden."

I started to say all right, but then I remembered how dark it would be there at night. And I remembered too about the boat that sailed by itself in the fountain. "No," I said, "not there."

"Wait, I know," Sara said. "We could go up on the roof. Have you ever been up on the roof?"

I said I never had, and I thought about it quickly and it seemed like a good idea. At least on the roof it would be wide open and you could know what was around you. It would be almost like being outside Alcott-Simpson's. Perhaps it *would* be like being outside Alcott-Simpson's, I thought—deliberately *not* thinking that perhaps They couldn't follow us there, as if I were afraid even to think what I really meant because the feeling was so strong that They were all around us, listening and watching. I nodded, "All right, let's go up on the roof."

Sara led the way to the emergency staircase, and we took the upward flight, up past the seventh floor where all the big offices were, to a little room that opened out onto the huge dark stretch of the open roof. To the West the horizon still glowed with sunset, and far to the East the sky was a clear blue-black, sparkling with stars, but the fog had settled again on the center of town and it was very dark. All around us the fog blotted out the edges of the roof so that it seemed endless, as if we were walking through dark clouds on a tar-paper and gravel infinity.

We walked for a way without talking. A slow damp wind lifted Sara's hair and the pale blue scarf, and mixed them with the mist that closed in like a wave behind our backs. Finally a low wall with a wide ledge took shape just ahead. We came to an edge of the roof and looked over. The lights of Palm Ave, blurred and hazy, shone up from what seemed much more than seven stories down below. We leaned on the ledge and looked down into the fog flooded canyon.

"Sara," I began, "since I saw you last, I've found out some very important things."

Sara turned towards me, and the scarf fell across her face leaving only her eyes unveiled. "Yes," she agreed, "I thought you had."

"I found out all about the ones you call the Others," I said. "I know all about it now—who They are and how They came here to Alcott-Simpson's."

She nodded sadly. "I didn't want you to find out," she said. "I tried to make them stay away from you. I was afraid you wouldn't like me any more if you found out. But They wouldn't remember."

"It doesn't matter. It doesn't change how I feel about you," I said. "It's not your fault."

"Yes, it's my fault. I shouldn't ever have come here. It wasn't right for me. And it isn't right for you."

"Well, maybe," I said, "but anyway—" I stopped and looked around, but nothing moved except the fog and there was no sound except the distant fog-muffled drone of the city. "Anyway it will all be over soon. They, the Others, are going to have to go away soon."

"I know," Sara said, "I am going to have to go away, too. I'll have to go with Them—"

"No!" I said, and it came out almost a shout. "You mustn't let Them make you think that. You don't belong with Them. They only want to make you think you do. You're going to come away right now with me. You just have to make up your mind that you are going with me no matter what. We'll go down the stairs very quickly, and if They lock the doors, we'll go down the escalator; and if you see Them or hear Them don't slow down, and we'll—"

I stopped. The wind had come up suddenly, and the air swirling around us was so heavy with white mist that Sara's dress and hair blended into the twisting fingers of fog. But I could still see her face clearly. She moved closer to me, and her eyes were shining with a kind of wild excitement. "Do you want to come with me, Dion?" she said, and her voice was strange, too high and light.

"Yes," I said. "Yes," and suddenly a wave of terrible excitement broke inside my mind. A part of me struggled and then drowned, and then the fog was full of small soft hands pushing me, and I moved with them willingly towards the edge. But when I looked down, far down to the dark street, a last stab of fear broke through the numb willingness. The fear of falling was a sharp pain in the backs of my legs, and I felt my face twist with terror.

"No," Sara said, and suddenly she was between me and the edge of the roof. The wild brightness was gone from her face, and her eyes were soft and steady and very sad. "I'm sorry," she said, but I only stared at her without saying anything, because suddenly I knew—and there was nothing to say.

"I'm sorry," she said again. "It's my fault. I shouldn't have let you come here. I shouldn't ever have let you see me." She was moving back, away from

me into the fog. "I should never have come here at all. Only the very little ones were sent for, but some of them were my brothers and sisters and so I came, too. But I was too old just to play—and then I saw you——"

The fog came down then and closed in between us, but in a moment I heard her voice calling, "Dion, Dion, this way." I followed the sound, and it led to the little shed where the emergency stairway came out onto the roof. Sara was not there. I wound my way down the stairs for what seemed like miles and miles. My mind felt numb, and my legs were so weak and shaky that sometimes I thought I would have to stop. When I finally got to the ground floor and started down the Mall to the east entrance, the numbness had gotten worse so that I felt I was fighting to stay conscious. I wasn't sure I could make it through the doors to the outside. Then, just as I was almost there, I heard someone call my name. It was Madame Stregovitch, coming towards me down the Mall. I didn't even wonder why she was there. I only remember her catching me by the arms and the fierce burning of her eyes. Then I began to slip down and down into a soft and sleepy darkness.

When I woke up, I was lying on the bench in the alcove behind Ladies Gloves. No one else was there. If Madame Stregovitch had really been in Alcott-Simpson's, she had gone off and left me there alone. I rushed to the east entrance in a panic. The door was unlocked, and I burst out into a clear, dark night.

Chapter 14

THE NEXT FEW DAYS HAVE FADED IN MY MIND. IT's strange because I've always had such a good memory. But those days, right after that last night at Alcott-Simpson's, are all jumbled up in a haze of events and feelings and fears. There are a few things that stand out clear and sharp, but I'm not sure about sequence and things like that.

I know I stayed out of school two more days that week. I hardly ever miss school so of course Dad wanted to know what the matter was. I guess it was the first day I stayed home that I ran into Dad in the kitchen about nine o'clock.

"Dion," he said. "What are you doing at home? Are you sick?"

"No" I said. "I just overslept. I had some trouble getting to sleep last night, and when I finally did, I guess I just overslept."

Dad looked worried. I'd been getting myself off in the mornings since I was a little kid, and I was never late. Of course, I didn't always go to school because of the operations; but if I was going at all, I got there on time. Dad put some coffee on to perk and fixed himself some cereal before he said anything more, but after he sat down at the table he said, "Well, then, why don't you take advantage of the opportunity and get a rest? You look tired. You know I've told you I think you're on much too strenuous a schedule. I have some home lessons this morning so the place should be fairly quiet for a while. Why don't you go back to bed and really catch up on your sleep?"

I shrugged. "I might. I don't much like to go into class late." So I stayed home that day and the next, not doing much except thinking. Dad asked questions once or twice, but he didn't pressure me to get back to school.

The second day I went back to Alcott-Simpson's, feeling very sure I'd find everything just the way it had always been. At that particular point I'd almost convinced myself that I'd had some kind of complicated nightmare, and that everything would be back to normal. But instead I found the store closed and locked and huge sheets of paper pasted over all the windows. I came home in a kind of panic.

Back at our house I picked up the morning paper and it was full of stuff about the sudden, startling failure of the fabulous Alcott-Simpson department store. The articles went on and on about the history of Alcott-Simpson's—how it had for so many years been almost a symbol of a way of life—and how it had stood for a kind of service and a standard of quality that were fast becoming unknown—and that its passing was a great loss to the discerning and particular shopper. There was another article about why the store had closed.

The story started CHANGING TIMES FORCE END OF GREAT STORE. It was full of quotes from the managers. They explained the whole thing by saying that Alcott-Simpson's was built on a lavish scale at a time when such things were more widely appreciated, and that in these modern times it was too difficult to maintain. This fact, plus the growing competition from suburban shopping centers, had finally become decisive. The article went on like that, quoting more or less the same thing said in slightly different ways by different owners and managers. I read it over three times. Someone did mention that there had also been an increase in the usual problems with thieves and vandals, but that was the closest any of them came to saying anything much at all.

It was the end of the week when I decided to go back to Madame Stregovitch's house. When I got there it looked at first as if there was no one at home. I knocked on the door several times without getting an answer, and when I peeked in through the little oval window it looked very dark and empty. Finally, just as I was about to give up and go away, I heard something moving and a light came on.

I had a definite shock when Madame opened the door. For a minute I almost didn't recognize her. She was wearing a long robe-like thing, and her black and silver hair, that I'd always seen piled up on top of her head, was hanging down her back. She looked tired, and there were dark shadows around her eyes.

"Hey, are you sick again or something?" I said. "I'm sorry I bothered you."

"No, no. Come in. I'm very glad you came," Madame said, and as soon as she began to talk, she seemed more like herself. "If you had not come soon I would have sent for you. I wanted to see you before I left."

"Before you left?" I said. "Are you going away?"

"Yes," she said. "Very soon."

"I'm sorry," I said. "I'll miss you. I guess you lost your job when the store closed. Have you found another job somewhere else?"

Madame nodded. "Yes. I have found other work to do. But I wanted very much to see you before I left. I wished to tell you good-by—and also, there are some explanations I feel I must make."

When she said that about explanations, I felt a kind of weight lift in my mind. "That's what I need," I said, "explanations! You know, the last few days have been pretty bad." I gave a little laugh so neither of us would take it too seriously, but I think I really meant it. "Sometimes I've been pretty sure I must be cracking up."

155

Madame frowned. "You must not think that. Hasn't it occurred to you that you are not alone in your affliction? Doesn't it seem strange to you that so many others at Alcott-Simpson's have at the same time become also insane?"

"Look," I said, "I don't know what happened to other people at Alcott-Simpson's. Sure, they had to shut it down, but you saw what the papers said about the reasons. I don't know what the real reasons were."

"The *real* reasons," Madame said slowly. "*Reality*. It is a strange word. Everyone supposes that they know its meaning, but in truth it has meant different things to every age and to every individual. What has been real today may, in the future, become only a dream, and things beyond belief may become tomorrow's realities."

I guess it was plain that I wasn't getting any less confused, because all at once Madame stopped and held up her hand. "Yes, yes, you must have a more direct answer. You will not understand fully, but I feel that I owe you at least such explanation as I can give."

"You owe me?" I asked.

"Yes," she said, "I owe you an explanation because I am to some extent responsible for your confusion." Madame's lips twitched with a flicker of her usual biting humor. "You see, I do not claim full responsibility, because I feel certain something of the sort would have had to happen, sooner or later. Those who accept without question so incredible a world as Alcott-Simpson's, must not expect to ignore forever other worlds no more incredible. But enough of that—as I said, you cannot hope to understand fully, but I can perhaps help you to see that it is not your sanity that has been at fault."

Madame paused as if she were collecting her thoughts, and then she suddenly pointed to the picture on the mantle, the one with the strange magnetic eyes. "You noticed, the other day, the picture of my mother?" I nodded. "Many years ago my mother was known in many countries as a person of unusual powers, psychic powers. When I was a young child, the country in which we were living fell under the control of evil leaders, and because my mother spoke freely of the events she was able to foresee—of the suffering these leaders would cause and the terrible fate that would finally be theirs—she was taken away. I managed to escape, and I lived in hiding for many years in several countries. Then, when I was almost a woman, I began to discover that I had to some extent inherited the gifts that had been my mother's. But like many young ones, I chose another way. I did not want the life, and the death, that had been my mother's. I was at an age when other forces, normal forces, are very strong, so I ran away. I finally arrived in this country, and I worked and lived in many ways and in many places. At last I came to Alcott-Simpson's, and there, as you know, I have been for many years."

I leaned forward and opened my mouth, but Madame held up her hand and went on. "Why did I stay in such a place?" I gulped because it was exactly what I was going to ask. "I stayed because, after all those years, I was still running away and I felt safer there. Better than in most places, I was able there to shut out knowledge that I did not want, contacts that I wished not to make. Alcott-Simpson's shuts out many things."

I nodded. "I've always had a feeling like that about it. Like it was a separate world."

"Exactly. And it was so for me until not long ago. Then one day I happened to see an article about some gifts in that special world—some very special and unusual gifts. And on the next page I read about what seemed, indeed, to be a very different world. It was a story about children in a country where for some years now there has been much famine."

All of a sudden I knew what she was talking about. "I remember," I said. "You gave me part of that magazine for my scrapbook. And I remember something strange about it. It was some eyes. Some eyes that came right through when you held it up to the light. Did you notice that?"

Madame's eyes whipped up at me so sharply that I jumped as if I'd been hit. "Indeed I did notice," she said. "Those eyes, those strangely misplaced eyes, were what gave me the inspiration to do what I did. For many years I had tried to forget things I was afraid to know, but such knowledge is not easily forgotten.

Among the things I remembered was the means used to send a particular invitation to a very special kind of visitor. Only one thing was lacking. In order for me to accomplish what I had decided to do, I needed the unknowing cooperation of an adolescent—the mind of a sleeping or unconscious child. Then one day as I walked through Alcott-Simpson's, there on a bench in an alcove was the missing ingredient."

"M-m-me?" I stammered in absolute amazement.

Madame nodded. "I am afraid that you are right. It was you. But you must believe that I did not anticipate that your involvement would be any more than the momentary use I put you to. I did not foresee the danger to which you would be exposed. I still do not understand why it happened."

"I think I know," I said. "It was only because of—of Sara." It hurt to say her name, and even to think about her brought a dull undimming pain. "She told me why she came—and why she shouldn't have. She said the Others were all younger. I guess they were happy enough with all the things to play with, but Sara was too old for just that."

I sat for a while staring at my hands. "And now—are they gone?" I asked. "Are they *all* gone?"

Madame nodded. "On that last day I, too, hid myself and stayed after closing in the store. I knew I dared wait no longer. I planned to try to send them back by other means; but as I had feared, it was not possible. Then once again, my missing ingredient appeared, just when he was needed—entirely against orders, but I must admit, most opportunely." Madame smiled, and I could tell she was trying to sound cheerful to make me feel better.

I tried. "That's me," I said, "always handy." But it didn't come off. I couldn't hide how I really felt.

"I'm sorry," Madame said, and I'd never heard her sound so gentle. "You must think of it as a sad but beautiful mystery. It is, indeed, a mystery—so complete a materialization. Such a thing is very rare. But then her reason was very strong—the strongest reason of all, for love in itself is the greatest of mysteries."

That was all. We sat there a little longer without saying anything, and then I got up to go. At the door Madame said, "Dion, I must tell you again that I am sorry. Very sorry for what I have done to you, and even a little sorry for the mischief I have done to Alcott-Simpson's."

It seemed to me that that was a strange way to put it. As far as I could see, "mischief" didn't begin to cover it. "Mischief?" I said.

Madame shrugged, and the corner of her mouth twitched in something like a smile. "Call it what you will. I meant it only as mischief. Had I meant something more, I could have opened the doors to very different visitors. I might have lowered a drawbridge to powerful and evil invaders. But instead, one could say, perhaps, that I only unlatched the back gate for the neighbor's children."

That was the way it ended.

I thought it through to the very end, and then I wrote the last verse. It goes like this:

The police are baffled, the management's frantic,
The watchmen will not stay.
All the scientific investigators,
Gave up and went away,
And they all pretend that they can't be certain,
For nobody wants to say
That the ghosts,
Little ghosts
Who lost their childhood,
Have been sent to Alcott's to play.

Chapter 15

IT HAS BEEN ABOUT SIX MONTHS NOW SINCE ALCOTT-Simpson's closed and Madame Stregovitch went away. Looking at just the outside of things, you might say that nothing has changed very much; but from another point of view everything is entirely different.

We still live in the same old place, and I still go to Randolph High School. The main difference at Randolph is A-Group. That's what we call the folk-rock band that Jerry and Brett and I have formed with another guy named Johnson on the drums. We've really been doing all right. We've played for a lot of school dances, and we've even had a few outside jobs for money. I've been writing music again lately, and a lot of my stuff we do in the group. But an even more startling development is that Brett and I do most of the singing. If anyone had told me a year ago that I'd be singing in front of several hundred people—particularly several hundred high school kids—I'd have told them they were crazy. But it wasn't so hard after the first few times. I guess I do all right.

I don't mean by that that I've turned into any big personality sensation or anything like that. As a matter of fact, except for the guys in the band, I still don't have any gang that I really belong to. But there are two or three bunches of kids that I see a little of now and then. The funny thing is I've found out that that's the way I like it. I have some friends here and there, and I don't have to get hung up on anybody else's action. I don't know how the whole thing happened, except that when I forgot to keep up the big social effort I'd been making ever since I came to Randolph, I just slid back into my own style; and the surprising part was that it was all right. It's not flashy, but it's comfortable and it comes out of what I am, instead of something I have to keep spreading around on top.

At home things look almost the same on the outside, too. My Dad still drifts along with pretty much the same bunch of students, not to mention the same little army of friends and acquaintances. He did have a spell of trying to make some changes a few months back, but nothing much came of it. It was pretty much to be expected—at his age and right here in the same old environment. But when I get fed up, and I still do now and then, I have to remember that I have only myself to blame. I had a chance to change things, and I didn't take it.

I had the chance a few months ago right after Alcott-Simpson's closed down. It happened at dinner one night towards the end of that week when I stayed home from school and just sat around thinking and worrying. I remember that Dad had made my favorite kind of stew, and while we were eating all of a sudden he said, "Di, I've been thinking about something, and I believe I've come to a decision. I was talking to John again yesterday and apparently that job in the music department at Wentworth still hasn't been filled. How would it be if I called up to see if I could arrange an appointment? Then you and I could get all slicked up and make a trip out there tomorrow to see if we can convince Mr. Marple that we would be worthy members of the Wentworth family."

Dad's friend John, who teaches at Wentworth, is always talking about this Marple guy. He is the principal at Wentworth, but he likes to call himself the "Headmaster," and he is always talking about the "Wentworth Family." John says Marple has a Father-Figure complex with a capital F; and if he's heard of academic freedom, he thinks it means letting his staff go home at night instead of locking them in the storeroom with the other school property. He's very big on things like "professional appearance" and being seen at the right places and *not* at any of the wrong ones.

All of a sudden I got a mental picture of scruffy old Dad with his hair slicked back, trying to put on some kind of an act for this Marple character. I didn't say anything for quite a while, and at last Dad said, "Di?"

"Well, go ahead if you want to," I said, "but as

far as I'm concerned I'd rather stay right here. Seems to me that for someone who's used to city life, the suburbs would be a real drag."

I got up then and put my dishes in the sink, and as I left the kitchen I got a glimpse of Dad's face. If you could have framed his expression, you would have had to label it, "The Last Minute Reprieve."

To tell the truth, what I did then—I mean turning down a chance to move—wasn't just pure heart on my part. Happening right at that particular moment, my mind was so crowded and confused that I didn't want to face any other big new change right then. But later on, when I'd had time to consider it, I began to get some ideas about what Dad's offer really represented, I mean for a guy like him. He might as well have volunteered for a stretch in Sing Sing. And then, after a while, when things began to change a little at Randolph and we got A-Group under way, I began to lose interest in changing schools anyway.

Like I say, I still get fed up at times, but in the last few months the trouble between my dad and me has begun to ease up a little. I've been doing some reading and thinking about the subject of rebellion, and it seems to me that the whole thing was probably inevitable. It seems to me that rebellion is usually inevitable, and that it only gets useless when you forget that it's just a doorway and not a destination. Because if you settle down in a doorway, your future is going to be pretty narrow.

And speaking of destinations—mine is a lot more up in the air than it used to be. I have at least half a dozen plans that I'm fooling around with. I can't seem to make up my mind. It's kind of funny actually, when I used to be so sure of what I wanted—all those years when I was planning to be an executive at Alcott-Simpson's someday. And now I have to start planning all over again. But I don't mind. There are a lot of things I'm interested in, and planning is still something that I like to do.

Just a few days ago they started tearing Alcott-Simpson's down. I guess they're going to build a huge new office building on the spot. I went by one day to watch, but I didn't stay long. I didn't like the way it made me feel. I don't mind thinking about the things that happened at the store last spring, but I didn't like thinking about it *there*, with the wrecking ball crashing into the walls. Last night, for instance, when I got the idea for the song, I started thinking about all of it, and I thought it through from beginning to end; and it didn't bother me at all. For one thing, I've quit worrying about what I believe.

I don't know what other people believe happened to Alcott-Simpson's, and maybe I don't even know for sure what I believe. But what *happened* to me was real, and Sara was real, and the difference in me is as real as the difference there'll be in Alcott-Simpson's when they've finished with that wrecking ball.

Now that I've thought about the song some more

The police are baffled the managment's
frantic. The watchmen will not stay
All the scientific investigators
gave up and went away.
And they all ~~pre~~ pretend that
they can't be certain for
nobody wants to say
that the ghosts, little
ghosts who lost
their childhood
have
been
sent to
alcotts to play.

—the Fishbowl Song—I don't think I'll show it to Brett and Jerry after all. It's a good song, but it wouldn't mean too much to them, or maybe to anyone else but me. Instead I guess I'll put it away in a box of important things I keep in my bottom desk drawer. I'll put it in my scrapbook with the magazine articles that Madame Stregovitch gave me—the ones with the fishbowl and the eyes.

The two articles have been there since right after Madame Stregovitch went away. That was when I took them out of the scrapbook and put them in the drawer where I could get them out and look at them now and then. Every time I do, it amazes me how I was able to look at them that first time and not have it tell me anything. Oh, I noticed the eyes, all right, looking out through the fur lining of the fishbowl—but it didn't mean a thing to me except an interesting accidental effect. And that just goes to show you how stupid a human being can be.

S0-BRY-140

4.00
C + H

ARGENTINA

The Royal Institute of International Affairs is an unofficial and non-political body, founded in 1920 to encourage and facilitate the scientific study of international questions. The Institute, as such, is precluded by the terms of its Royal Charter from expressing an opinion on any aspect of international affairs. Any opinions expressed in this publication are not, therefore, those of the Institute.

ARGENTINA

by

GEORGE PENDLE

Third Edition

Issued under the auspices of the
Royal Institute of International Affairs

OXFORD UNIVERSITY PRESS

LONDON NEW YORK TORONTO

WINGATE COLLEGE LIBRARY
WINGATE, N. C.

Oxford University Press, Amen House, London E.C.4

GLASGOW NEW YORK TORONTO MELBOURNE WELLINGTON
BOMBAY CALCUTTA MADRAS KARACHI LAHORE DACCA
CAPE TOWN SALISBURY NAIROBI IBADAN ACCRA
KUALA LUMPUR HONG KONG

New material in these editions
© Royal Institute of International Affairs 1961, 1963

First published 1955
Second edition 1961
Third edition 1963
Reprinted (with corrections) 1965

PRINTED IN GREAT BRITAIN

TO
OLWEN

35832

CONTENTS

Contents

PREFACE TO SECOND EDITION

I FIRST went to Argentina in 1930 and I have returned again and again. Always someone tells me that I shall find things greatly altered. Of course, many changes do occur. Between my last two visits a military junta had been superseded by an elected president (though the military hierarchy still were the power behind the presidency); on a railway journey across the country from Mendoza to Buenos Aires I noticed that diesel engines had replaced the old steam locomotives and that many more trees were growing on the pampa (the pastures stretching to the flat horizon still shimmered in the sun and wind); the mechanization of agriculture had progressed (the tractor drivers had not ceased to be gauchos in spirit); urban industry had expanded; the oilfields at last were in active production; and so on. Yet it seems to me that in all essential qualities Argentina is the same as when I first landed in the Río de la Plata in 1930. Indeed, I believe that the character of the Argentine nation was formed as long ago as the days of General San Martín and the wars of independence. San Martín, as described by his contemporaries in their journals, can be recognized today as an Argentine—an outstanding citizen, but unmistakably from Argentina.

The historian Frederick Jackson Turner argued that settlers in the United States were not simply transplanted Europeans: the existence of an area of free land and the advance of settlement westward gave the North Americans a distinctive outlook. The United States character was created by the practical everyday life on the free soil of the frontier, and it was permanently fixed by the time that the frontier closed in the 1880's. The influence of the pampa is tremendous. W. H. Hudson was born in the province of Buenos Aires and lived his first thirty years or so in Argentina. But he was of immigrant stock and he wrote all of his books in England and in the English language. Neverthe-less, when we read the books it is apparent to us that, in his dingy London lodgings, he was thinking as an Argentine.[1] Since the middle of the nineteenth century Argentina has absorbed many immigrants from many lands, and many new ideas; but, in the local *ambiente*, they have all acquired a recognizably Argentine quality.

Argentine history is a continuous process, but it is re-lated to world trends. The social and economic upheaval initiated by Juan and Eva Perón was bound to have hap-pened sooner or later, in one way or another. If the Peróns had not appeared on the scene, someone else would have carried out their function—more efficiently, perhaps, and (it might be hoped) more disinterestedly; but that is beside the point, because until 1945 no one seized the opportunity. By then the time had arrived when, in Professor W. W. Rostow's words,

a new leading élite must emerge and be given scope to begin the building of a modern industrial society. This élite must to a degree supersede in authority the old land-based élite, whose grasp on income above minimum levels of consumption must be loosened or broken if they do not themselves divert this surplus into the modern society. Generally, the horizon of expectation must lift; and men must accept a life of change and specialized function.

And Rostow adds:

As a matter of historical fact, xenophobic nationalism has been the most important motive force in the transition from traditional to modern societies—vastly more important than the profit motive. Men have been willing to uproot traditional societies primarily not to make more money, but because the traditional society failed, or threatened to fail, to protect them from humiliation by foreigners.[2]

It may be said that the eventual transformation of Argen-tina into an industrialized state will not convert the Argen-

---

[1] cf. Enrique Espinoza, *Tres Clásicos Ingleses de la Pampa* (1951), pp. 23–54.
[2] *The Economist*, 15 Aug. 1959, p. 411.

tine people into better or happier people. That is doubtless true. In the days of much smaller population and smaller towns, the patriarchal community of the estancia was, in many respects, idyllic. The majority of the people were poor, so that the few might be rich; but the poor had all that they needed for their simple lives and bore no resentment against their masters, who, for their part, took a fatherly pride in the *peones'* loyalty and equestrian skill. But Argentina, in spite of its geographical remoteness, and no matter how strongly the national characteristics may persist, cannot avoid passing through the stages of social development that are seen to be the experience of other modern states. Likewise 150 years ago discontented citizens in Buenos Aires found themselves following a course similar to that already taken by the revolutionary leaders in North America and carrying out ideas of freedom that had spread across the Atlantic from France.

I hope that the reader of this little book will gain a true and an adequate impression of what Argentina is—and that he will be enabled, moreover, to understand why the Argentine people are what they are, and why they behave as they do.

The Perón passages of the first edition have been reconsidered in the light of subsequent revelations; a chapter covering the post-Perón period has been added; the Appendices are new; and the Bibliography has been enlarged.

In connexion with the present edition I am indebted to B.O.A.C., who enabled me to re-visit Argentina at the time of the inauguration of their Comet service to South America, and the Research Department of the Bank of London and South America, who supplied and checked statistics. I thank Miss M. B. James for help at every stage.

G. P.

PREFACE TO THIRD EDITION[1]

BETWEEN the publication of the second edition and the preparation of the present edition the leaders of the armed forces—observing that the social classes which Juan and Eva Perón had brought into politics were rising again—deposed the President of the Republic, Dr Arturo Frondizi, who had facilitated the resurgence of the Peronistas by allowing them to nominate and vote for their own candidates at the congressional and provincial elections for the first time since Perón's downfall.[2] Such drastic military intervention shocked the majority of liberal-minded citizens but, as readers of this book will understand, it did not come as a great surprise to anyone.

The military allowed the holding of elections in July 1963, but restored the ban on Peronista participation. These elections were won by the anti-Frondizi Radical faction, the Unión Cívica Radical del Pueblo, whose presidential candidate was Dr Arturo Illia, a medical practitioner from Córdoba. President Illia, who took office in October, chose many of his Cabinet ministers from among provincial politicians, with the intention of trying to reduce the traditional dominating role of Buenos Aires and to demonstrate the national character of his administration.

G.P.

---

[1] In the 1965 impression the Tables in Appendix VII have been brought up to 1963. Other statistics have been reprinted without alteration.
[2] See pp. 145–6

xii

Chapter I

PAMPA AND MOUNTAINS

THE PAMPA

FEW countries contain so many different kinds of land—
and so many climates—as Argentina.[1] In the north are the
sub-tropical scrub-forests of the Chaco, on whose southern
fringe lie plantations of oranges, *yerba*,[2] tobacco, and sugar.
To the west is the majestic Cordillera of the Andes with,
amidst its arid foothills, occasional oases and irrigated vineyards. In the south are mountain lakes and pine-trees,
wind-swept sheep ranches, Argentina's principal oilfields
and, finally, the bleak near-Antarctic latitudes where the
Andean range breaks up into rocky bays and islets. But the
heart of this great country is the fertile central plain, the
pampa,[3] which, from the wide east-coast estuary of the Río
de la Plata, extends towards the northern plantations, the
Cordillera and the Patagonian plateaux in a huge semi-
circle whose radius is of 500 miles or more.

A traveller who in the 1820's rode on horseback from
Buenos Aires to the western town of Mendoza (a distance of
650 miles by railway today) described the appearance of the
pampa before the systematic development of cattle-raising
and agriculture had begun:

The part which I have visited . . . is divided into regions of
different climate and produce. On leaving Buenos Aires, the
first of these regions is covered for one hundred and eighty miles
with clover and thistles;[4] the second region, which extends for

---

[1] The total area of the republic is about 1,080,000 square miles.

[2] *Yerba: Ilex paraguariensis* or Paraguay tea. The leaves are infused in a
mate or gourd to produce a favourite South American beverage. cf. George
Pendle, *Paraguay* (London, R.I.I.A., 1954), pp. 64–65.

[3] The word *pampa*—or *bamba*—is of Quechua Indian origin, meaning a
flat area or steppe.

[4] The thistle is not indigenous to the pampa. The seeds are believed to

four hundred and fifty miles, produces long grass; and the third region, which reaches the base of the Cordillera, is a grove of low trees and shrubs. The second and third of these regions have nearly the same appearance throughout the year, for the trees and shrubs are evergreens, and the immense plain of grass only changes its colour from green to brown; but the first region varies with the four seasons of the year in a most extraordinary manner. In winter, the leaves of the thistles are large and luxuriant, and the whole surface of the country has the rough appearance of a turnip-field. The clover in this season is extremely rich and strong; and the sight of the wild cattle grazing in full liberty on such pasture is very beautiful. In spring, the clover has vanished, the leaves of the thistles have extended along the ground, and the country still looks like a rough crop of turnips. In less than a month the change is most extraordinary; the whole region becomes a luxuriant wood of enormous thistles, which have suddenly shot up to a height of ten or eleven feet, and are in full bloom. The road or path is hemmed in on both sides; the view is completely obstructed; not an animal is to be seen; and the stems of the thistles are so close to each other, and so strong, that, independent of the prickles with which they are armed, they form an impenetrable barrier. The sudden growth of these plants is quite astonishing; and though it would be an unusual misfortune in military history, yet it is really possible that an invading army, unacquainted with this country, might be imprisoned by these thistles before they had time to escape from them. The summer is not over before the scene undergoes another rapid change: the thistles suddenly lose their sap and verdure, their heads droop, the leaves shrink and fade, the stems become black and dead, and they remain rattling with the breeze one against another, until the violence of the pampero or hurricane levels them to the ground, where they rapidly decompose and disappear—the clover rushes up, and the scene is again verdant.[5]

The soil of the pampa consists mostly of fine sand, clay, and silt washed down towards the Atlantic by the great

---

have been introduced accidentally by the Spaniards, perhaps in the coats of animals brought from Europe.

[5] Captain F. B. Head, *Rough Notes taken during some rapid Journeys across the Pampas and among the Andes* (1826), pp. 2–4.

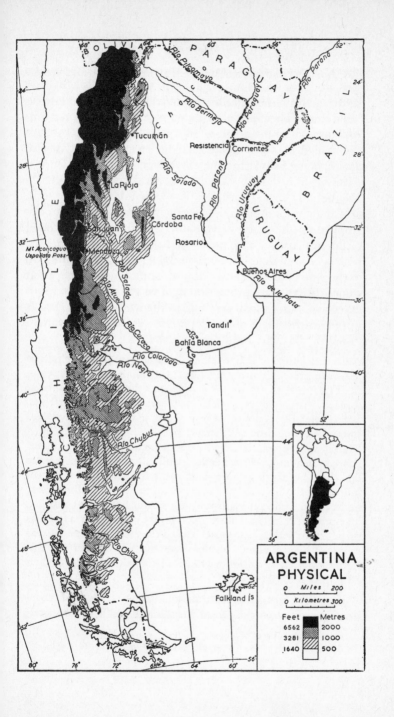

ARGENTINA
PHYSICAL

| Miles | 200 |
| Kilometres | 300 |

Feet	Metres
6562	2000
3281	1000
1640	500

rivers, or blown in dust storms from the west. There are no stones or pebbles, so that it has been said that a plough could be driven from the Atlantic shore to Mendoza without striking a stone. The climate of the pampa is not uniform: summers are hot in the north-west, but near the east coast they are cooled by the Falkland Island current. Rainfall also varies, being heaviest in the north-west (40 in.) and Buenos Aires (37 in.), though even in these areas severe droughts do occasionally occur. Periodically cool winds from the south, crossing the pampa and meeting the warm air from the tropical north, create violent storms in the neighbourhood of Buenos Aires. These gales—*pamperos*—are accompanied by heavy rainfall and sometimes by a remarkable piling up of the waters in the Plata estuary. Today the waterfront at Buenos Aires gives protection against the rising flood, but extensive damage can be done to the fruit-farming islands in the nearby Tigre delta. Previously, as an Englishwoman noted in 1881, the results were graver:

On the return of fine weather the streets in the lower part of the town presented a strange sight; the inhabitants putting out their furniture to dry on the azoteas,[6] as their houses had been flooded. We saw more than a dozen dead horses in the streets, and in one place a shattered brougham, of which the driver and horses had been drowned. Storms of this kind occur generally in March and September, very often preceded by extraordinary signs, such as a shower of beetles, dead mice, or fish. The beetles fall almost as thick as snow-flakes; the fish rise in waterspouts in front of the city, and are then blown inland over the houses; and as for the mice, it is supposed they come from Patagonia.... The present storm had done much injury to shipping, as well as on land. An Italian war vessel, called the *Principe Tommaso*, was found in a gentleman's garden near the Retiro, and the San Fernando railway station was carried a mile farther north than its proper site.[7]

How the pampa was transformed from a fertile wilderness into one of the world's most productive pastoral and agri-

[6] *Azotea*: the flat roof of a house.
[7] [Mrs] M. G. Mulhall, *Between the Amazon and the Andes* (1881), pp. 2–3.

cultural areas will be described in a later chapter. Today the pampa is used approximately in the following manner,[8] the different forms of usage in the four main districts being determined by each district's climate, drainage, and soil. First, a south-eastern zone between Mar del Plata and Tandil, being relatively cool and containing a large amount of swampy land, is devoted to the breeding of high-grade sheep and cattle, with almost no agriculture. A second, western, belt which extends in a curve for some 600 miles from Santa Fe in the north to Bahía Blanca in the south is used principally for the cultivation of *alfalfa*[9] and wheat, with some cattle-raising. In a third area, around Rosario, maize and flax are the chief crops, with some cattle. A fourth major district, in the vicinity of Buenos Aires, has been developed to supply the capital with vegetables, fruit, and milk: the market gardens start on the outskirts of the city; dairying is concentrated towards the south-east; and the orchards are situated chiefly on the islands of the Paraná delta, which is a favourable site because in that region the warm river waters from the north make it possible to grow peaches and a variety of sub-tropical fruits as well as apples, pears, and plums.

THE ANDES AND PATAGONIA

There can be no greater contrast than that presented by the flat fertile pampa of central Argentina on the one hand and the huge, arid mass of the Andes which is its boundary on the west. The Cordillera rises behind each of the old colonial cities of western Argentina. These cities are situated in oases in the foothills where streams, formed by the melting Andean snows, serve to irrigate limited areas of the piedmont. After the dusty journey across the pampa from Buenos Aires, the traveller, accustomed for so long to the featureless horizon of the plain, suddenly catches sight of the mountains and then, in due time, enters the haven of

[8] cf. Preston E. James, *Latin America*, rev. ed. (1950), pp. 317–29.
[9] *Alfalfa*: lucerne.

Mendoza, which has always been the main transit-city on the route to Chile. The following description was published in 1825: the scene is the same today.

Nobody can imagine the effect the view of this stupendous barrier of mountains produces on the traveller. I discovered it quite by accident, for while the peons went for horses, our time was spent in rambling in the neighbourhood: at last my eye was caught by what appeared, on a transient glance, to be stationary white pillars of clouds. However, having been practised a little at sea in looking out for land, I thought that there was a resemblance to it, and the intervening mists clearing away, a spectacle was presented which I shall never forget. The enormous mountains were entirely covered with snow, and rose to such a height that we were obliged to strain our necks to look up at them: they seemed to belong to a different world. . . . As we proceeded on our journey this day, we began to observe some appearance of comfort and cultivation—a house here and there neatly planted with poplars, and a few irrigated enclosures. . . . The approach to this city [Mendoza] is very beautiful: in the foreground were the green fields of lucern and clover, mixed with the vineyards bending under their purple burden, and watered by innumerable streams in all directions from the mountains: further on over this rich country was seen the city of Mendoza, whose towers and minarets rose above the bright green of the surrounding poplars. These again were finely contrasted with the majestic Cordillera ascending proudly in the background in noble masses of light and shade, while the snow-capped summits of the Andes towered over all.[10]

The eerie Uspallata Pass, situated at an altitude of 12,600 feet amidst the peaks that rise behind Mendoza, provides access to Chile. The precipitous and desolate Uspallata route was used by the Spaniards—who named it the *Camino de los Andes*—and, during the war of liberation, by one of the principal columns of San Martín's famous army. By these same ravines the trans-Andine railway now scales the Cordillera and descends into the Vale of Chile. Even the aeroplanes on the regular services between Buenos Aires and

[10] Robert Proctor, *Narrative of a Journey across the Cordillera of the Andes* (1825), pp. 45–48.

Santiago usually make their crossing at this point, flying over the pass and beside Mount Aconcagua (22,835 ft), the highest summit in the western hemisphere.

Northwards of Mendoza a desert extends as far as Córdoba and Tucumán. Rainfall in this region is slight, the annual average at Mendoza being 7·6 inches, and 3·5 inches at San Juan. But in the far north-west the mountain wall is broken at several places by valleys which bring water to Tucumán's sugar plantations and to the maizefields around Salta and Jujuy.

South of Uspallata the Cordillera continues as the backbone of the tapering continent, flanking the south-western pampa and (beyond latitude 40°) the cool, dry, windy plateaux of Patagonia. In this section the eastern piedmont contains spectacular lakes—such as Lake Nahuel Huapí—which are inset in heavily-wooded canyons. Glaciers still exist in the southern mountains.

In spite of the high latitude, however, winters on the Patagonian table-lands (which stretch from the Andean foothills to the Atlantic shore) are relatively mild because, as the continent narrows towards the south, the temperature is moderated by the two great oceans that close in upon it. Even in Tierra del Fuego, the coldest month averages above 32°F. The Patagonian scenery was described by Charles Darwin who in the year 1833 landed from H.M.S. *Beagle* at Puerto Deseado and climbed the high cliff on to the plain.

[Its] surface is quite level [he wrote] and is composed of well-rounded shingle mixed with whitish earth. Here and there scattered tufts of brown wiry grass are supported, and, still more rarely, some low thorny bushes. . . . When standing in the middle of one of these desert plains and looking towards the interior, the view is generally bounded by the escarpment of another plain, rather higher, but equally level and desolate; and in every other direction the horizon is indistinct from the trembling mirage which seems to rise from the heated surface.[11]

---

[11] Ch. 8 of Charles Darwin's *Journal* of the voyage of the *Beagle*, of which many editions have appeared since it was first published in 1839.

Here Darwin for the first time saw the *guanaco*, a species of llama roaming over the plateaux in small herds. Later, the solitude and silence of this empty world attracted W. H. Hudson.[12] The plains are swept by boisterous winds and dust storms. There is little rain, but a few rivers cross the country eastwards in deep canyons which, since the extermination of the wild Indian nomads in the campaigns of 1879–83, have provided shelter, water, and pasture to hardy sheep-farmers and their animals. Many of these farmers are of Welsh or Scottish origin, some of the Scotsmen having come to Argentina from the British-owned Falkland Islands (situated opposite the coast of southern Patagonia), others from southern Chile. The sheep ranches are of enormous size, but they suffer from severe and prolonged droughts, as in 1953–4, when large numbers of sheep were lost.[13] Population is sparse.[14] Wool—the main local product—is shipped to Buenos Aires in coastal steamers from small ports along the Atlantic shore. Other sources of wealth are the oil wells of Comodoro Rivadavia (where oil was first discovered in 1907) and the vineyards and orchards of the Río Negro which came into existence as the result of an ambitious irrigation scheme undertaken between 1910 and 1921. The Río Negro district now produces valuable supplies of grapes, pears, and apples.

MESOPOTAMIA

Northern Argentina is neither pampa nor mountain. It has two chief divisions: first, the Chaco; secondly, a region which is bounded on the one hand by the Río Paraná and on the other by the Río Uruguay.

The Chaco is a great lowland plain lying between the

[12] W. H. Hudson, *Idle Days in Patagonia* (1893).

[13] In northern and central Patagonia the average rainfall for 1953 did not reach 100 millimetres (*Review of the River Plate* (later referred to as *R.R.P.*), 19 March 1954, p. 23). On many farms in 1954 it was decided not to let the rams go with the ewes, as the ewes were in such a weak condition that they would not have been able to survive the rearing of a lamb (ibid. 30 April 1954).

[14] Patagonia includes more than 25 per cent of the territory of Argentina but contains scarcely 1 per cent of the population of the republic.

north-western piedmont of the Andes and the Paraguay–
Paraná river system, overlapping into eastern Bolivia,
western Brazil, and Paraguay. It is covered with sub-
tropical scrub-forest and areas of grass. The temperature is
very high in summer, and the summer rains cause the flood-
ing of vast tracts; but the winters are dry, and in the parts
that are remote from rivers the rapid evaporation of mois-
ture makes agriculture impossible. The most important of
the scrub trees is the *quebracho*, 'the axe-breaker', so named
because its wood is extremely hard. One species of this tree
is of exceptional commercial value because it contains as
much as 30 per cent of tannin, an extract used in the tan-
ning of leather. But the tannin industry has a grave problem: each year the *quebracho*-cutters have to travel farther
from the rivers into the forest in search of the trees, and as
the *quebracho* takes a century to reach maturity, no afforesta-
tion has been attempted.[15] A second species of *quebracho*,
having a lower percentage of tannin, is cut for sale to the inhabitants of the treeless pampa, where it is used for telegraph poles, railway sleepers, and fences, and also as fuel.
Cattle are grazed on the Chaco's grassy savannas, and there
is sufficient rainfall to permit the growing of cotton in a
fairly wide district to the north-west of the 'mushroom'
town of Resistencia and westwards of Formosa.

The land that lies between the Paraná and Uruguay
rivers is a region of abundant rain, swampy valleys, forests,
and rolling grassy plains. The summers are hot and wet, the
winters mild. The country around the river port of Corrientes is mainly pastoral, but the Upper Paraná district of
Misiones (of which the town of Posadas is the commercial

[15] In 1954 the biggest of the *quebracho* companies announced the closing of
one of its factories 'due to the exhaustion of woods from our own forests and
the impossibility of obtaining supplies from other sources which could war-
rant economic production. Consequently a start has been made on the dis-
mantling of the factory together with the sale of the buildings in the town
and the lifting for sale of the railway's lines which previously served for the
transportation of woods from the forests' (Annual Report of the Chairman
of the Forestal Land, Timber and Railways Company, *The Times*, 1 July
1954).

9

centre) is largely devoted to the growing of *yerba*—as it was in the time of the Jesuits, from whose missions its name is derived.[16] Tobacco, tung, and citrus fruits are also grown in Misiones. From Posadas, tourists travel upstream to the Iguazú Falls, which are of greater height than Niagara and are, in their tropical setting, a magnificent spectacle. Spray from the numerous cascades of which the Falls are composed soaks the surrounding virgin forest, which is adorned with orchids, festooned with creepers, and is alive with brightly-plumaged birds: parrots, toucans, humming-birds, kingfishers.

The eastern and southern parts of the country that lie between the rivers Paraná and Uruguay are devoted to the raising of cattle and sheep and the cultivation of maize and flax. The chief town in this region is the river port of Paraná, which at one time was the capital of the Argentine Confederation.

In the foregoing description of the country great distances have been covered. The north-western town of Jujuy is 1,000 miles by railway from Buenos Aires, while, in the opposite direction, the south Patagonian port of Gallegos[17] (whence wool is shipped to the capital) is 1,600 miles by sea from the Río de la Plata. The size of the republic is nearly six times that of Spain.

[16] The Jesuits were in the Paraná neighbourhood from 1588 to 1767.
[17] Gallegos is also known as Puerto Gallegos and as Río Gallegos.

Chapter II

SPANIARDS AND CRIOLLOS

THE COMING OF THE SPANIARDS

MODERN Argentina is a product of the late nineteenth century and of the present century, but the origins of the national character can be traced to the colonial period, when this country was the 'poor relation' of Peru, whose gold and silver had attracted the *conquistadores* and whose capital city, Lima, was famous for wealth and luxury. The method of settlement was itself destined to have important consequences.

The territory that is now Argentina was entered during the sixteenth century by Spaniards coming from two directions. Expeditions from the already well-established Spanish communities on the Pacific coast crossed the high ranges of the Andes by the old Inca route and founded, in the foothills to the east of the Cordillera, the cities of Santiago del Estero (1553), Tucumán (1565), Córdoba (1573), Salta (1582), La Rioja (1591), and Jujuy (1592) and, approaching from Chile, Mendoza (1561), San Juan (1562), San Luis (1596). In these cities the colonists built fine churches and convents and taught the local Indians useful handicrafts. Thus Santiago del Estero, for example, became well known in South America for its woollen *ponchos*[1] and its stirrups. Mules, bred on the eastern prairie, were fed on the pastures in the vicinity of Salta before being driven up into the arid altitudes of Peru, where mules were the only means of transportation. Indeed, for more than 200 years the economic life of Argentina was orientated towards these north-western towns, and in spite of the barrier of the

---

[1] *Poncho*: a piece of cloth with a slit in the middle to put the head through, used as a cape.

Andes the people of the north-west were linked economically and politically to the communities of the Pacific coast,
whose offspring they were.

A second stream of settlers came from quite a different
direction. The natural entry into the country was on the
opposite side of the continent, by way of the wide brown
estuary to which explorers from Spain, imagining that it
might lead them to the precious metals that they coveted,
gave the name of Río de la Plata, the River of Silver. This
estuary had been discovered in 1516 by Juan de Solís, who
landed with a few companions and was killed by the Indians. Ten years later Sebastián Cabot sailed into the river
and built a fort. The fort was destroyed by the Indians, and
Cabot returned to Spain. A determined attempt at settlement was then made in 1536, when an expedition under
Pedro de Mendoza arrived and established the little river-
side town of Puerto de Santa María del Buen Aire, so
named either because of the fresh Plata breezes or in honour
of the patron saint of navigators: Santa María of Fair
Winds. But the land was a disappointment. It contained no
gold or silver, and the nomadic Indians who had killed
Solís were as savage and warlike as ever. A German who was
among the party later wrote of the hardship experienced
by the settlers in their fort of Buen Aire: 'So great was the
suffering and disastrous the hunger that there were not even
enough rats or mice, nor snakes nor other reptiles [for food],
and [therefore] even shoes and hides, everything had to
be eaten.'[2] Meanwhile Mendoza had dispatched a recon-
naissance force upstream to seek a short cut to Peru. No
such passage was discovered, but a more luxuriant country
was entered where the Indians were amenable. In this
region the town of Asunción del Paraguay was established
(1537).[3] Buenos Aires was evacuated, the horses and mares
which Mendoza had brought from Spain being left on the

[2] Ulrich Schmidl, *Derrotero y Viaje a España y las Indias*, trans. by Edmundo
Wernicke (1944), p. 41.
[3] cf. Pendle, *Paraguay*, p. 10.

grassy pampa, where they multiplied. Asunción, in spite of its remote inland position 1,000 miles from the Atlantic Ocean, now became the centre of Spanish settlement in south-eastern South America. From this rapidly-growing city expeditions sailed downstream to found towns on the margin of the Argentine plains. In 1573 Juan de Garay led a party of 9 Spaniards and 75 *criollos* (young men born in South America of European parentage)[4] down the rivers Paraguay and Paraná to establish the town of Santa Fe. In 1580 Garay again set forth, this time with 10 Spaniards, 50 *criollos*, 1,000 horses, and 500 cows for the final founding of Buenos Aires on the river bank where the modern city stands today. Of course the new town of Buenos Aires could not compare with the distant and flourishing cities in the Andean foothills. For many decades it was a precarious beach-head, constantly subject to attack by the Indians and later apprehensive of the Portuguese and English. In these circumstances the population—so predominantly *criollo* in origin—developed a self-reliant and independent spirit.

Thus by the end of the sixteenth century the foundations of Argentine history had been surely laid: the people of the future capital city and the people of the interior were already living quite separate and distinct lives; the town of Buenos Aires had been established on a strategic site which ensured its becoming one of the world's great ports; the herds of cattle which were to provide Buenos Aires with such wealth that it would automatically assume leadership of the nation were now multiplying on the pampa; and the inhabitants of Buenos Aires already possessed the spirit of independence which was destined later to inspire them to expel British invaders and overthrow the rule of Spain.

THE VICEREGAL PERIOD

The Spanish territories in America technically were not colonies or dependencies of Spain: they were kingdoms

[4] Today the word *criollo* is applied to any person or thing considered to be typically local. The expression *muy criollo* (very criollo) indicates approval of the person or thing so described.

13

WINGATE COLLEGE LIBRARY
WINGATE, N. C.

belonging to the Crown of Castile, and the Spanish king appointed viceroys to administer them on his behalf. Until as late as the eighteenth century the whole great empire was divided into no more than two such vice-royalties: the Vice-Royalty of New Spain (Mexico) and the Vice-Royalty of Peru. The viceroy of Peru not only ruled nominally over a vast Pacific coast territory stretching from Panama to Chile: his domain also extended eastwards across the Cordillera of the Andes and the wide pampa to include the town of Buenos Aires itself, some 3,000 miles distant from the viceregal city of Lima. The Crown enforced—or attempted to enforce—a monopoly of trade throughout the empire, and with disastrous consequences. For the sake of safety and to ensure the strictest possible supervision, direct commerce between Buenos Aires and the outside world was prohibited, trade to and from the Río de la Plata being confined to a single, circuitous route via Lima. Goods shipped from Spain for Buenos Aires were unloaded at a remote Caribbean port, Porto Bello, and were conveyed thence over the Isthmus of Panama, carried by sea down the Pacific coast to Callao, and then transported on muleback across the continent to the Atlantic-estuary town that was their destination.[5] Not only was this procedure absurdly long and costly, but the quantities of goods so received were quite insufficient for the requirements of the population, and there was ever-increasing resentment at the exorbitant profit made by the Lima merchants through whose hands all the traffic passed. But Spain was unable to maintain indefinitely her too stringent monopolistic regulations, and so, as Buenos Aires was a natural and an easily accessible port, it became a centre for contraband. Large amounts of foreign merchandise were smuggled into the Río de la Plata, as they were from the islands of the West Indies to the Spanish Main, and attempts to prevent the direct exportation of local products—notably hides and tallow—and of

[5] In the latter half of the eighteenth century mule-trains began to be replaced by covered wagons—*carretas*—drawn by oxen.

specie and bullion, were ineffective. Smugglers reaped the rewards that should have gone to Lima and Spain; and by the beginning of the eighteenth century Spain's overseas trade had declined to such an extent that the authorities at Madrid at last decided to introduce a more liberal policy. In the 1720's a few ships were permitted to sail directly to Buenos Aires, and after 1740 the new system of allowing specially-registered vessels to engage in direct trade with South American ports became general. In 1777 and 1778 the prohibition on traffic between Buenos Aires and other Spanish possessions was lifted, and in the latter year a so-called decree of free trade opened all the more important South and Central American ports to direct trade with the principal ports in Spain. The effect of these changes was to free the Río de la Plata from the economic domination of Peru; and Buenos Aires entered a period of unprecedented commercial activity. Adequate supplies of manufactured goods were now received, and at prices that were about one-third of those which had previously prevailed. The exportation of hides, skins, tallow, horns, and wool was stimulated.[6]

In 1776, as a part of the general reorganization of the Empire, and in spite of protests from Lima, Spain severed from Peru and Chile an area comprising approximately the territories of the present-day republics of Argentina, Bolivia, Paraguay, and Uruguay, and formed this extensive region into a new vice-royalty: the Vice-Royalty of the Río de la Plata, with Buenos Aires as the seat of the administration. This measure resulted from an improved knowledge of the geography of the New World and of local conditions, and from the recent growth in the economic importance of Buenos Aires. There was also an evident need to strengthen the Spanish position in the Río de la Plata against the Portuguese, who were constantly pressing southwards from

[6] For commerce during the colonial period, see R. A. Humphreys, *British Consular Reports on the Trade and Politics of Latin America, 1824–1826* (1940), pp. 28–32 and 352–3; also Ricardo Levene, *A History of Argentina*, trans. and ed. by W. S. Robertson (1937), pp. 101–16.

Brazil, and against the English, Spain's traditional rivals, whose maritime power constituted a permanent threat in the South Atlantic.

But the inauguration of the new vice-royalty did not signify that the local people were to have any greater share than formerly in the management of their own affairs. All the high functionaries continued to be Peninsular-born Spaniards, appointed by Madrid, and the *criollos* were still almost excluded from the work of government. It is true that in each town the *cabildo*, or municipal council, contained locally-born citizens; but these town councillors were not elected by the people: usually, on retirement, the councillors nominated their own successors (subject to confirmation by the Spanish governor); and the functions of the *cabildo*, except in a moment of emergency, were purely municipal.[7] Nevertheless, this body did provide an outlet for local aspirations and discontent, and the *cabildo* of Buenos Aires eventually played an influential part in the overthrow of Spanish authority.

The spirit of rebellion had long existed among the *criollos* of the Río de la Plata. As early as the year 1580 the people of Santa Fe (largely *criollo* in origin)[8] deposed, though only temporarily, all the chief Spanish office-holders in that town.[9] In 1589 the *cabildo* of Buenos Aires passed a significant resolution. They had been asked to cede all the wild horses of the pampa to a Spanish religious order. In their reply, refusing to make such a grant, the town councillors stated that 'it pertains to the children of the first conquerors to enjoy these wild horses as persons who inherited them from their fathers and as persons who sustained the said land at their own cost without being aided by his Majesty or any other person.'[10] In the following centuries the local people naturally were dissatisfied with their humiliating position under Spain's economic and political régime. The

[7] For a neat evaluation of the *cabildo*, see F. A. Kirkpatrick, *Latin America* (1938), p. 23, and C. H. Haring, *The Spanish Empire in America* (1947), pp. 158–78.
[8] See above, p. 13.   [9] Levene, p. 42.   [10] Ibid. pp. 42–43.

reforms in the eighteenth century came too late, and in fact they served to weaken Spanish authority. As Professor Humphreys has said,

The reforms stimulated an efflorescence of colonial society, a greater economic activity, an increasing regional self-consciousness. They contributed, with subsequent events, to a freer play of ideas, of which the foundation of clubs and newspapers at the end of the century was a sign; and they made yet more glaring the anomalies in the imperial structure and yet more odious the efforts of the merchants of the mother country and in the colonies to maintain a monopolistic control.[11]

In 1796 Spain was again at war with England, and English control of the seas interrupted communication between the mother country and her American possessions. There followed a great scarcity of foreign manufactures in the Río de la Plata, and the value of exports from Buenos Aires, which had amounted to $5\frac{1}{2}$ million pesos in 1796, fell to 335,000 pesos in 1797. In these circumstances the *cabildo* urgently demanded permission of the viceroy to carry on trade in 'neutral' ships without restriction, and to export local products to any countries that would accept them. The administrator of the Buenos Aires Customs supported the *cabildo's* request:

When [he wrote] great numbers of ships are tied up at the wharves, accumulating as much expense as they are worth, and entirely unable to procure supplies necessary for their preservation; when bumper crops that farmers produce go to waste and do not bring in enough to meet their needs; when merchants have no business and when mercantile transactions bring no profit; then commerce will commit the crime of placing itself outside the law, for our lawgivers have nothing to say about unforeseen cases, when international justice and nature itself cry out and cannot support the law.[12]

In 1797, in response to this appeal, a royal order was issued permitting trade in neutral vessels, but only on condition

[11] R. A. Humphreys, *The Evolution of Modern Latin America* (1946), p. 36.
[12] Quoted by Levene, p. 134.

that the ships should 'return to the ports of Spain', and that they should pay the usual duties upon importation into Spain and the import and export duties in America. As Spain at that time was virtually blockaded by England, the new regulations were impracticable; the vice-royalty continued to suffer a shortage of imports; and instead of preventing contraband, the royal order made it inevitable that the *criollos* should engage in illicit trade as a means of alleviating their distress. When peace was signed between Spain and England, in 1802, commercial relations with the motherland were resumed; but a new war with England broke out in 1804, and the Spanish Empire thereupon entered its last phase.

Already a number of *criollos* in various parts of Spanish America—encouraged by the North American example and the ideology of the French Revolution—had dreamed of and plotted emancipation. Some of these *precursores* had received a sympathetic hearing in London. In 1797, indeed, the British Government wrote to the Governor of Trinidad directing him

to promote the measures most suitable to liberate the Spanish colonies, and to place them in a position to resist the oppressive authority of their government, in the certainty that they could count upon all the resources to be expected from H.B. Majesty, be it with forces, or with arms and ammunition to any extent, with the assurance that the views of H.B. Majesty go no further than to secure to them their independence, without pretending to any sovereignty over their country or even to interfere in the privileges of the people, either in their political, civil, or religious rights.[13]

The object of this proposed intervention was twofold: to inflict a crippling wound on Spain, and to provide Britain's rapidly-expanding industries with new markets and new sources of supplies. The resumption of the war in 1804 provided the opportunity for action to be taken—at first unofficially—against the Spaniards in the Río de la Plata.

[13] Quoted in ibid. p. 193.

Spaniards and Criollos

Among the most enthusiastic advocates of various schemes for the invasion of Spain's American dominions was Commodore Sir Home Popham—'a restless officer of insinuating manners, who had early in his career gained favour in high places'.[14] Popham's popularity in the Navy is attributed to the fact that 'he looked carefully to the interest of the men and officers under his immediate command, particularly in the matter of prize-money, which was frequently the main object of his operations. . . . [And] constant employment in more or less independent stations had given him an opportunity of dabbling in mercantile transactions.'[15] It was not surprising that a man of this disposition should be attracted by the commercial possibilities of South America and in 1806, after taking part in the capture of Cape Town from the Dutch and having no immediate work to be done, the Commodore on his own responsibility set sail from South Africa with his whole squadron, crossed the South Atlantic, and entered the Río de la Plata. With him he had brought the veteran Highland 71st Regiment under Brigadier-General William Carr Beresford, a few artillerymen, four guns, and seven dragoons. The Spanish authorities at Buenos Aires, although they had been warned that a British force was approaching, allowed themselves to be taken by surprise; the viceroy, the Marqués de Sobremonte, fled ignominiously to the interior; and on 27 June 1806 Beresford's troops occupied the town. The British general immediately issued a wisely-worded proclamation wherein he offered to the people of the Río de la Plata the right to administer justice for themselves, the right of private property, freedom to practise the Roman Catholic religion, and freedom of commerce. Without delay, Popham and Beresford dispatched to London glowing reports of the wealth and other attractions of the 'New Arcadia', and they sent home nearly $1,100,000 of prize money, seized from the fleeing Sobremonte, as evidence that their enthusiasm was not un-

[14] J. W. Fortescue, *The History of the British Army* (1910), v. 310.
[15] Ibid. p. 311.

founded. On 20 September this booty was paraded through the streets of the West End and City of London in eight waggons, each drawn by six horses, adorned with ribbons and flags whereon the word 'TREASURE' was inscribed in letters of gold.[16] Visions of El Dorado caught the imagination of business men and adventurers, who hastened to ship large cargoes of British manufactures to the Plata. The British Government, deeply committed by Popham's unauthorized action, had no option but to send out reinforcements under Sir Samuel Auchmuty to consolidate the position.

Meanwhile, however, the people of Buenos Aires—aided by Santiago Liniers (a Frenchman in the Spanish service), who landed with an expeditionary force from the Banda Oriental (modern Uruguay)—had risen against the British invaders and, on 12 August, had compelled them to surrender, together with their arms and their regimental colours, some of which are still displayed in the church of Santo Domingo, Buenos Aires. In the annals of Argentina this action is referred to as the *Reconquista*, the Reconquest.[17] Most of the British prisoners were sent far into the interior, where one of the officers, Major Alexander Gillespie, kept a diary of his experiences and wrote vivid descriptions of the country. He marvelled at the 'fertile wastes' of the pampa, the abundant wild life, and the indolence of the people. 'Computed by the eye,' he wrote, 'we may fairly reckon ten thousand heads [of cattle] to be the fortune of every [human being], from his birth. Unconscious of his own wealth, he slumbers through his days.' During a part of his internment Gillespie was billeted in an adobe hut in a typical Argentine village, San Antonio de Areco, where he and his brother officers occupied their time in fishing, cricket, hunting, and riding. He noted:

The village of San Antonio is admirably placed for any

---

[16] *An Authentic and interesting Description of the City of Buenos Ayres and the Adjacent Country* . . . (London, John Fairburn, 1806), pp. 55–56.
[17] The British Embassy is now situated in the Calle Reconquista.

manufactury that requires a regular supply of water, but no
business is carried on by the population, who amount to six
hundred, except the knitting of stockings, which belongs to the
females. The males seemed to have no pursuit, and no visible
means of existence but from rapine, and the lasso. The liquor
shops are many, and thither the multitude repair upon Sun-
days, to carouse after worship, and then to play, until one or
another loses his all, even to the tatters upon his back.[18]

The news of the defeat of Beresford caused consternation
in London. Popham was recalled to England to be court-
martialled; further reinforcements were hurriedly dispatched; and Lieut.-General John Whitelocke was appointed to command all the troops in the Río de la Plata
area. While these measures were being taken, the earlier
reinforcements had arrived off the coast of the Banda
Oriental and, as they were insufficient in strength for an
attempt to recapture Buenos Aires, Auchmuty had been
obliged to limit his action to the assault and occupation of
the smaller town of Montevideo, on the Uruguayan shore
of the Plata estuary (3 February 1807). In the harbour of
Montevideo all the British warships and transports and a
large fleet of British merchantmen—loaded with goods for
the inaccessible golden market across the river—now lay at
anchor, awaiting Whitelocke's arrival.

The people of Buenos Aires, naturally, had gained a new
feeling of confidence by their successful uprising against the
invaders, and they were determined to resist the second on-
slaught, which they knew must be imminent. The Spanish
viceroy, who on Beresford's arrival had abandoned the
criollos to their fate, was in disgrace, and, after the fall of
Montevideo, they deposed him, nominating their own
'viceroy'—Santiago Liniers—in his place. It was evident
that Spain could not defend the vice-royalty, so the local
citizens proceeded to enlist and train their own militia.
Whitelocke arrived at Montevideo in May 1807 and was
joined by another expedition, under Brigadier-General

[18] Alexander Gillespie, *Gleanings and Remarks during many Months of Residence at Buenos Ayres* (1818), pp. 138–42.

Robert Craufurd, in the following month, by which time the total force under his command amounted to more than 10,000 men. The population of Buenos Aires was between 40,000 and 50,000, Liniers's raw militia numbering about 8,000.

Whitelocke was a weak and vacillating commander; and the British Government, in ignorance of local conditions, had addressed to him instructions which even a capable general would have found to be quite unrealistic:

> He was to reduce the province of Buenos Ayres by force of arms and exile the authors of the insurrection which had overthrown Beresford; and yet he was to consider that his main object was not to distress or annoy the enemy but only to occupy a portion of his territory. Again, he was to attach the inhabitants to British rule, but was forbidden to give them assurance of protection against the vengeance of Old Spain after the conclusion of peace.[19]

H.M. Government failed to understand that Beresford had been defeated, not by the machinations of a few pro-Spanish conspirators, but by an uprising of the mass of the population; and when Whitelocke's red-coated columns entered the narrow streets of Buenos Aires on 5 July 1807, having previously overcome the resistance of the militia stationed on the outskirts of the town, it was the citizens crowding on the flat house-tops who destroyed them.

The Commander-in-Chief's delay in launching the final assault had provided the mayor of Buenos Aires with time in which to prepare the defence. A British officer, Major Vandeleur, later described the experiences of one of the invading columns on the fatal day:

> On my arrival about a third [of the distance] down the street, a fire opened on me from the tops and windows of the houses on each side directly over me. I immediately ordered the column to advance double quick time, which was immediately executed and answered by our men by cheering. As we advanced through the streets we were continually assailed from

[19] Fortescue, v. 435.

the windows, on both sides of the street, with musketry, hand grenades, stink pots, brick bats and all sorts of combustibles. When we arrived at the last square of houses in that street, there was a breast-work thrown up directly across the front, made of bags of hides filled with earth. On our ascending this breast-work, on the opposite side we descended into a ditch of about six feet deep and twelve wide, likewise cut across the street. [The corner houses here were flanked with cannon. Every man who tried to enter the houses to reach the roofs was shot down from the roofs across the way.] Having so few men left, and a retreat appearing entirely impossible, or even if it was possible, that so many officers and men lying about wounded, it would be a breach of humanity, we therefore agreed to enter into a parley with the enemy.[20]

The other small columns into which Whitelocke had imprudently divided his force were similarly treated, and, having been ordered to enter the town by a number of widely separated streets, these columns were unable to support one another. The casualties were appalling. During this one day the British Army lost over 400 killed, 650 wounded, and 1,925 taken prisoner, of whom 250 were wounded. Faced by a calamity of such dimensions, Whitelocke decided to negotiate a truce with Liniers, and on 7 July he signed an agreement whereby he undertook that the entire British expedition—troops, warships, and merchantmen alike—would evacuate the Río de la Plata.

When the British convoy sailed for home from Montevideo on 9 September, it comprised more than 200 vessels. The troops were indignant at the humiliating terms that their commander had accepted from the leaders of the rabble against whom they had been fighting; but Whitelocke's decision to abandon the whole enterprise was perhaps the one instance of wisdom that he had manifested since his arrival in South America. Business men and speculators in London, who had invested their fortunes in the ship-loads of goods which (excepting those that had been

[20] *The Proceedings of a General Court Martial . . . for the Trial of Lieut-Gen. Whitelocke*, taken in shorthand by Mr Gurney (London, 1808), ii. 509-10.

liquidated in Montevideo) were now returned to them unsold, demanded an inquiry. At a court martial at Chelsea Hospital at the beginning of the year 1808 Whitelocke was cashiered and declared 'totally unfit and unworthy to serve His Majesty in any military capacity whatever'.

This second victory over the British Army is known to Argentines as the *Defensa*, and the street which was the scene of some of the bitterest fighting is so named. The *Defensa* was essentially a *criollo* victory. At his court martial Whitelocke admitted that he had been warned that the house-tops of Buenos Aires would be manned by the local people, but he claimed that there was no precedent in recent military history to suggest that the resistance of a civilian population could be so effective:

> Not one [instance] can, I will venture to say, be produced like the present, in which it is no exaggeration to say that every male inhabitant, whether free or slave, fought with a resolution and perseverance which could not have been expected even from the enthusiasm of religion and national prejudice, or the most inveterate and implacable hostility.[21]

The so-called *invasiones inglesas* are an important event in Argentine history. By twice defeating the British, the people of Buenos Aires discovered their own strength; and Spanish rule was felt to be even more irksome than before. And although, after the first moment of surprise, the British invaders were fiercely opposed by the inhabitants, nevertheless the liberal ideas expressed and put into practice by General Beresford during his brief administration had been eagerly welcomed: not only did Beresford preach free trade and demonstrate the advantages to be derived from unrestricted commerce with Great Britain, he lowered the local Customs duties and abolished State monopolies of certain basic commodities, thereby showing that Spanish policy in such matters had been unnecessarily oppressive. It was evident that the life of Buenos Aires could never be the same again. Mariano Moreno and other members of a small,

[21] Ibid. p. 727.

liberal-minded intelligentsia who in the late eighteenth century had translated and debated a number of prohibited books by French and British authors, now in fact became revolutionary agitators, sharing with the unprivileged business men of the port the conviction that the domination of Spain must be brought to an end. For many of these *criollos* allegiance to the Spanish Crown seemed a mockery indeed when in 1808 the French army invaded the mother country, imprisoned King Ferdinand VII, and installed Napoleon's brother Joseph Bonaparte on the throne at Madrid; and in the middle of May 1810 the position of the Spanish viceroy Cisneros, who had been sent out from Europe to replace the locally-appointed Santiago Liniers, was hopelessly weakened by the news that the French had occupied the town of Seville, which was almost the last refuge of Spanish authority in the Peninsula. In an atmosphere of excitement and anticipation the *cabildo* or municipal council of Buenos Aires thereupon summoned a general assembly of leading citizens—a *cabildo abierto*; but for three days the conservative councillors (half of the councillors were Spaniards, and half *criollos*) resisted the popular clamour for the formation of a national junta of government. On the fourth day, 25 May 1810, because of the threatening attitude of the crowd in the main square of the town (now appropriately named the Plaza de Mayo), they withdrew their opposition. Thus there came into being Argentina's first *criollo* Government, chosen by the leaders of the revolution and supported by the people of Buenos Aires. In practice the new junta merely took the place of the viceroy and nominally operated on behalf of the captive King Ferdinand.

Napoleon's invasion of Spain in 1808 had brought about a sudden and radical alteration in British policy: an army which Arthur Wellesley (the future Duke of Wellington) was preparing to lead to South America in the wake of those of Beresford, Auchmuty, Whitelocke, and Craufurd was dispatched instead to the Peninsula, and on a contrary errand: to liberate Spain. Great Britain and Spain were now allies, and Viscount Strangford, H.M. Minister at Rio de Janeiro, found that one of his main tasks was to protect Spanish interests in the Río de la Plata, where H.M. Government was not yet represented and where French interference would have deprived Great Britain of an increasingly valuable market and source of raw materials. Strangford was aided in his work by the fact that the Buenos Aires junta—and subsequent local governments—continued to profess loyalty to the Spanish royal house. Also, Buenos Aires needed British trade, had no desire to become a dependency of France, and was anxious to have assistance (which this able and conscientious diplomat provided) against Portuguese schemes to annex the Banda Oriental (Uruguay) to Brazil, whose 'natural frontier' in the south was considered by the Portuguese-Brazilians to be the Río de la Plata. There were suspicions and misunderstandings, but for some seven years Strangford managed to maintain amicable relations with successive Governments at Buenos Aires without alienating the Spaniards at Montevideo or in Europe, or the Portuguese at Rio de Janeiro. Largely because of his skill and perseverance the Plata—except during short periods—remained open to British shipping.[22]

THE EMANCIPATION

The *cabildo abierto* of 25 May 1810 was the origin of Argentine independence (though this was not formally declared until six years later) and it had another far-reaching consequence: by setting up an ostensibly 'national' Government without having yet invited the cities of the interior to participate in it, the Buenos Aires leaders perpetuated the old cleavage between their town and the hinterland, thereby preparing the way for years of anarchy and a permanent disequilibrium in the State.

The events of 25 May 1810 were followed by a long period

[22] For an admirable estimate of Strangford's achievement, see J. Street, 'Lord Strangford and the Río de la Plata, 1808–1815', *Hispanic American Historical Review* (later referred to as *H.A.H.R.*), Nov. 1853, pp. 477–510.

of political confusion and warfare. The most urgent problems were military. The revolutionaries—or, as they now
became, the patriots—had to eliminate the Spanish or
Spanish-led forces still remaining in the western and northern regions of the country; they had to try to safeguard the
land against invasion by the powerful Spanish armies still
existing in Peru; after the restoration of King Ferdinand to
the throne in 1814, the arrival of an expedition from Europe
to crush the revolution seemed imminent; and Portuguese
ambitions in the Banda Oriental were a permanent cause
of anxiety. One of the first acts of the junta was to dispatch
an improvised army to destroy a counter-revolutionary
movement at Córdoba, where Santiago Liniers, who had
thrown in his lot with the Spanish governor, was captured
and summarily executed. Three months later, on 7 November 1810, the patriots routed the Spaniards farther north, at
Suipacha—an event which is celebrated as the first victory
won by an Argentine army. But in the following years there
were defeats as well as victories. The constantly changing
Governments at Buenos Aires did not succeed in their endeavours to incorporate the whole of the former vice-royalty
in the new nation: they were unable to keep control of the
Andean region that is now Bolivia; an army led by Manuel
Belgrano—one of the intellectuals of the revolution, and
still a novice in the art of war—failed to 'liberate' Paraguay;
and the people of the Banda Oriental, after the overthrow
of the Spanish governor at Montevideo, resisted Argentine
and Brazilian domination alike. Moreover, defensive action
against Spanish troops descending upon the northern cities
from the Altiplano of the Andes had been inconclusive, and
General San Martín soon recognized that the only way to
safeguard the independence of the Plata was by expelling
the Spaniards from their strongholds on the far side of the
Cordillera.

While the military campaigns were in progress, attempts
were made to organize the nation internally. There were
insurrections almost without number. Juntas were followed

27

by Triumvirates, and they in turn gave way to Supreme Directors. Representatives were sent to Europe to search for a suitable and willing monarch for the Río de la Plata; but they returned empty-handed. The provinces were given opportunities to collaborate with Buenos Aires in the task of organizing the country, but they were unwilling to accept *porteño*[23] leadership, each provincial city wishing to be either autonomous or an equal partner in some loose form of federation. When a constitutional congress met at Tucumán in 1816, the members did at last declare that the 'United Provinces of the Río de la Plata' had become an independent State and no longer owed allegiance to Spain; but the majority of the deputies still favoured the adoption of a monarchical system, although this was not acceptable to the mass of the population; and when in 1819 the congress finally produced a constitution, it was of a centralized type so that, as was to be expected, the provincial *caudillos* promptly rejected it. On the margin of the confusion San Martín, at Mendoza, prepared his great military campaign.

All the descriptions of José de San Martín by English travellers who met him indicate that he was a man of outstanding personality and charm. John Miers, the botanist, who called upon him at Mendoza in 1819, wrote:

He was a tall well-made man, very broad across the shoulders, and upright in his carriage; his complexion was sallow, and he possessed a remarkably sharp and penetrating eye; his hair was dark, and he had large whiskers. His address was quick and lively; his manners affable and polite . . . what more particularly excited my attention [in the General's private study] was a large miniature likeness of himself, hung up between prints of Napoleon Buonaparte and Lord Wellington, all three being framed in a corresponding manner.[24]

Captain Basil Hall, R.N., was equally impressed:

He is a tall, erect, well-proportioned, handsome man, with a

---

[23] *Porteño*: belonging to the port. The inhabitants of Buenos Aires are referred to as *porteños*.

[24] *Travels in Chile and La Plata* . . . (London, Baldwin, 1826), i. 158–60.

large aquiline nose, thick black hair, and immensely bushy dark whiskers, extending from ear to ear under the chin; his complexion is deep olive, and his eye, which is large, prominent, and piercing, is jet black; his whole appearance being highly military. He is thoroughly well-bred and unaffectedly simple in his manners; exceedingly cordial and engaging, and possessed evidently of great kindliness of disposition: in short, I have never seen any person, the enchantment of whose address was more irresistible.[25]

Even Maria Graham, later the author of *Little Arthur's History of England*, though she had personal reasons for disapproving of San Martín, could not conceal her admiration.[26] Such was the man who is now Argentina's national hero.

San Martín had settled at Mendoza in 1814, and he spent nearly two and a half years at that small provincial town patiently and methodically plotting to attack the Spaniards on the Pacific coast. He raised his own army and imposed special taxes to maintain it. To equip it, he built an arsenal, a powder-factory, and a textile mill, and he set the male and female population to work making cannon, shot, horseshoes and bayonets, knapsacks, shoes, and uniforms. He dispatched agents into Chile to spread false rumours to mislead the enemy. The ladies of Mendoza contributed their jewels. From Buenos Aires the Supreme Director, Juan Martín de Pueyrredón, sent military equipment and supplies in response to San Martín's voracious demands. Every detail was planned: nothing was left to chance. At last in January 1817 the Army of the Andes, numbering 4,000 soldiers with an auxiliary militia of 1,400 more, went forth to scale the Cordillera, which rises majestically in full view of the town. The crossing was made by four principal passes on a front of some 500 miles. The artillery was dragged nearly 200 miles by almost impassable mountain trails over

[25] *Extracts from a Journal written on the Coasts of Chili, Peru, and Mexico* . . . 4th ed. (Edinburgh, Constable, 1825), i. 213–14.
[26] Maria Graham, *Journal of a Residence in Chile* . . . (London, Longman & Murray, 1824), pp. 280–4.

altitudes of 12,000 feet. Of more than 9,000 mules that left Mendoza with the expedition, less than half reached Chile; and less than a third of the 1,600 horses survived the journey. But the whole operation was carried out with mathematical precision. The main columns joined forces on the western side of the Cordillera exactly at the appointed time and place. They took the Spaniards by surprise and routed them at Chacabuco on 12 February. Two days later San Martín entered Santiago (the Chilean capital) in triumph. He obtained a second and, on this occasion, a decisive, victory at Maipú on 5 April 1818. Chile was now free, and the Argentine general was already planning the final stage of his campaign: the invasion, by sea, of Spain's greatest stronghold in South America—the Peruvian capital of Lima.[27]

San Martín entered Lima on 10 July 1821. Meanwhile the Venezuelan Liberator, Simón Bolívar, had been defeating the Spaniards in northern South America, and he forestalled San Martín by seizing the Ecuadorian port of Guayaquil before it could be incorporated in the new independent State of Peru. The two men met in secret conference at Guayaquil on 26–7 July 1822, and they disagreed. San Martín, disillusioned and weary, returned to Lima and resigned his command, stating in his farewell address: 'My promises to the countries for which I have fought are fulfilled: to secure their independence and to leave them to select their own governments.' He took no further part in South American affairs and died, a lonely exile, at Boulogne-sur-Mer.

The liberation of Chile and the invasion of Peru by Argentine-led and, partly, Argentine-composed armies did not imply that Buenos Aires or San Martín had any intention of annexing those Pacific Coast countries to the so-called 'United'—though in fact they were very disunited— 'Provinces of the Río de la Plata'. But the Argentines under-

[27] cf. R. A. Humphreys, *Liberation in South America 1806–1827* (1952), pp. 68–81.

standably have taken pride in San Martín's far-flung achievement, and if today they feel that their nation has a continental mission, it is partly because they truly had such a mission—and effectively fulfilled it—in the vital years 1817–22.

Chapter III

GAUCHOS AND TOWNSMEN

DURING the 1820's there was no national Government in Argentina, at least not one which survived for long. In the year 1820, the 'year of anarchy', the province of Buenos Aires itself had at least twenty-four governors. In the rest of the country government was in the hands of local gaucho leaders—caudillos. The rivalry, which for so long had prevailed, between the city of Buenos Aires and the 'camp',[1] broke out in civil war. As Domingo Faustino Sarmiento wrote in his classic work on the period,[2] two incompatible types of society existed side by side: on the one hand, there was an urban civilization on the Spanish and European model; on the other hand, the wild life of the untutored and lawless gauchos. The gaucho, the South American cowboy, was, so to say, the human expression of the vast and desolate pampa, his way of living determined by the presence of the great herds of cattle and horses which roamed over the unfenced plains. He was of mixed Spanish and Indian blood, accustomed to attack by Indian raiders, indifferent to his neighbour's life, and constantly risking his own. He had no wants that the horses and cattle of the pampa could not provide. 'Vain is the endeavour to explain to him the luxuries and blessings of a more civilized life', wrote one English traveller; 'his ideas are, that the noblest effort of man is to raise himself off the ground and ride instead of walk—that no rich garments or variety of food can atone for the want

[1] The 'camp', a word used by British settlers and Anglo-Argentines generally, is the Anglicized form of the Spanish *campo*, or country, and refers to all the country outside the city of Buenos Aires.

[2] *Facundo* (Buenos Aires, Editorial Tor), p. 58. (*Facundo* was first published in 1845, the full title being: *Civilización y Barbarie: Vida de Juan Facundo Quiroga*.)

of a horse—and that the print of the human foot on the ground is in his mind the symbol of uncivilization.'[3] The gaucho's equipment was primitive. On most nights he slept on the ground in the open air, using his saddle as a pillow. His boot (the *bota de potro*) was the hide stripped from a colt's hind leg and pulled on to his own leg while still moist, so that it dried to the appropriate shape, the upper part forming the boot's leg, the hock fitting over the heel, and the remainder covering the foot, with an aperture for the big toe. Often his stirrup was merely a bone hanging from a leather thong, gripped by the free toe. His diet was meat. His sports were equestrian. If he had a hut, the door was a cow's hide. His only instrument, when eating, was his knife. Another of the many British visitors who were enthralled by the habits of the gaucho explained: 'The use of a fork is avoided, because . . . a knife and fork require a plate, which needs to be placed on a table. . . . This want creates another: a table involves the necessity of a chair; and thus the consequences resulting from the use of forks involve a complete revolution in the household.'[4] In short, when the *criollo* intellectuals and merchants of Buenos Aires began to try to put the country in order, 'the gaucho, inured by his style of living to the stress of weather and to the struggle with savage animals, became the right hand of the petty chiefs of party faction, ever joining the side in conflict with the ruling power. The words law and order signified for him oppression and servitude, and he became the declared enemy of all authority.'[5] In later years José Hernández, in his epic poem *Martín Fierro*, immortalized the gaucho spirit:

> It is my pride that I live as free
> As the bird in the sky. . . .[6]

[3] Head, p. 21.

[4] William MacCann, *Two Thousand Miles' Ride through the Argentine Provinces* (1853), i. 102–3.

[5] Herbert Gibson, 'Monograph attached to the Argentine Agricultural and Live Stock Census of 1908', quoted in Gordon Ross, *Argentina and Uruguay* (1917), p. 171.

[6] *Martín Fierro* was published in two parts: the first in 1872, the second in 1879.

In political terms, the incompatibility of *porteños* and gauchos now became a conflict between *Unitarios* and *Federales*: the *Unitarios* were those who wished to have a strong central Government at Buenos Aires dominating the whole country; the *Federales*, living outside the city, had no desire to be dominated by men who (in the phrase of Sarmiento, himself on the side of 'Europeanization') wore frock coats instead of *ponchos*.

With the emancipation from Spain and the opening of the port of Buenos Aires to European trade, the poverty of the old cities of the interior was aggravated. Buenos Aires looked towards Europe. Maritime communication with Great Britain was easy, by comparison with the slow journeying of the ox-carts overland to Santiago del Estero, Tucumán, Salta, and Jujuy; and so those western towns, whose prosperity had depended on the Spanish monopoly and the use of the Panama–Lima line of traffic, suffered and languished. It was now cheaper to obtain *ponchos* from Yorkshire than from Santiago del Estero, wine from France than from Mendoza, sugar from Brazil than from Tucumán. Buenos Aires drew from the 'camp' the produce that it shipped abroad, and in exchange for these exports European manufactured goods poured into the city. The contrast between the life of the well-to-do *porteños* and that of the country people became increasingly marked.

Buenos Aires learned what to wear, and how to heat her houses, from the English. She took her poetry and literature from the French. Where the provincial ate his beef without bread, without vegetables, and drank Correntine caña and wine from Mendoza, the porteño ate bread and fruit and vegetables as well as the finest beef, and drank the best that Spain and France had to offer. In the city the poor might dress like the gauchos, but the estanciero and merchant class wore satins and silks. The campesino drank from a gourd mate, and the porteño from a mate of wrought silver. The gaucho wore *botas de potro*, the porteño silver-buckled shoes. And so was born the porteño mentality, which may be roughly summed up as the inner conviction that Argentina exists for Buenos Aires, and that all outside the limits of Buenos Aires is outside the limits of civilization.[7]

Furthermore, the province of Buenos Aires, containing the only port in the whole country, received and appropriated to itself all the Customs duties, leaving the other provinces almost without public income. Thus in spite of the general anarchy and of being engaged in a war against the Portuguese, who had annexed the Banda Oriental, Buenos Aires prospered during the 1820's, and Great Britain's first official representative to the Río de la Plata[8] was able to report in 1824 that the local revenue was progressively increasing. Meanwhile Bernardino Rivadavia, a far-sighted patriot, introduced many reforms in finance and education, and did his utmost to encourage immigration and to attract foreign investment. In 1826 this distinguished statesman was nominated the first President of the United Provinces of the Río de la Plata and, being in favour of strong centralized rule, he at once persuaded Congress to abolish the provincial government of Buenos Aires, thereby making the city the capital of the nation. But Rivadavia was a townsman, ignorant of conditions in the 'camp'. A British traveller described him as

about five feet in height, and much about that measure in circumference; his countenance is dark, but not unpleasing, it denotes acuteness; . . . his coat is green, buttoned *à la Napoleon*; his small clothes, if such they can be called, are fastened at the knee with silver buckles, and the short remainder of his person is clad in silk hose, dress shoes, and silver buckles.[9]

Such was the man who had known and admired Jeremy Bentham and who now provoked the landowners of the province of Buenos Aires—jealous of their autonomy and unwilling to share the Customs revenue of the port with the people of the interior—to resist him. The caudillos in the

---

[7] Ysabel F. Rennie, *The Argentine Republic* (1945), pp. 19–20.

[8] Woodbine Parish was appointed Consul-General at Buenos Aires in 1823 and chargé d'affaires two years later.

[9] J. A. B. Beaumont, *Travels in Buenos Ayres and the adjacent Provinces of the Rio de la Plata* (1828), p. 158.

other provinces were equally determined not to tolerate a 'unitarian' form of government. Rivadavia resigned, and civil war again broke out.

Many of the plans sponsored by Rivadavia, though enlightened, were premature, and their collapse caused hardship and financial loss. For example, in 1824 two Scottish merchants, the Parish Robertson brothers, had agreed to establish an agricultural settlement at Monte Grande in the province of Buenos Aires. The colonists, who came chiefly from the west and south of Scotland, 'were chosen with a view at once to their agricultural skill and their religious and moral character'.[10] They were farmers, bricklayers, blacksmiths, carpenters, and servants, men, women, and children numbering 220 in all. They sailed from Leith in 1825 together with all the necessary agricultural implements and machinery, and on arrival at Monte Grande they set to work to transform the pampa. But the scheme was too ambitious; funds were inadequate; and during the wars which followed the fall of Rivadavia the colony was invaded time after time by rival bands of horsemen who plundered and sacked the farms. So the colonists dispersed, and the Parish Robertsons lost the £60,000 that they had invested in the project.

The Río de la Plata, so recently freed from colonial rule, was not yet ready for representative institutions of the British or North American kind, or for the social reforms which the intellectuals of the revolution had imagined that they could carry out forthwith; and in the Plata, as elsewhere in Spanish America, anarchy inevitably prepared the way for despotism. It has been said that 'From one point of view . . . the dictators who so early arose were as much the expression of the Spanish American revolutions as Napoleon was an expression of the French Revolution. From another, dictatorship represented the triumph of experience over theory.'[11] In the revolutionary wars the

---

[10] James Dodds, *Records of the Scottish Settlers in the River Plate* (1897), p. 3.
[11] Humphreys, *Evolution of Modern Latin America*, p. 84.

people had grown accustomed to military leadership, and during the civil wars the provinces were dominated by caudillos. Thus by the end of the 1820's the personal rule of a military chief was generally accepted as a natural form of government. Indeed, the tradition of *caudillismo* is still not extinct today.

Rivadavia's high-handed attempt to impose a 'unitarian' pattern on the country had produced unparalleled chaos, and now was the opportunity for his opponents, the *Federales*, to endeavour to create order after their chosen fashion. However, the leader of this reaction—Juan Manuel Ortiz de Rosas—did not come from a province of the interior, but from the province of Buenos Aires itself, and, paradoxically, although he styled himself a *Federal*, throughout his long period of power he was almost constantly at war with one or more of the caudillos of the inland provinces. Furthermore, although Rosas was supported by the gauchos and the urban working class of Buenos Aires, he was in fact one of the wealthiest *estancieros*[12] in the land, the owner of a valuable *saladero*[13] and of the ships in which he exported his salted meat to Brazil and Cuba. But this offspring of aristocratic families had spent his childhood in the 'camp', where he became a consummate horseman and won the admiration of the gauchos and Indians, whom he formed into a courageous and devoted militia. A traveller who met Rosas when he was at the height of his power wrote:

In his character of a country gentleman he gained the hearts of the peasantry: he surpassed them all in feats of activity and address, in taming wild horses, and throwing the lasso; and his management of an estancia was excellent. Throughout his entire career, his administrative skill, and his art of ingratiating himself with his associates, obtaining their confidence and securing implicit obedience from all under his control, have been very remarkable. My first interview with General Rosas was in one of the avenues in his pleasure grounds. . . . On this

[12] In Spain the word *estancia* means a stay or sojourn. In South America it signifies a large country estate; its owner is called an *estanciero*.
[13] *Saladero*: meat-salting plant.

occasion he wore a sailor's jacket, with blue trousers and cap, and carried a long crooked stick in his hand. His handsome ruddy countenance and portly aspect (he is of sanguineous temperament), gave him the appearance of an English country gentleman. . . . In referring to the motto, which is worn by all citizens: '*Viva la Confederación Argentina! Mueran los Salvajes Unitarios!*' ('Live the Argentine Confederation! Death to the Savage Unitarians!') he explained to me . . . that on occasions of popular excitement it had been the means of saving many lives—it was a token of brotherhood, he explained; illustrating it very forcibly by embracing me. The word death was only meant to express a wish that the Unitarians, as a political party, in opposition to the government, should be destroyed. Many Unitarians, it was true, had been executed; but only because twenty drops of blood shed at a proper moment might save the spilling of twenty thousand.[14]

During the civil disturbances following Rivadavia's fall the authorities at Buenos Aires had appealed to Rosas, with his militia, to restore order, and so he had come to be recognized as the strong man of the province. In 1829 the legislature appointed him for three years Governor of the Province and Captain-General, with dictatorial powers. At the end of this term he led a campaign against the Indians in the south, thereby adding to his territorial possessions and to his reputation. In 1835 he was again summoned to assume the governorship, and his rule continued without interruption until the year 1852. Although Rosas was a *Federal*, no more 'unitarian' régime than his can be imagined. Everyone in Buenos Aires was obliged to wear as a sign of loyalty a red ribbon inscribed, as mentioned above, with a denunciation of the '*salvajes Unitarios*'. Even the ladies of the aristocracy did not dare to be seen in the street without their red ribbon or sash. Doña Encarnación, Rosas's wife and ardent assistant, wore evening dresses of scarlet satin. *Estancieros* wore scarlet *ponchos*. The dictator's spies and secret police, the *Mazorca*, intimidated and assassinated his enemies. His portrait was exhibited throughout the city, and

[14] MacCann, ii. 4–5.

was even displayed on the altars in the churches; intellectual activity was discouraged; schools were closed. Rosas quarrelled with France, and the French fleet—later joined by the British—blockaded Buenos Aires, bringing disaster to local commerce; he himself prohibited traffic up the river to Paraguay, in an unsuccessful attempt to subdue that country; and for nine years—unsuccessfully, also—he laid siege to Montevideo, where many of his opponents had sought refuge. Rebellions by provincial caudillos and by *estancieros* were ruthlessly crushed, the leaders being decapitated and their heads exhibited in public. Then suddenly in May 1851 one of the caudillos whom the dictator imagined that he had permanently tamed—General Urquiza, of Entre Rios—renounced his allegiance and began to collect together a formidable army. Rosas was decisively beaten by Urquiza's forces at the battle of Monte Caseros on 3 February 1852. He went to live in England in exile near Southampton, where he died in 1877 at the age of eighty-four.

Rosas lived in violent times, when it was not unusual for a victorious leader to execute his defeated rivals; but never before had terror been organized systematically. It can be argued, however, that the tyranny of Rosas had beneficial consequences. This *estanciero*, who governed with a gaucho's violence and lack of respect for human life, did remind the people of the city of Buenos Aires that in future they would ignore the provinces at their peril; and although the only interests that the tyrant served were his own, the provinces did at least learn during his rule that one government in Argentina at a time was enough.

THE CONSTITUTION OF 1853

After the battle of Monte Caseros the Argentines were ready to enter the modern period in their evolution. At this stage four fundamental characteristics may be noted:[15] first, the population was still small, there being only about

[15] James, *Latin America*, p. 307.

1,200,000 inhabitants; second, the people still despised agriculture and were almost exclusively interested in horses, cattle, and sheep; third, there was an abundance of free land of excellent quality for cattle-raising and for the cultivation of grain; and fourth, as a result of the distribution of vast tracts of public land by Rivadavia (to secure collateral for a British loan) and Rosas (to reward his supporters), the large private *estancia* had become an established feature of the country. Another circumstance was to have vital consequences: there was now a growing recognition, alike among the 'unitarian' *émigrés* who returned to their homeland from Montevideo and Chile and among the victorious provincial leaders, that some form of constitutional compromise must be negotiated. Because of the traditional rivalry between Buenos Aires and the interior, this process of adjustment was delayed by suspicion and jealousy and disturbed by civil war; but the foundations of national union were quickly laid.

In May 1852 General Urquiza invited the provincial governors to meet at San Nicolás de los Arroyos, and at this conference it was agreed that a Constituent Convention should be convoked forthwith. The Convention began its deliberations at Santa Fe in November, but without the participation of the province of Buenos Aires, which rejected Urquiza's leadership, continued to refuse to be merged with the less prosperous inland provinces, and proceeded to organize itself as a separate State. The delegates at Santa Fe, however, were undeterred: they set to work to draw up a constitution which, with only minor modifications, eventually became the basic law of the whole nation and survived as such until the year 1949. As their model they took the Constitution of the United States, adapting it to local conditions in accordance with the recommendations of the Argentine publicist Juan Bautista Alberdi, who argued that, while the republic must be organized on a federal basis (because the provinces were so diverse physically and had experienced such long periods of isolation and autonomy), there must nevertheless be a strong central authority to prevent a recurrence of anarchy. The Constitution was proclaimed in May 1853. As Buenos Aires would not yet join the so-called 'Argentine Confederation', a temporary capital was established at the small town of Paraná. Elections were held in November 1853, and General Urquiza was proclaimed the first constitutional President of the Confederation.

The points at which the Constitution[16] differed from that of the United States were significant. In particular, so that he might be able to maintain national unity, the Argentine President was given considerably more power than that accorded to the President of the United States; and this arrangement followed Spanish tradition, it being contrary to Spanish ideas (and South American custom) that an executive should be subordinate to the legislature. Thus the Argentine President was authorized to frame and introduce his own bills in Congress (Art. 68); he was empowered to appoint and remove the ministers of his cabinet, and many other officials, without requiring the approval of the Senate (Art. 86, cl. 10); and in certain circumstances he might suspend constitutional guarantees by declaring a state of siege (Art. 86, cl. 19). The function and nature of the state of siege were defined in the following terms:

In case of internal commotion or foreign attack, endangering the exercise of this Constitution and of the authorities created by it, the province or territory in which the disturbance of order exists shall be declared in a state of siege, the constitutional guarantees there being suspended. But during this suspension the President of the Republic shall not condemn by himself nor apply penalties. His power shall be limited in such a case, with respect to persons, to arresting them or conveying them from one point of the nation to another, if they should not prefer to leave the Argentine territory. (Art. 23.)

The state of siege is still frequently used today, enabling the

[16] For an English translation of the complete text of the Constitution of 1853, see R. H. Fitzgibbon, ed., *The Constitutions of the Americas* (1948); also Austin F. Macdonald, *Government of the Argentine Republic* (1942), pp. 429–52.

President to dispense with such democratic forms as he may declare to be contrary to the national interest.

Another provision of the Constitution of 1853 gave additional power to the federal government—i.e. to the President, since the members of the cabinet were merely his nominees. For the preservation of order and unity the executive was to be permitted, whenever he should consider the step to be necessary, to 'intervene' in the provinces (Art. 6). When these occasions have arisen in practice it has been customary for the President to remove the governor, the members of the local legislature, the municipal officials, and the judges of the provincial courts, and to appoint his own federal representative—an *interventor*—with full authority to manage all provincial affairs and to supervise elections so as to make certain that the results should be favourable to the candidates enjoying federal support.[17] Thus, under the cover of one of the articles of an essentially 'federalist' Constitution, it has been possible for 'unitarian' presidents at Buenos Aires to dominate the provinces to a degree which would not have been tolerated in pre-constitutional times.

In other respects the Constitution of 1853 was remarkably liberal, and many of its clauses revealed the influence of the far-sighted intellectual, Alberdi. The opening section was a bill of rights wherein all the inhabitants of the nation were guaranteed the right to work, trade, enter, remain, or leave, 'to publish their ideas through the press without previous censorship'; and 'of freely professing their religion' (Art. 14). Further it was stated that 'the Argentine Nation does not admit prerogatives of blood or of birth; in it there are no personal privileges nor titles of nobility. All its inhabitants are equal before the law, and admissible for employment without any other requisite than fitness. Equality is the basis of taxation and of the public burdens' (Art. 16), and 'no inhabitant of the Nation may be punished without previous trial, based on an earlier law than the date of the offense. . . . The prisons of the Nation shall be healthy and

[17] Fitzgibbon, p. 169.

clean, for the safety and not for the punishment of the prisoners confined in them' (Art. 18). 'Aliens enjoy in the territory of the Nation all of the civil rights of the citizen; they may exercise their industry, commerce, and profession; own landed property, purchase it and sell it; navigate the rivers and coasts; freely practise their religion' (Art. 20). Alberdi had declared that the country required immigration and foreign capital, and that railways would unite the people better than any political measures could do. His ideas inspired, among many other clauses, the following:

Congress shall have power . . . to provide whatever is conducive to the prosperity of the country, for the progress and welfare of all of the Provinces, and for the advancement of learning, enacting programs of general university instruction, and promoting industry, immigration, the construction of railways and navigable canals, the colonization of lands of the national domain, the introduction and establishment of new industries, the importation of foreign capital, and the exploration of the interior rivers, by protective laws and by temporary concessions of privileges and the offering of rewards (Art. 67, cl. 16).

Moreover, the Constituent Convention boldly dealt with many of the economic causes of disunion. The inter-provincial tariffs, which had crippled internal trade, were abolished (Arts. 10–12). The income from the Buenos Aires Customs was to belong to the nation, instead of being retained by the province of Buenos Aires (Art. 9). And, with the long tyranny of Rosas in mind, the delegates at Santa Fe decreed that: 'The President and Vice-President shall hold their office for the term of six years, and can be re-elected only after a similar intervening period' (Art. 77).

Argentina was now split into two separate states: the wealthy province of Buenos Aires and the inland Argentine Confederation. Urquiza's Government at Paraná made an honest and vigorous attempt to develop the economy of the territory under their control; but, as Buenos Aires monopolized the overseas trade of the Río de la Plata—and, thereby, the Customs duties—the Confederate provinces lacked the financial resources necessary for their projects for agricultural settlement, railway construction, education, and so forth. In 1856, hoping to attract shipping directly to their upstream port of Rosario, the Paraná Congress introduced a system of 'differential duties', imposing a higher rate of duty on all 'indirect' imports—i.e. on all European merchandise entering the Confederation via Buenos Aires. This measure naturally caused resentment and a further deterioration in the relations between the *porteños* and the Confederates. In 1859 Congress authorized Urquiza to subdue Buenos Aires by force. A *porteño* army, under General Bartolomé Mitre, was routed at the battle of Cepeda (October 1859), and a pact was then signed by the two parties, Buenos Aires agreeing to join the Confederation. The constitution of 1853, with some very slight modifications, requested by the *porteños*, was finally adopted for the whole nation in October 1860. The old conflict was then revived, however, because the province of Buenos Aires insisted on electing its deputies to the first national Congress in accordance with its own provincial electoral laws. The national Congress therefore refused to recognize the Buenos Aires deputies. On this pretext the *porteños* renounced the pact of 1859; civil war broke out again; and, reversing the previous outcome, General Bartolomé Mitre defeated the Confederate army at Pavón (September 1861). This had been an unnecessary war, caused, in part at least, by Mitre's personal antipathy for Urquiza; but after the victory at Pavón the *porteño* leader magnanimously and wisely refused to follow up his military success: instead, he entered into negotiations with Urquiza and formally accepted, once again, the Constitution of 1853. National elections were held in 1862, as a result of which Mitre became the first constitutional President of a united Argentine republic.

THE RULE OF THE TOWNSMEN

In 1862 the townsmen—*porteños, Unitarios,* Liberals—were in power at last. President Mitre—who besides being the leading soldier of the day, was a distinguished scholar and historian—appointed a talented and public-spirited cabinet. This Government nationalized the Buenos Aires Customs, in accordance with the Constitution; encouraged European immigration and foreign trade and investment; began to construct railways; built schools; and organized a national system of posts and telegraphs. The impetuous educator Domingo Faustino Sarmiento—famous author of *Facundo*—went to serve as Governor in his native San Juan. But while Mitre and his colleagues devoted themselves to the national interests, resistance to *porteño* rule continued in many parts of the country. The legislature of the province of Buenos Aires would not abdicate in favour of the national Congress, though permitting the latter to assemble in the city which everyone agreed must ultimately become the capital of the republic. Rural caudillos—and notably the gaucho Angel Vicente Peñaloza, nicknamed 'El Chacho', of La Rioja—persisted in their customary guerrilla warfare.

Nowhere was the conflict between the new ideas and the old tradition more intense than in San Juan, which town Sarmiento was determined to convert into a South American Boston—the city which for him symbolized the ideal of public education and representative government.[18] Sarmiento had travelled widely in Europe and the United States and had marvelled at the cultural and material achievements of the people of those regions. During years of exile he had meditated on the needs of his homeland; drawn up plans for reforming every branch of the national life; and published in newspapers of his own founding and in innumerable pamphlets and books his opinions on every subject under the sun. In the campaign of Caseros he had followed the army with a printing press in a cart and had poured forth a stream of bulletins and broadsheets denouncing the dictator Rosas—publications which were at the same time first-class war propaganda, historical documents,

[18] A. W. Bunkley, *The Life of Sarmiento* (1952), p. 288.

and literature. Before joining Urquiza's forces Sarmiento had bought a full European uniform and outfit. In his view clothes were the symbol of culture, and if his compatriots were to be civilized they must be compelled to change the *poncho* and the *chiripá*[19] for European clothing. He explained: '[My] saddle, spurs, polished sword, buttoned coat, gloves, French képi and overcoat, everything was a protest against the gauchesque spirit. . . . This seems like a small thing, but it was a part of my campaign against Rosas and the caudillos.'[20] A daguerreotype which is still in existence[21] shows the educator in his imported uniform: he was a short, thick-set man with a massive head, large features, beetle brows and a high forehead, a bull-like neck, broad but bent shoulders, piercing dark eyes and a sad, stubborn expression. Two years after the fall of Rosas, Sarmiento had begun to play an active part in the legislature of Buenos Aires, where he proposed and supported all manner of reforms, from the introduction of the metric system of weights and measures to the institution of the secret ballot. He spoke eloquently in debates on the most diverse matters and came to be recognized as a statesman and political leader of the future. During this period he sponsored a law to create a model agricultural community around the town of Chivilcoy, where hundreds of farmers lacked deeds to give them possession of the land that they worked, while others paid rent to absentee landlords. Sarmiento suggested the awarding of definite titles to the workers of the soil, the division and sale of the lands at a low price, and aid in the organization and improvement of the community. The proposal was accepted, and within eight years Chivilcoy had become one of the richest and most productive districts in the province of Buenos Aires. The principles governing that experiment became the basis of Sarmiento's later programme of

---

[19] The *chiripá*, or primitive substitute for trousers, was formed of a shawl-like blanket. This was wrapped around the waist like a kilt, after which it was brought up between the legs, from back to front, and the end tucked through the girdle, to hang down again in front.

[20] Bunkley, p. 335.   [21] This portrait is reproduced in Bunkley.

colonization and land reform.[22] His general plan for educational development was equally enlightened. Teaching was still looked upon as an inferior profession. Sarmiento insisted that it must be raised to a position of dignity, and that an adequate and independent revenue must be assured for state schools. He was convinced of the civilizing influence of women teachers and of the desirability that book-learning should be supplemented by training in manual crafts. And not only must the farmer be provided with land of his own: he too must be educated. In every rural area of two and a half leagues[23] enough land should be set aside to support a school. On this land, apart from the school itself, there should be built an establishment for the experimental cultivation of plants, a dairy, a library, a chapel and a vaccination centre.[24] As chief of the Department of Schools, between 1856 and 1861 Sarmiento founded thirty-six new schools in Buenos Aires; caused the latest and best texts to be translated into Spanish; and introduced the teaching of foreign languages, music, and singing.

But it was when he became Governor of San Juan in 1862 that, for the first time in his life, Sarmiento had the power personally to put into practice the whole of his programme for improving the lot of mankind. For a number of reasons, his endeavours were unsuccessful. Sarmiento was too impatient and disagreeable in manner. A self-made man, of unlimited energy, and with a justifiably high opinion of his own worth,[25] he was, in spite of his love of civilization, barbarously intransigent. The little Andean province of San Juan was not ready for many of the changes that he imposed upon it. Sarmiento's primary preoccupation was always the preparation of the human being for the new age of

[22] Ibid. pp. 369–70.
[23] A league is 5 km. or about 3 miles. A sq. league is 2,500 hectares or 6,176 acres.   [24] Bunkley, p. 374.
[25] Sir Richard Burton, who admired Sarmiento's honesty of purpose and his belief in progress, recorded that he was referred to in Buenos Aires as 'Don Yo' (Mr I) (*Letters from the Battle-Fields of Paraguay* (1870), p. 164). Burton dedicated this book to Sarmiento.

civilization that he was ushering in, so education and information came first; but during his two-year governorship he also devoted much effort to the moulding of the province into a model district. He created new offices such as those of justice of the peace, the defender of minors, the district attorney and a topographical department, which drew up the first map of the province and the first important plan of the town of San Juan, with its adjacent agricultural lands. He founded an office of statistics, established agricultural communities, organized the rural and urban police, paved streets, put name signs on street corners and benches in the parks, laid pavements, constructed hundreds of bridges, inaugurated mail services to Mendoza and San Luís, public baths, a 'house of correction' for women, and so on.[26] It soon became evident that the poverty-stricken province would not be able to provide financially for all these undertakings, and by 1863 the landowners were complaining of the burden that the reforms placed upon them. For his biggest school, Sarmiento had chosen to renovate and convert a former convent, and this choice enabled his political opponents and the clergy to claim that he was an atheistic liberal. Simultaneously, the caudillo El Chacho was sending gaucho guerrillas from La Rioja to raid the territory of San Juan. In the eyes of Sarmiento, El Chacho was the embodiment of barbarism: he could not read or write, signed his name with a mark, wore the *chiripá*, and had brought terror into the province that the Governor was trying, against already formidable odds, to civilize. The Government at Buenos Aires authorized Sarmiento to direct a 'police' campaign to pacify the northern regions of the republic, and late in 1863 the national forces finally cornered El Chacho while he was imbibing *yerba maté* in a remote village, where they captured and subsequently executed him. Sarmiento was not personally responsible for this assassination, which horrified the nation; but to his other troubles was now added the accusation that the severe measures that

[26] Bunkley, pp. 398–9.

he had introduced during the emergency—such as the declaration of a 'state of siege', which was perhaps an abuse of his constitutional powers—had led to the outrage. In December 1863 President Mitre, conscious of the difficult position of the Governor—their friendship dated from the years of exile under Rosas—named him Argentine Minister to the United States, where Sarmiento eagerly resumed his study of North American culture, educational methods, social organization, and economy.

An international war now overshadowed the danger of rebellion by provincial caudillos. Shortly after Sarmiento's departure for his new post, Brazilian forces invaded Uruguay—a buffer state on the estuary of the Río de la Plata. This action provoked the Paraguayan dictator Francisco Solano López to ask President Mitre for permission to send troops across the province of Corrientes to attack Brazil in the south, with the purpose of compelling the Brazilians to withdraw from Uruguayan territory. Mitre in February 1865 refused to authorize this passage across Argentine soil. López nevertheless landed an expeditionary force in Corrientes, thereby bringing into existence an anti-Paraguayan triple alliance of Brazil, Argentina, and Brazil's 'satellite' Uruguay. The war declared by these three nations against Paraguay became a nightmare for all concerned. Hostilities continued year after year until at last in 1870 López was hunted down and killed in a distant valley in his own country.[27] Meanwhile, in 1868, Sarmiento was chosen as the next President of Argentina. Mitre had been almost constantly in the field commanding the allied armies; but in spite of the war, economic progress had continued, and a period of prodigious economic development was about to begin.

Sarmiento, returning from his diplomatic post in the United States, had embarked for Buenos Aires without having heard the outcome of the presidential elections. One

[27] For a brief account of the Paraguayan war see Pendle, *Paraguay*, pp. 22–24.

day on the long southward voyage his ship entered the harbour of Bahia, Brazil, where it was greeted by a United States frigate with a salute of twenty-one guns, and Sarmiento then knew that he was to be Mitre's successor. He had taken no part in the campaign and his candidacy had received the support neither of the Government nor of any political party. He had issued no programme—when asked to do so in New York he had simply replied: 'My programme is in the atmosphere, in twenty years of life, actions and writings.'[28] He was chosen because it was in the interests of the growing bourgeoisie of Buenos Aires and the powerful landowners who in recent years had taken charge of much of the pampa that there should be an end of factional strife, so that they might develop their businesses and their *estancias* in peace. Sarmiento's career had proved him to be opposed both to the narrow provincialism of the *Federales* and to the narrow 'unitarianism' of the *porteños*. He represented the nineteenth-century bourgeois desire for orderly and efficient government and material progress.[29]

Of course Sarmiento had many enemies, and when he came to power caudillos in the provinces were still ready to take up arms in defiance of the central authority. When Urquiza of Entre Rios magnanimously offered to co-operate with the President for the sake of national unity, this seemed to many local *Federales* to be a betrayal, with the result that Urquiza was assassinated (1870), and rebellion spread. Time after time Sarmiento was obliged to send troops into the interior to restore order. Gradually the caudillos were suppressed, and at the end of Sarmiento's term of office they had little desire left to fight the national Government. Nor had Sarmiento any sympathy for the Indians of Patagonia, who were constantly pressing northwards against Argentina's southern internal 'frontier'. He launched a campaign against them also. The cost of this civil warfare, combined with that of the Paraguayan war and the expense incurred as the result of a disastrous

[28] Bunkley, p. 446.   [29] Ibid. p. 439.

epidemic of yellow fever in 1871, gravely weakened the country's finances, thereby hampering Sarmiento in the carrying out of his cherished programmes. Nevertheless, he went ahead with many of his plans. He began by ordering the first census ever to be taken in Argentina. This census of 1869 revealed that there were 1,800,000 inhabitants, of whom one-tenth lived in the city of Buenos Aires and one-third in the city and province of Buenos Aires. Four-fifths of the people lived in huts of twigs, cane or straw, with earth floors; and at least 78 per cent were illiterate.[30] During his presidency, as he had dreamed to do, Sarmiento created Argentina's primary educational system, doubling the number of schools during his six years in office. He founded free libraries all over the country and brought North American teachers to organize normal schools. He opened the Naval Academy, the Military Academy, the Academy of Exact Sciences, and the Schools of Mining and Agronomy. He began the system of school inspection, night schools, the teaching of civics, physics, and physical education. He built the first observatory.[31] Sarmiento believed that one way to overcome the gaucho mentality was to introduce more European blood into the race, and during his term of office immigration increased: when he became President in 1868 about 26,000 immigrants were entering Argentina annually: by 1874 the number had risen to 40,000.[32] Great progress was made in the construction of railways and the spreading of telegraph lines.

Sarmiento's innovations were not uniformly successful. He lacked organizing ability and efficient collaborators.[33] His influence on the evolution of Argentina was profound and far-reaching, but although his troops and police—assisted by the advance across the pampa of land ownership, railways, and immigrants—were able to complete the

[30] Rennie, p. 115.   [31] Ibid. p. 116.
[32] Mark Jefferson, *Peopling the Argentina Pampa* (1930), p. 197.
[33] Extract from Leopoldo Lugones, *Historia de Sarmiento*, in Germán Arciniegas, ed., *The Green Continent*, trs. by H. de Onís and others (1947), p. 327.

subjugation of the 'camp', yet Sarmiento was mistaken in his belief that he could change the character of the Argentine people. In his own *Facundo* he had acknowledged—and with evident approval—that the national character was already distinctive and pronounced and that it had acquired its special quality from the gauchos themselves:

The habit of triumphing over resistance, of constantly showing a superiority to Nature, of defying and subduing her, prodigiously develops the consciousness of individual consequence and superior prowess. The Argentine people of every class, civilized and ignorant alike, have a high opinion of their national importance. All the other people of South America throw this vanity of theirs in their teeth and take offense at their presumption and arrogance. I believe the charge not to be wholly unfounded, but I do not object to the trait. Alas for the nation without faith in itself! Great things were not made for such a people! To what extent may not the independence of that part of America be attributed to the arrogance of these Argentine gauchos, who have never seen anything beneath the sun superior to themselves in wisdom or in power? The European is in their eyes the most contemptible of all men, for a horse gets the better of him in a couple of plunges. . . . During the French blockade [i.e. in the time of Rosas] General Mansilla exclaimed: 'What have we to apprehend from those Europeans, who are not equal to one night's gallop?' and the vast plebeian audience drowned the speaker's voice with thunders of applause.[34]

The Argentines might be taught to read and write and to wear trousers, but they retained the traditional preference of the gaucho (to whose make-up the Spanish *hidalgo*, as well as the life of the pampa, had made a vital contribution) for personal independence and personal rule. They continued to be more ready to follow a leader than to give their allegiance to a political programme. The Argentine caudillo henceforth was dressed in a frock-coat—or in the uniform of an officer of the national army—but he remained a

[34] Mrs Horace Mann, *Life in the Argentine Republic in the Days of the Tyrants*, from the Spanish of Domingo F. Sarmiento (New York, Hurd & Houghton, 1868).

caudillo at heart. Indeed, Sarmiento never recognized the degree in which he himself was one of those 'personalist' rulers against whom for so many years he had so tirelessly and so fiercely campaigned. In his knowledge that his cause was right and that it must ultimately triumph, it seemed to him again and again that he was justified in resorting to the methods which, when they were practised by other men, never failed to shock and infuriate him. Though his aim was to introduce government by law, he frequently governed by decree, so as to by-pass parliamentary opposition. In a similar manner, 'Sarmiento thought nothing of using his powers of intervention to overcome opposition to his Government and his programme in the provinces.'[35] In 1869, to prevent disorder, he declared martial law in San Juan—a step which the former President Bartolomé Mitre denounced as unconstitutional. In fact Sarmiento, in spite of his democratic intentions, belonged, like Juan Manuel de Rosas and Juan D. Perón, to the true line of Argentina's 'personalist' presidents.

Caudillismo—caudillismo in trousers—now entered Argentine politics with a vengeance. The elections of 1874 were violent and fraudulent. Sarmiento supported as the official candidate for the presidency Nicolás Avellaneda, who had been his Minister of Justice and Public Instruction and was his most enthusiastic disciple in educational matters. After the voting, it was announced that Avellaneda had secured a substantial majority, whereupon Mitre—who had been a rival candidate—placed himself at the head of a revolution. Sarmiento acted with his customary vigour, but the uprising had not yet been suppressed when he handed over the office of President to Avellaneda.[36]

President Avellaneda's forces soon defeated Mitre, who was still a popular figure among the *porteños* and was pardoned by the new Government. The next problem was

[35] Bunkley, p. 473.
[36] Sarmiento's later life was active, but an anti-climax. In 1887, for the sake of his health, he went to settle in Paraguay, where he died in the following year at the age of seventy-seven.

presented by the Indians of Patagonia who now were again advancing northwards, overrunning one *estancia* after another. An efficient plan for combating the Indians—who, in the event, were found to be surprisingly few—was drawn up by Avellaneda's Minister of War, General Julio A. Roca, and the latter himself directed the campaign. In this so-called 'War of the Desert' (1879–83) the Indians were ruthlessly exterminated 'and consequently', as one Argentine historian light-heartedly explains, 'that factor was eliminated from the miscegenation of races which is taking place in our country'.[37] However, President Avellaneda also continued the constructive work begun by Mitre and Sarmiento, and during his term of office large numbers of immigrants—mainly Italians and Spaniards—entered the country.

In the presidential elections of 1880 the old rivalry between the national Government and the Government of the province of Buenos Aires reached its climax. The two principal candidates were General Roca ('The Hero of the Desert') and the Governor of Buenos Aires, Carlos Tejedor. The latter's supporters threatened violence, and President Avellaneda was compelled to remove his Government and the national Congress (who had been the 'guests' of the city since the beginning of Mitre's presidency) to the suburb of Belgrano. The national army, after some fighting on the outskirts, defeated the provincial forces and captured the city. A new Congress then voted a law separating the municipality of Buenos Aires from the province. The city thus became the capital of the nation, and the province of Buenos Aires founded its own provincial capital of La Plata[38] thirty-five miles down-stream on the Plata estuary. General Roca was sworn in as President of the Republic, which he ruled with a soldier's firm hand.

The *Unitarios* had won the contest: the provinces were

[37] Levene, p. 483.
[38] After the death of the wife of President Perón in 1952, La Plata was renamed 'Eva Perón'; its former name was restored in September 1955.

doomed henceforth to be the satellites of the *porteño* metropolis. Provincial governors who carried out the President's wishes received financial assistance from the State; those who did not were removed from office. Indeed, an era had begun in which Argentina's presidents habitually respected only such parts of the constitution as they found to be convenient. In the words of Ricardo Levene: 'The presidency absorbed and centralized all the power of the democracy, in such a manner that the fortunes of the candidates did not depend upon the electoral struggle of political parties but upon the wish of the president'.

THE TRANSFORMATION OF THE PAMPA

A tale of the Pampa tells how a River Plate farmer of bygone days, seeing his wife and child dead of pestilence and his pastures blackened by fire, fell into a magic slumber born of the lethargy of despair. He was awakened, many years afterwards, by the scream of a railway engine at his boundary; to find his land fenced in, his flocks and herds improved beyond recognition, and maize and wheat waving where only coarse grass had been before.[39]

In the five decades that followed the fall of Rosas (1852) the pampa was transformed. It remained, of course, a vast, stoneless plain whose grasses bent before the constant breeze; as before, cattle and sheep grazed upon it; the distant, flat horizon still shimmered—uncertain, but ever promising—in the southern sunlight; the habitations of men were still few and squalid. But, by the end of the century, although so much appeared to be unchanged, the pampa in fact had been tamed, organized, and virtually harnessed to the economy of far-away Great Britain. The grass was no longer the wild, tough prairie grass of Rosas's day: landowners had sown more tender varieties and were now cultivating *alfalfa* for the fattening of their cattle.[40] French inventors had proved, by the experimental voyages

---

[39] Godofredo Daireaux, quoted in Ross, p. 1.   [40] Rennie, p. 147.

55

of a small refrigerator ship—*Le Frigorifique*—in 1876-7, that it was possible to transport South American meat across the tropics and to deliver it in edible condition to the industrial populations of the Old World;[41] and as the refrigerator traffic increased, Argentina's cattle-raisers and sheep-breeders had become convinced that greater benefit was to be derived from the meat of shorthorns and Lincolns than from the hides, tallow and wool of lean *criollo* animals. In the last decades of the nineteenth century, therefore, land-owners imported from Great Britain pedigree stock which provided the type of meat preferred by British consumers. Further, so that breeding and feeding might be controlled, the *estancieros* went to the expense of erecting barbed wire fencing (likewise purchased in Britain) to divide their wide territories into manageable segments.[42] The cattlemen, though they still lived on horseback, were no longer no-madic gauchos: they were employees, *peones*, their activities restricted by wire fences and the law.[43] Land, which form-erly had been almost worthless, was increasingly valuable.

By 1887, fifty-seven refrigerator ships were in regular ser-vice between Buenos Aires and British ports, and by the end of the century the number had risen to 278.[44] But the spec-

[41] The pioneering voyage was made in the opposite direction: *Le Frigori-fique* carried a load of meat from Rouen to Buenos Aires. The Argentine word *frigorífico*, meaning a packing-plant for meat, comes from the name of this ship.

[42] For the importance of fencing, and a detailed account of the develop-ment of the meat trade, see Simon G. Hanson, *Argentine Meat and the British Market* (1938). See also Herbert Gibson, *The History and Present State of the Sheep-breeding Industry in the Argentine Republic* (1893). An Englishman, Richard Newton, in 1844 put up the first wire fence in Argentina, enclosing the cultivated areas of his estate. It was another Englishman, William White, who imported, in 1848, the first shorthorn bull.

[43] The sons of the gaucho were not always willing to live the life of fenced-in farm-hands: 'Now his sons are mostly to be found in the army, the police, or that very useful body of firemen and soldiers too, the corps of "Bomberos", men who can be relied on at any moment to quell a fire or a riot in their own very effective way. They fear neither flames nor turbulent strikers, and are only too ready, in the case of the latter, to shoot first and listen to orders afterwards. Another body of men drawn almost exclusively from gaucho source is the "Squadron of Security"; a mounted corps of steel-cuirassed and helmeted semi-military police, also used to clear the streets of political or other disturbances' (Ross, p. 14).

[44] Rennie, p. 146.

tacular development of the export trade in meat could not have occurred if the only means of internal transport had continued to be the ox-cart and the mule train following deeply-worn tracks in dust or mud (according to the season) across the plain. Alberdi—whose ideas contributed so greatly to the constitution of 1853 and to the policies of Mitre, Sarmiento, and their successors—had stated that the real obstacle to progress was 'not Rosas, but distance', and the expansion of the meat industry was made possible by the fact that for some years before the momentous first voyage of *Le Frigorifique* British engineers and investors—encouraged by the Argentine Government—had been opening up the interior of the republic by the construction of railways, which enabled the national authorities to maintain order in the 'camp' and facilitated the carriage of animals and agricultural produce to the port of Buenos Aires. Roads, in a stoneless country, were difficult and costly to make and to maintain; but the building of railways was simple: on the nearly level surface of the pampa there was no need for cuts, fills, bridges, tunnels, or even curves. In few parts of the world were construction costs lower. Great Britain supplied most of the capital, technicians, and equipment; and the fuel was British coal. The first railroad had started operations in 1857: it ran for merely six miles southwestwards from Buenos Aires and was on a broad gauge. (The legend that the 5 ft 6 in. gauge was adopted to accommodate second-hand British rolling-stock previously used in the Crimean war has been disproved.)[45] Shortly afterwards a line was built along the old, traditional mule route from Rosario to Córdoba and Tucumán; and with extraordinary rapidity a fan of railways spread from Buenos Aires to the limits of the pampa. By 1890 5,848 miles of railways had been built. In 1900 the total mileage was 10,269; in 1912 20,400.[46]

[45] See Michael Robins, 'The Balaklava Railway', *J. of Transport Hist.* (Univ. Coll. of Leicester), May 1953, pp. 41–42.
[46] Frederic M. Halsey, *The Railways of South and Central America* (1914), p. 9.

The opening up of the interior and the development of the high-grade cattle industry increased the need for immigrant labour. It was Alberdi, again, who had said 'to govern is to populate', and from 1853 onwards successive Governments had devised measures for attracting immigrants. Contracts were made for the bringing of families of agricultural workers from Europe; land was granted to these colonists; and many of the colonies—sometimes after years of disappointment and hardship—flourished.[47] One of the most remarkable of these ventures was undertaken from Great Britain when a Welsh nationalist, Michael D. Jones, became convinced that somewhere in the world an isolated place must be found where a Welsh colony could be established with the purpose of preserving, uncontaminated, the national language, customs, and nonconformist religion. Jones, who at that time had not yet visited South America, chose the desolate territory of Patagonia as being sufficiently out of reach of other peoples and cultures; the Argentine Government offered generous terms, promising land, sheep, horses, and grain; and so, in May 1865, 153 Welsh emigrants—men, women, and children—set forth from Liverpool in the bark *Mimosa*, singing hymns as they sailed towards the New World. Although the colonists were destined to settle in an uncultivated land where they would have to grow their own food, only four of the adult males were farm labourers. After two months at sea this courageous but ill-selected company landed on the barren, wind-swept Patagonian coast, where for a while they camped in caves and then planted crops which, because of the lack of rain and their own inexperience, were a calamitous failure. For several years the settlers suffered privation, and they would probably have starved, but for the supplies of food sent to them annually by the Argentine Government or left occasionally by a British warship that had been warned of their plight. It was the local Indians, however, who helped

[47] For a summary of the principal colonies see Rennie, pp. 130–5; also Jefferson, *Peopling the Argentine Pampa*.

them most—teaching them to manage horses, to use the
bolas and lasso, and to hunt wild animals, such as the *guana-co*.[48] Then, at last, they learned to canalize the waters of the
river Chubut for the irrigation of their fields. Slowly the
farms progressed. The colonists acquired a ship and dispatched their agricultural products to the Buenos Aires
market. They imported agricultural machinery, and, having lost their homes in previous floods, they built houses on
ground above the river. As the news of the increasing prosperity reached Wales, additional groups of emigrants set
sail to join the colony, who by the year 1880 numbered 800.
At first the settlers were allowed to govern themselves; but
in 1884 Chubut was declared a Territory of the Argentine
Republic and came under closer supervision from Buenos
Aires. Argentine schools were established by the federal
authorities, and the colonists were required to do military
drill—though, after a personal visit by President Roca in
1899, their protests were heeded and they were excused
from parading on the Sabbath. In 1887 a light railway was
completed, joining Port Madryn with the Chubut Valley.
Then the settlement was extended farther inland, into the
foothills of the Andes; and wool began to compete with agricultural products in importance. Non-Celtic immigrants
were now infiltrating into the colony. Some of the Welsh
intermarried with Spanish-speaking Argentines and Italians; and their children spoke Spanish rather than Welsh.
Many families, however, succeeded in an extraordinary
degree in fulfilling the original aims expressed by Michael
D. Jones, and even until today they have preserved their
language, the customs of their ancestors, and their religion.[49]

[48] During the Conquest of the Desert (see above, p. 54) the colonists
did not take up arms against the Indians. The *guanaco* (like the *vicuña*) is a
small representative of the camel tribe, a graceful, timid animal with long,
fawn-coloured hair above and white hair below. Its meat was eaten
by the Indians and the Welsh, and its droppings were used as fuel by the
Indians.
[49] An interesting investigation into the history of the Welsh colony in
Patagonia is John E. Baur, 'The Welsh in Patagonia: an Example of
Nationalistic Migration', *H.A.H.R.*, Nov. 1954, pp. 468–92. The journal of
one of the original colonists—previously only available in Welsh—was

Meanwhile, as political conditions in the Río de la Plata region became more stable, the tide of immigration into the pampa rose ever more rapidly. The total population of Argentina, which had been 1,200,000 in 1852, was 2½ million in 1880, and of these some 173,000 were people born in Europe.[50] According to the census of 1895 the population in that year numbered 3,954,811, of whom 1,005,427 were foreigners.[51] Immigration reached a peak in 1889, when 218,744 second- and third-class passengers came to Buenos Aires. In that year 40,649 left the country; but, although emigration was always considerable, between 1857 and 1900 the net increase in population by immigration amounted to about 1,200,000.[52] Almost 80 per cent of the newcomers were Italians and Spaniards (the former slightly outnumbering the latter), the other principal nationalities being French, German, Austrian, Russian, British, and Swiss. Together, of course, these settlers radically altered the composition of the Argentine race.

The Spanish immigrants of the second half of the nineteenth century were of a different type from the adventurers from Spain who had sailed to the New World 300 years earlier: the later voyagers were mostly peasants from the province of Galicia, and today Argentines call all Spaniards (a little contemptuously) *Gallegos*. But it was in particular the incoming Italian peasants[53] who—in combination with the refrigerator ships, the wire fencing, and the railways—were responsible for the transformation of the pampa. Some of these Italians were merely temporary

---

published in Spanish in 1954: Rev. A. Matthews, *Crónica de la Colonia Galesa de la Patagonia*, trans. by F. E. Roberts (1954). A simple account of the colony's history (very unfair in regard to the behaviour of the Argentine authorities) is given in Idris Jones, *Modern Welsh History* (1934), Ch. IV. Cf. also (in Welsh) R. Bryn Williams, *Cymry Patagonia* (1945); and a version in novel form (in Spanish): Carlos A. Bertomeu, *El Valle de la Esperanza* (1943).

[50] James, *Latin America*, p. 314.   [51] Levene, p. 518.

[52] James, *Latin America*, pp. 314–15.

[53] North Italians went to the pampa; South Italians (*Napolitanos*) remained in the towns. cf. Walter Larden, *Argentine Plains and Andine Glaciers* (1911).

hands who travelled to Argentina for the southern hemisphere harvest and then returned to Europe in time for the Italian wheat harvest. They were known as *golondrinas*, or swallows, and their seasonal homeward journeys partly explain the extent of emigration referred to above. The majority of Italian immigrants, however, worked as tenant farmers, and they converted vast areas of the pampa to agricultural land. The native Argentines still despised farming. An Englishman who had the opportunity to observe the effects of the new immigration in the 'camp' wrote: 'The estanciero worked the stock with his staff of natives—of the old gaucho class—while the Italians, a race apart, drew their profit out of the soil in maize, wheat, and linseed, paying their rent in kind, and, when they moved on, left the land transformed and fit for sheep or cattle of the best breeds.'[54] The landowners needed in particular agricultural labourers to prepare the land for the planting of *alfalfa* for their high-grade beef animals, and the most effective way to do this was to rent it for a period of four or five years to tenants and to permit them, for a share in the crop, to raise grain. Thereby, in addition to increasing their *alfalfa* acreage, the *estancieros* were provided with a profitable by-product in the form of their share in the crops of wheat, maize, and linseed. The contracts obliged the tenants to plant the land with *alfalfa* and to move away after a specified number of years. The *alfalfa* fields yielded well for five or ten years, after which time new tenants would be secured, and the cycle repeated.[55] It was a hard life. Walter Larden wrote:

The industry of these colonists is wonderful; man, woman, and child, all work; and, though they are obliged to ride and to deal with cattle to some extent, they seem to take to agricultural work as naturally as the Spanish-American did to hunting and stock work. . . . August [when the immigrants take over the land] . . . is in general a month of bad weather, . . . and these colonists, arriving, will find nothing ready for them. There is

---

[54] Ibid. p. 80.   [55] James, *Latin America*, p. 316.

the bare plain of tussocky grass; some kind of a hut has to be built, a well has to be dug, fences to be set up, and the land to be ploughed. . . . It must be a curious life that these men lead. They have no real homes, but merely uncomfortable adobe and mud hovels in which they live for some four years; and they don't know where they are going next. Yet there is plenty of money to be made, there is abundance of food, and they are their own masters (pp. 72–79).

The pampa was not the only part of the country to be transformed during the later decades of the nineteenth century: the building of railways in lines radiating from Buenos Aires brought more and more of the interior within the region where cultivation was economically worth while. The distant north, for instance, could now send its sugar and *caña* (rum) to market by train. The sugar industry of Tucumán had languished because transport by ox-cart to Buenos Aires doubled the cost of the produce. In 1876 the railway arrived. Six years later the sugar fields had doubled in area, iron machinery and generators had been brought in. Thus the development of Tucumán's large modern sugar industry was made possible.[56]

During this period of economic progress successive national and provincial Governments had continued to give away land in large units to political favourites and military heroes. For example, vast tracts in the south were presented to the officers of the Army of the Desert who had cleared that part of the country of Indians. It was hoped that the generous distribution of uninhabited land would hasten its population; instead, however, the recipients of the more remote estates disposed of them for a nominal price to speculators, who amassed *estancias* often measuring many square miles. In this way, and by the auctioning of huge territories in the Chaco and elsewhere, the Governments of the republic perpetuated the system of large-scale private landownership which had been initiated by Rivadavia and Rosas.

[56] cf. Rennie, pp. 142–3.

Nor was speculation confined to rural real estate. In the 1880's Buenos Aires experienced a building fever in the course of which most of the Spanish-colonial architecture in the centre of the city was replaced by imitation Parisian. There were now tramways and parks. The wife of an English railway director who arrived in Buenos Aires in 1890 was amazed. 'We are delighted with everything we see,' she wrote. 'The ladies all look very pretty, and are beautifully dressed in the latest Parisian fashions. I am indeed pleased to find everything much more civilized than I expected.'[57] Rosas's dreary, one-storey town had become almost a modern city,[58] and from its new railway stations luxury trains set out across the plain. The English visitor who travelled on the Western Railway in 1890 noted in her diary: 'Before starting we inspect the different carriages, which are very comfortable, consisting of sleeper, and dining car, with a pretty kitchen, looked after by the *chef*, who is very smart, with his pretty white cap and apron.'[59] It was a time of the utmost optimism and extravagance, in which the Government shared. President Miguel Juárez Celman proudly told Congress in 1889: 'Everything goes up: the value of land, of livestock, of agriculture, of industry, commerce, credit, the accumulation of capital, public and private incomes. . . . For this I congratulate the country and I congratulate you, *señores diputados y senadores*.'[60] The President never dreamt that the bubble was about to burst. But there were in fact abundant signs of impending financial disaster. Banks and companies had been organized without capital, speculators being confident that future profits would cover their obligations. Credit had been freely granted by the mortgage banks, because everyone believed that the value

[57] [Aline Todd], *Journal of a Tour to and from South America*, [? 1892], pp. 48–49.
[58] The population of Buenos Aires increased as follows:

1855	90,000
1870	270,000
1890	668,000

(James, *Latin America*, p. 331.)
[59] Todd, p. 80.   [60] Quoted in Rennie, p. 174.

of all property would continue to rise at the same speed indefinitely. Favouritism and corruption were rife. To finance its own lavish undertakings—such as the construction of dams, bridges, ports, and public buildings—the Government had long been borrowing excessively from abroad and had printed paper money quite recklessly. Inflation had developed fast, with a continuous fall in the value of the paper peso. In this situation the traditional conflict between the interests of town and 'camp' was again very apparent. With the transformation of the pampa, the *estancieros*—a class to which President Juárez Celman himself belonged—had become the most powerful section of the community. As they sold their meat and grain for British sterling and French francs, they now welcomed the depreciation of the Argentine currency, which meant that they received a higher peso income for their exports. On the other hand, the inflation was ruining the Buenos Aires merchants, who had to pay at soaring peso rates for the manufactured goods, the French wines, and the olive oil which they imported from the British Isles and Europe. The crash occurred in 1890–1. Business firms suspended payment. Banks closed.[61] Export earnings of foreign exchange were insufficient to finance the nation's debt-service charges. The London house of Baring, which had lent millions to Argentina, collapsed.[62] It was inevitable that the economic crisis should have political repercussions.

[61] Of the major banking institutions, only the London & River Plate Bank remained open. This bank—which had been founded, as the London, Buenos Ayres & River Plate Bank, in 1862—subsequently became the Bank of London & South America. cf. Bank of London & South America Ltd, *A Short Account of the Bank's Growth and Formation* (London, 1954).

[62] See A. G. Ford, 'Argentina and the Baring Crisis of 1890' in *Oxford Economic Papers*, June 1956, pp. 127–50.

Chapter IV

CONSERVATIVES AND RADICALS

WITH the rising prosperity, Argentina's urban middle class had become, of course, increasingly numerous and substantial. A high proportion of the merchants and shopkeepers were of European birth, or were the sons of immigrant parents, and their outlook differed fundamentally from that of the old landowning families who were in permanent control of the Government. When, in the growing financial disorder of 1889, a group of young men (mostly university graduates) met together to form an anti-Government 'Unión Cívica de la Juventud', the business men of Buenos Aires and the small tenant farmers and shopkeepers of the interior gave to them their enthusiastic support. Meetings were held; an experienced and idealistic politician, Leandro N. Além, was elected head of the party's executive council; and in 1890 the aged Bartolomé Mitre emerged from his retirement to join the movement to overthrow President Juárez Celman. The main item in the new party's policy was a demand for free suffrage and honest elections—in other words, that the middle class should be given an opportunity to share in the government of the country. Hitherto, opponents of the long line of conservative Governments had taken little part in elections, because the army or police prevented them from going to the polls. If they were allowed to vote, fraud in any case would ensure a result favourable to the established régime. In the provinces the use of the presidential powers of intervention served the same purpose. In these conditions, despairing of attaining their democratic ends by democratic methods, the Unión Cívica in July 1890 attempted to depose President Juárez Celman by force. The revolution was mismanaged and was quickly suppressed, amnesty being granted to the rebels. By now, however, the economic crisis referred to in the previous chapter was at its height, and the President of the republic had been so discredited that he resigned; but power remained in the hands of the landowners.[1]

Although the revolution had failed, the section of the community which had backed it continued to develop in size and self-assurance; and the causes of discontent remained. Silently, shrewdly, and relentlessly, Além's nephew Hipólito Irigoyen built up an efficient party machine for the Unión Cívica in the all-important province of Buenos Aires. Irigoyen, a former *comisario* of police, while he professed devotion to democratic principles became in fact the political caudillo of the province. In 1891 he was among the outstanding younger men who, the aged Mitre having betrayed the Unión Cívica by negotiating a personal agreement with the conservative General Roca, broke away to found the Radical Party, which—under the title Unión Cívica Radical—was to become Argentina's biggest political movement. Another revolutionary attempt was made in 1893. This also failed. Além lost heart, and later committed suicide. Thereafter, Irigoyen was the acknowledged leader of the Radicals. Solemn, enigmatic, autocratic, biding his time, he earned the fanatical loyalty of large numbers of the middle and poorer classes, but not even his close associates knew what really was in his mind: he seems not to have been a man of great intelligence, but he possessed the flair of the old Argentine caudillos for personal leadership, though he wore a townsman's sombre clothes. Always convinced that he and his party could not defeat the landowning oligarchy at the polls, Irigoyen re-

[1] Juárez Celman was succeeded by his Vice-President, Carlos Pellegrini, son of the French engineer who built the extravagant Colón Theatre at Buenos Aires in imitation of the Paris Opéra. Pellegrini was an able statesman, and during his brief term of office he devoted special attention to much-needed financial reforms (he was responsible for the creation of the national Bank, the Banco de la Nación); but he was a confirmed conservative who did not believe in popular suffrage.

peatedly refused to allow the Radicals to take part in the elections. He thereby emphasized his contention that 'minority' elections (i.e. elections controlled by the land-owning class) were improper. Several prominent members of the Radical Party, disapproving of the leader's dictatorial methods, left it. In 1894 Juan B. Justo, considering the Radical policy to be too moderate, broke away and founded Argentina's Socialist Party. Nevertheless, Irigoyen retained his reputation as a power behind the scenes.

The mid-1890's were years of political uncertainty but also of steady economic recovery. The *estancieros* as a class had welcomed the inflation during the presidency of Juárez Celman, but thereafter more enlightened conservative statesmen, recognizing that this trend would eventually bring disaster to the landowners as well as to the merchants, introduced measures to stabilize the currency. By the end of the century Argentina was able to resume payments on the foreign debt, which had been in suspense. Immigration, which in the depression of 1891 had been exceeded by emigration, soon revived.[2] By 1895 the population had risen to nearly 4 million.[3] The rebuilding of Buenos Aires, the expansion of the railways, and the general economic development continued. More and more land was brought under cultivation, the pedigree livestock multiplied; the economic setback of 1889–91 was forgotten, and this fabulously fertile country—which the Spanish *conquistadores* had rejected as a wilderness—was indeed fulfilling the prophecies of the

[2] cf. Jefferson, p. 197:

Year	Immigrants	Emigrants
1891	28,266	72,380
1892	39,973	29,893
1893	52,067	26,055
1894	54,720	20,586
1895	61,226	20,390
1896	102,673	20,415

Argentine immigration and emigration statistics are notoriously unreliable. The foregoing figures represent the number of second- and third-class passengers arriving at Buenos Aires from Europe and leaving Buenos Aires for Europe, such being the official method of calculation. There is no record of the numbers coming and going by the land frontiers.

[3] Levene, p. 518.

much-abused Sir Home Popham, who at the beginning of the nineteenth century had assured H.M. Government and the City of London that the Río de la Plata was potentially a commercial El Dorado. That such rapid economic progress should have been achieved under a political system that was oligarchical and corrupt indicates that the system was not so unsuited to the national needs as its critics maintained. Faced with a never-ending swarm of immigrants of many diverse nationalities and a locally-born population which for the most part was illiterate and quite inexperienced in public affairs, the ruling class perhaps acted wisely in retaining power in their own hands; and their rule, though selfish, was benign. Immigrants enjoyed personal liberty to come and go, to do and think as they pleased, and they were completely free from political or racial persecution. At the turn of the century, however, it was evident that the urban middle class, at least, could not permanently be denied participation in the management of the republic.

In 1910 Roque Sáenz Peña—a man with an honourable record of public service—was inaugurated as President. He was, of course, the outgoing President's nominee and a member of the conservative minority; yet he had been genuinely troubled to observe that year after year such a large and important section of the population abstained from the elections in protest against the use of force and fraud at the polls. In his campaign speeches he referred to the need for clean politics, and he promised honest elections. Others had often spoken after that fashion without feeling under any obligation to fulfil their promises, and the supporters of Sáenz Peña cannot have imagined that he was more in earnest than his predecessors. The Radicals, certainly, had no faith in his assurances. Nevertheless, no sooner had he assumed office than the new President began to draw up a plan for electoral reform. His law—known as the Sáenz Peña Law—provided for universal and compulsory male suffrage, the secret ballot, and a strict system for the registration of voters. All men were to be required to register for one year's military service on reaching the age of eighteen, when an enrolment book was to be issued to them. This *libreta de enrolamiento* would then serve as proof of identity at the polls, where it would be marked to indicate that the holder had duly cast his vote.[4] In spite of strong opposition from those who maintained that the Argentine masses were unfit to partake in the responsibility of selecting their own rulers, the Sáenz Peña Law was passed in 1912.

The passing of this law was one of the crucial events in the evolution of Argentina, leading to yet another adjustment in the social equilibrium. Soon the landowning aristocracy would not have a monopoly of political power: they would be obliged to share it with the sons of merchants and shop-keepers. In 1916, for the first time in their history, the Argentine people freely elected a President. Their choice was Hipólito Irigoyen. On the day of his inauguration, disapproving of the popular jubilation, Irigoyen—who was a tall, heavily-built man with a stern countenance—tried to quieten the crowds; but they unhitched the horses from his carriage and dragged it and the protesting passenger through the streets with their own hands.

Irigoyen began his term of office with no clear policy: indeed, he was incapable of clear thinking, and his public and private utterances were often so confused as to be unintelligible. He had received the votes of the middle class, for reasons mentioned above; and, although the Socialist Party were strong in Buenos Aires, he had the backing of the majority of the poorer classes, for whom he was a saintly figure, shrouded in mystery, with a reputation for simplicity and generosity (he always remained a poor man); but he had no programme for converting into practical measures the general feeling of liberalism with which he and his colleagues entered upon their duties. There was one subject, however, on which his mind was firmly made up: he was

[4] In practice, although voting became obligatory, many did not vote, the system of punishing non-voters being too complicated for easy application to large numbers of persons.

determined to continue the previous Government's policy of neutrality in the world war, which had been in progress for two years at the time of his election. In spite of pressure at home and from abroad, he never wavered on this issue; and so Argentina peacefully prospered. The war did cause serious inconvenience by depriving the people of a wide range of manufactured goods which normally they imported from Great Britain and continental Europe, and there was an alarming rise in the cost of living; but the value of exports of meat and hides to Great Britain and France rose spectacularly, and from 1916 to 1919 the Argentine peso was quoted above every other major currency in the world. The lack of imported manufactures also stimulated the growth of local light industries, which had been few and very small, with the result that when later emergencies occurred Argentina was no longer completely dependent on overseas suppliers. After the end of the war even Irigoyen's bitterest critics admitted that neutrality had been economically beneficial; and his policy was quoted as a precedent during the second world war.

Irigoyen's attempts at social reform were timid, but projects for arbitration in labour disputes, minimum wages, maximum working hours, and so on, were sent to Congress and they did represent a new departure in a country whose previous rulers had given no thought to such matters. The workers, aware that they had the President's sympathy, sought to hasten the course of events by means of strikes. In January 1919 the strikes in Buenos Aires became so numerous and so violent that, during a so-called *Semana Trágica* (the Tragic Week), the police were instructed to use their firearms. They caused many deaths, and the mobs in the streets killed many more. When the week was over, there was general agreement that the Government had acted incompetently.

Nor was Irigoyen's treatment of the strikes the only, or even the principal, cause for complaint during his presidency. Although he had so constantly denounced the high-handed methods of the conservatives, he proceeded to rule his 8 million compatriots[5] as autocratically as he had run the Radical Party during its years in the wilderness. He outdid all his predecessors but one in the use—or abuse—of his constitutional powers of intervention in the provinces; he had no respect for the democratic rights of Congress; and the horde of hangers-on whom he appointed to ministerial and lesser posts were allowed to engage in an orgy of corruption and favouritism which disgusted not only his opponents, but also the best elements in the Radical Party itself. Yet there was never any suggestion that Irigoyen derived any personal benefit, and the masses who had acclaimed him at the time of his election still looked upon him as the champion of the unprivileged.

In 1922 Irigoyen nominated as his successor a wealthy and elegant *porteño*, Marcelo T. de Alvear, who had been one of the original members of the Unión Cívica but had since lived for many years in Paris. It was a time of post-war prosperity: business was booming in Buenos Aires: *estancieros* were spending fortunes at home and abroad. Irigoyen, now an old man, had intended that his nominee should be a mere puppet and that he himself should continue to direct the Government from behind the scenes; but Alvear refused to submit to this dictatorial management, recognized the rights of Congress, and in 1924 separated from the Unión Cívica Radical to organize a Radical 'anti-personalist' party of his own: the U.C.R. Anti-Personalista. At the end of Alvear's term in 1928, however, the combined forces of the Anti-Personalista and Conservative Parties could not prevent the re-election of Irigoyen. This second term brought to a close the brief period of Radical rule and demonstrated that Argentina was not prepared for democratic government of the British or North American kind. The President, who had never been clear-headed, was now senile; his rapacious subordinates, without his knowledge, robbed every department of the administration; and he

[5] In 1914 the population was 7,905,502. cf. Levene, p. 518.

himself was incapable of fulfilling the ordinary routine of his office—papers remained unsigned, salaries unpaid, and appointments with his ministers ignored. 'In the Aduana [Customs] there were 3,500 employees unauthorized by law. In one office of the State Railways there were 300 employees where the budget authorized six.'[6] The President of the republic had become a recluse—and at a time when, once again, Argentina was suffering from the effects of being too dependent on the countries to which she sold her primary products. The world depression of 1930 caused a steep decline in exports and in the value of the peso. Now, at last, the workers were disillusioned, blaming Irigoyen for the rise in the cost of living and in unemployment. Business men complained of the higher costs resulting from the President's occasional attempts to help the workers. Some of the criticism was unjust, for the chief cause of the crisis was the world-wide economic slump; but it certainly was true that the Radicals had wasted their opportunity in office. Probably they failed mainly through lack of experience. Corruption itself was not fatal—the habit had always prevailed since colonial days, when *criollos* resorted to illicit trade to circumvent the restrictions imposed by Spain; and bribery and favouritism had always been used as a means of 'humanizing' the law. A country with such vast natural wealth could afford the luxury of corruption in government circles, but not gross and prolonged incompetence. So, yet again, revolution was in the air. Another new phase was about to begin in Argentina's struggle to reconcile her tradition of caudillismo with her growing desire for a governmental system that would satisfy the requirements of the population as a whole. The immediate development, however, was to be a conservative reaction.

[6] Rennie, p. 222.

Chapter V

ARMY AND WORKERS

THE REVOLUTION OF 1930

THE revolution which overthrew Hipólito Irigoyen in September 1930 was supported not only by the conservative families but by the leaders of other opposition parties, students, and the discontented masses. Although it was therefore a popular uprising, its real organizers were a small group of military officers (among whom was a Captain Juan D. Perón), and the leading figure was General José F. Uriburu, an extreme conservative closely associated with the Catholic hierarchy. Uriburu at once took over the Government, declared a state of siege,[1] and made a number of arrests. He had proposed to abolish universal suffrage and the secret ballot (i.e. the Sáenz Peña Law), but during his brief period as *de facto* President he found that he could attain the same ends by the old practices of intervention, the control of the lists of electoral candidates, and the annulment of any provincial elections that did not result in his favour. Under the pressure of public opinion he was reluctantly compelled to call presidential elections for November 1931; but he announced that the Radical candidates were ineligible, so the contest was between General Agustín P. Justo (an Anti-Personalista who had the backing of the conservatives) and a coalition led by Lisandro de la Torre (a former member of the Unión Cívica who had created his own Partido Demócrata Progresista) and Dr Nicolás Repetto (then at the head of the Socialist Party).[2]

[1] The state of siege is a modified form of martial law. It suspends all constitutional guarantees, but differs from martial law in that the civil courts continue to operate.

[2] For a journalistic impression of the electoral campaign of 1931 see Pendle, *Much Sky* (London, Blue Moon Press, 1932), pp. 19–23.

73

The Radicals abstained; the conservatives, aided by the police (who confiscated the enrolment books of undesirable voters), resorted to various forms of fraud; and Justo won.

Wishing to give a correctly constitutional appearance to his régime, General Justo—a genial man—cancelled the state of siege and released Uriburu's political prisoners; but his rule none the less was that of a dictator. The new President had the co-operation of the landowners, who were determined to prevent the Radicals from ever again attaining power. These *estancieros* were of a different calibre from their ancestors—from the conservative class that had produced statesmen of dignity and intelligence such as Pellegrini[3] and Sáenz Peña. As a class, they had been spoiled by decades of easy prosperity, and their sons were apt to be *niños bien*, young men-about-town. In the eyes of the *niño bien*, every worker was a Bolshevik—or, at least, every urban worker, for the *peones* in the 'camp' were still ignorant of trade unionism and lived far away from the centres of contamination. Even before the fraudulent 'election' of General Justo, the mass of the population—who remembered enjoying a taste of democracy, however slight, between 1916 and 1930 —recognized that whatever progress had been made towards social reform since the founding of Unión Cívica had already been undone. The conservatives—who now gave their political organization the inappropriate name of 'National Democrat Party'—had come back, and the days of Irigoyen, with all their disappointments, were seen to have been infinitely preferable to the new state of affairs. When Irigoyen died in 1933 at the age of eighty-one, the demonstration of popular grief was as great as that of jubilation which had attended his first election to the presidency in 1916. The Justo Government refused to allow the body of the ex-President to lie in state in the cathedral at Buenos Aires; but thousands of mourners climbed the narrow stairs to his modest apartment to file past the coffin. A quarter of

[3] See above, p. 66 n.

a million people formed the funeral procession, while an equal number crowded the balconies, windows, roofs, and trees along the route.[4]

In spite of the popular devotion to the memory of the great Radical caudillo and the widespread desire for social reform, the condition of the Radicals—like that of the conservatives—had deteriorated. The leaders of the party were no longer of the same quality as the idealist Além, and the U.C.R. was split into factions. The leadership lacked vigour, youthful talent, and the faculty for adapting itself to changed circumstances. Moreover, basically the interests of the commercial class who formed the backbone of the party were not so different from those of their conservative opponents as was imagined: the *estancieros'* pastoral and agricultural exports provided the means whereby the merchants were enabled to import the goods from which they derived their own livelihood. For this reason the members of the U.C.R. did not really desire any radical alteration in the economic system—indeed, the title 'Radical' was a misnomer—and so lacking were they now in progressive ideas that they failed to attract to their party not only the workers but also the rising class of industrialists who, as a result of the reduction of imports of manufactured articles during the first world war and the depression of the early 1930's, played an increasingly important role in the national economy. In reality, the Radicals were almost as much a part of the old order as the conservatives.

The alliance—under Uriburu and Justo—of the army and the National Democrat Party was a formidable combination. By means of favouritism and intimidation the conservatives were again installed in control of all the departments of Government. Nevertheless, during the 1930's the urban working class was becoming a power which could not indefinitely be denied participation in public affairs; and when in the 1940's Colonel Perón, recognizing the bankruptcy of the conservative and Radical movements,

[4] See John W. White, *Argentina, the Life Story of a Nation* (1942), pp. 149–50.

75

sought the support of the *descamisados* (workers), this was the logical consequence of the negative character of the revolution of 1930—and also of developments in the composition and outlook of Argentina's proletariat. The economic depression of 1930, together with drastic restrictions which were then imposed, brought immigration almost to a standstill.[5] This interruption in the influx of foreign peasants and labourers was welcomed by the landowners who—no longer short of hands to plant and harvest their crops— knew that incoming European workers would bring with them revolutionary ideas of which the nineteenth-century advocates of immigration had never dreamed. It was certainly true that

the Spanish and Italian workers who came to the country before, during, and just after the First World War had in many cases taken part in the trade union and political movements of the Old Countries. They were familiar with the ideas of socialism, syndicalism, anarchism then current in their native countries, and they naturally attempted to transplant those ideas and movements to their new home. Thus to a very large degree the Socialists, anarchists, syndicalists who led the labor movement of Argentina during its formative years were immigrants.[6]

At the first meetings of the Argentine Socialist Party speeches were made in Italian, French, Spanish, and German, and committees were called 'internationals'.[7] With the passage of time—and, particularly, after the imposition of restrictions on immigration in the early 1930's—a change took place in the nature of the working-class movements. As Robert J. Alexander has said:

---

[5] The movement of 2nd and 3rd class maritime passengers during the critical years appears to have been as follows:

Year	Immigrants	Emigrants
1931	63,665	59,706
1932	37,334	48,926
1933	29,903	40,285
1934	33,209	31,730

(SOURCE: R. García-Mata and E. Llorens, *Argentina Económica 1939* (1939), p. 21.)

[6] R. J. Alexander, *The Perón Era* (1952), p. 7.　　　[7] Rennie, p. 199.

More and more of the urban workers were sons of immigrants instead of immigrants themselves. And these second-generation Argentines were above all anxious to prove to themselves, to the rest of the Argentines, and to the world at large that they were 'Argentinos'. In all too many cases they regarded their fathers' allegiance to anarchism, socialism, syndicalism as part and parcel of 'foreignness'. Hence, they tended to discard these 'imported' ideas and became ready material for some native movement of apparent social reform. [Moreover,] since there was no longer any great stream of immigration, new workers to man Argentina's growing industries had to come from the hinterland. . . . These new city dwellers were different from the old. Many more of them were illiterate. All that most of them knew of politics was what they had learned from being marched to the ballot box by their 'patrones' to vote for the local Conservative Party dignitary.[8]

Thus the depression of 1930 and the policy of the conservative Governments which followed it combined to prepare the urban working class for a leader who would appeal to their nationalist sentiments and incite them to treat as their mortal enemies the conservative oligarchy who had neglected their welfare for so long.

A DIRECTED ECONOMY

Another consequence of the depression of 1930 was the introduction of a 'directed economy' to meet the emergency. In Argentina the crisis took the usual form: exports declined catastrophically; the prices of agricultural products fell; farmers were threatened with the foreclosure of their mortgages; unemployment increased; the budget was unbalanced; government revenue shrank; and the peso depreciated. The situation was aggravated by the Ottawa agreements of 1932 whereby the United Kingdom undertook to give preferential treatment to the produce of the British Empire. The Argentine landowners naturally were alarmed by this new policy of imperial preference, which threatened to cause a reduction in Great Britain's demand

[8] Alexander, pp. 7–8.

for their meat. The Vice-President of the republic, Julio A. Roca (son of the 'Conqueror of the Desert') was therefore sent urgently to London to negotiate with the British Government's representative, Walter Runciman, President of the Board of Trade. Runciman's chief argument was that year after year Great Britain had an unfavourable balance of trade with Argentina, and that in future the United Kingdom intended to 'buy from those who buy from us'. As a result of the discussions a trade treaty between the two countries—the so-called Roca–Runciman Treaty[9]—was signed in May 1933. Three years later the treaty was renewed.[10] Its main provisions were as follows. First: the United Kingdom would not reduce its imports of Argentine chilled beef in any quarter below the quantity imported in the corresponding quarter of the year ended 30 June 1932. Second: the sterling earned from Argentine exports to the United Kingdom was to be reserved for remittances to the United Kingdom, with the exception of a limited sum which might be deducted for the servicing of Argentina's public debt to other countries. Third: British funds which were still blocked at the time of the signing of the treaty were to be converted into a 4 per cent sterling loan, repayable in twenty years. Fourth: in a supplementary agreement[11] Argentina undertook to reduce her tariffs on British goods to 1930 levels and to leave coal on the free list, while Great Britain promised not to levy new duties on the principal products imported from Argentina. Finally, to placate British shareholders whose dividends from investments in tramways, railways, and other public utilities in Argentina had sadly dwindled, a protocol was drawn up in the following terms:

The Argentine Government, fully appreciating the benefits rendered by the collaboration of British capital in public

---

[9] Cmd. 4492. The full text of the Roca–Runciman Treaty is also printed in White, pp. 342–5.

[10] Regarding the renewal of the treaty in 1936, see Hanson, *Argentine Meat*, p. 269.

[11] Cmd. 4494.

utility and other undertakings . . . hereby declare their intention to accord to those undertakings . . . such benevolent treatment as may conduce to the further economic development of the country, and to the due and legitimate protection of the interests concerned in their operation.

The Roca–Runciman Treaty was attacked by almost everyone except the Argentine conservatives. The United States denounced it as an act of discrimination against her own trade. To this accusation the Argentine cattle-raisers were able to retort that the United States was guilty of discrimination against Argentina by the refusal (which had long been in force, and continued so) to import Argentine chilled beef, on the pretext that the cattle of the pampa suffered from *aftosa* (foot-and-mouth disease). The Argentines were well aware that the real purpose of this so-called 'sanitary embargo' was to protect the United States cattle industry; and they argued that other measures, such as the Smoot–Hawley Tariff of 1930, were likewise designed primarily to prevent the entry into the United States of competitive farm products from Argentina. Thus the Roca–Runciman Treaty served indirectly to aggravate Argentine resentment against the 'Colossus of the North'. It also caused much bitterness for other reasons. With the growth of nationalism in Argentina, there was dissatisfaction that the nation's economy should be so subservient to that of Great Britain, and it was considered an indignity that Roca should have promised 'benevolent treatment' to the alien capitalists. British complaints that the British-owned tramways, railways, etc., had been victimized (by, for example, excessive taxation and prohibition against charging 'adequate' fares) were countered by accusations that the shareholders and their local representatives had long been guilty of the grossest exploitation; that their tramcars were antiquated and dilapidated (which was true); and that their railways were now quite insufficient for the requirements of the nation's fast-expanding economy (this also was true, but the railways had made the expansion possible in the first instance). In retrospect, present-day Argentine nationalists might look upon the much-criticized Roca–Runciman Treaty as having been doubly beneficial; on the one hand it helped to save the cattle industry and the national balance of trade in a moment of grave crisis; on the other hand it stimulated the popular desire for 'economic independence' and thus facilitated the subsequent rise to power of Juan D. Perón, whose denunciation of the 'British Octopus' at a time when Great Britain was weakened by consequence of the second world war had a particularly wide appeal.

The Roca–Runciman Treaty became the basis of General Justo's plan for national recovery. This recovery plan was comprehensive, and was remarkably successful. In November 1933 the Government depreciated the peso by 20 per cent, fixed minimum prices for grain, and, by assuming control of all operations in foreign exchange, established a system of import licensing. Conversion operations in the foreign and internal debt substantially reduced the sums needed by the State for the payment of interest; foreign owners of blocked funds were persuaded to lend them to the Government, to whom these loans were most useful for the financing of a number of large-scale undertakings, the solution of the unemployment problem being reached by means of an extensive programme of public works. Under President Justo an unprecedented number of roads were built, supplementing—and competing with—the railways; military establishments (including, notably, the officers' quarters at garrisons throughout the country) were modernized; even at the height of the crisis, payments on the foreign debt were maintained; and the financial mechanism of the nation was greatly strengthened by the creation, in 1934, of a Central Bank designed to act as a bank of issue and controller of credit operations (by the discounting of the paper of private banks). The Central Bank performed a highly profitable revaluation of gold reserves. Thus by 1938 the Justo dictatorship—assisted by favourable market conditions overseas—had lifted Argentina to yet another peak of prosperity. The Radicals still were divided and demoralized, and the workers were beyond the pale; intimidation of the press was so persistent that it was a form of censorship;[12] and sympathy with the European ideologies of Fascism and Nazism was spreading among army officers and young conservative nationalists; but, as a nation, Argentina had never been so prosperous as she was in the last year of General Justo's presidency.

THE SECOND WORLD WAR

In 1937 President Justo nominated as his successor Dr Roberto M. Ortiz—a well-to-do lawyer who had acted for British companies and was acceptable to the landowners—and for the vice-presidency he chose Dr Ramón S. Castillo —a conservative of the most reactionary type. Ortiz and Castillo were duly 'elected' and the continuance of the oligarchy's rule seemed assured. But Ortiz soon revealed that —like Sáenz Peña before him—he had unorthodox notions: although he owed his own position in the presidency to fraud, he was convinced that the time had come to restore freedom of suffrage. To the disgust of the conservatives, he instructed the provincial governors that henceforth the secrecy of the ballot must be respected; and when fraudulent elections occurred in the provinces, he did in fact intervene and annul them. Thus Ortiz won the affection of the mass of the population, while the class who had placed him in power did their utmost to obstruct him in the Senate and elsewhere. In 1940, however—to the conservatives' satisfaction—he was compelled by ill health to hand over his office to Castillo,[13] who reverted to the customary undemocratic practices and in December 1941, on the pretext that the entry of the United States into the world war had creat-

[12] At this time many newspapers in Buenos Aires and the provinces refused to be cowed. Some resisted too long. Their fate is recorded below, pp. 114 f.
[13] At first this was only a provisional arrangement. Ortiz did not finally resign the presidency until 1942. He died shortly afterwards.

ed a condition of emergency throughout the hemisphere, declared a state of siege, suspending constitutional guarantees. At the outbreak of war Ortiz—following Irigoyen's precedent—had proclaimed Argentina's neutrality. This was a popular decision, for, although there was widespread sympathy with the Allied cause, the war was remote and Argentines were aware of the prosperity that previously came to them as neutrals. Castillo, who likewise refused to break off relations with the United States' enemies, was also supported by a considerable number who believed in or hoped for an Axis victory.

At this point it will be convenient to examine Argentina's traditional position in international affairs.

Her attitude towards the rest of Latin America is that of a superior Power. Arrogance has already been referred to as an acknowledged national trait. Nevertheless, Argentines take pride in demonstrating that they have not abused their strength, and that they have a long record of non-aggression. They claim (however much the claim may be disputed) that Rosas's campaign against Montevideo was a defensive action, launched to prevent the estuary of the Plata from falling into unfriendly hands. They are able to show that the Paraguayan war was not of Argentina's seeking, and they quote as an example of their magnanimity the words of the Argentine Foreign Minister who, when Paraguay had been vanquished by the Triple Alliance, declared that 'victory does not confer rights'.[14] They point out that in 1902 their most serious frontier dispute—concerning the Patagonian frontier with Chile—was settled not on the battlefield but by arbitration.[15] Finally, in more recent times, they maintained that President Perón's pacts of 'economic union' with his weaker neighbours were designed to be of reciprocal benefit and had no political implications.

[14] Levene, p. 480.
[15] cf. Colonel Sir Thomas Hungerford Holdich, *The Countries of the King's Award* (1904).

The Argentines have no doubt that they are destined to lead the Latin American world, and therefore they are inclined to view with suspicion any international organization wherein the United States may appear to be stealing the limelight. So it is not surprising that by 1943 Argentina had ratified only six out of the ninety conventions concluded since 1890 by the Pan American Union.[16] But although national pride has played an important part in Buenos Aires' relations with foreign Powers, Argentine policy—especially towards countries outside Latin America—has been determined primarily by economic considerations: by the desire to stimulate the flow of exports to Great Britain and continental Europe and (except during a period of extreme nationalism) the influx of capital from abroad. At the end of 1939, British investments in Argentina amounted to about £428,500,000;[17] but by that time the economic ascendancy of the United States in the hemisphere was already assured. The Roca–Runciman Treaty had temporarily reaffirmed Argentina's dependence on the United Kingdom and had served incidentally as a protest against anti-Argentine discrimination by the United States; but when the economic crisis passed it was evident that South America had moved into the orbit of the United States, both economically and strategically. With the years, the rivalry between the Colossus of the North and the prospective Colossus of the South was likely to become more acute.

During the second world war the majority of Argentines were pro-Ally. The conservative families were connected commercially and socially with Great Britain; and Paris had been the Mecca alike of the wealthy and of the artistic. The children of the well-to-do had been brought up by English nannies and governesses;[18] the principal literary

---

[16] Humphreys, *Evolution of Modern Latin America*, p. 156.
[17] J. Fred Rippy, 'British Investments in Latin America: a Decade of Rapid Reduction', *H.A.H.R.*, May 1952, p. 286.
[18] For the influence of an English governess on the development of a well-known daughter of the landowning aristocracy (Victoria Ocampo, owner

influence was from France; and some aristocratic Argentines even preferred to speak and write in French, rather than in Spanish. All the chief newspapers were anti-Nazi and relied on United States news agencies for their information on world affairs. Nevertheless, just as at the end of the eighteenth century the North American and French revolutions put new ideas into *criollo* heads, so did totalitarian ideologies affect the outlook of a large number in the 1930's. The British retreat from Dunkirk in 1940 pleased the nationalists, who had now resurrected the dictator Rosas as a national hero and were denouncing Alberdi, Mitre, and Sarmiento as traitors who 'sold the country to the foreigner'. By others besides extreme nationalists it was felt to be an indignity that the British—who often were inclined to treat Argentina almost as an additional colony—should be in control of so many of the public services and that they should have tied the Argentine economy so tightly to their own. The fall of France seemed to prove conclusively that the Axis would win the war, and there were many who welcomed that prospect. The doctrine of Fascism appealed to some of the young men-about-town, to anti-liberal employers of labour, and to a certain type of intellectual; and although the majority of Argentines of Italian origin deplored Mussolini's régime, to others the Duce appeared to be a glamorous caudillo, a leader whom they themselves would gladly follow. The Argentine army was mainly German-trained; and officers who had visited Germany and Italy (Juan D. Perón served as an attaché in Italy from 1939 to 1941) had complete faith in the military superiority of the Axis. The clergy—who for the most part were of Spanish origin—were pro-Franco and anti-Communist; they abominated the North American way of life as represented —or misrepresented—by Hollywood; and they detested the Protestant missionaries who came from the United States to proselytize in this Catholic land. Even among those who

and editor of the literary magazine *Sur*), see Bea Howe, *A Galaxy of Governesses* (London, 1954), pp. 186–8.

supported the cause of the Allies, there were many who feared 'dollar imperialism' and recalled past instances of United States intervention in the internal affairs of the Central American and island republics and in Colombia. The German Embassy at Buenos Aires, influential German business men residing in Argentina, and the numerous general German-Argentine colony, naturally did their utmost to encourage ill-feeling towards Great Britain and the United States in all these sections of the population.[19]

Castillo has been accused, rightly or wrongly, of having Fascist inclinations: certainly he did not doubt that the Allies would be defeated. In the name of neutrality he allowed the Germans to conduct their propaganda campaign in Argentina unhindered; but in fairness it must be recognized that British residents, Anglo-Argentines, and other friends of the democracies also were permitted to organize their own movements.[20] Although the landowners—who were the mainstay of the Castillo Government—wished for a British victory, there was a great gulf between that wish and any desire to take an active part in a European war; and they had scant respect for the United States. Therefore Castillo met with little disapproval from his supporters when he opposed Washington's suggestion that the whole of Latin America should cease to have political, commercial,

[19] For divergences between British and United States policy towards Argentina during the war, see Sir David Kelly, *The Ruling Few* (1952), Ch. XIV.

[20] 'The British Colony ... was still the largest ... outside the Empire. ... Between three and four thousand English businessmen [in Argentina] had imposed on themselves a voluntary levy, and the English women had organized themselves in 130 working guilds. Before the end of the War ... they had already contributed three million pounds' worth of goods and provisions for the victims of the War and were virtually maintaining twenty thousand prisoners of war by their special levy. Apart from these patriotic activities, the community still maintained its own hospital and charitable institutions, and still had a number of flourishing English schools, clubs and associations ... while the British Chamber of Commerce held every month a public lunch attended by from five hundred to one thousand guests. ... They maintained two daily and one weekly English language papers' (ibid. p. 290). Many volunteers travelled to the United Kingdom to join the British forces; and, among other substantial contributions, Argentine sympathizers subscribed the cost of a whole squadron for the R.A.F. (ibid. p. 299).

G

and financial dealings with Germany, Italy, and Japan. When, in January 1942, representatives of the republics met at Rio de Janeiro to consider the situation created by the entry of the United States into the war, Argentina's Foreign Minister, Dr Enrique Ruiz Guiñazú, refused to sign an undertaking to break off relations with the Axis. To satisfy the United States' desire for a united American front, a compromise formula had to be devised, and this final resolution—which all the Latin American nations, including Argentina, signed—merely 'recommended' a rupture of relations. Castillo's comment on what amounted to a diplomatic defeat for the United States was significant. He said:

The optional rupture approved at Rio ... has given me logical satisfaction. . . . We said clearly at the beginning and maintained at all times that *Argentina would not go to war nor break off relations*, but was disposed to accept, in consequence of its never absent American sentiments, whatever formula for the future reaffirmed continental solidarity and unity and at the same time left each country free, *in the exercise of its sovereignty*, to adopt the special resolutions which the particular situations and circumstances of each country made best in each case.[21]

Meanwhile, the economic effects of the war were disturbing and disappointing. The United Kingdom bought at high prices all the meat that was available, but was unable to supply in exchange the goods that Argentina wished to import, with the result that Argentine credits accumulated in London. Most of the European markets, of course, were inaccessible, and consequently large stocks of unsold grain piled up in the ports. The United States—now Argentina's principal supplier—could not offer adequate quantities of the goods that were needed. In these circumstances there was great scarcity of certain kinds of merchandise in the shops; local industrialists and speculators profited by the shortages; prices rose, and discontent developed among the under-paid urban working class. But

[21] Quoted in Rennie, p. 294.

the workers had no hope of a change by peaceful means: Castillo's friends were in power throughout the country.

THE COMING OF PERÓN

Only once—during the short period of Radical government—had Argentina experienced parliamentary democracy, and that interlude had ended in corruption, ineptitude, disillusionment, and the revolution of 1930. At all other times—except in the two years of Ortiz's active presidency—the country had been ruled by civilian or military caudillos who in varying degrees made a mockery of the Constitution of 1853. Under Castillo, institutional decadence reached new depths. In the Chamber of Deputies Radical and Socialist members—representing a majority of the electorate—fought the régime as best they could; but they were impotent to influence government policy. Thus democracy was further discredited. Political frustration, wartime shortages, the rising cost of living, and the certainty that Dr Castillo would ensure that a representative of the conservative oligarchy should succeed him in the presidency in 1944, prepared the way for yet another revolution. The only uncertainty was, which section of the population would be able to organize a coup d'état. For their part, the *estancieros* had no desire for an upheaval: Castillo, they now knew, had selected as the next President of the republic one of their own number—a wealthy, feudalistic, pro-British owner of sugar plantations, Robustiano Patrón Costas. The Radicals were still demoralized. The General Confederation of Labour (the C.G.T.) had split into two rival factions and, as explained above,[22] the mass of the workers now had scant sympathy for the orthodox, European-inspired socialism of the old Argentine Socialist Party. As for the anti-Nazis and anti-Fascists, they were to be found scattered among all the foregoing political and social groups, but they had little else in common except their dislike of Castillo's régime and their suspicion of one another. The *es-*

[22] See above, pp. 76–77.

tancieros did not wish for parliamentary democracy—which would have provided the Radicals with the opportunity to return to power. Neither the landowners nor the Radicals were willing to allow labour to have a share in government. And, while the urban workers would have welcomed the overthrow of the conservative 'oligarchy', they were not attracted by the form of democracy advocated by the Radicals. In short, the army alone could stage the revolution—and it was probably Castillo's choice of Patrón Costas as the next President which finally provoked them to act.

Basically, however, the coup d'état of 1943 was the result of the revolution of 1930, because that event had restored the monopoly of government to the old landed aristocracy,[23] who refused to acknowledge that a change had occurred in the country's sources of wealth. Of the one hundred persons paying the highest income tax in 1941, only ten were *estancieros*. The others were manufacturers of textiles, beer, bags, and shoes; financiers and importers; operators of mines; owners of casinos, cinemas, and radio stations. More people were now employed in industry than in cattle-raising and farming.[24] Thus economic power was moving into

[23] cf. Sir David Kelly's comment (p. 287): 'When I returned [to Argentina] as Ambassador in June 1942, the outstanding phenomenon for me in the Argentine situation was that the group of great estancieros and lawyers, known collectively as the "distinguidos", who had when I was there in 1919 and 1920 formed the opposition to the radical demagogue President, Irigoyen, were in 1942 apparently firmly in the saddle again and had been for many years. The Jockey Club and its more select and more expensive inner circle, the Circulo de Armas, were again, as before the days of Irigoyen, the great centres of political gossip and the power behind the scenes. The second interesting fact was that whereas in 1919 the Jockey Club and the Circulo de Armas fiercely criticized President Irigoyen for having kept the country neutral, now in 1942 their own Government under President Castillo was just as determined as President Irigoyen had been to keep out of the War, whereas what remained of the old radical Irigoyenist party was now being backed by the Americans as the party that would bring Argentina into the War. Whilst the smart society in general backed the neutrality of the Castillo Government only very few of them were pro-German; the vast majority, though resenting at that period the constant admonitions of Cordell Hull and Sumner Welles in Washington, were thoroughly pro-allied and especially pro-British in their personal sympathies.'

[24] cf. Rennie, p. 317.

different hands, and the political situation was bound to be affected. Nevertheless, the landowning minority continued to behave as though nothing had altered, as though Irigoyen had never existed, and as though the new industries—whose development was so vitally important during the second world war—were of no account.

The army officers who in 1943 decided to overthrow Castillo were not yet fully aware of the economic shift that had taken place, or of its significance, and their future policy was confused; but they did at least now recognize and agree that monopoly rule by the conservative oligarchy was out of date. It is noteworthy that these military schemers did not come from landowning but from middle- and lower-class families. Their collaboration with the conservatives against the Radicals in the 1930 revolution had seemed at that time to be a natural alliance; it was only when the army—through lack of political experience and organization—lost control of the situation after the elections of 1931, that they began to understand that the *estancieros* could not satisfy the needs of the modern State. They made better preparations to hold power in 1943. A directive group of officers—the Grupo de Oficiales Unidos, or 'G.O.U.'—drew up thoroughly efficient plans for action. Among these men the most forceful was Colonel Perón, whose influence is apparent in a document which was circulated in May 1943 and which deserves to be quoted here in full in Blanksten's translation:

COMRADES:
The war has fully demonstrated that the nations are not able now to defend themselves alone. Hence the uncertain play of the alliances that lessen, but do not amend, the grave evil. The era of the NATION is slowly being substituted by the era of the CONTINENT. Yesterday the feudals united to form the nation. Today the nations join to form the CONTINENT. That will be the end achieved by this war.

Germany is making a titanic effort to unite the European

continent. The strongest and best-equipped nation should control the destinies of the continent in its new formation. In Europe it will be Germany.

In America, in the north, the controller will be, for a time, the United States of North America. But in the south there is no nation sufficiently strong to accept this guardianship without discussion. There are only two nations that could do so: ARGENTINA and BRAZIL.

OUR AIM IS TO MAKE POSSIBLE AND UNQUESTIONABLE OUR POSITION AS GUARDIANS.

The work is hard and full of sacrifices. But we cannot make our country great without sacrificing everything. The great men of our independence sacrificed wealth and life. In our time Germany has given life a heroic meaning. All this should be an example to us.

The first step to be taken, which shall lead us toward a strong and powerful Argentina, is to get the reins of Government into our hands. A civilian will never understand the greatness of our ideal, we shall therefore have to eliminate them from the Government, and give them the only mission which corresponds to them: WORK and OBEDIENCE.

Once we have obtained power, our aim will be to be STRONG: STRONGER THAN ALL THE OTHER NATIONS UNITED. We shall have to arm, and continue to arm, fighting and overcoming difficulties, both internal and external. Hitler's fight in peace and war shall be our guide. The alliances shall be the first step. We already have Paraguay, and we shall have Bolivia and Chile. With Argentina, Paraguay, Bolivia, and Chile, we shall have no difficulty in bringing in Brazil, owing to the form of its government and the large nucleus of Germans. With Brazil on our side, the South American continent will be ours. Our guardianship will be a fact, a glorious fact, without precedent, realized by the political genius and the heroism of the ARGENTINE ARMY.

Mirages! Ideals! you will say. Nevertheless let us look again at Germany. Beaten in 1919 she was obliged to sign the Versailles Treaty, which was to keep her under Allied domination as a second-class state for at least fifty years. In less than twenty years she has had a fantastic career. By 1939 she was armed as no other nation, and in peace time she annexed Austria and Czechoslovakia. Then, in war she imposed her will on the entire continent of Europe. But it was not accomplished without a hard struggle. Strong dictatorship was necessary to make the people realize the sacrifices necessary to accomplish this great program. SO IT WILL BE IN ARGENTINA.

Our Government shall be a firm dictatorship, although at the beginning, in order to become firmly established, it will concede the necessary allowances. We shall attract the public, but eventually the people will have to work, make sacrifices, and obey. Work more and sacrifice more than any other country. Only thus will it be possible to carry out the armament program, indispensable for the domination of the continent. With Germany's example, the right spirit will be instilled into the people through the RADIO, by the CONTROLLED PRESS, by LITERATURE, by the CHURCH, and by EDUCATION, and so they will venture upon the heroic road they will be made to travel. Only in this way will they forego the easy life they now enjoy. Our generation will be a generation sacrificed on the altar of a high ideal. ARGENTINE PATRIOTISM will shine like a brilliant star for the good of the continent and of the whole of humanity. VIVA LA PATRIA![25]

On 4 June 1943 troops from the suburban garrison of Campo de Mayo marched into Buenos Aires and surrounded the presidential palace, the Casa Rosada; but Castillo had already fled. And so a struggle for leadership began among the officers themselves. The details of that contest— which lasted for two years—do not need to receive attention in the present study. The important fact is that Colonel Perón finally emerged as the undisputed head of the régime.

[25] George I. Blanksten, *Perón's Argentina* (1953), pp. 47–49.

PERÓN'S ARGENTINA

THE CONSOLIDATION OF POWER

CASTILLO was followed in the presidency by a succession of three generals (Rawson, Ramírez, and Fárrell), while behind the scenes Colonel Perón and the G.O.U. directed the Government's programme for 'renewing the national spirit'. Army officers were sent to 'intervene' in the provinces, the trade unions, and the universities. Congress was dissolved and elections indefinitely postponed. Decrees were issued regulating even the most trivial aspects of the

[1] This chapter has a new heading and has been slightly altered, as the years can now be seen in better perspective; but it is substantially the same as in the first edition. When originally published in 1955, these pages aroused numerous protests that the author was 'a Peronista'. The chapter has been retained, however, because it was widely regarded as a useful record of the development of the Perón régime. Thus, even at the height of the anti-Peronista purge in Argentina, the following review appeared prominently in the Buenos Aires newspaper *La Razón* (28 January 1956):

'After the welter of books published in the last few months about our present political and social situation, it is an English writer, George Pendle, who has produced in one organic and intelligent volume the most responsible work on the subject. Although its aim is to present a complete, condensed picture of our past and present, Pendle not only achieves a concise but fundamental analysis of our geography and history, but also ventures into a profound description of our obscure present. The essential feature of the work is the author's study of the years from 1930 to today. No aspect of our country is unknown to him. With the same sure touch, he analyses economic and social phenomena, the means used by Perón to achieve power, and his administration. Objection can be raised to these chapters from one or other passionately biassed point of view; but whoever a few years hence may wish to get a coherent view of this period, will be obliged to return to these pages as to the most impartial source on the subject. Pendle, the author of this controversial but honest study, has lived for many years in our country and has known prominent figures of our public life. As evidence of his care and responsibility, an extensive and select bibliography accompanies the volume which is proof of his conscientiousness in carrying out the work, as well as a guarantee of the sometimes disconcerting knowledge its author possesses of our most intimate reactions as a nation. Certain aspects of his judgements may give rise to bitter discussions, but the value of these pages as a whole is enhanced by the fewness of the errors, which are attributable to the distance at which the author lives.'

national life. Newspapers which criticized the Government were suspended. Teachers and other State employees whose loyalty to the régime was in doubt were dismissed wholesale. People who protested at the manner in which the republic was being treated as though it were an army corps were arrested or were obliged to flee into exile. In December 1943, to secure the support of the Catholic Church, the Government decreed that religious instruction—which had been rejected alike by statesmen of the Sarmiento era and the Radicals—was to be compulsory in all national schools.

The administration was unashamedly pro-Axis, though in January 1944 diplomatic relations with Germany and Japan were severed.[2] There were two main motives for this rupture. First, Washington had threatened to publish evidence of Argentina's clandestine traffic with Germany (an agent named Hellmuth had been arrested at Trinidad in November 1943 while travelling from Buenos Aires to Europe) and of Argentine plotting to set up 'friendly' Governments in neighbouring countries (in particular in Bolivia, where a successful revolution in December 1943 had undoubtedly received support from Buenos Aires).[3] Second, the Government hoped—though their hope was unfulfilled—that the rupture would encourage the United States to supply the goods which Argentina urgently required but could no longer obtain from Europe.

Colonel Perón was not a prominent public figure during the first months of the régime, but his name was already familiar to foreign diplomats and newspaper correspondents in Buenos Aires.

Juan D. Perón was born at Lobos in the Province of Buenos Aires in 1895, the son of a small-scale farmer of

[2] All the Latin American republics except Argentina and Chile had ceased to have diplomatic relations with the Axis by the time that the Rio de Janeiro conference of 1942 closed. Chile had severed relations in January 1943.
[3] This evidence was later included in the notorious 'Blue Book'. See below, pp. 102–3.

Italian origin.[4] He graduated from the National Military Academy, subsequently serving as military attaché in Chile and Italy. He was known as an expert skier and became the fencing champion of the Argentine army. He taught at the Army War College (Escuela Superior de Guerra); for a while held the chair of combined operations at the Naval War College (Escuela de Guerra Naval); and wrote several books on military history and strategy. Indeed, he seems early to have acquired a taste (which grew with the years) for expounding his own interpretation of history and for advising people how they should live their lives. In view of later developments, this aspect of Perón's character deserves attention. During his Italian assignment

he took extensive courses on economics, sociology and politics at the Universities of Bologna and Turin. . . . In the 1920's he had studied history under one of the leading Argentine historians, Ricardo Levene. In 1937 he contributed an article on San Martín's famous crossing of the Andes in 1817 to the International Congress of the History of America, which met in Buenos Aires under the chairmanship of Levene. Shortly thereafter the latter engaged Perón to contribute several chapters to the monumental and scholarly *History of the Argentine Nation* (1936–1942) which Levene was then editing. Perón accepted, but his trip to Europe diverted his attention to other matters.[5]

Thus, long before entering politics, this military officer was already an inveterate theorist and lecturer, and as early as 1944 his public pronouncements had acquired more than a merely military significance. In that year he caused something of a sensation when, in the act of dedicating the chair of National Defence at the University of La Plata, he said:

The words 'national defence' may make some of you think this is a problem whose presentation and solution are of interest only to the nation's armed forces. The truth is very different: into its solution go all the inhabitants, all their energies, all their

---

[4] For summary of President Perón's career, see *Who's Who in Latin America*, Part V (1950), p. 151.
[5] Arthur P. Whitaker, *The United States and Argentina* (1954), p. 119.

wealth, all their industries and production, all their means of transport and communication, the armed forces being merely . . . the fighting instrument of that great whole which is 'the nation in arms'.[6]

Subsequent lectures confidently covered such vast subjects as the entire history of philosophy.[7]

In addition to all his other qualities, Perón also possessed great personal charm, being handsome and masculine, with—in the true tradition of the Argentine caudillo—a facility for arousing the enthusiasm of the people whom he aspired to lead. Among the many personal impressions of Perón that have been written, a portrait by a British poet who met him in 1947 is one of the most revealing:

As the doors were flung open, the General came forward to greet us, shaking each of us heartily by the hand. He looks a man in his late thirties. . . . He is not tall, but very broad and strong. He has a very likeable, slightly shy smile. . . . His eyes are wary and tired. . . . He managed to put us at our ease, to build up a coherent case for himself, and as a man to capture our sympathy. He had a frank and open way with him and gave us an impression, new to us in our discussions of Argentine politics, of practical common sense. He has a certain disarming ordinariness, and knows how to make what he has been doing sound the natural thing to do. . . . He is genial. One is aware of unusual energy and capacity, and also, after a time, of certain limitations. The limitations spring, I think, from the fact that he is a professional soldier, though with a political intelligence quite unusual in soldiers. But he thinks of the morale of the regiment; and he thinks of the citizen as existing for the state, as the soldier exists for the regiment. Again, his tactics are military rather than strictly political ones; he thinks of dividing and dispersing the opposition, not of finding some basis of agreement with it. He has no sympathy, that is to say, for what one calls in a wide sense the liberal attitude to life.[8]

[6] Quoted in Rennie, p. 375.

[7] For example: *Conferencia del . . . General Juan Perón . . . Primer Congreso Nacional de Filosofía* (Buenos Aires, Presidencia de la Nación, Subsecretaría de Informaciones, 1949).

[8] G. S. Fraser, *News from South America* (1949), pp. 128–33.

During the early months of the military régime Perón—who at that time was chief of the secretariat of the Ministry of War and president of the National Department of Labour —soon saw that the high-handed methods of the administration were alienating the population. He recognized that the movement, if it were to attain its object of forging a 'New Argentina', must somehow find popular support. In the course of his work at the Department of Labour, therefore, he appealed to the labour leaders, whose unions were now safely under the supervision of military 'interventors'. He arranged for his Department to be promoted to the rank of Ministry, with the title of Secretariat of Labour and Social Welfare (the Secretariat could not be officially named a ministry, as the constitution did not yet permit the creation of additional ministries). Perón himself was in charge of this new body, later occupying also—and simultaneously—the posts of Minister of War and Vice-President of the republic. At the Secretariat he proceeded to tighten his hold on the unions while undertaking many long-overdue social reforms and obtaining other benefits for the workers, who reciprocated by hailing him as their champion.

A list of some of the measures introduced by Colonel Perón during this critical period will show how thoroughly he prepared his ground.[9] During 1944–5 he built up a National Institute of Social Security, thereby converting Argentina from one of the most backward countries in South America in social insurance matters to one of the most advanced. He contrived that his Secretariat should be increasingly utilized to supervise collective bargaining; that during those negotiations the workers should usually obtain substantial concessions; and that the new wage agreements so concluded should have the widest possible publicity. At the same time workers who went on strike and refused to avail themselves of the facilities offered by the Secretariat were roughly handled. In the meat-packing

[9] For a more detailed account of Perón's activity at the Secretariat of Labour and Social Welfare, see Alexander, *Perón Era*, pp. 23–32.

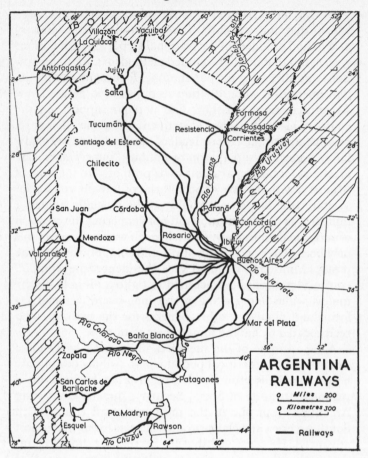

ARGENTINA
RAILWAYS

0   *Miles* 200
0   *Kilometres* 300

——— Railways

plants and in other industries where the employers had prevented the workers from forming unions, Perón enabled
them to do so. But he maintained his control over the
unions by the introduction of a regulation that collective
bargaining contracts would only be recognized as valid
when the unions signing them had been officially approved
by the Secretariat. He supported amenable union leaders,
giving them posts in the Secretariat, and he refused official

recognition to unfriendly unions, while encouraging the formation of rival unions in the industries in question. Gradually, as the number of friendly unions increased, Perón gathered them together into a reconstituted General Confederation of Labour (C.G.T.), which was dominated by loyal Perón men. He arranged the appropriation of a large sum for the construction of inexpensive houses. In 1945 a decree was issued providing compulsory annual holidays with pay for all wage-earners. It was not surprising that by October 1945 the majority of workers considered Colonel Perón to be a more important man than their traditional leaders. And, no matter how demagogic his methods, he had accomplished more for them in two years than the Socialist Party had achieved in decades of patient and constantly obstructed legislative effort. Perón was now ready for an open trial of strength.

Outside the working class, the military administration—usually referred to as the *de facto* Government—had become increasingly unpopular. Not only was there widespread dissatisfaction at the continuance of unconstitutional rule, but middle-class Argentines were humiliated when they saw that, as a result of the G.O.U.'s mistaken assumption that the Axis would win the war, the country was in a state of isolation unparalleled since the time of Rosas. The *de facto* Government had declared war on the Axis at the eleventh hour,[10] but Argentina nevertheless was still boycotted by the United States, and relations with the other western democracies and even with the majority of the Latin American republics were less than cordial. The officers at the garrison of Campo de Mayo, ashamed of the little respect in which their country was now held abroad and aware of the régime's failure to win approval at home, became restive;

[10] Argentina declared war in March 1945 and was the last Latin American republic to do so. The six Central American republics and the three island republics of the Caribbean had declared war in December 1941; Mexico in May and Brazil in August 1942; Bolivia in April and Colombia in November 1943; Chile, Peru, Ecuador, Paraguay, Venezuela, and Uruguay in February 1945.

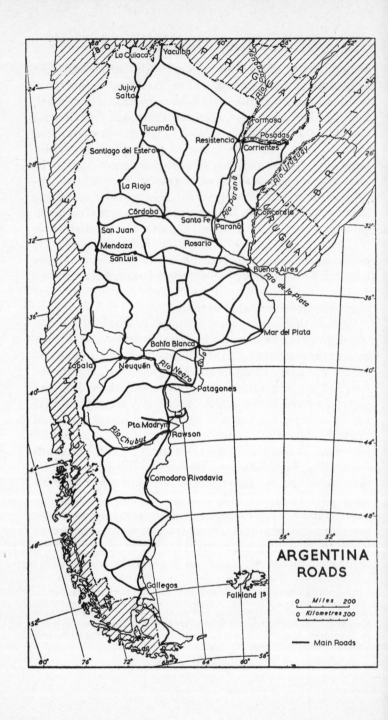

ARGENTINA
ROADS

Miles 200

Kilometres 300

Main Roads

many of them were jealous of Colonel Perón's political ascendancy; and so, on 9 October 1945, they obliged Perón to resign from all his three government posts. On 10 October Perón defiantly appealed to the workers for support. He was then placed under arrest. Working-class riots followed, and the union leaders—feverishly assisted by Eva Duarte, a twenty-six-year-old radio performer who was a close friend of Perón and, like him, of humble social origin—organized large-scale demonstrations. Men in shirt-sleeves—henceforth to be known as *descamisados* (literally, men without shirts)—poured into Buenos Aires from the working-class districts and, in particular, from the meat-packing suburb of Avellaneda. Soon these *descamisados* were virtually in control of the capital. The Government—which now consisted of Perón's rivals—hesitated to use force. Then, to appease the crowds who were constantly shouting his name, Perón was released from 'protective custody' and, on the evening of 17 October, appeared on the balcony of the Casa Rosada in company with the *de facto* President, General Fárrell. He received a tumultuous welcome. A few days later he and Eva Duarte were married.

After the triumph of 17 October, Perón placed his friends in key positions in the Government but did not himself take office: instead, he devoted his energies to preparing for elections which were to be held in February 1946. His supporters formed a new party, the Partido Laborista, which nominated him its candidate for the presidency. The party pledged itself to work for the nationalization of the public services (notably, the railways), the building of hospitals and homes for the workers, the aged, and the infirm, and the defence of the social gains made while Perón was Secretary of Labour. By claiming that his aim was to carry on the reforms begun by Hipólito Irigoyen, Perón managed to secure the collaboration of a group of dissident Radicals. And to a considerable extent his candidacy was favoured by the Church, which of course disapproved of certain opposition politicians who were said to advocate the separation of

Church and State, the abolition of religious education, and the legalization of divorce. The Peronistas warned the electorate that, if they were defeated, the *estanciero* oligarchy would resume its hold upon the country. Three opposition parties—the Radicals, Socialists, and Communists—formed a coalition, Unión Democrática, whose propaganda was rather lacking in constructive proposals, being largely devoted to denouncing Perón as a Fascist. The contest between the Peronistas and Unión Democrática was bitter and violent. Two weeks before Christmas 1945 the Government—which was known to be operating under Perón's direction—ordered all employers to pay a Christmas bonus of one month's wages to their workers. This astute political move delighted the workers but caused consternation among the employers, some of whom ill-advisedly instituted a lock-out by way of protest. Meanwhile, the United States Ambassador to Argentina, Spruille Braden, had on several occasions openly declared that Perón and his colleagues were enemies of the free world who throughout the war had been in contact with Axis agents; and the Ambassador made a point of being seen in the company of anti-Perón politicians. Braden had left the country in August; but he was now Assistant Secretary of State at Washington and the United States Government's chief adviser on Argentina. It was undeniable that Braden wished to interfere in Argentine affairs. Playing on the traditional fear of intervention by the 'Colossus of the North', the Peronistas claimed that the elections were in fact a contest between Perón and Braden. The State Department at Washington then supplied Perón with a further opportunity for appealing to national pride by issuing a Blue Book[11] analysing the conduct of Argentina's *de facto* Government during the war and listing the names of Nazis and Fascists to whom the régime had given protection. This Blue Book was published just

[11] The title of the Blue Book is *Consultation among the American Republics with Respect to the Argentine Situation*. Copies of the book were handed by the U.S. Secretary of State to each of the Latin American Ambassadors at Washington.

two weeks before the elections, with the unconcealed intention of influencing the voters. Instead of assisting the Unión Democrática and damaging Perón's chances, however, it reinforced the latter's argument that he was standing up to the United States in defence of his country's independence.

The elections took place on 24 February 1946 under the supervision of the army and were, by common consent, the cleanest since 1916. The voting was fairly even, but the electoral college system gave an overwhelming victory to Perón, who won the presidency for himself[12] and secured almost two-thirds of the seats in the Chamber of Deputies and all but two of the seats in the Senate. His success in the provinces was equally remarkable. Thus was the military revolution of 1943 at last legalized. Juan Domingo Perón—with the rank of brigadier-general—was inaugurated President of the republic on 4 June.

PERÓN'S ECONOMIC PROGRAMME AND THE CONSTITUTION OF 1949

It will be unnecessary to give a detailed account of the early years of General Perón's presidency, and it would be impossible to enumerate all the ways in which his rule affected the life of the Argentine people—each year thousands of laws and decrees, covering almost every imaginable subject, were promulgated by his Government. But from the moment when he began to dabble in politics, Perón appears to have had one major purpose which never altered—though the methods that he adopted often changed. His aim was to organize a social and economic revolution that would con-

[12] In the ballot for members of the presidential electoral college Perón received 1·5 million votes, while his rival (the Unión Democrática leader, Dr José P. Tamborini, who was an elderly physician and a Radical) received 1·2 million. In the electoral college—operating in accordance with the Constitution of 1853—Perón had 304 votes against 72.

The Peronista Constitution of 1949 (see below, pp. 108 ff.) abolished the electoral college system and provided that in the future the President of the republic should be elected by direct popular vote.

vert Argentina into a powerful and self-sufficient modern state. Necessarily, therefore, the revolution—particularly in its first phase—was strongly nationalist in character and opposed alike to the foreign ownership of public services, to the (undoubtedly excessive) dependence of the Argentine economy on foreign markets and imports, and to the privileged position of the *estanciero* class who wished to keep the country in this condition of so-called 'colonial' dependence so that the export trade in their own pastoral and agricultural products might continue to flourish. Thus, to attain 'economic independence' Perón relied on two main expedients: the elimination of foreign finance and the expansion of local industry. A few examples will suffice to show how the dual process was carried out. In March 1946 (i.e. after Perón's electoral victory but more than two months before his inauguration) the Government nationalized the Central Bank, which had been directed by a board most of whom were representatives of important foreign banks operating in Argentina.[13] This Bank was given control over all other banks and over all bank deposits and was empowered to withhold loans and to seize bank accounts if necessary. Thereby the Government in fact took charge of all the financial resources of the nation. Insurance was likewise centralized and became almost a State monopoly.[14] Perón next proceeded to pay off Argentina's foreign debt. Much of this debt was held in London, so the President was able to redeem it largely by means of blocked sterling which, as Great Britain was as yet unable adequately to resume her pre-war export trade, could not be used immediately for importing the goods that Argentina required. Perón then, with the currency which had accumulated from favourable trading in wartime and immediate post-war years, purchased the North American-owned telephone system and other foreign-owned services. In 1947–8 he negotiated the

[13] Perón subsequently claimed that only four members of this board spoke the language of the country (Alexander, *Perón Era*, p. 156).

[14] For details of the insurance law of 1947 see J. G. Lomax, *Argentina* (London, H.M.S.O., 1948), pp. 17–18.

purchase of the British railways, which had contributed so greatly to the prosperity of the republic but were now in urgent need of extensive and expensive rehabilitation.[15] In connexion with his economic programme he set up a series of official institutions whose names and precise duties were changed from time to time but whose general purpose was always to supervise the development of the national economy. The most important of these government agencies was the Instituto Argentino de Promoción del Intercambio (Argentine Institute for the Promotion of Trade), known as I.A.P.I., which was created by decree in May 1946. I.A.P.I. was given the right to buy virtually the whole of Argentina's agricultural and pastoral production and to sell it wherever the best price could be found. In this manner the Institute, which in the first years paid low prices to local producers and obtained high prices from foreign buyers, exerted an anti-inflationary influence while at the same time earning substantial profits. I.A.P.I.'s earnings of foreign currency were chiefly used for the importing of ships, vehicles, machinery, and equipment for industrialization projects. By 1950 it became apparent that the low prices paid to farmers and cattle-raisers were having a discouraging effect on the production of cereals and meat, and in subsequent years more attractive prices were therefore guaranteed to the producers. I.A.P.I. continued to operate on a very extensive scale. In 1953, for instance, the Institute was responsible for 63 per cent of Argentina's total exports and 20 per cent of her imports.[16] By 1953, however, international commodity prices had become weak and unstable,[17] and in that year I.A.P.I. incurred a trading loss of

[15] The Anglo-Argentine Agreement (the so-called 'Andes Agreement') was published as a White Paper, Cmd. 7346 (1948).

[16] *R.R.P.*, 11 May 1954, pp. 13–14. I.A.P.I.'s principal exports in 1953 were cereals, vegetable oils, meat, and hides. The Institute's most important imports were hessians (for bags, and for the manufacture of the rope-soled shoes—*alpargatas*—worn universally in the 'camp'), iron, bananas, newsprint, sugar, tractors, copper, and rubber.

[17] The extent of the deterioration in the terms of trade for Argentina is indicated in the following table, the basic year being 1950=100:

2,184 million pesos.[18] Thus did the Institute at that time protect the national economic structure against the effects —which in the past had so often been disastrous—of falling world prices for the country's basic exports. By law, the Government was authorized to reimburse I.A.P.I. 'the amount of the losses it may incur in the marketing of agricultural and pastoral produce in the domestic or international markets, purchased from the producers at prices fixed by the Executive Power.'[19]

Another government agency, the National Economic Council, was created in July 1947 to co-ordinate all the financial and economic policies of the régime, including the operations of I.A.P.I. The first chairman of this Council was Miguel Miranda, a prosperous industrialist and 'self-made man' who was the senior Argentine negotiator of the purchase of the British railways and other foreign-owned public utility enterprises, and Perón's principal economic adviser during the first phase of his rule.[20] Miranda believed that improvement in the living conditions of the working class—whose interests were of such personal concern, and of such political significance, to the President and Señora Eva de Perón—could best be attained by industrialization. He despised the old-fashioned 'colonial' occupations of farming and cattle-raising and did not care that the production of the 'camp' would suffer through under-payment so that urban industry might be financed and equipped. He was convinced that, to consolidate the Peronista revolution, money must be spent quickly and generously on industriali-

	1948	*1949*	*1950*	*1951*	*1952*	*1953*
Export prices	139	122	100	133	119	105
Import prices	119	121	100	135	159	142
Terms of trade	117	101	100	99	95	74
Volume of exports	115	85	100	93	59	102
Capacity to import	135	86	100	92	44	76

Thus, relative to 1948, which was the peak year of Argentina's post-war prosperity, the terms of trade had declined by 36 per cent by 1953 (*R.R.P.*, 11 Jan. 1955, pp. 10–11).

[18] Ibid. pp. 12–13.   [19] Ibid. p. 13.

[20] For an informative biographical note on Miguel Miranda, see *R.R.P.*, 27 Feb. 1953, p. 10.

zation; and it was only when the nation's reserves of foreign currency had been exhausted, when the increasingly rapid depreciation of the peso was felt and the rise in the cost of living was causing discontent throughout the land, that this 'financial wizard'—in January 1949—fell from favour.

One of the main functions of Miranda's National Economic Council was to supervise the Five Year Plan which Perón presented to Congress in October 1946.[21] The Plan consisted of a catalogue of all the reforms which the Government hoped to accomplish during its term of office. It included such items as the granting of the vote to women (a provision sponsored by the President's wife) and measures designed, on the one hand, to enable the poorer classes to attend the universities and, on the other hand, to bring the universities even more closely under Peronista control. It covered public health and immigration. But the main object of the Plan was to further the campaign for Argentina's 'economic independence'—an aim which, as indicated above, was enthusiastically shared by Perón's nationalist colleagues, and which previous economic crises had proved to be desirable.

The Government participated in the carrying out of Perón's vast economic programme in various ways, and especially by direct investment (through administrative departments), the forming of state-owned or mixed corporations, preferential Customs treatment for companies establishing new industries, and loans granted to approved enterprises by the official Banco de Credito Industrial Argentino. Great progress was made in expanding such undertakings as the state-owned merchant navy,[22] the production of electric power,[23] the manufacture of motor-

[21] The complete text of the Plan was published as *Plan Quinquenal del Gobierno del Presidente Perón, 1947–1951* (1946).

[22] In 1943 the Argentine merchant fleet amounted to 233,700 tons (Alexander, p. 162). At the end of 1953 the ocean and river fleet consisted of 5,219 vessels of a total of 1,167,298 tons (*Business Conditions in Argentina*, Buenos Aires, Ernesto Tornquist, quarterly report no. 282, June 1954, p. 36).

[23] In 1948 power-houses providing a public service, and accounting for

cycles, motor-cars, lorries, and aircraft by the state-owned Industrias Aeronáuticas y Mecánicas del Estado (I.A.M.E.), and the services of the state-owned civil air lines. In January 1954 it was announced that under the first Five Year Plan the Government had advanced to its industrial dependencies and the public services sums totalling 4,104 million pesos, the principal recipients being the Teléfonos del Estado (the nationalized telephone system), Ferrocarriles Nacionales (railways), Aerolíneas Argentinas (air lines), Flota Mercante del Estado (merchant navy), Yacimientos Petrolíferos Fiscales (the national petroleum organization) and Industrias del Estado (the group of state-owned manufacturing industries).[24]

The revolution was carried into every branch of the national life. In 1948 Perón's supporters argued that the constitution of 1853 must be brought up to date. As a result of congressional elections in March 1948 the Peronistas now held more than two-thirds of the 158 seats in the Chamber of Deputies, and they already controlled all but two of the 30 seats in the Senate; so they were able to secure the necessary number of votes in favour of a Constitutional Convention. The Convention was duly appointed in December 1948, and a new Constitution went into force in March of the following year.[25]

In the Constitution of 1949 the framework and much of the wording of the 1853 document were preserved; and many of the changes—such as an alteration in the terms of office of senators and deputies and a provision for the direct

---

practically the whole of the national production, had an output of 3,911 million kwh. In 1953 production amounted to 4,927 million kwh. (*R.R.P.*, 20 Aug. 1954, pp. 9–10). Production in 1954 and 1955 was still inadequate for the national requirements.

[24] Bank of London & South America, *Fortnightly Review*, 20 Feb. 1954, pp. 115–16. At the time of this announcement the official free market rate of the £ was about 39 pesos, the rate of the U.S. $ being about 14 pesos.

[25] The text of the Constitution was published in English by the Argentine Under-Secretariat of Information, entitled *The Constitution of the Argentine Nation, approved by the National Constituent Assembly, March 11th, 1949* (1949).

popular election of the President and senators instead of their nomination by an electoral college—were of little significance. There were, however, certain important modifications. The President's already strong position in relation to Congress was further strengthened—for example, the new Constitution stated that, should Congress question the executive's behaviour, a reply might be sent by letter, whereas formerly a responsible minister was supposed to appear in person to be interrogated. Of general interest was the new Article 78 which—contrary to the stipulation in the 1853 Constitution that a President could only be re-elected after an intervening period of six years—declared that the President was eligible for immediate re-election at the end of his term of office. The executive was given greater latitude in other aspects of government. The old Constitution had provided that the President could only establish a 'state of siege' in the event of foreign invasion or internal rebellion; the Constitution of 1949 gave him that right also 'in the event of a disturbance of public order threatening to disrupt the normal course of life or the essential activities of the population'. The new Constitution contained statements on the rights of workers and the aged which were in fact a reproduction of speeches made by President Perón and his wife and an outline of the social welfare legislation which they had promoted. An opportunity for the inculcation of the Peronista 'ideology' was provided in a clause on education: 'The universities shall establish obligatory and ordinary courses designed for the students of all the faculties for their political formation.' The liberal definition in the 1853 Constitution of the right to private property ('Property is inviolable') was altered to read: 'Private property has a social function. . . . It is incumbent on the State to control the distribution and utilization of the land.' Every rural worker was to be given a chance to own the land which he worked. The extension of State intervention in economic affairs was authorized: foreign trade (the new Constitution declared) 'shall be in the hands of the State in accordance with the limitations and rulings that may be established by law', and such resources as minerals, waterfalls, petroleum fields, coalfields, and gas deposits were described as being 'the imprescriptible and inalienable property of the Nation'. Public services were to be State-owned.

'In the new constitution', writes Robert J. Alexander, 'Perón has left a monument to himself',[26] and it is certainly true that he succeeded in incorporating in that document all his favourite doctrines regarding social welfare and economic nationalism. By means of the new Constitution, moreover, he acquired greater powers to prevent the growth of an effective opposition and secured the legal right to prolong his rule indefinitely.

THE PRESERVATION OF POWER

Perón had to struggle to survive. In retrospect, it can be judged that his decline was already beginning in 1948-9, with the economic deterioration. The threat of subversive action existed in a number of different quarters. Well-established and powerful groups recognized that his policy, if it were carried out in practice, would be detrimental to their interests; and in the view of liberal-minded persons in many walks of life *Peronismo* represented the introduction of abhorrent totalitarian ideas and methods of government into their country. Perón was constantly faced, too, with the danger of the emergence of a dissident faction under rival leadership within his own party—as in the early days of the régime when Cipriano Reyes, the leader of the packing-house workers, proclaimed that the President's proposal to widen the party to include a following of non-Labour Peronista supporters signified a betrayal of the working-class movement which had raised him to the presidency.[27] If Perón had allowed his enemies and rivals free-

[26] *Perón Era*, p. 83. The Constitution of 1949 was abolished after Perón's downfall in 1955.
[27] Concerning Cipriano Reyes's conflict with Perón, see Alexander, *Perón Era*, pp. 54-60 and 128, and Blanksten, pp. 334-5 and 346-7.

dom of expression and action, he would have been quite unable to complete the social and economic revolution on which he had embarked. But the principal reason why his treatment of opponents in (for example) the judiciary, the press, the universities, the army, and the Church deserves attention here, is because in the process of defending himself against them he indicated the role which he considered that those institutions should perform in the 'New Argentina'; and the measures that he took profoundly affected their status and their operation.

At this point it is necessary to present the Peronista case concerning the manner in which the President maintained himself in office. It is true, of course, that he was working in an abnormal, revolutionary atmosphere. But Peronistas argued that even when out-manœuvring or crushing his enemies—and at all other times—Perón invariably acted within the law and in accordance with the will of the people. The very considerable powers of the executive under the Constitution of 1853 have been referred to in a previous chapter; and although the further extension of those powers in the revised Constitution of 1949 was the work of the President's own party, the constitutional amendments were passed by a Constituent Assembly which had been duly appointed by popular vote and whose decisions therefore were legally valid. Subsequent laws which assisted Perón to suppress the opposition and to carry out his social and economic revolution were likewise devised by the President and his colleagues; but those laws were formally approved by successive Congresses which had been chosen by the people in elections acknowledged by the opposition leaders themselves to be among the cleanest in Argentine history. Perón's conception of democracy differed greatly from that which prevails in the United Kingdom or the United States; but, as we have seen, he was not the first Argentine President to combine *caudillismo* with the ballot, and his claim that he enabled the workers to participate in the Government and that he widened the franchise by giving the vote to women[28] must be accepted. Perón did introduce certain 'totalitarian' ideas which formerly had not exercised much influence in Argentina; and he did rely on the federal police to intimidate his opponents. But since the days of the American and French revolutions the Argentines had constantly imported and adapted new ideas and techniques from overseas, and although Perón often used methods which he had learned during his residence in Mussolini's Italy, it would be a mistake to imagine that his rule was purely Fascist, in the European meaning of that term. He remarked of his own rise to power: 'We collected all the good ideas that we found on our road to Government House; and when we arrived there, we contributed what was needed.'[29] And Peronistas have been apt—too apt—to make light of the activities of the police under Perón, protesting that they were mild by comparison with the behaviour of the Mazorca in the time of Rosas, when Argentina was a 'Police State' indeed.

There are two judicial systems in Argentina: national tribunals deal with cases that arise under the federal Constitution and federal laws, while provincial tribunals attend to other cases. All the members of the national tribunals are appointed by the President of the republic, with the approval of the Senate.[30] The senior national tribunal is the Supreme Court of Justice, which theoretically has the power to decide whether new legislation is or is not constitutional—though its chief function is appellate. In 1945, while Perón as Vice-President of the republic was the dominant

[28] By the women's suffrage law, passed in 1947, the right to vote was granted to all women over the age of 18.

[29] *South American J.*, 9 June 1951, p. 271.

[30] 1853 Constitution, Art. 86, cl. 5, and 1949 Constitution, Art. 83, cl. 5. The 1853 Constitution provided (Art. 102) that criminal cases be tried by jury 'as soon as this institution is established'; but in practice trial by jury was only very rarely adopted, and this provision was omitted from the 1949 Constitution. In general, Argentine justice is on a Roman Law basis. For a brief account of its evolution, see Ricardo Levene, 'Notas para la Historia del Derecho Argentino e Hispano Americano', in *Atlante*, Apr. 1954, pp. 102–6.

personality in the administration, the Supreme Court declared that several of the Government's decrees were unconstitutional. By the end of that year the Court had in fact shown that it was hostile to the revolution; and even before his inauguration as President, Perón had declared that the supreme judicial authority had been guilty of political bias. In the same manner as he had already claimed that a democracy which tolerated class privilege and poverty was a sham democracy, so did he now state that the 'spirit of justice' was more important than the law and that a Supreme Court which did not acknowledge this truth was unworthy to exercise judicial power. On his recommendation, therefore, the Peronista majority in Congress voted, in 1947, the impeachment of the members of the Supreme Court; and from that date onwards the highest tribunal was composed exclusively of Perón's nominees. The lower national courts were likewise purged, and by the end of 1947 seventy-one judges had been dismissed.[31]

Perón then proceeded to protect his régime against too violent criticism in and outside Congress by strengthening two laws (which were already in existence) against *lèse-majesté* and treason. The first of these laws—the statute against *desacato* or 'disrespect'—was amended in October 1949 so as to prohibit the public utterance of expressions of disrespect concerning not only the President of the republic but also the régime and its officials. *Desacato* was defined as 'anything which offends the dignity of any public official, whether the statement refers directly to the person or by allusion to him or the governmental organization of which he forms a part.'[32] Penalties under this law ranged from two months' to three years' imprisonment. In September 1950 another statute of a similar nature was rendered more severe, the ostensible purpose being to punish espionage, sabotage, and treason. Under this law the following maxi-

[31] cf. Blanksten, pp. 122–30.
[32] Ibid. pp. 175–6. Blanksten incorrectly gives 1948 as the date of the law of *desacato*.

mum penalties were established. For obtaining or revealing political, social, military or economic secrets involving the security of the state: ten years' imprisonment in peace-time and life imprisonment or death during war; for sabotage generally: twenty-five years' imprisonment in peace-time and death during war; for causing public alarm or despondency: eight years' imprisonment.[33] These two laws naturally caused anxiety to members of the opposition, and their concern was justified: in subsequent years many of them spent short periods in prison, and in times of crisis the federal police—which had been greatly enlarged by Perón—were kept busy rounding up Radicals and conservatives, the sons of *estancieros*, students, intellectuals, and dissident labour leaders. A particularly large number of arrests was made after the events of 15 April 1953, when two bombs exploded during a mass meeting of Peronistas in Buenos Aires and, in retaliation, a mob roamed the streets of the capital, sacking premises belonging to supposed perpetrators of the explosions and setting fire to the luxurious Jockey Club, which was the traditional stronghold of the landowning 'oligarchy'. Among those arrested after that night of arson was Victoria Ocampo, a well-known author and publisher, who spent three weeks in gaol. Señora Ocampo, although not an active politician, was looked upon with disfavour for three reasons: she was a member of a family of the 'oligarchy', she had made no secret of her sympathy with the democracies during the second world war, and she was a friend of many of the leading democratically-minded writers in France, England, and the United States.[34]

Early in his political career Perón showed his dislike of press criticism; and as President he soon took action to pre-

[33] *The Times*, 29 September 1950. Until then the death penalty was reserved for military offenders, the last execution in Argentina having occurred more than twenty years before.

[34] Victoria Ocampo made a dignified and non-political reference to her experiences in prison in her own literary review *Sur* (Buenos Aires), July–Aug. 1953, pp. 121–2.

vent it. Various direct and devious methods were adopted
to intimidate, obstruct and, finally, close down the anti-
Peronista newspapers. Señora Perón herself purchased
three Buenos Aires dailies, one of which—*Democracia*—became the 'mouthpiece' of the Casa Rosada (Government
House). A committee which was set up by Congress to in-
vestigate the provincial newspapers found reasons for closing most of them. The Socialist *Vanguardia* (Buenos Aires)
was closed on the pretext that the premises in which it was
printed were 'dirty and unhealthy', violating the municipal health regulations. As almost no newsprint is manufactured in Argentina, the threat by the Government that
supplies of imported paper would be withheld from unfriendly editors became a favourite means of intimidation.
But the bitterest of the campaigns against an opposition
newspaper was that which culminated, in 1951, in the closing of *La Prensa*—a substantial Buenos Aires daily which
had an international reputation for its high journalistic
standards. *La Prensa*—founded in 1869, and the property of
a family of the old landowning class—had little sympathy
with those who advocated social changes. In spite of constant molestation, it continued to criticize—stubbornly,
and in a rather ponderous manner—the policy of Perón's
Government; and, unlike the remainder of the press (with
the exception, to some extent, of another distinguished and
independent newspaper, *La Nación*), it published news
items—such as reports of police violence—liable to bring
discredit on the administration. The fact that *La Prensa*
obtained its foreign news from a United States source (the
United Press) was declared by Peronistas to be proof that its
editors were 'tools of Wall Street' and guilty of treason. In
January 1951 the contest reached its climax: the news-
vendors' union (which was affiliated to the Government-
controlled C.G.T.) refused to distribute *La Prensa* unless
the owners agreed to close their branch offices, give up their
mail subscription lists, and contribute 20 per cent of their
advertising revenue to the union's 'social assistance' fund.

The staff of *La Prensa* remained loyal to their employers, but the Government maintained that the suspension of the publication of the newspaper was the result not of political pressure but of a labour dispute; and when armed guards fired upon members of the staff to prevent them from returning to work, this was referred to as action by strike 'pickets'. In April 1951 Congress voted the expropriation of *La Prensa*. The newspaper was then handed over to the C.G.T. by the authorities, and it reappeared in November as one more of the many organs of information—including radio stations —which the Peronistas now owned or controlled.[35]

Perón also set to work to ensure that the nation's educational establishments should serve his cause. Primary and secondary education were already in the hands of the State (though there were and still are a number of private, foreign, and religious schools), and Perón and his colleagues had no difficulty in compelling all schools to use government-approved text-books which were designed to 'exalt the sentiment of the fatherland'. Teachers who disagreed with Peronista policy were dismissed. But the universities— which since 1918 had been a breeding-ground of political unrest—resisted the military régime. There are six universities in Argentina, namely those of Córdoba (Córdoba University was founded in 1613 and has long been of continental fame), Buenos Aires (created by Rivadavia in 1812), La Plata (founded in 1897), and the twentieth-century universities of Tucumán, The Litoral (situated at Santa Fe, with branches in Rosario and Corrientes), and Cuyo (at Mendoza). These are all national institutions, the President of the republic having the right to 'intervene' in them and to remove the university authorities. When Irigoyen sent an 'interventor' to Córdoba University in 1918, however, the students (encouraged by the liberal ideas

[35] The proprietors' point of view in regard to the victimization of their newspaper is given in *Defense of Freedom*, by the editors of *La Prensa* (London and N.Y., Boardman, 1952).

which Irigoyen's own party had recently brought into politics) went on strike and secured the adoption of a new system whereby students were to share with the professors the responsibilities of university administration. This so-called movement of University Reform (always spelt with capitals) afterwards spread to the other universities, and at the time of the 1943 revolution all universities except that of Cuyo were administered by mixed councils composed of professors and students. There was general hostility to the 1943 revolution in university circles; but the national Government had retained the right of intervention, and both before and after Perón's electoral victory of 1945 (in October of which year the most serious student riots occurred) all of the universities were placed under the control of interventors, aided, on occasion, by the police. Hundreds of professors and lecturers were replaced by Peronista nominees. Meanwhile Perón delivered speeches on the function of higher education, and introduced certain beneficial reforms of his own. He argued that the scholarship system should be expanded so that any Argentine youth who wished to attend a university might do so, no matter how humble his social position. He criticized the prevailing custom whereby the university faculties were staffed by persons who earned their living in practising professions (law, medicine, etc.) and merely taught in their spare time. He sponsored a plan providing for the establishment of full-time teaching staffs; and in 1949 all university fees were abolished.[36] But in 1947 a law was passed by the Peronista-dominated Congress which provided that in future each of the universities should be under the direction of a rector appointed for a three-year term by the President of the republic himself, and it was to be the duty of the rector to

[36] Details published by the University of Buenos Aires in 1954 indicated a considerable increase in university education. The number of students rose from 16,631 in 1940 to 64,425 in 1953. Argentina then had 601 university students for every 100,000 inhabitants. But there was a noticeable lack of increased interest in the Agricultural and Veterinary Sciences, in spite of the fact that the national economy was so dependent on agricultural and pastoral production.

nominate the members of the administrative and teaching staffs. By these and other means the universities were to a considerable extent—though not entirely[37]—subdued.[38]

In modern times no President of Argentina could stay in power without at least the passive support of the army, and since the revolution of 1930 the army have not been content with a passive role: they have taken an active part in politics. Five of the seven Presidents between Irigoyen and Perón were generals, and during the period following the military revolution of 1943 about one-half of the federal interventors and provincial governors were military officers. To please the officers (as well as because, being himself a soldier by career, he had military leanings), Perón increased the size of the army and its budget, raised the officers' pay, improved their barracks and living quarters, purchased large quantities of military equipment, and expanded the local factories producing military materials. Nevertheless, the danger of opposition in the army was a frequent cause for anxiety. The formation of political clubs and cliques—such as the G.O.U., which had plotted the 1943 revolution and prepared the way for Perón's own rise to power—has long been an accepted practice in Argentina, and it continued during Perón's presidency. Some of these cliques opposed various aspects of Peronista policy—for example, many officers considered that too much favouritism was being shown to the workers—and in August 1951 there was widespread disapproval of the nomination of the President's wife as candidate for the vice-presidency of the republic. Apart from their objection to the appointment of a woman to such a high position in the state, the army were mindful that in the event of the President's death or absence the Vice-President, in accordance with the Constitution, would become acting President and Commander-in-Chief of the armed forces. At the end of August military pressure com-

[37] For example, demonstrations against the régime occurred in the universities in October 1954, when many students were arrested.

[38] For more detailed accounts of Perón's educational policy see Alexander, *Perón Era*, pp. 133–40 and Blanksten, pp. 186–9.

pelled Señora Perón to withdraw her candidacy. But tension still continued between a certain section of the army and Perón's administration. When a military coup d'état was attempted in September 1951, thousands of indignant workers poured into the streets of Buenos Aires and built barricades to halt the rebels; but the small insurgent force was routed by loyal troops before it could reach the outskirts of the city. Perón declared martial law, and ninety-seven officers who had been arrested were sentenced to terms of imprisonment and were cashiered. The elections in November then proved that Perón's popularity was undiminished: he was elected to the presidency for a second six-year term (as provided by the revised Constitution of 1949), receiving 4·6 million votes against his Radical opponent's 2·3 million. At these elections, moreover, the Peronista Party secured all the seats in the Senate and reduced the Radical minority in the Chamber of Deputies from 45 to 14. His position thus reaffirmed, Perón three days later took energetic action to show that he had not forgotten the abortive September rising and that he did not intend to tolerate further opposition in the army. On 14 November he placed the entire higher command of the army on the retired list and appointed nine new generals.

The Catholic Church (Roman Catholicism is the official religion in Argentina) at first caused little trouble to Perón, who naturally took care to flatter an institution which had so great an influence over the population. By a decree issued in December 1943, religious instruction was made compulsory in all national schools. From the beginning of the Perón era, priests were invited to Peronista Party and trade union meetings to give their blessing to the proceedings. But when it was revealed that the Government required school-teachers to inculcate in their pupils the belief that *Peronismo* was the 'one true faith of all Argentines', the Catholic hierarchy began to wonder whether their confidence had been misplaced. A crisis finally occurred in 1954, after the passing in September of a law which—contrary to the Church's conception of the sanctity of family life—gave to illegitimate children the same rights as those enjoyed by children born in wedlock. In November the Peronista newspapers began to accuse the clergy of meddling in politics and of having 'aristocratic and oligarchic preferences'.[39] Perón himself announced that a few bishops and priests were conducting a campaign against his régime, that they were planning to create an opposition political party, and that by means of a Catholic workers' federation they were trying to suborn the trade union movement. The centre of this conspiracy was stated to be the old colonial city of Córdoba, where (as in most of the other cities of the interior) the people in general are more devout than the cosmopolitan inhabitants of Buenos Aires. Conflicts between Church and State previously had been avoided in Argentina, but a clash was now seen to be inevitable. In religious demonstrations the cry was heard 'Christ, or Perón' —just as at another time it had been 'Perón, or Braden'. The President retaliated in typical fashion. Priests were imprisoned for short periods; the entire judiciary of Córdoba province was suspended; Catholic newspapers were charged with various abuses, and some (notably *El Pueblo* of Buenos Aires) were closed; Catholic students' clubs at the universities were raided by the police; religious processions were prohibited; religious teachers were dismissed. At Córdoba University the rector and several deans of faculties resigned.[40] To the Peronista *avant-garde* it seemed not only that the clergy had become a rival force in the struggle to direct the life of the people, but that the priests' ideas were out of date and incompatible with the needs of a twentieth-century industrialized nation. Now that the support of the clerical hierarchy had obviously been lost, these Peronistas went ahead with the work of 'modernizing' the social code, each new measure being designed further to

[39] *The Times*, 8 Nov. 1954.   [40] Ibid. 15 Nov. 1954.

weaken the hold of the clergy upon the population. In December 1954 Congress passed a bill legalizing divorce.[41] A fortnight later Perón signed a decree authorizing the provincial governments and the municipality of Buenos Aires to re-establish brothels.[42] A campaign was launched against Catholic schools; and in March 1955 a decree was published removing most of the religious festivals from the list of public holidays and relegating Good Friday and Christmas Day to the rank of 'lesser holidays'.[43] In May a Bill was passed by Congress providing for the disestablishment of the Church and for a plebiscite to elect a constituent assembly to make the corresponding alteration to the national Constitution.[44] Catholic Action (a militant and mainly lay organization) defied the police and marshalled anti-Peronista processions in the streets of Buenos Aires. Further arrests were made; two bishops were expelled from the country; and the Vatican excommunicated all those responsible for the 'crimes' and violence against the Roman Catholic Church.[45]

LABOUR AND EMPLOYERS

Perón and his collaborators were responsible for a steady improvement in the conditions of employment of urban workers and (in spite of persistent inflation) in their standard of living. Already during his pre-presidential period Colonel Perón had championed the poor; and thereafter,

[41] Ibid. 15 and 17 Dec. 1954. Previously persons wishing to obtain divorce were obliged to go abroad—for instance, to Uruguay—for that purpose.   [42] Ibid. 31 Dec. 1954.
[43] This decree abolished the holidays of Epiphany, Corpus Christi, the Assumption, All Saints' Day and the Immaculate Conception. The remaining holidays were classified according to two grades:

(i) *National Holidays*, consisting of Labour Day and the anniversaries of the revolution of 1810, the Declaration of Independence, the death of Señora Perón, and Perón's return from internment in 1945.
(ii) *Lesser Holidays or non-working days*. These were Christmas Day, New Year's Day, the Monday and Tuesday of Carnival Week, Good Friday, and the anniversary of the death of General San Martín. (Ibid. 22 March 1955.)

[44] Ibid. 21 May 1955.   [45] Ibid. 17 June 1955.

spurred on by his wife, he continued to do so. Señora Eva Perón—a glamorous, energetic, resourceful, and warm-hearted young woman, not devoid of feminine vindictiveness towards her enemies in the 'oligarchy' and elsewhere—was herself particularly active in this sphere. Soon after her husband's inauguration in 1946 she installed herself in his former centre of power, the Secretariat of Labour and Social Welfare, where she became for all practical purposes the Secretary of Labour, controlling the General Confederation of Labour, and with her friends at the head of the various unions. From that strategic position she effectively supported the workers' claims for higher wages and sponsored a host of social welfare schemes. She also supervised the affairs of the newly-created Ministry of Health, encouraging the building of hospitals and the launching of campaigns (some of which were remarkably successful) against diseases such as malaria, tuberculosis, and leprosy. 'Evita'—as the *descamisados* affectionately called her—also ran her own Social Aid Foundation, a huge philanthropic organization financed mainly by contributions from the trade unions and industrial and commercial companies in response to her very forceful appeals. Through the Foundation, Señora Perón distributed clothes, food, medicine, and money to needy people in all parts of the republic—and occasionally, for political reasons, abroad.[46] She opened shops which sold food and clothes at lower prices than those charged by the ordinary grocers and drapers. In the event of a railway accident or some other public disaster she rushed emergency supplies, doctors, and nurses to the scene of the tragedy. It is no exaggeration to say that the poorer classes worshipped her.

One of the most vivid sketches of Eva Perón has been provided by a United States Ambassador, James Bruce, who was sent to Argentina in 1947 with President Truman's in-

[46] For example, on the occasion of the revolution in Bolivia in April 1952 the Foundation sent aeroplanes to La Paz loaded with medicine, food, clothing, doctors, and nurses to care for the wounded.

structions that he should 'make friends with those people'. Mr Bruce wrote:

Blonde, diminutive, brown-eyed Evita had a highly vivacious nature which covered a cool and calculating personality. She, far more than the President, was driven by the desire to dominate those [i.e. the 'oligarchy'] who had once rejected her. In many cases she forced her husband to make shrewd decisions, to resolve problems over which he worried and hesitated. Through her efforts in the Labor Ministry, the General Confederation of Labor, the Peronista Women's Party, her social welfare foundation, the press, radio, and newsreels, she directly intervened in almost every phase of Argentine life except the Army. . . . The bitterness and adoration she aroused made her career so dazzling as to have been matched by few women in history. She was so set on achieving her ambitions that she could not compromise. Frequently she told friends: 'Without fanaticism one cannot accomplish anything'. . . . Evita's desire to assert herself was matched by seemingly boundless energy. . . . It forced her to follow the rigorous diet that undermined her health. She wanted to have one of the loveliest figures in the world and to be the world's most expensively dressed woman. Constantly and astutely she told her *descamisados*, or shirtless followers, that she wore her elaborate wardrobe only in trust for them . . . and that some day they would have similar luxuries. . . . Her diet sapped her youth and energy, weakened her already overworked body, and paved the way for the ravages first of pernicious anemia and later of cancer.[47]

She died, at the age of about thirty-three, in 1952. The influence of Evita as a driving force had been tremendous. If she had lived three years longer she might have led the *descamisados* to the barricades, in a desperate attempt to prevent her husband's deposition.

Social welfare legislation completed under Perón's direction was so vast that it cannot be dealt with in detail in the present study. Holidays with pay and a forty-hour work-

[47] James Bruce, *Those Perplexing Argentines* (1954), pp. 280–9. For a woman's impressions of Señora Perón see Fleur Cowles, *Bloody Precedent* (1952).

ing week were decreed for urban workers. Minimum wages were established not only in the towns but also in the 'camp'. A scale of indemnities was drawn up for dismissed employees and for those injured while at work. Laws were passed to protect expectant and nursing mothers and to restrict child labour. Especially important was the legislation —which until 1954 applied only to urban labour—creating a system of pension funds to which workers were to contribute 10 per cent of their wages and employers 15 per cent, the funds being grouped under the jurisdiction of a National Welfare Institute (Instituto Nacional de Previsión Social). In general, the retirement age was fixed at fifty-five; but a Pensions Reform Law passed in 1954[48] offered a bonus to those who continued at work until the age of sixty. Pensions were linked with the cost of living: that is to say, they were to be calculated in relation to the wages currently in force and not to those which the pensioner received when in employment. In practice, the contributions collected by the National Welfare Institute were always greatly in excess of the annual amount needed for the payment of pensions and administrative expenses. In 1954, for example, revenue totalled 9,645 million pesos, while only 3,236 million was disbursed.[49] The Institute's surplus was regularly loaned to the state against Social Welfare Bonds (*Bonos de Previsión Social*, bearing 4 per cent interest until July 1954 and 5 per cent thereafter). In this manner large sums became available to the Government for the financing of its public works programmes and for compensating the losses incurred by state-owned enterprises. In 1954 a pension scheme for employers and independent workers was introduced,[50] making it obligatory for all such persons over the age of eighteen to contribute 10 per cent of their earnings. In the same year the national pension system was expanded to cover rural labour, the employer's contribution being fixed

[48] For the text of the Pensions Reform Law see *R.R.P.*, 8 Oct. 1954, pp. 41–55.
[49] Ibid. 10 May 1955, p. 13.
[50] Ibid. 19 Oct. 1954, pp. 25–30 and 31 Dec. 1954, p. 27.

at 7 per cent and the worker's at 5 per cent.[51] From the beginning of 1955, therefore, virtually the whole of Argentina's population—numbering at that time about 18·7 million—were assured of financial assistance in their old age. (If the money could be found.) The importance of the pension system, of course, was not only in the benefits that it conferred upon the aged but also in the fact that it absorbed and redistributed—by means of the Government's development projects—a substantial proportion of the national income.

Perón made many attempts to stabilize the cost of living, and although his efforts were only partly—or only temporarily—successful, they were appreciated in particular by the poorer sections of the community. Frequently he used threats, and sometimes fines and imprisonment, to induce manufacturers, merchants, and shopkeepers to lower their prices. Eventually the inflation, combined with and intensified by a deterioration in the balance of trade, caused him to modify his attitude towards workers and employers, industry and agriculture. The effects of this change in outlook were far-reaching.

During 1952 the Argentine economy suffered from a severe drought (the second in three years); in the shops and markets there was a shortage of some kinds of food—notably, meat—and of foreign manufactured articles; speculation increased and prices rose. The 1952 balance of trade showed a deficit of 3,969 million pesos,[52] and the cost of living continued to mount until in February 1953 the index figure, on the basis of 1943 = 100, reached 615.[53] In this critical situation Perón made two main adjustments to his policy. Recognizing, rather belatedly, that industrial expansion (which was so dependent on imports of machinery, fuel, and raw materials, and therefore on the availability of foreign currency) must be slowed down pending a revival of

[51] Ibid. 31 Jan. 1955, p. 9.
[52] Bank of London & South America, *Fortnightly Review*, 17 Apr. 1954, p. 242.   [53] Ibid. 17 Oct. 1953, p. 693.

pastoral and agricultural exports, he suspended the provision of credit to industry and commerce, while allowing the banks still to grant credit facilities to farmers. Indeed, a depression in urban industry and commerce was deliberately fostered by the Government in the hope that unemployment would drive workers back to the land, from which in recent years they had been attracted to the fast-developing cities.[54] In the second place, Perón abandoned his habit of almost unreservedly supporting the workers' demands against their employers. Not only prices but also (and more effectively) wages were now 'frozen'—the latter for a period of two years. To counterbalance to some extent the power of the manual workers represented in the General Confederation of Labour, a separate federation was created for 'white collar' workers; and the formation of a series of employers' associations—grouped as the Confederación General Económica—was officially initiated. Thus, while Perón continued to express his concern for the welfare of the *descamisados*—and especially for the 'submerged ones', *los sumergidos*—his speeches on economic affairs became noticeably more sober and orthodox. He frequently ex-

[54] The effect of the discouragement of urban industry will be seen in the following table:

ECONOMICALLY ACTIVE POPULATION

	1947		*1954*		*Per cent difference of 1954 in relation to 1947*
	No. (*'ooo*)	*Per cent of general total*	*No.* (*'ooo*)	*Per cent of general total*	
Agriculture, &c.	1,622	10·3	1,770	9·4	+ 9·1
Manufacturing industry, building, and mining	1,827	11·6	1,701	9·1	− 6·9
Trade and commerce	1,071	6·8	1,230	6·6	+14·8
Other activities*	1,747	11·0	2,899	15·5	+66·0

* Consisted of the professions, government service, transport, communications, domestic service, &c.

(SOURCE: *R.R.P.*, 18 Feb. 1955, p. 12.)

horted the workers to increase their output (which had shown a tendency to decline), and he told them that in future they must settle their wage claims by negotiation with the employers' associations. When he first came to power (Perón said), prevailing conditions had made it necessary for him to assist the workers in their struggle for 'social justice'; but they were now able to defend themselves.

This important new trend in government policy caused surprise among those who had not taken seriously the rather verbose and imprecise Peronista 'philosophy' of *justicialismo*, which in recent years had been expounded in countless speeches and publications. The basis of 'justicialist philosophy' was never more clearly expressed, perhaps, than in the following presidential assertion:

For us there is nothing fixed and nothing to deny. We are anti-Communist because Communists are sectarians, and anti-capitalist because capitalists are sectarians. Our Third Position is not a central position. It is an ideological position which is in the centre, on the right or on the left, according to specific circumstances.[55]

The need for such 'fluidity' was explained by Perón and his technical adviser, Raúl Mende, as being the result of the fact that there were four conflicting forces in human society: materialism and idealism, individualism and collectivism. Each of the four forces had a useful function to perform; but none of them should be allowed to become too powerful; none of the four must be suppressed; nor should any two of them be permitted to combine to dominate the national life. The unique merit of *justicialismo* was said to be that it constituted 'a doctrine whose objective is the happiness of man in human society achieved through the harmony of materialist and spiritual, individualist and collectivist forces, each valued in a Christian way.'[56] The doctrine was re-

[55] Quoted by Blanksten, p. 292.
[56] Raúl A. Mende, *El Justicialismo: Doctrina y Realidad Peronista* (1950), p. 106.

ceived with little enthusiasm by the majority of Argentines
—except in regard to foreign affairs—but it was useful as a
standard vindication of Perón's habit of playing off one
section of the community against another in turn: for example, the *descamisados* and the industrialists against the
landowning 'oligarchy' and army officers; the general public against the industrialists, merchants, and shopkeepers;
and later (for reasons indicated in this chapter), the employers against the workers.

The second Five Year Plan, passed by Congress in December 1952,[57] was even more ambitious and varied than
its predecessor: its text contained the expression of aspirations and principles which were intended to guide the
people and their rulers for generations to come. More important than the 500-page Plan itself, however, was the
executive's interpretation of its clauses in the years immediately following its publication, during which time a
system of priorities was established which coincided with
the change of emphasis in President Perón's general policy
referred to in the foregoing pages.

Each section of the second Plan was divided into three
parts: (1) the elaboration of a 'fundamental objective' (for
example, the ultimate aim of education was to be 'to realize
the moral, intellectual and physical formation of the people
on the basis of national Peronista doctrine');[58] (2) a statement of the general ways and means required for achieving
the 'fundamental objective'; and (3) a list of the practical
measures to be completed by 31 December 1957. These
practical measures were to involve an expenditure of
33,500 million pesos during the five-year period.[59] In practice, the most important clauses of the Plan proved to be

[57] For the text see Argentina, Presidencia, *Segundo Plan Quinquenal* (1953).
Extensive extracts were published in an English translation over a period of
months in *R.R.P.*, 9 Dec. 1952–20 Mar. 1953.

[58] *R.R.P.*, 9 Dec. 1952, p. 5.

[59] At the beginning of 1955 authorized expenditure was increased to
34,524 million pesos (Bank of London & South America, *Fortnightly Review*,
19 Feb. 1955, p. 91).

those which were designed to increase the production of petroleum and electric power, agricultural and pastoral commodities, tractors and other agricultural machinery, and the development of transport and communications.

In the carrying out of the second Five Year Plan particular attention was given to petroleum, for which the demand was constantly growing as a consequence of industrialization and agricultural mechanization. The 'fundamental objective' in this department was that the country should be rendered self-sufficient in fuel; and although at the end of 1953 Argentina was still producing only about 42 per cent of her petroleum requirements,[60] considerable progress was already made in that year. In 1953 the national output of crude petroleum amounted to 4,530,000 cubic metres, which represented an increase of 15 per cent over the preceding year. More than three-quarters of that total was produced by the Yacimientos Petrolíferos Fiscales ('Y.P.F.'—the 'State Oilfields') from the oilfields of Comodoro Rivadavia in Patagonia (which were the main source), Plaza Huincul (Neuquén), Salta, and Mendoza.[61] The second Five Year Plan also provided for the expansion of oil-refining plant and of the means of transporting petroleum from the oilfields: refining in 1953 showed an increase of 8 per cent over the previous year.[62] The backwardness of petroleum production in Argentina—which caused a corresponding high expenditure of foreign currency on fuel imports[63]—had resulted from a narrowly nationalist policy

[60] U.N., E.C.L.A., *Economic Survey of Latin America, 1953* (1954), p. 237.

[61] *R.R.P.*, 11 May 1954, p. 7. In addition to these domestic supplies of crude oil, a pipeline, inaugurated in 1949, brought natural gas from Comodoro Rivadavia to Buenos Aires, a distance of some 1,800 kilometres.

[62] E.C.L.A., *Economic Survey, 1953*, p. 237.

[63] Argentine fuel imports in 1954 were as follows:

	Tons		Tons
Fuel oil	2,172,421	Brought forward	6,258,566
Crude petroleum	3,678,436	Kerosene	41,077
Aviation spirit	40,531	Coal	1,403,644
Diesel oil	67,932	Coke	24,323
Gas oil	276,113	Anthracite	14,900
Petrol	23,133		
Carried forward	6,258,566		7,742,510

(*R.R.P.*, 21 Jan. 1955, p. 25.) About two-thirds of Argentina's petroleum

which had denied to foreign companies a reasonable opportunity to explore and exploit the very substantial local resources. With the introduction of the second Five Year Plan, President Perón set about changing this situation. In August 1953 a law was passed with the purpose of attracting foreign capital for the financing of industry, and especially of the petroleum industry. This law established that foreign capital might enter Argentina for Government-approved projects in the form either of liquid funds or of equipment; that after two years the foreign investor would be entitled to remit annually to the country of origin profits up to 8 per cent of the registered capital; and that the capital itself might be repatriated in instalments after the expiry of ten years.[64] When seeking to justify this revision of policy towards foreign capital, President Perón argued: 'The Government has arrived at the conclusion that it is necessary to extract rapidly all the petroleum from our own subsoil, by any means compatible with the Constitution which we ourselves submitted to the people's approval, and which assures us the ownership of the oil and its marketing.'[65] In other words, the nationalists were promised that the foreign companies would act not as proprietors but as contractors, selling their output to the state for distribution.

In accordance with his new trend of stimulating agriculture and livestock-raising, Perón in the second Five Year Plan and in his subsequent pronouncements was now at pains to reassure the landowning 'oligarchy' regarding agrarian reform. In the past, Peronistas had talked rather wildly about their intentions of expropriating the large estates and dividing them up among the *descamisados*; but the second Plan went no further than to declare that assistance would be given to tenant farmers to purchase the land that

imports usually came from the sterling area (E.C.L.A., *Economic Survey, 1953*, p. 237).

[64] An English translation of the foreign investment law (No. 14,222) and additional regulations was published as a supplement to the Bank of London & South America's *Fortnightly Review*, 12 Dec. 1953.

[65] *R.R.P.*, 11 May 1954, p. 8.

they cultivated if they wished to do so,[66] though there was a vague reference to settlement on lands 'which do not fulfil their social function'.[67] A Colonization Law passed in December 1954 was equally mild.[68]

Throughout the year 1954 President Perón, anxious to create conditions of stability which would favour an increase in production, frequently expressed his solicitude for 'private enterprise'. In August 1954 *The Review of the River Plate* reported one of his more illuminating statements on this subject:

The President emphasized the difference between the First Five Year Plan, in which the State itself undertook the execution of a vast number of public works, and the Second, in which this aspect of the Plan accounts for only a small proportion of the whole, whereas the State will support, through credit schemes, private initiative, as in the case of housing construction, or will proceed to hand over to private enterprise the industries created by the State as soon as they become economically productive. The two plans, he asserted, had been drawn up bearing in mind the special circumstances attendant on their respective periods of application, with a view to fostering national activity in all its aspects. 'A plan of a certain nature cannot be followed by another of a similar character.' As a rule, a stimulating plan must be followed by a period of capitalization.[69]

Business men were heartened by this unexpectedly encouraging exhibition of the doctrine of *justicialismo* in application, and there was a noticeable increase in Perón's following among the middle class.[70] In 1954 Arthur P. Whitaker expressed the opinion that by that date 'even

[66] An instance of this policy was the publication of a decree in December 1954 announcing that agricultural land in Patagonia *owned by the State* would be sold to those who had occupied and developed it for ten years. Buyers would be granted a 50 per cent rebate on the official valuation of the land and in certain cases deferred payment up to 25 years would be allowed (Bank of London & South America, *Fortnightly Review*, 8 Jan. 1955, p. 4).

[67] *R.R.P.*, 9 Dec. 1952, p. 32.   [68] Ibid. 21 Jan. 1955, pp. 5–7.

[69] Ibid. 31 Aug. 1954, p. 7.

[70] As a result of the deflationary policy, drastic import restrictions, and good weather, which produced a bumper 1952–3 harvest, there was a marked improvement in economic conditions during 1953. The balance of trade showed a favourable trend:

among Perón opponents the majority now endorse his changes [i.e. his reforms] in principle, though not in many of their current applications', and he was convinced that the social welfare system, the extension of the powers of the national Government, and the organization of labour effected during Perón's rule would survive a change of régime.[71] Even the conservative Bolsa de Comercio de Buenos Aires (the Stock Exchange) in its annual report for 1954 indicated its approval of Perón's general economic policy. The authors of the report considered that Argentina was 'in a stronger position than many [primary producing] countries, since here, thanks to the action of I.A.P.I., the primary producer is protected from the adversities implicit in the trend of international prices for the commodities that he produces, while the Government's forward-looking industrialization policy of the past decade or so has gone far towards reducing Argentina's former dependence on imported supplies of consumer goods'.[72] In this phase of his régime Perón even went so far as to begin negotiating a contract with a subsidiary of the Standard Oil Company of

---

	Imports	Exports	Balance
	(in million of *pesos*)		
1952	8,361	4,392	−3,969
1953	5,655	7,107	+1,452

(Bank of London & South America, *Fortnightly Review*, 17 Apr. 1954, p. 242.)

By June 1953 the cost of living index had dropped from the February peak figure of 615 to 575·9 (ibid. 17 Oct. 1953, p. 693).

In spite of the President's refusal to intervene in the numerous wage disputes which broke out during the first half of 1954, the workers in general remained loyal to the régime, which they still looked upon as their own; and in April 1954 the Peronistas won another convincing victory in elections for the partial renewal of Congress. In June and July of that year new agreements for higher wages were reached between the employers' associations and the trade unions, thus ending the 1952 two-year 'freeze'; and, to preserve the equilibrium, President Perón assured the employers that a corresponding rise in prices would be permitted, when necessary. In February 1955 a decree was published authorizing the Ministry of Commerce to place the sum of 300 million pesos at the disposal of the meat-packing companies to cover operating losses during 1954 caused by circumstances affecting the industry as a whole. This measure was in fact introduced to ensure the payment of the scales of wages and allowances fixed in the labour contracts of 1954 (ibid. 5 Mar. 1955, pp. 127–8).

[71] *U.S. and Argentina*, p. 252.   [72] *R.R.P.*, 22 Apr. 1955, p. 17.

California for the urgently-needed exploitation of petroleum resources in Patagonia. This enabled his Radical enemy, Dr Arturo Frondizi, to accuse him of preparing an agreement that would permit Yankee imperialists to create 'a wide colonial zone' across the southern part of the country. Military officers maintained that in reality Perón was authorizing the establishment of 'foreign bases' on Argentine soil.

Although, to meet new emergencies, Perón from time to time was compelled to change the emphasis in his immediate policy, yet he always professed that 'social justice' and 'economic independence' were his main concern. And he clung to certain theories of government which had attracted him early in his career. For example, during his period of service in Italy Perón had become a believer in Syndicalism and the Corporate State; and although he was prevented by circumstances from putting his Syndicalist proposals immediately and fully into practice, yet the influence of Mussolini's teaching was repeatedly apparent in his declarations of policy and in his actions. Thus when addressing a group of labour delegates in 1951, he assured them: 'We are moving towards the Syndicalist State, the ancient aspiration of the human community, in which all will be represented in the Legislature and in the Administration by their own people.'[73] In December of that year, in accordance with the President's convictions, the new Presidente Perón province[74] was in fact given a Syndicalist constitution which decreed that one-half of the members of the provincial legislature should be chosen by the electorate while the other half were to be representatives of trades and occupations. This predilection for corporate methods was then reflected in the creation of the Confederación General

[73] Ibid. 18 July 1952, p. 11.
[74] In July 1951 the federal territories of El Chaco and La Pampa were promoted to the rank of federal provinces, under the names Presidente Perón Province and Eva Perón Province. Their former names were restored after the revolution of September 1955.

Económica—although on this occasion, as always, Perón's motives were practical as well as 'ideological': he aimed at stimulating production by calling in the employers to participate in national economic planning, whereby, moreover, he hoped to broaden and stabilize the foundations of his régime.

Perón was also convinced of the usefulness of Co-operatives, and he returned to this subject again and again. In 1951 he said that his Government intended that

agricultural and pastoral farming production should be totally in the hands of the actual producers and this would only be achieved when the co-operative organizations covered the whole country and protected production, from the land to the consumer, Argentine or foreign, replacing the State [i.e. I.A.P.I.] in the commercialization process which should now be realized

and Perón added that I.A.P.I. had been merely the first step towards the transferring of the marketing of the country's produce from the hands of intermediaries to those of the producers themselves. The credits granted to Co-operatives by official banks increased tenfold in the five years 1948–52, and the 1952 figure was doubled in 1953. By the year 1952 there were some 2,000 Co-operatives in existence with a total of more than 800,000 members, and in 1953 the list of grain exporters included, for the first time, the names of co-operative concerns.[75] Government support took the form not only of credits, but also of the preferential distribution to Co-operatives of scarce commodities such as burlap sacks, tractors, and other farm machinery.[76] At a Co-operative Congress at Buenos Aires in 1954 the delegates recommended 'the stimulation of "production co-operatives" in all sectors of the national economy, with a view to the eventual replacement of salaried labour by associated workmen'.[77]

[75] *R.R.P.*, 28 Aug. 1953, pp. 7–8.
[76] E.C.L.A., *Economic Survey, 1953*, p. 150.
[77] *R.R.P.*, 11 June 1954, pp. 16–17. An important instance of this tendency occurred in May 1955, when a large area of land in the Province of

16 JUNE 1955 AND AFTER

In previous pages it has been demonstrated that adverse economic events compelled Perón to modify and moderate his policy; to reduce his concessions to the C.G.T. (General Confederation of Labour); to widen the basis of his régime by adopting a more orthodox programme, which would gain the approval of the managerial classes; and thereby to create conditions of stability that would be likely to attract foreign investors. From the middle of 1953 onwards, it was mainly in his efforts to crush the opposition of the Catholic Church that Perón continued to show his former intransigence. As it grew more bitter, this quarrel with the Church produced an atmosphere of unrest which encouraged other opponents to attempt a coup d'état.

In the cloudy winter's afternoon of 16 June 1955 successive groups of naval aircraft appeared over the centre of Buenos Aires and dropped a large number of bombs, the chief target being the presidential office in the old pink Government House (the Casa Rosada) in the Plaza de Mayo. The attack on this building from the air was synchronized with an assault by land from the near-by Ministry of the Navy. The Casa Rosada was seriously damaged, but poor visibility interfered with the airmen's aim, and many bombs fell in the streets. As the vicinity of the Plaza de Mayo was crowded with traffic and pedestrians, several hundred civilians were killed and many more wounded by the bombing and machine-gunning. Shortly before the first attack, Perón had left his office and had entered the Ministry of the Army, which now became the headquarters from which the Government's defence was organized by the Minister of the Army, General Franklin Lucero. The army

---

Misiones which formerly belonged to the Bemberg Group was sold by the State to a workers' Co-operative. Ten per cent of the price was to be paid within 90 days, and the rest in twenty-four equal yearly instalments. The chief crop on this estate was yerba mate (Bank of London & South America, *Fortnightly Review*, 28 May 1955, p. 317). The entire property of the Bemberg Group—until that time Argentina's largest commercial and industrial combine—had been nationalized in 1953 for alleged tax evasion.

leaders—with their traditional horror of civil war—apparently had convinced Perón that it would be unwise and unnecessary for him to summon the C.G.T. to throw its loyal *descamisados* into the resistance.[78] The suppression of the revolt was therefore left exclusively to the army. Anti-aircraft guns, troops, tanks, and artillery were quickly brought into action against the rebels, and before nightfall the insurgent land forces had surrendered, while the rebel aircraft were seeking asylum in accordance with custom, in the neighbouring republic of Uruguay. During the evening of 16 June, parties of Peronista hooligans set fire to several of the finest churches and to other religious institutions in the capital, as though wreaking vengeance against the Catholics for having fostered the development of the revolutionary situation. Perón at once disowned these acts of arson; appealed to the *descamisados* for restraint; and seemed to be glad of the opportunity to make it clear that he now wished to end his dispute with the Church, whom he was careful not to accuse of direct participation in the revolt. A delegation from the C.G.T. formally thanked the army for having restored order.

It was immediately evident that the leaders of the insurrection were high officials of the navy. Argentine naval officers generally came from liberal, middle-class families. They are traditionally unpolitical and have been inclined to disapprove of the army's constant participation in politics. The Argentine Navy was founded by an audacious Irish seaman, Admiral William Brown, who played a prominent part in the River Plate during the war of independence against Spain;[79] and while local army officers have come under the influence of German instructors, Argentine naval officers have travelled more widely and have been on friendly terms with their British and United States colleagues. They acted against Perón's authoritarian

[78] Subsequent events indicated, however, that the *descamisados* might not have responded to his call.
[79] For a biographical sketch of Admiral Brown see M. G. Mullhall, *The English in South America* (1878), pp. 144–69.

military government on 16 June because they disliked it; and because they considered Perón's campaign against the Catholic Church to be a final and intolerable provocation. But they over-estimated the support that they would receive from the other diverse sections of the opposition.

Although it had been expected by foreign journalists that the army, being now in supreme power, would refuse to recognize the continued leadership of the Government by Perón (whose favouring of the workers some officers had always deprecated), no military officer stepped forward to take his place. The Peronista Party and the C.G.T., although long accustomed to displaying their strength in public in times of emergency, still agreed to respect the President's request that they should leave the maintenance of order in the hands of the army. Thereupon Perón—perhaps as a tactical move; or pressed, perhaps, by his military and economic advisers—resumed with ever greater emphasis his policy of moderation.

The President announced his decisions day by day, leaving his supporters and opponents to draw their own conclusions. He accepted the resignation of Ministers who had been closely associated with the most extreme Peronista measures—such as Angel Gabriel Borlenghi, Minister of the Interior and Justice; Armando Méndez San Martín, Minister of Education; and Raúl Alejandro Apold, Under-Secretary of Information of the Presidency. (The outgoing Ministers were replaced by somewhat obscure Peronistas.) Radical and Catholic prisoners were released from gaol. On 5 July Perón asked his followers to show their good will and party discipline by observing a truce in the party struggle.[80] A week later, taking advantage of the official declarations regarding conciliation and pacification, a group of Catholics announced the foundation of the Argentine Christian Democratic Party,[81] but the hierarchy tactfully renounced any connexion with this new organization in a document wherein they stated: 'The Argentine Episcopate has not

[80] *The Times*, 6 July 1955.   [81] Ibid. 14 July 1955.

accepted, nor can it ever accept, any understanding with any political party to defend the liberties and the rights of the Church against the legitimate Government of the nation in any case, even if persecution and oppression continued.'[82] On 15 July Perón told representatives of Congress that he intended to resign his leadership of the Peronista Party. According to an official communiqué, he said:

A new phase of constitutional character without revolutions is now starting because the country cannot be in a permanent state of revolution. How does this affect me? The answer is simple: I cease to be head of a revolution in order to become President of all Argentines—friends and foes. I must put an end to all limitations imposed on the ways and behaviour of our opponents. Henceforth they will act freely within the law with all guarantees, rights and freedoms.

That is proper, and that is what we shall do. They will be allowed to reassemble their forces and challenge the political forces of our movement within limitations imposed by good manners, decency, and the need for appeasement. Let them say whether they want pacification in a friendly way. If they refuse, we will do it by ourselves. Henceforth the Government will act merely as a Government, and politics will be left in the hands of political organizations.[83]

Following the publication of this statement, other Government officials reluctantly were persuaded to resign their membership of the superior council of the Peronista Party. On 27 July, to the general astonishment, the Radical leader, Dr Arturo Frondizi, was allowed to broadcast to the nation. In his message Frondizi fearlessly criticized the Government, but also he informed the Conservatives that his own party were not willing to return to the state of affairs that prevailed under Conservative rule before 1943 'which they [the Radicals] had fought for thirteen years and which had led to the present situation'. He only mentioned the Roman Catholic question to say that there should be freedom of religion. The correspondent of *The Times* in Buenos Aires commented:

[82] *New York Times*, 14 July 1955.   [83] *Manchester Guardian*, 16 July 1955.

When President Perón proposed pacification, many people thought it might be an astute way of weakening and dividing the Opposition. This impression will be increased by Dr Frondizi's message, because of his attacks on the Conservatives and his omission to mention the sufferings of the Roman Catholic Church.[84]

Frondizi refused to conciliate other sectors of the opposition or to compromise with anyone. He rather arrogantly demanded the full restoration of constitutional government; the repeal of all laws and police edicts suppressing freedom; equal freedom of the press for all, and freedom to speak for all parties. But it was evident, once again, that Argentina was not yet ready for complete democracy. Even the slight relaxation of control allowed in the weeks following the June revolt had resulted in an increase in political tension and rioting.

Indeed, the troubled months of Argentina's 1955 winter revealed that, whatever other consequences there might be of his long rule, under Perón the old political jealousies, far from being abandoned for the sake of forming a united opposition to the régime, had been nourished. By 'playing off' group against group; by adopting, and adapting to his own needs, some of the favourite theories of one party and another; by persuading prominent men from opposing factions to join him; by using the turbulent force of the trade unions as a threat—Perón had maintained a state of disunity in the nation which only a 'strong man', a caudillo, could hope to dominate. Effective pacification now was obviously out of the question, and on 31 August the President addressed the assembled masses in the Plaza de Mayo, Buenos Aires, and authorized them to suppress the enemies of the régime by violence if necessary. Shortly afterwards the General Confederation of Labour announced that arms would be issued to the workers for this purpose. But Perón had spread disunion more widely than he knew; and the military revolution which broke out on 16 September 1955 showed that even the much-purged army was far from being

[84] *The Times*, 29 July 1955.

united in his support. To forestall the forming of the trade unions into a virtual militia, General Eduardo Lonardi and other retired or disgruntled officers led the chief provincial garrisons to rise in rebellion, while Admiral Isaac Rojas brought rebel warships from the naval base at Puerto Belgrano (Bahía Blanca) to blockade the Plata estuary. Thus encircled, Buenos Aires alone remained under the Government's domination; and on 19 September Perón offered to resign.[85] He then sought refuge on a Paraguayan gunboat that was in Buenos Aires harbour and, in accordance with Latin American practice, claimed the right of political asylum. A fortnight later he was allowed to travel into exile.

Some of the reasons for Perón's downfall have already been indicated. Other reasons became apparent after the event. Important factors were, first, the determination of nationalist officers in the armed forces to prevent the granting of concessions to the Standard Oil Company and, second, the indignation felt by many proud Argentines at the abundant evidence of corruption in Perón's entourage. Graft had always existed in Argentine government circles, but the Peróns vastly enlarged the field by bringing commerce and industry more and more under state control. Neither the beneficiaries of Rosas's largesse in land nor Irigoyen's corrupt hangers-on had ever envisaged such opportunities for personal enrichment as were provided by I.A.P.I. and the Eva Perón Social Aid Foundation. The reaction was correspondingly whole-hearted: Argentina has rarely been governed as honourably as in the years that followed Perón's departure.

[85] In the first edition of this book it was stated that Perón 'resigned the presidency'. Subsequently the late G. A. Hinkson—highly-respected Buenos Aires correspondent of *The Times*—pointed out to the author that Perón in fact never did resign. On 19 September he merely wrote a rather ambiguous letter in which he suggested that he might withdraw from the scene to facilitate a settlement and avoid further bloodshed. Perón's letter was published in facsimile in the newspaper *Noticias Gráficas* (Buenos Aires), 20 Sept. 1955. Hinkson commented: 'It seems that he still hoped that he might worm his way back to power, as he did in 1945.'

Chapter VII

AFTER PERÓN

THE September 1955 revolution—like so many earlier up-risings, including the movement which overthrew Rosas in 1852—was planned in, and directed from, the provinces.[1] The rebel headquarters were at the old university city of Córdoba, where Perón's campaign against the Church had aroused the greatest opposition. The revolutionary leader, General Lonardi, was a devout Catholic. When he entered Buenos Aires in triumph to be inaugurated as provisional President of the republic, the Papal flag was flown side by side with that of Argentina, and the aircraft passing over Government House took the form of the cross followed by the letter V. Lonardi's slogan was *Christus vincit*. Admiral Rojas became vice-president. Lonardi appointed a Government consisting mainly of Catholic nationalists; but real power remained with a group of military leaders. When, at the beginning of October 1955, the present author went to interview Lonardi, the corridors and ante-chambers of Government House were crowded with officers, priests, and *Cordobeses*, who had come to the capital to seek favours. Soon the anti-clerical Radicals—who had suffered more than anyone else during Perón's rule, while the Church officially was still supporting the régime—began pressing for the removal of Catholics and 'reactionaries' from the administration.

Lonardi's first speeches were high-minded and concilia-tory. 'Ni vencedores, ni vencidos', he said, in the hope that he might unite the whole Argentine people for the good of all. He promised freedom of speech and assembly, liberty

[1] cf. Arthur P. Whitaker, *Argentine Upheaval* (1956), pp. 28–29.

for the trade unions to conduct their own affairs, and free elections to be held in about six months' time. His military associates, however, would not agree to the bringing of the Peronistas into the national fold: the country must be purged of every trace of Peronismo. Lonardi was soon obliged to modify his policy.[2]

Already the anti-Peronista measures had been quite severe. Congress had been dissolved and Peronista deputies arrested for interrogation; persons connected with the Perón régime had been dismissed from the federal and provincial administrations and from universities, law courts, and embassies abroad; government commissioners had been placed in charge of the newspapers and radio stations; it had been announced that the agreement with the Standard Oil Company would be cancelled and the I.A.P.I. trading organization liquidated. Government, of course, was by decree.

As the anti-Peronista measures multiplied, they provoked riots in working-class quarters, with the result that the military junta at Government House complained that Lonardi was still behaving too leniently towards the basically Peronista trade unions. He was also criticized for not dismissing some officers in the army who had served loyally under Perón. Democrats in the armed forces and outside considered that Lonardi's Catholic entourage had no real desire to establish democracy, which, after all, was one of the principal aims of the revolution. This dissatisfaction culminated in a palace coup on 13 November 1955, when Lonardi was deposed by the military junta, his place being taken by General Pedro Aramburu. Admiral Rojas remained vice-president. Thus did the brief provincial incursion come to an end. The *Cordobeses* returned to their hills.

[2] In the course of an interview on 11 October 1955 the author asked Lonardi: 'Will your government allow complete freedom to all political parties, including the Peronista Party, in the forthcoming elections?' The President replied: 'All parties will enjoy the fullest freedom.' He then qualified his reply by adding: 'But these guarantees will not benefit the supporters of totalitarianism, or those who make excuses for the deposed régime.'

Aramburu at once set to work to intensify the 'de-Peronization' of the country. The Peronista workers knew that they could now only expect violent repression; so they, too, became more violent. Aramburu broke a general strike by sending troops into the industrial districts. He placed *interventores* in charge of the unions. He arrested hundreds of working-class leaders, military officers, and Catholics, who were accused of subversive activities. Many of them were shipped to detention camps in southern Patagonia. The proscription of the Peronista Party was decreed. In June 1956 an attempt by several military garrisons to overthrow the Government was quickly crushed, and although it had long been a matter for pride in Argentina that the Constitution of 1853 had abolished the death penalty 'for ever', a number of the rebels were court-martialled and summarily shot by firing-squads. The increasing severity distressed many even of those Argentines who had been prominent in the movement against Perón. Ernesto Sábato, for example, in a book published in 1956 appealed for

a national reconciliation based on an understanding of all classes, a new meaning for the word 'liberty' (formerly so glibly pronounced but not practised by the political parties), a return of the unions to the workers, a cessation of persecutions and the feeling of revenge, a recognition that *all* Argentines were responsible for the rise of Perón to power, and a respect for the anti-Peronista (the anti-Peronista millions being as much a part of the country as the Peronista masses).[3]

Perón's Constitution of 1949 had been cancelled in May 1956, and the Constitution of 1853 reinstated—but it needed to be adjusted to modern conditions. Election of a Constituent Assembly therefore took place in July 1957. The poll was headed by the two rival factions into which the Radical Party was split. The moderate faction received 2·1 million votes. The left-wing group, led by Dr Arturo Frondizi, polled 1·8 million. Blank votes numbered 2·1

[3] From Fritz L. Hoffmann's review of Sábato's *El otro rostro del Peronismo* (Buenos Aires, Imprenta López) in *H.A.H.R.*, May 1959, p. 219.

million, and it was generally believed that most of these were cast by Peronistas who, their own party being illegal, had no other means of demonstrating their strength. The Constituent Assembly was dissolved without having reached any decisions.

Aramburu had promised that elections for the presidency and Congress would be held in February 1958; that no members of his own *de facto* Government would be eligible for election; and that he would surrender power to the successful candidate, no matter who he might be. Aramburu did his utmost to persuade the politicians to behave with a greater sense of responsibility than they were displaying in their reckless, vote-seeking speeches. He particularly disapproved of the manner in which Frondizi was propounding Peronista policies in an endeavour to gain the support of the 2 million voters who had cast blank ballots in the previous year. The elections were duly held on 23 February. Polling was free—except that, once more, the Peronista Party was not allowed to participate. From his refuge in the Dominican Republic, Perón instructed his followers to vote for Frondizi, who, it was understood, had indicated that he would give the Peronistas a fair deal if he won the presidency. With this assistance, Frondizi obtained 4·1 million votes and an overwhelming victory over the rival Radicals (2·6 million). Because of the victor's Peronista connexion, some members of the military junta tried to persuade Aramburu to refuse to hand over the presidency. But Aramburu, again, was true to his word, and Frondizi was inaugurated on 1 May 1958.

FRONDIZI

Frondizi—the son of an Italian who settled in Argentina during the great migration from Italy in the 1890's—was born in the province of Corrientes in 1908. A lawyer by training, he was involved in politics while still a student, joining the Irigoyen branch of the Radical Party.[4] He

[4] See above, p. 71.

rapidly became a leading Radical personality; fearlessly attacked Perón; and was equally bitter in his attacks on the Conservative 'oligarchs'.[5]

When the results of the February 1958 elections were announced, Frondizi declared that he would govern, not for any one party, but for the nation. It was evident that he intended to try to bring the Peronistas back into the community. Soon after his inauguration, he ordered a general wage increase of 60 per cent., granted amnesty to Peronistas who were in prison or exile for political offences, and enabled Peronistas to regain influential positions in the trade unions and the judiciary. The military leaders objected to these concessions and began to force him to adopt a harsher policy. Stage by stage, but not without resistance, he gave in to their pressure.

It is unnecessary to continue to follow political developments in detail. Politically, Frondizi was faced with the dilemma that so often has confronted public-spirited civilian statesmen in Argentina: on the one hand, he seriously wished to establish the principle of government accountability to the people; on the other hand, he knew that he only held office by permission of the military. In March 1962 he authorized the *Justicialistas*—i.e. the followers of Perón—to nominate their own candidates for the congressional and provincial elections, which they had not been allowed to do since Perón's downfall. He underestimated their strength. At the elections the *Justicialistas* won more than half of the available seats in the Chamber of Deputies and the majority of the provincial governorships, including that of Buenos Aires. The military leaders, fearing that Frondizi would permit the revival of Peronismo to continue, deposed him from the presidency and imprisoned him on the island of Martín García in the Río de la Plata, a naval base which the military had used as a prison for President Irigoyen

[5] See above, p. 102.

when they overthrew him in 1930[6] and for Colonel
Perón when he was becoming too popular with the masses
in 1945[7]. After the removal of Frondizi a decree was issued
annulling the March elections. Thus a suggestion that the
military hierarchy were no longer interested in taking
command of government[8] proved premature.

ECONOMIC RECONSTRUCTION

Much of the unrest in Argentina in the later months of the
Perón régime and in the years that followed arose from the
deterioration in the nation's economy; and the unrest, in
turn, hampered the endeavours of successive governments
to solve the economic problems.

Most of the problems were not suddenly created: their origin was in the course taken by Argentina's development in
the past, and in certain physical deficiencies of the country.
But the troubles were aggravated in a considerable degree
by Perón and the Peronistas. The manner in which these
various factors combined to bring about the economic crisis
of 1955–60 can be indicated in a few paragraphs.

The conservative classes for many years had opposed
industrialization—such as the establishment of a steel industry. Argentina, therefore, continued to be much too
dependent on the exporting of primary products. But the
carrying out of Perón's plans for diversifying the economy—
for example, by the construction of a steel plant at San
Nicolás—was slowed down by the inadequacy of export
earnings to pay for the importing of machinery and raw
materials. Often, too, his industrial projects were vitiated
by needless extravagance, and corruption.

[6] See above, p. 73.   [7] See above, p. 101.
[8] John J. Kennedy, 'Accountable Government in Argentina', *Foreign
Affairs*, Apr. 1959, p. 458. For an opinion on the changing character of the
officer corps in Latin America generally, see John J. Johnson, *Political
Change in Latin America* (1958).

There were three main reasons for the decline in export earnings:

1. Landowners in general (though there were many honourable exceptions) had failed to adopt the modern agricultural techniques which would have raised production and increased surpluses for export; and Perón, using export profits to finance his industrial programme, discouraged agricultural improvement, until the drought of 1952 forced him to reconsider his economic priorities.[9]

2. The terms of trade (1950 = 100) declined from 144 in 1948 to 88 in 1955. The adverse trend continued thereafter,[10] emphasizing the vulnerability of the agriculturally-based economy.

3. The growth in the population and Perón's effective raising of the standard of living of the urban working class[11] caused an increase in the local consumption of the traditional export products—notably, meat—thereby reducing the amount available for export.[12]

Thus the value of exports, in million U.S. dollars, fell from the 1947 total of 1,613 to a 1955 total of 929.[13]

The Central Bank's gold and foreign exchange reserves shrank from nearly U.S. $1,700 million in 1946[14] to U.S. $457 million in December 1955.[15]

[9] See above, pp. 125 ff.

[10] Bank of London & South America, *The Economic Situation in Argentina*, Sept. 1959, p. 45.

[11] 'It is frequently maintained in Argentina that the economic position of the working classes has not improved, but such is not the case. There has been a definite improvement. . . . During the past decade, according to national statistics, the real income of industrial workers increased by 37 per cent. This is an incontrovertible fact'—Dr. Raúl Prebisch, reported in *R.R.P.*, 29 June 1956.

[12] For the fluctuation in cattle numbers see Appendix IV. In 1955 the Minister of Agriculture declared that, as a result of the increase in the population and in domestic purchasing power, 85 per cent. of Argentina's meat production was now being consumed at home (Bank of London & South America, *Fortnightly Review*, 5 Mar. 1955, p. 127). In 1954 the average annual consumption of beef was 84 kilogrammes per inhabitant. The consumption of beef in Greater Buenos Aires alone required the daily slaughtering of 12,000 head of cattle, the rest of the country requiring 16,000 head per day (*R.R.P.*, 22 Apr. 1955, pp. 5–11).

[13] *The Economic Situation in Argentina*, p. 43.

[14] F. Benham and H. A. Holley, *A Short Introduction to the Economy of Latin America* (1960), p. 96.   [15] Bank of London & South America.

If the Argentine economy is to progress on modern lines, industrialization is essential;[16] but although the country still is in many respects the most highly developed of the Latin American republics, it is not well equipped to keep its economic leadership in the present industrial age. There is a lack (which does not exist to anything like the same extent in South America's other major republic, Brazil) of the raw materials necessary for the creation of heavy industry; and the sources of hydro-electric power are remote from the industrial centres. In an earlier period foreign investment made a vitally important contribution to the expansion of the Argentine economy. In the 1950's foreign capital was again required for the launching of a new economic phase. But financial losses experienced during the depression of the 1930's and Perón's campaign to free his country from foreign financial influence[17] naturally had created an unfavourable impression abroad. Moreover, even when Perón decided that the cost of importing petroleum had become too great a burden, Argentine nationalists (as we have seen) still refused to admit that foreign aid was needed for the more intensive exploitation of the oilfields.

As a result of all those adverse conditions the cost of living in Buenos Aires, on the basis of 1953 = 100, rose to 124 in December 1955. Subsequently, with the continual depreciation of the peso during the régimes of Lonardi, Aramburu, and Frondizi, the rise was even steeper, the index reaching 275 in December 1958 and 482 in June 1959.[18] It is not surprising that the urban workers repeatedly agitated for higher pay, and that the Government's occasional attempts to control inflation by 'freezing' wages was one of the chief causes of social unrest.

Immediately after the revolution of September 1955 Lonardi called upon a distinguished Argentine economist,

[16] 'Latin American industrialization is an indispensable condition of economic growth'—Raúl Prebisch, referring specifically to Argentina, quoted in *R.R.P.*, 29 June 1956.
[17] See above, p. 107.　　[18] *Economic Situation in Argentina*, p. 47.

Dr. Raúl Prebisch (a former General Manager of the Central Bank, actually serving as Executive Secretary of the United Nations Economic Commission for Latin America), to examine the state of the economy and recommend measures for its improvement. Prebisch continued as economic adviser to the Government after Lonardi's downfall, but he refused to take ministerial office, preferring to remain the *éminence grise*. One cannot blame this economic theorist for his reluctance to leave his E.C.L.A. study and put his ideas into practice in the political mêlée of that time.

Perón's second Five Year Plan, it will be remembered, was designed to stimulate the production of the traditional pastoral and agricultural commodities, the output of petroleum and electric power, the manufacture of tractors and other agricultural machinery, and the development of transport and communications.[19] 'Although this Plan was abandoned after the fall of the régime in 1955, these are the lines on which subsequent Governments have endeavoured to proceed.'[20] Some of Prebisch's proposals, however, were a reversal of Peronista policy.[21] In a long list of recommendations, Prebisch emphasized that various State enterprises (though not Y.P.F. or the railways) should be transferred to private ownership; that the independence of the Central Bank should be restored; that all price controls, subsidies, and exchange controls should be removed; that Argentina should join the World Bank and the International Monetary Fund; that non-essential imports should continue to be severely restricted; and that the number of civil servants should be drastically cut. The most urgent requirement was 'the restoration of a sound currency'. As a step towards this end, the official rate of the peso was devalued to a more realistic level in October 1955.

[19] See above, p. 128.   [20] Benham and Holley, p. 92.
[21] Prebisch's preliminary report on the state of the national economy was issued in two instalments and published in *R.R.P.* 3235, 31 Oct. 1955, and 3326, 11 Nov. 1955. His Economic Recovery Programme and a final report (entitled 'Sound Money or Uncontainable Inflation') were published in *R.R.P.* 3243, 20 Jan. 1956.

The effect was quickly seen in the free rate of the peso, which dropped from about 75 pesos to about 100 pesos to the £. The devaluation encouraged the farmers to increase their production for export; but it caused a substantial rise in the cost of living. Prebisch recognized that some wage increases would therefore have to be authorized for the lower-paid workers, but he insisted that the increases should be small and that their cost should come out of profits and not be passed on to the consumer. The harshness of this proposal rendered it politically impracticable. A series of strikes in 1956 forced the Government to permit wage increases greatly in excess of Prebisch's recommendation; retail prices rose correspondingly; the Government made an attempt to fix maximum prices, which led to the granting of subsidies to producers; and inflation continued on its course,[22] punctuated by experiments at wage 'freezing', and by strikes and more wage increases. Disagreements on the Prebisch programme occurred in the Aramburu Government, some ministers advocating that it should be put into operation in its entirety at once, and a completely free economy decreed; others—and their influence prevailed—advocating a more gradual procedure.

Although the carrying out of the full Prebisch programme was postponed again and again, several of his recommendations were put into effect during the Aramburu régime, and with satisfactory results. Thus Argentina joined the World Bank and the I.M.F.; the Export–Import Bank made a substantial loan for the purchase of transport and power equipment; and as the official attitude to foreign capital became more reassuring, further loans were obtained from the United States and Europe, and private foreign investment increased.

Immediately after his inauguration in May 1958, Frondizi—to demonstrate his concern for the workers' interests—decreed, as already mentioned, a 60 per cent. rise in wages, thus imparting new impetus to the wage-cost spiral. In July, however, he made a courageous decision which was

[22] See Appendix III.

contrary to all the ideas that he had previously expressed regarding the exploitation of the local oilfields.[23] In that month he announced that Argentina could no longer afford to spend some U.S. $300 million per annum on petroleum imports, and that he was therefore negotiating a number of contracts of limited duration with foreign (mainly U.S.-owned) oil companies which would enable Argentina to become self-sufficient in petroleum by about 1961. The contracts would be for the drilling of new wells, the establishment of a plant for manufacturing oil-industry equipment, and the construction of pipelines. Frondizi assured his compatriots that the foreign companies would not be operating for their own account, but merely as agents of Y.P.F., so that the nation's sovereignty over its own oil resources would be safeguarded. In spite of this assurance, there were widespread protests that the contracts would be a 'betrayal'. Nevertheless, it was evident that even the nationalist-minded military hierarchy were at last persuaded that Argentina's economic predicament was so grave that they could not reject Frondizi's programme. The contracts therefore were signed, and the foreign companies began work without delay. 'This undoubtedly represented the most important single move towards a solution of the country's economic problems that had been taken up to that time.'[24]

The oil programme—although in the event it provided spectacularly quick results—was designed as a relatively long-term contribution to economic recovery. Meanwhile, the general state of affairs was still in decline. One indication of the trend was the uninterrupted depreciation of the national currency, the free market rate of the peso dropping to 206 to the £ in December 1958, while the official rate stood at 50. The economic deterioration had reached a point where more drastic action could no longer be postponed. The military leaders were restive. And Frondizi—

[23] For his previous arguments that Argentina did not need the assistance of foreign oil companies see, in particular: Arturo Frondizi, *Petróleo y Política* (1955).
[24] Benham and Holley, p. 98.

who in his oil programme already had proved that he had ceased to be bound by the ideological convictions of his pre-presidential period—announced an austere and strictly orthodox 'stabilization plan' drawn up on the I.M.F. pattern. The official rate of exchange was to be abolished; credit was to be confined to essential production; price controls and subsidies were to be removed; and economies were to be effected in government expenditure. To support this plan the I.M.F., the U.S. Government, and a group of North American banks agreed to provide credits totalling U.S. $329 million.[25]

Frondizi's stabilization plan was launched in January 1959. The peso, set free to 'find its own level', soon dropped to 256 to the £; the cost of living rose again; many strikes occurred; and new wage increases were granted. Understandably, the public were opposed to the austerity measures, and the military leaders claimed that Peronistas still occupying influential positions in the administration and the trade unions were obstructing the economic recovery. Under military pressure Frondizi in May 1959 effected yet another purge of such persons. In June he appointed as Minister of Economy and acting Minister of Labour one of his bitterest critics, Álvaro Alsogaray—a former air force engineer, latterly a successful business man, and always a strong advocate of economic liberalism and free enterprise.

Alsogaray agreed to adopt the stabilization plan; declared that he would discontinue the previous practice of using force to break industrial strikes; began, in a series of 'fireside chats' on television, to explain in simple terms the nation's problems and his ideas for overcoming them; and

[25] The credits to be granted were as follows:

	U.S.$ millions
I.M.F.	75
Export–Import Bank	125
Exchange agreement with the U.S. Treasury	50
U.S. Development Loan Fund	25
Private North American Banks	54

(SOURCE: *Economic Situation in Argentina*, p. 21.)

gradually created a greater feeling of confidence at home and abroad.

On 1 May 1960 Frondizi was at last able to deliver a reasonably optimistic address to Congress. Argentina, he said, was rapidly approaching self-sufficiency in oil fuels; oil production, which in 1948 had amounted to 5½ million cubic metres, rose in 1959 to 7 million, with, in addition, an output of natural gas equivalent to about 3 million cubic metres. The construction of the oil and gas lines across the country from Campo Durán (Salta) to San Lorenzo (near Rosario) and Buenos Aires had been completed, and other pipelines were planned. The building of two large electric power stations in the Buenos Aires dock area was well advanced. Considerable foreign capital had been invested in the setting up of essential industries.[26] The San Nicolás steel plant would soon be in operation. Schemes for providing hydro-electric power and establishing new industries in the provinces were progressing. The 1959 balance of trade showed a small surplus.[27] In recent months the peso had remained fairly steady at a rate of about 230 to the £. The cost of living rose alarmingly during 1959,[28] but subsequently the rise had been relatively small. Frondizi admitted that it had not yet been possible to deal adequately with the rehabilitation of the railway system or the repairing and extending of roads. And there still existed a budgetary deficit, resulting from the cost of an overgrown bureaucracy and the inability of certain state enterprises (such as the railways) to cover their expenses.[29]

In 1961, with the next year's elections in mind,[30] Frondizi dismissed Alsogaray, who had become extremely unpopular among those whose living standards and businesses had suffered from the effects of the austerity programme.

[26] For foreign investment in 1959 see Appendix V.
[27] See Appendix VII. There had been a slight improvement in the terms of trade. See Appendix VI.   [28] See Appendix III.
[29] Frondizi's message was published in *R.R.P.*, 20 May 1960.
[30] See above, p. 145.

Chapter VIII

FOREIGN RELATIONS

FOR reasons that have already been explained,[1] Argentina's prestige abroad had never been lower than it was towards the end of the second world war. Perón, however, rapidly began to assert himself in international affairs. Having been admitted to the United Nations in 1945, Argentina led the opposition to the policy of boycotting General Franco's Spain, and Perón refused to recall his Ambassador from Madrid.[2] In 1948 the Argentine Minister of Foreign Affairs,[3] as President of the Security Council, created an impression in international quarters by his determined, though unsuccessful, attempt to end the Berlin blockade. In several international organizations the Argentine representatives acted as spokesmen of the 'underdeveloped' nations not only of Latin America but of other parts of the world,[4] and they met with considerable approval in Latin America when accusing the United States of wishing to prevent the growth of new industries in such countries. In successive negotiations with Great Britain concerning meat, the nationalization of the British-owned railways, and other commercial and financial matters, Argentina took a firm

[1] See above, p. 99.

[2] Subsequently relations between Perón and Franco became far from amicable, Spain having failed to fulfil her financial commitments.

[3] Juan Atilio Bramuglia.

[4] For example, in November 1952 the Economic Commission of the United Nations adopted an Argentine resolution that industrialized countries should create a system for ensuring a 'just and equitable relationship' between the prices of their manufactured exports and the prices of raw materials imported from the underdeveloped countries. This Argentine proposal—made at a time when world prices for certain basic commodities were falling—was directed primarily against the United States, and it received enthusiastic support from the underdeveloped nations not only on this occasion but when subsequently repeated. (cf. *Hispanic American Report*, Dec. 1952, pp. 32–33.)

stand and drove hard bargains. To reduce the republic's dependence on the British market, Perón sought new customers abroad—and, at the same time, new sources of essential imports—and signed bilateral agreements with a number of countries, including the U.S.S.R. Recognizing the failure of Ambassador Braden's aggressive treatment of Perón, the United States now adopted a conciliatory attitude towards Argentina, and a series of friendly Ambassadors were sent to Buenos Aires, several of them being genial business men; but Perón, while ready to accept whatever the United States had to offer, gave no sign that he was sorry for his past behaviour or that he intended to be less antagonistic to so-called 'Yanqui Imperialism' in the future. During the Korean War Argentina rejected the suggestion that she should send troops to join the United Nations forces. At Inter-American Conferences (and notably at Caracas in 1954) Perón's delegates aroused widespread sympathy by denouncing the existence of European colonies—such as British Honduras, British Guiana, and the Falkland Islands—in the western hemisphere. In all matters connected with the cold war, Argentina claimed that—in accordance with the doctrine of *justicialismo*[5]—she occupied a 'Third Position' between the United States and the U.S.S.R.; and this theory appealed to the majority of Latin Americans, who had no desire to be associated with either side. Thus did Argentina, by a display of independence and leadership, try to enhance her prestige in international affairs.

Political rather than economic motives have prevailed particularly in Argentina's dealings with the other Latin American republics, partly because commerce with those countries (except Brazil and Chile) is relatively slight, and partly because—as mentioned earlier in this book—the Argentines have long been convinced that they have a 'manifest destiny' to lead the continent. In 1953 President Perón made a determined effort towards the creation of a

[5] See above, p. 127.

southern bloc. Like many of his other projects, this was an old scheme revived; but he gave it an up-to-date 'justicialist' appearance, proclaiming that his object was to complete the task of Latin American emancipation: as in the last century the army of San Martín crossed the Andes to liberate Chile and Peru politically, so now would the Peronistas go forth to foster 'social justice' and 'economic independence'. Perón began his campaign in February 1953 by crossing the Andes to Chile, where he and the President of that country drew up the Act of Santiago in which they expressed their intention to promote the 'progress and wellbeing of their peoples by means of the common and coordinated action of their Governments'. Measures were to be taken forthwith to 'integrate and stimulate' the economies of the two republics, whose 'economic union' was now declared. Customs duties and exchange differences were to be eliminated. The 'union' was to 'remain open, so that other fraternal peoples may join it'.[6] This agreement foreshadowed the treaty establishing a Free Trade Association drawn up at Montevideo in 1960.[7] The Act of Santiago itself, however, proved in practice to be little more than a bilateral trade agreement; and it was received unfavourably by the Chilean public, who had serious misgivings as to the ultimate ambitions of their powerful neighbour.[8] The next nation to join the 'justicialist' block was Paraguay, which has always been economically at the mercy of Argentina because its life-line—the Plata–Paraná–Río Paraguay river system—runs through Argentine territory. The Argentines traditionally despise the backward, upstream republic and have never been reconciled to its refusal—at the time of the break-up of the Vice-Royalty of the Río de la Plata—to remain a part of the *porteño* patrimony. Paraguay signed the

[6] The text of the Act of Santiago was published in Argentina, Ministerio de Relaciones Exteriores y Culto, *Mensaje a los Pueblos de América de los Presidentes Perón e Ibáñez* (1953).
[7] See below, p. 162.
[8] For a statement of the Chilean attitude see Alejandro Magnet, *Nuestros Vecinos Justicialistas* (1953).

Act in August 1953, and two months later Perón issued an 'Argentine–Paraguayan Decalogue' which clearly revealed his desire that that stubborn little nation should become in all but name a part of Argentina. In this Decalogue he addressed his fellow citizens in the following terms:

Every Argentine citizen should know that the Paraguayan people and the Argentine people, fully retaining their national sovereignties, are really and effectively brothers. Therefore, we Argentines must all work for the greatness of Paraguay, and for the happiness of its people, with the same faith and love as animate us when working for our own greatness and happiness.

From today all Paraguayans will be compatriots of all Argentines.

The Government, the State, and the people of Argentina will make available all such resources and means as may help Paraguay to consolidate social justice, economic independence, and political sovereignty.[9]

Paraguay's adherence to the Act of Santiago brought immediate economic benefits. Argentine goods, which had long been withheld, began to arrive in abundance, payment being accepted at an advantageous rate of exchange; and Argentine financial and technical aid was promptly supplied for a number of useful public works. The dictator of Nicaragua and General Perón signed a 'justicialist' Declaration in October 1953,[10] and Ecuador joined Argentina in theoretical 'economic union' in December.[11] Bolivia became a member of the bloc in September 1954.

Thus Perón did make some progress in asserting his country's claim to be recognized as a leading Power in Latin America. The truth was, of course, that the social and economic features of the Peronista revolution appealed to other Latin American caudillos who were faced with prob-

[9] Argentina, Ministerio de Relaciones Exteriores y Culto, *Expresiones de una Política Continental: Discursos de los Presidentes Chaves y Perón* (1953), pp. 25–27.

[10] Argentina, Ministerio de Relaciones Exteriores y Culto, *Expresiones de una Política Continental: Argentina y Nicaragua bajo el Signo de América* (1953).

[11] Argentina, Ministerio de Relaciones Exteriores y Culto, *Unión Económica Argentina Ecuatoriana: Afirmación de un Destino Común* (1953).

lems similar to those existing in Argentina; and although the Argentines were regarded with suspicion by their neighbours, there was general agreement that if the Latin American republics were to combine in some form of coalition they would be better able to defend their interests when negotiating with the United States.

Besides signing fraternal pacts with Heads of State, Perón sought to extend his influence in Latin America on another level: as Robert J. Alexander has written, he 'conceived the idea of setting himself up as a Hemispheric protector of the working man.'[12] Peronista labour attachés were sent to Argentine Embassies throughout the New World, their main function being to enter into close contact with the local trade union movements;[13] and Perón even founded his own international labour federation. Two other such federations already existed in Latin America: these were the Confederación de Trabajadores de América Latina (C.T.A.L.), which had a Communist tendency, and the Organización Regional Interamericano de Trabajadores (O.R.I.T.), which was anti-Communist and had United States approval. In conformity with 'justicialist' teaching, Perón's federation—the Agrupación de Trabajadores Latino-Americanos Sindicalistas, or A.T.L.A.S.—was said to occupy a 'Third Position' between the other two; and A.T.L.A.S. did attract a considerable number of adherents outside Argentina because it was genuinely a Latin American entity, whereas C.T.A.L. was looked upon as being in some degree connected with the U.S.S.R., while O.R.I.T. was considered to be a protégé of the United States. When Perón needed financial aid and therefore adopted a more kindly attitude towards Washington, his

[12] Alexander, *Perón Era*, p. 187.

[13] Sometimes these labour attachés were accused of interfering in the internal affairs of the countries to which they were accredited. For example, in September 1952 the Argentine labour attaché at Montevideo and his secretary were declared *personae non gratae* by the Uruguayan Government, proof having been found that they had intervened to provoke disorders in a strike for higher wages at the Alpargatas factory in that country. (cf. *The Times*, 15 Sept. 1952, and *Hispanic American Report*, Oct. 1952, p. 32.)

influence on 'anti-Yanqui' foreign labour movements tended to decline, but it had been surprisingly effective:

For several years Peronist propaganda among the Latin American masses met with considerable success. In virtually every country Perón succeeded in building up a group of labour leaders who not only were in sympathy with his régime, but worked actively on its behalf in the trade unions and other social organizations of their respective countries. In their heyday, the Peronists had been able to win over or build up significant labour organizations in Mexico, Nicaragua, Panama, Colombia and Paraguay. They had won wide sympathy among the Ibañist masses in Chile. They had established friendly relations with virtually the whole trade union movement of Bolivia, and they had rallied considerable mass support in Cuba and a few other countries, including Costa Rica, where they narrowly missed taking control of the country's principal labour organization.[14]

The Peronistas were only moderately successful in gathering these sympathizers into their own continental federation, nevertheless A.T.L.A.S. did continue to receive support. In January 1955, when Perón was in the midst of his dispute with the Argentine Church, the National Workers' Confederation of Colombia, an affiliate of A.T.L.A.S., was accused by the Archbishop of Antioquia and the Primate of Colombia of being anti-Catholic and guilty of Peronismo, *justicialismo*, and Communism.[15]

Perón's treatment of the U.S.S.R. and of Argentine Communists was of course in keeping with his theory of the 'Third Position'. He renewed diplomatic relations with Moscow in 1946 (they had been interrupted for nearly thirty years in consequence of an insult to the Argentine flag at the time of the Russian Revolution of 1917) and he allowed an Argentine Communist Party to exist; but he did not become a Soviet partisan in the cold war, and his police periodically arrested groups of Communists on one pretext

[14] Alexander, 'Peronism and Argentina's Quest for Leadership in Latin America', *J. of International Affairs*, vol. 9, no. 1, 1955, p. 54.
[15] *Hispanic American Report*, Feb. 1955, p. 31.

or another. The Communist Party remained small—a high proportion of its members being of Slav and Jewish origin—and it never secured a seat in Congress. Many Communists and potential Communists—particularly those of Spanish and Italian stock—were content to join the Peronista Party.[16]

The growth of Argentine prestige and influence caused anxiety not only to the smaller and weaker neighbouring republics, but also to Brazil, which was alarmed by Perón's increasing domination over Paraguay's economy and administration and by his prolonged campaign to persuade the other of the two buffer states of the Río de la Plata region—the republic of Uruguay—to carry out his wishes. Rivalry between Buenos Aires and Rio de Janeiro for the possession of the strategically-placed territory that now constitutes Uruguay had begun in colonial times and continued after the emancipation, with the *porteños* besieging the capital, Montevideo, and the Brazilians repeatedly invading the land from the north. By the middle of the nineteenth century it began to be recognized that the independence of Uruguay was essential for the creation and preservation of peace in the Plata.[17] Tension between Buenos Aires and Montevideo revived during the second world war. The Uruguayan Government had clearly shown that their sympathies lay with the Allies, and they were accused by Argentina's rulers of allowing their country to become a United States outpost. Relations worsened after 1946. Montevideo was the traditional refuge of Argentine political exiles, and during the presidency of Perón it was the chief centre from which his enemies directed their propaganda against him. The Uruguayan authorities stubbornly rejected Argentine demands that they should prevent these refugees from engaging in anti-Peronista activities. To-

[16] For a brief study of Perón's policy towards Communism, see 'Left Wing Movements in South America', *The Times*, 27 Mar. 1953.
[17] Concerning Argentine–Brazilian rivalry see Robert N. Burr, 'The Balance of Power in Nineteenth-Century South America', *H.A.H.R.*, Feb. 1955, pp. 37–60 and Pendle, *Uruguay*, pp. 7–14.

wards the end of 1952 Perón retaliated by imposing a boy-
cott on trade with Uruguay and by introducing passport
formalities which were so stringent that travel between the
two republics was brought virtually to a standstill, the
Uruguayan economy suffering gravely from the suspension
of Argentine tourist traffic which in the past had been an
important 'invisible export'.[18] In April 1955, however,
Perón adopted a more lenient attitude permitting the resumption of normal diplomatic relations with Montevideo
which had been interrupted for several years. When he was
overthrown, all travel restrictions were removed. It was
early summer, and many Argentines soon resumed their
practice of crossing the Río de la Plata to spend their holidays at the Uruguayan coastal resorts.

With the departure of Perón, Argentina's new leaders
were at great pains to demonstrate their desire to work in
harmony with the United States and the Western European
Powers—on whom they counted for financial aid—and
with other Latin American nations.

After 1955 new plans for Latin American economic co-
operation were drawn up, with the keen encouragement of
Raúl Prebisch (in his capacity as Executive Secretary of
the United Nations Economic Commission for Latin
America). Argentina took part in all of the negotiations,
although the prospect of any immediate benefit was slight.[19]

[18] For Uruguay's tourist trade see Pendle, *Uruguay*, pp. 76–77.
[19] To a considerable degree the economies of Argentina and Brazil—who
exchange, for example, wheat for tropical produce and minerals—are
complementary; and Argentina needs Chilean copper, while Chile requires
Argentine cattle. But in general intra-regional trade in Latin America is
limited by the fact that the republics produce identical goods, and by the
existence of natural as well as artificial barriers. Most of these countries
have protected their new industries by import restrictions of one kind or another, and transport within the continent is still extremely difficult. Trade
among the southern republics amounts to only about 10 per cent. of their
total international commerce, and approximately 80 per cent. of the merchandise which they exchange has to be transported by sea. And this maritime traffic is unbalanced. It is characteristic of the trade between the
southern countries that goods going to the Pacific coast (for instance, wool,
vegetable oil, and meat) have a much higher specific value than most of
those carried in the opposite direction (which are largely minerals). This

As a step towards the creation of a Latin American 'common market',[20] a treaty establishing a Free Trade Association was signed at Montevideo in February 1960 by Argentina and six other Latin American republics.[21] This provided for the liberalization of trade between the member countries in not more than twelve years.[22]

THE FALKLAND ISLANDS AND DEPENDENCIES

A minor but perennial cause of trouble in Argentina's relations with Great Britain is the British occupation of the Falkland Islands—a matter in which the republic of Uruguay became involved during the Perón régime. In October 1952 Perón complained that Uruguay had been guilty of acts that implied recognition of the British ownership of the islands, which Argentina had always claimed as being a part of her own rightful inheritance from Spain. Successive Argentine Governments, in protest against the British occupation, have for many years prohibited direct communication between the Argentine mainland and the

means that for the balancing of payments there must necessarily be inequality in the volume of cargo transported in the two directions, and ships sailing from the South Atlantic to the South Pacific customarily make the voyage with half-empty holds. Sometimes vessels even sail from Argentine to Chile in ballast (cf. U.N., E.C.L.A., *Study of the Prospects of Inter-Latin-American Trade (Southern Zone of the Region)*, 1954).

Argentine wheat is the most important single commodity in South American intra-regional trade. In the past, Argentine Governments have been accused on occasion of withholding supplies of this grain as a means of bringing pressure to bear upon the Governments of other southern countries (cf. Alexander, *Perón Era*, pp. 184–5).

[20] Regarding the proposed Latin American common market and the various meetings of groups of countries within the area, see the Bank of London & South America's *Quarterly R.*, July 1960, pp. 1–7.

[21] Those six republics were Brazil, Chile, Mexico, Paraguay, Peru, and Uruguay. The treaty was open to accession by all the remaining Latin American republics.

[22] The text of the treaty was published as a supplement to the Bank of London & South America's *Fortnightly Review*, vol. 25, no. 611. The principal clauses were:

1. Arts. 2 and 3, which declared that during the period of not more than twelve years the contracting parties would gradually eliminate from the essential part of their reciprocal trade all types of duties and restrictions affecting the importation of goods between them.

2. Art. 16, which stated that the contracting parties would endeavour to co-ordinate their industrialization policies.

islands; therefore it has been customary for all communication between South America and Port Stanley to be conducted through the Uruguayan port of Montevideo, the principal means of transport for the voyage of more than 1,000 miles being the British-owned 600-ton vessel *Fitzroy*. The Argentine Note delivered in October 1952 named two causes for complaint: first, the Uruguayans had given offence by ratifying a treaty of aerial navigation with Great Britain whereby Montevideo was designated a port of call for flights between the United Kingdom and the Falklands; and second, the Uruguayan Government had shown disregard for Argentina's rights by maintaining a consular office at Port Stanley. Uruguay replied that her actions had been misinterpreted. The exchange of Notes on this subject ended at last in December;[23] but Argentina reiterated the annually-repeated claim against Great Britain.

The Falkland Islands are situated in the South Atlantic some 300 miles to the east of the southern coast of Argentina. It is generally agreed (except in Argentina) that the islands were sighted by British navigators towards the end of the sixteenth century. A British captain landed in 1690 and bestowed the name of Falkland, after Lord Falkland the then Treasurer of the Navy. The islands were also seen by adventurers from St Malo, becoming known in France as *les Iles Malouines* and in Spain as the Malvinas. In 1764 a French expedition under Louis-Antoine de Bougainville founded Port Louis in East Falkland and in 1765 Commodore John Byron took formal possession of West Falkland and founded Port Egmont. French claims were ceded to Spain in 1767 and in 1770 a Spanish expedition from Buenos Aires expelled the British garrison. An Anglo-Spanish agreement was concluded in 1771, under which the British garrison was reinstated, without prejudice, however, to the question of sovereignty. But the garrison was withdrawn in 1774, and thereafter West Falkland remained

[23] This Argentine-Uruguayan dispute over the Falklands was fully reported in *The Times*, 23, 24, 25, and 29 Oct. 1952 and 13 Dec. 1952.

without regular inhabitants. In East Falkland a small Spanish community was maintained at Soledad (Port Louis) until its withdrawal by the authorities at Buenos Aires in 1811.

For a number of years the Falkland Islands thus became in practice a *terra nullius*. In the 1820's, however, the Government of Buenos Aires hoisted their flag as a sign that the islands were a part of the Plata vice-regal territory whose independence from Spain had now been declared. A settlement at Soledad was now re-established. But its governor, in 1831, seized three United States sealers operating in surrounding waters, whereupon a United States sloop-of-war landed an armed party at Soledad, dismantled the fort, and dispersed the colonists. Finally, in December 1832, the British Government having formally protested against Argentine claims to the islands, two British warships arrived, the officer in command taking formal possession of Port Egmont, and then, in January 1833, of Soledad, where a small Argentine garrison was forced to yield. Since that date these bleak, windswept, treeless moorland isles[24] have been a British Colony, the inhabitants being mainly sheep-farmers of British stock who export wool, hides, and tallow and are obliged to import almost all of the commodities that they need, except meat.

The Falklands may be lacking in residential attraction and natural resources, but their strategic importance for Great Britain has been demonstrated again and again. Control of the islands is essential in time of war for keeping open the South American trade routes and the Straits of Magellan, and in 1914 and 1939 two British naval victories —the battles of the Falkland Islands and the River Plate— were won by squadrons based on Port Stanley. The United States, while expressing a pious hope that European colon-

[24] In 1771 Dr Johnson accurately referred to the Falklands as 'islands thrown aside from human use, stormy in winter, barren in summer, islands which not even the southern savages have dignified with habitation'. Four years earlier a Spanish priest, then stationed in East Falkland, wrote: 'I tarry in this unhappy desert, suffering everything for the love of God.'

ies in the western hemisphere will eventually become self-governing nations, has no desire that the Falklands shall be transferred to the sovereignty of a potentially troublesome Power such as Argentina: the Panama Canal is not invulnerable, and if it should be blocked by enemy action in time of war, the southern passage— dominated by whoever holds the Falklands—would be the only alternative maritime route joining the east and west coasts of the continent.

On Argentine maps and postage stamps, and in Argentine schoolchildren's text-books, the 'Islas Malvinas' are shown as belonging to the Argentine Republic; and their population is often included in the national census returns. Falkland islanders visiting Argentina are treated as Argentine citizens, are refused Argentine visas for their British passports, and are liable to be called up for military service. Under the régime of General Perón the demand for the 'repatriation' of the Malvinas became increasingly insistent and, in addition to the usual official Notes re-stating Argentina's claim, public demonstrations against the British occupation took place outside H.M. Embassy in Buenos Aires. The dispute, as we have seen, is of no recent origin: indeed, Argentines of all political parties have always been united in condemning Britain's seizure of the islands and have produced a copious literature on the subject.[25]

Closely linked with—though legally distinct from—the question of the Falkland Islands is that of the Antarctic area lying to the south, south-east, and east of Cape Horn.[26] Britain's so-called Falkland Island Dependencies in this region were defined by Letters Patent issued in 1908 and 1917. The Dependencies, thus determined, include a huge segment of the ice-covered Antarctic mainland extending southwards to the South Pole; the peninsula of Graham Land (jutting some 800 miles northwards from the Ant-

---

[25] The titles of some books on the Malvinas by Argentine writers will be found in the Bibliography. The best book in English is Julius Goebel, *The Struggle for the Falkland Islands* (1927).

[26] For a general study of the Antarctic question see E. W. Hunter Christie, *The Antarctic Problem* (1951).

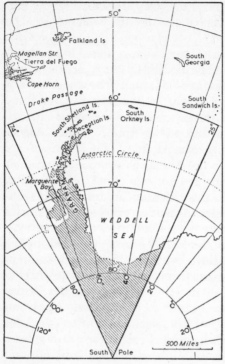

arctic mainland towards Cape Horn), with the islands along its coast; the groups of islands known as the South Shetlands, South Orkneys, and South Sandwich Islands; and the remote sub-Antarctic island of South Georgia, situated in the South Atlantic Ocean 800 miles to the east of the Falkland group. British bases were originally established at various points for the prosecution of the whaling industry

THE ANTARCTIC SECTOR CLAIMED
BY ARGENTINA

and its proper regulation, and for the conducting of meteorological and other scientific investigations. Britain's sovereignty over the area is founded on priority of discovery, followed by formal claims and the establishment of a local administration, acting under the Governor of the Falkland Islands, to control the British and foreign whaling and sealing industries by a system of licensing. In the past the Dependencies have been of importance as forming a part of the British strategic position—of which the Falkland Islands are the centre of operations—on the flank of the Straits of Magellan and the Drake Passage. In the future they might again have strategic significance if air routes were opened

166

up across Antarctica, and they might one day be of economic value if exploitable mineral deposits were discovered in this region.

Great Britain's possession of Antarctic territory is challenged, however, by Argentina and Chile,[27] who argue that the Graham Land peninsula and adjacent islands are legally their property because of their proximity to the South American continent. There are also certain very dubious claims regarding inheritance from Spain. For nationalistic reasons the two South American republics have pressed their Antarctic demands against Great Britain with increasing vigour in recent years, and many expeditions from both countries have visited the area since General Perón came to power in Argentina. In 1954 Perón announced that his aim was gradually to acquire Argentina's so-called 'Antarctic Sector' by 'saturating' this inhospitable region with Argentine occupants,[28] and by January 1955 he had already established eight permanently occupied Argentine bases (as against eight British and four Chilean) in the British Dependencies.[29] Protests have been exchanged annually; but in 1949, with the object of preventing 'any misunderstanding in Antarctica which might affect the friendly relations between the United Kingdom, Argentina and Chile', the Governments of those three nations agreed formally to notify one another that 'in present circumstances they foresee no need to send warships South of latitude 60 deg. . . . apart, of course, from routine movements such as have been customary for a number of years.'[30] These declarations have been renewed year by year since that date. Meanwhile, the British Government has repeatedly invited Argentina and Chile to place their Antarctic claims before the International Court at The Hague. As

[27] The claims of Argentina and Chile overlap. The Argentine claims are set out in J. C. Rodríguez, *La Republica Argentina y las adquisiciones territoriales en el Continente Antártico* (1941). For the Chilean case, see Oscar Pinochet de la Barra, *La Antártica Chilena* (1948).
[28] *The Times*, 9 Apr. 1954.   [29] Ibid. 18 Jan. 1955.
[30] Ibid. 19 Jan. 1949.

this invitation has always been rejected by the South Americans, H.M. Government decided in 1955 to make a direct application to The Hague. On 4 May 1955, therefore, documents establishing the British title were submitted to the Court.[31] Once again the Argentine Government refused to accept the International Court's jurisdiction, and in June a law was passed wherein the Falkland Islands and Dependencies were declared to form part of a new Argentine province incorporating all the mainland and islands lying to the south of latitude 46°.[32]

At Washington on 1 December 1959 Argentina and eleven other interested countries[33] signed a thirty-year Antarctic treaty. The main objects of the treaty were to suspend all territorial claims and disputes in the Antarctic area; to guarantee the free use of the whole continent for scientific research; and to set up an inspection system to prevent any military activities. The area covered by this agreement included the Falkland Island Dependencies, but did not include the Falkland Islands.[34]

[31] *The Times*, 7 May 1955.
[32] Bank of London & South America, *Fortnightly Review*, 11 June 1955, p. 357.
[33] The other signatories were Australia, Belgium, Chile, France, Japan, New Zealand, Norway, the Union of South Africa, the Soviet Union, the United Kingdom, and the United States.
[34] The text of the treaty was published in *New York Times* (European ed.), 3 Dec. 1959.

Chapter IX

THE REMOTE COLOSSUS

Dr [Ricardo] Rojas thought of Argentina as the repository of all that was richest in European culture, as a nursery, in which seedlings, transplanted from that great cramped forest, would have room to grow and spread. To the European, Argentina offered what Europe no longer offered him, space, hope, and a future still to be shaped. Into the Argentine constitution there had been written an invitation to men of good will in all countries to come and shape that future.[1]

The fundamental problem of our life is distances, quantities, size and solitude.[2]

To some, even today, the far-off city of Buenos Aires is another Paris. Much of its late nineteenth-century architecture comes straight from the Madeleine and Neuilly. Its women are chic. Its shops are gay. Until recent times the smart set in Buenos Aires imported French works of art and French lecturers. Many wealthy Argentine families lived a part of the year in Paris and on the Riviera. Some authors, like Victoria Ocampo, even preferred to write in French rather than in Spanish, and they chose Paris, not Buenos Aires, as the scene for their novels.

To others, 'B.A.' still signifies British businesses and clubs, the London Bank, *Buenos Aires Herald*, English-named suburbs, cricket and polo at Hurlingham, amateur performances of English plays.

For millions, Buenos Aires is the most wonderful home in the world: the white skyscrapers with their luxury flats; the wide tree-lined avenues and elegant parks; the rich food

[1] Fraser, p. 76.
[2] Ezequiel Martínez Estrada, *Radiografía de la Pampa* (1942), i. 65.

169

served at small restaurants in narrow streets that might belong to Genoa or Marseilles or Barcelona; the display of wealth at the races, the cattle-shows, the military parades; the excitement, the noise; the miles of modern docks crowded with trans-Atlantic shipping; the lavish cinemas; the families sitting in wicker chairs at the gates of their suburban gardens in the evening; gardenias growing by the porch, lemon-trees against the window; the Southern Cross at night above the palm-trees; fire-flies, the *bombilla*.

But when you approach Buenos Aires by air from the west, over the flat green-brown pampa, you observe that it is a lonely city, placed between the immensity of the empty plain and that other vast brown expanse, the Río de la Plata estuary.

Raúl Scalabrini Ortiz has described the *porteño* as *el hombre que está solo, y espera*,[3] 'the man who is alone, and waits'—or it may be 'hopes', for the Spanish verb *esperar* means both 'to hope' and 'to wait'. The Argentines, even while they possess unbounded faith in their country's future, are aware of their geographical remoteness. The man of Buenos Aires, in his solitude, is bewildered when he attempts to imagine what are the characteristics of the nation that he and his compatriots are forging.

As for the man of the 'camp', he too inhabits a lonely world. The pampa is so huge and so empty. The villages of the interior consist of sad, mud-coloured shacks of crude brick, or adobe, or corrugated iron, with earthen floors. The wide earth streets are only visited at rare intervals by horsemen who ride in from distant *estancias* to purchase supplies and to drink. And life in the 'camp' still retains something of that violent, desolate, uncultured quality which Sarmiento named *barbarie*. The poet Jorge Luis Borges has written:

According to *criollo* ethics . . . the spilling of blood is not especially memorable, and it is in man's nature that he should kill. . . . One afternoon I heard an old man gently grumble 'In

[3] *El Hombre que está solo, y espera* (1931).

my day, who was there who hadn't a death to his account.' Nor shall I forget the uncouth fellow who said to me gravely: 'Señor Borges, I may have been in prison many times; but always for homicide.'[4]

The nation as a whole is conscious of its isolation, its remoteness from the present-day centre of power. It is as a result of their geographical position on the margin of our civilization that the Argentines have generally been reluctant to become involved in the northern hemisphere's international movements and organizations. Sarmiento and many others—including a number of twentieth-century intellectuals—tried to Europeanize or North-Americanize the republic; but the mass of the people resisted their endeavours. *Barbarie* still survives in the heart of the townsman and the *peón*.

The 1930's (Scalabrini Ortiz's book was published in 1931) were years of economic crisis, political retrogression, and intellectual uncertainty. To the dismay of many who desired a liberal way of life for Argentina, the practical response to the problems of the decade came in the form, not of a Radical revival, but of the military revolution of 1943. Juan D. Perón denounced the ruling caste and the social system that they represented for the same faults as the poets and essayists—among them, Ezequiel Martínez Estrada—had criticized in the 1930's. Martínez Estrada's investigation of Argentine history and of the prevailing state of affairs was first published in 1933. In this book the author complained that the resources of the country were being exploited for the benefit of foreign investors; that the people's occupations and their movement from one part of the country to another were determined by the requirements of overseas markets; and that Argentina was increasingly unable to organize her independent existence or to produce any materials other than those which the world demanded of her.[5] The British-owned railways had been planned not

[4] *Aspectos de la Literatura Gauchesca* (1950), p. 29.
[5] Martínez Estrada, i. 53.

with the purpose of developing the national economy, but with the object of carrying the produce of the 'camp' by the straightest possible route to the port of Buenos Aires for shipment to Europe. Thus an unnatural pattern of communications was imposed on the country, accentuating its already-existing divisions rather than assisting its unification, neglecting the inhabitants of vast areas, and augmenting out of all proportion the predominance of Buenos Aires. 'Our railways are the equivalent of pounds sterling in steel [and it is their function] to produce more pounds sterling, not wealth.'[6] Martínez Estrada believed that the fathers of the nation, with their faith in European and North American civilization, embarked on a mistaken course, and that 'the progress of the Republic is contrary to the interests of those who made it prosper.'[7]

The widespread *malaise* of the 1930's (the period which, more than any other, explains the events of the 1940's and the present-day situation) was expressed by many other writers and in many different ways. The distinguished novelist Eduardo Mallea, in an interpretative essay (first published in 1937), argued that since about the beginning of the century the nation had been in a state of decadence. To illustrate this contention Mallea compared the veneration in which Argentina had been held by the nineteenth-century immigrants with the apathy with which it was treated by later generations of foreign settlers. Those who had arrived in Buenos Aires from overseas 'when the voices of our forebears of major intelligence could still be heard'[8] had found themselves in a vital young country where everything was still to be done: the parks in the city, the residential suburbs, the martial songs, a political system—everything was in the process of creation. And those immigrants, marvelling and venerating, dedicated themselves to the common enterprise. 'In their old age [wrote Mallea] I have noticed in their faces the signs of this fervour, so simple, so moving and

[6] Martínez Estrada, p. 61.   [7] Ibid. p. 67.
[8] *Historia de una pasión Argentina* (1945), p. 25.

so pure.'⁹ But (in Mallea's interpretation) the newcomers who disembarked at Buenos Aires in later years did not receive the same inspiration: they found themselves among a people who in general were content with material comforts and who failed to carry forward the high ideals and ambitions of previous generations, their motto now being 'God will provide'. The consequence was that the newcomers themselves acquired this same frame of mind. Mallea appealed to his countrymen to recover a sense of their destiny, not to be satisfied with 'an easy Argentina', but to work for 'a difficult Argentina'.¹⁰ To Mallea, as to Martínez Estrada, the answer was provided by Perón, who told the Argentines what their destiny was to be.

The reaction against Sarmiento and his collaborators and successors was accompanied, as was to be expected, by a certain nostalgia for early times, for the gaucho, for the old heroic Argentina which had been transformed with the coming of the barbed-wire fence, the railway, and the *frigorífico*. The revival of the gaucho as a symbolic figure had begun before the 1930's and had served to stimulate the growth of those nationalist sentiments which later were to find expression in *Peronismo*. The poet Leopoldo Lugones had resuscitated the epic *Martín Fierro* in 1913, and to some of his contemporaries it seemed that these verses had a new political significance. The gaucho was a man without property, a vagabond who had no sympathy for Sarmiento's form of society and who was persecuted by the authorities from Buenos Aires. *Martín Fierro* symbolized resistance to the prevailing order. In 1926 Ricardo Güiraldes, a 'highbrow' poet known previously only to a few small groups and in the little magazines, unexpectedly produced a book which was to become the most popular of all Argentine novels, *Don Segundo Sombra*.¹¹ This was the story of a boy named Fabio who, as a protégé of an old gaucho, Don

⁹ Ibid.　　¹⁰ Ibid. p. 20.
¹¹ An English translation by Harriet de Onís, *Don Segundo Sombra: Shadows on the Pampas*, was published by Penguin Books, London, in 1948.

Segundo, roamed the pampa, breaking in horses and driving herds of cattle from place to place. One day Fabio inherited an *estancia*; but he did not wish to be a landowner, and at night he continued to sleep on the ground in the open air, refusing to live indoors. For a short while Don Segundo stayed with him, helping him to run his estate; but the old gaucho could not for long tolerate being tied to the ranch, in spite of his affection for the boy. And so at the end of the book we see Don Segundo going away on his horse, cantering towards the horizon to live again the rough and lonely life to which he and his ancestors had been accustomed. Tales such as this appealed to the Argentines who (as stated at the beginning of the present chapter) had inherited something of the gaucho's dislike of the modern social system, his natural loneliness, and the sadness engendered by it.

The Argentine film industry also became interested in gaucho themes. The film *Nobleza Gaucho* (1915) 'struck the same rhetorical note and displayed the same emotional intensity which we still associate, almost invariably, with every attempt by the Argentine cinema to extol the qualities of endurance, generosity and courage that are inherent in the rough country folk whose ways it depicts'.[12] Outstanding later films were *The Gaucho War* (1942) and *Barbaric Pampa* (1946) by Lucas Demare.

Historically, the gaucho was unhappy in his origin and in his fate. The word 'gaucho' is probably of Quechuan Indian derivation and signifies an orphan, a lost soul. The gaucho originally was the offspring of the Spanish invader and the Indian woman, whom the Spaniard subjugated but rarely married. Therefore, as Carlos Octavio Bunge wrote, he was from birth 'an orphan of civilization'.[13] But this nomadic

[12] Giselda Zani, 'Latin America on the Cinema Screen', in the *Geographical Magazine* (London), Mar. 1955, p. 569.

[13] *Nuestra América*, 6th ed. (1918), p. 185. Another possible explanation is that there may have existed formerly a Spanish architectural term *gaucho*, designating a rough and irregular surface. Spaniards arriving in the Río de la Plata may have used this word to describe the half-Indian cowboys in that region.

horseman had his revenge on 'civilization': he communi-
cated the sadness of the desolate pampa, and of his own experience, to the inhabitants of the city; and the melancholy
of his *tristes*, or laments, accompanied on the guitar,[14] was
echoed in the urban tangos,[15] whose verses almost invariably expressed disillusion and frustration. Thus:

> Brother, what things
> there are in life!
> I didn't love her
> when I met her,
> until one night
> she said to me, determined:
> *I'm very tired*
> *of it all*, and went away. . . .

The lonely, indigenous tree of the pampa, the *ombú*, has
become almost a national emblem. The *ombú* is known as
the 'lighthouse' of the pampa, because (until groves of fast-
growing eucalyptus trees were planted around occasional
estancia houses) it was the only object to be seen on the sea-
like plains. It has an enormous trunk and its widely-spread-
ing branches cover a large space of ground, while its knotted
roots, protruding above the surface of the land, offer a convenient resting-place to weary horsemen. The *ombú* lives
for innumerable years: no cyclone can blow it down, nor
can fire destroy it; and its pulpy wood is useless to man even
as fuel. Thus although it is a friendly tree for the rider and
his mount when the sun is high, the *ombú* in reality is a lonely
weed, a fit symbol of Argentina's solitude.

With the growth of nostalgia and nationalism in the

---

[14] 'Set a Gaucho to dance, and he moves as if he were on a procession to
his execution; ask him to sing, and he gives utterance to sounds resembling
an Irish keen, accompanied by nasal drones suggestive of croup; put him to
play the guitar, and you feel your flesh beginning to creep, for the tinkling
elicited is as if a number of sick crickets were crackling their legs over the
fingers of the player' (Thomas J. Hutchinson, *Buenos Ayres and Argentine
Gleanings* (1865), p. 123).

[15] The origin of the tango is disputed. For one interpretation see Waldo
Frank, *America Hispana* (1931), pp. 114–16.

1930's and 1940's, it is not surprising that there should have developed concurrently a campaign to rehabilitate the caudillo Rosas as a national hero. Books were now written to demonstrate that Rosas was a sincere champion of the local way of life, a patriotic opponent of foreign intervention, and a forerunner of the Peronista movement.[16] It was appropriate, too, that Señora Perón should have declared that the *descamisados* from the Buenos Aires meat-packing suburb of Avellaneda were fulfilling the same role as that which, a hundred years before, was played by Rosas's gauchos. By 1945, indeed, the stage was well set. The local oligarchs, the absentee foreign investors, and Argentina's conscientious intellectual fraternity in their various ways had provided all the justification that Perón needed for his undertaking of remodelling the nation. Moreover, the Argentine political parties for so long had been used by caudillos as mere instruments for attaining and keeping personal power, that no reliable institutional basis for representative government existed. Political decadence had continued almost without interruption since the death of Sáenz Peña in 1914, and when Perón appeared on the scene the traditional parties were thoroughly discredited.[17]

Ultimately Perón's rule will be judged very largely by his treatment of the problems that troubled such writers as Martínez Estrada and Mallea in the years preceding his rise to power. One of the main requirements was that the

[16] At this time many Argentines were horrified that Rosas should be set up as a hero—so appalling were the barbarities committed during his rule. There is disagreement on the degree of and the explanation for his villainy. W. H. Hudson, who remembered something of the last days of the tyranny and pondered on the character of the man, wrote that 'Some of his acts are inexplicable, as for instance, the public execution in the interests of religion and morality of a charming lady of good family and her lover. . . . There were many other acts which to foreigners and those born in later times might seem the result of insanity, but which were really the outcome of a peculiar, sardonic, and somewhat primitive sense of humour on his part which appeals powerfully to the men of the plains, the gauchos, among whom Rosas lived from boyhood' (*Far Away and Long Ago*, Everyman ed., 1939, p. 112).

[17] See Lucio A. Rubirosa, *Fronteras Democráticas* (1957), and Frank Tannenbaum, 'The Political Dilemma in Latin America', *Foreign Affairs*, Apr. 1960.

country should secure freedom to plan its own economic development. In this respect the verdict is likely to be that Perón's policy of nationalization, industrialization, state trading, and wider marketing did reduce the Argentines' dependence on foreign suppliers and protect them to some extent from the effects of fluctuations in world demand and prices. Second, it will be asked, did Perón assist the provinces of the interior to recover from the neglect that they had experienced for many decades while Buenos Aires prospered? Although he did not halt the growth in the size and influence of Buenos Aires, he did hasten the exploitation of the mineral resources of the far-away Andean region, encourage the development of important engineering and other industries in provincial towns such as Córdoba, and construct at least a few roads in areas which the old railways did not adequately serve. The benefits of the new social-welfare legislation were gradually extended to rural workers. And in the second phase of the Peronista régime vigorous action was taken in favour of the agricultural and pastoral industries. Finally, did Perón provide the nation with the inspiration and the high ideals which Mallea had considered to be lacking in the 1930's? 'Social justice' was certainly a worthy ideal; and under Perón—especially in the first phase of his rule—not only did the workers appreciate that the state was mindful of their needs, but they also felt that they themselves were at last being allowed to share in the responsibilities of Government. Argentina's destiny to become a great Power was repeatedly proclaimed, and the population were exhorted to behave with magnanimity towards their weaker neighbours. During the long course of the revolution many people who disapproved of it suffered for their convictions; and education, the press, the radio, and the films became, in varying degrees, the instruments of the régime. Nevertheless, as the 1955 revolution showed, liberal aspirations were not extinguished. Perón's undoubted disservice to Argentina was that by his methods of government he lowered the nation's moral standards: corruption during his rule was unparalleled in its extent, and his fall was preceded by semi-official gangsterism. Aramburu's great merit was that throughout his presidency (unconstitutional though it was) he set an example of incorruptibility and dignity.

There is some justification for the belief that Argentina is destined to be the 'Colossus of the South'; but continental recognition of Argentine hegemony has not occurred so soon as the prophets foretold. In 1864 the jurist Carlos Calvo wrote to Mitre:

The Argentine Republic is called upon to be, within a half century, if we have peace, as considerable a power in South America as are the United States in the North, and then will be the moment to settle accounts with that colossus with feet of paper, the Empire of Brazil.[18]

Latterly Brazil has grown faster than Argentina in population and industrial development. Her mineral deposits are more abundant and her sources of hydro-electric power more accessible than those of the southern republic. Nevertheless, the Argentines are still convinced that Brazil, in spite of its greater size and its many natural advantages, will never be a serious rival because (as the sociologist José Ingenieros wrote some forty years ago) 'the formation of great nations is incompatible with the climatic conditions of the tropics', and because of the existence of a high proportion of negro blood in the race.[19] Argentines, wherever they may be—in the distant pampa or the even more remote Andes, in the crowded cities or the desolate Antarctic outposts—have unshakeable faith in the superiority of their own people, their soil, and their climate. They already display, indeed, the self-confidence that will come from the achievements of tomorrow.

[18] Quoted by Magnet, p. 30.
[19] Magnet, pp. 22–23. cf. James, *Latin America* p. 359: 'In no part of Brazil are to be found those conditions of temperature and humidity which Huntington and others have shown to have a favourable effect on human energy.' James refers to Ellsworth Huntington, *Mainsprings of Civilization* (New York, 1945).

APPENDIX I

POLITICAL DIVISIONS

The Argentine republic is divided into the Federal Capital District of Buenos Aires, 22 Provinces, and the Territory of Tierra del Fuego (see political map, p. 93).

The Federal Capital and the Provinces have the right to elect senators and deputies to the national congress, and each of the Provinces has its own provincial chamber of senators and deputies.

In a decree of 6 March 1957 the Argentine part of Tierra del Fuego (the other part belongs to Chile) was defined as including the islands of the South Atlantic—namely, the Islas Malvinas (Falkland Islands), South Georgia, the South Shetlands, and the Argentine Antarctic Sector (see map, p. 166).[1]

APPENDIX II

POPULATION, FOREIGN RESIDENTS, AND IMMIGRATION

(A) Official Estimates, 1954 and 1959
(There was no national census between 1947 and 1960)

POPULATION

Total Population of the Republic

('000)

| | | 1954 | 18,939.5 | |
| | | 1959 | 20,775.2 | |

	Men	*Women*	*Argentines*	*Foreigners*
1954	9,643.9	9,295.7	16,106.8	2,832.7
1959	10,531.1	10,244.1	17,925.0	2,850.2

Federal Capital of Buenos Aires

| 1954 | 3,553.3 |
| 1959 | 3,845.3 |

The 1954 total includes the estimated population of Argentina's

[1] Bank of London & South America, *Fortnightly Review*, 30 Mar. 1957.

Appendices

so-called 'Antarctic Sector' and the islands of the South Atlantic. These were omitted in 1959, but a footnote in the *Boletín Mensual de Estadística* gave the number of persons in that area as 3,300.

By 1959 the population of 'Greater Buenos Aires' (i.e. the Federal Capital plus the suburbs, such as Avellaneda) was nearly 6 million, and Buenos Aires was said to be the most populous 'Latin' city in the world.

FOREIGN RESIDENTS

The largest Latin American foreign community in Argentina is Paraguayan.[1]

In 1954, among the other foreign-born residents of the republic, 2,005,367 were Italian, 820,616 Spanish, 114,837 Polish, 87,330 Russian, 58,524 German, 35,728 Yugoslav, 34,719 French, 29,727 Portuguese, 29,472 Syrian, and 18,277 Turkish.[2]

Jus solis has always been the basis of nationality in Argentina.

IMMIGRATION

Official statistics of the migratory movement to and from Argentina, 1947–59 ('000)

Year	Entries	Departures	Net Change
1947	452.3	406.2	46.1
1948	611.2	473.0	138.2
1949	641.9	484.7	157.2
1950	692.5	532.6	159.9
1951	594.9	466.6	128.3
1952	405.1	338.0	67.1
1953	242.9	213.3	29.6
1954	328.3	279.3	49.0
1955	426.0	371.6	54.4
1956	638.4	585.7	52.7
1957	726.7	662.0	64.7
1958	767.8	711.4	56.4
1959	849.3	841.3	8.0

(SOURCE: *R.R.P.*, 10 June 1960)

[1] cf. Pendle, *Paraguay*, 2nd ed. (1956), pp. 48 and 95.
[2] *R.R.P.*, 31 May 1954.

Appendices

(B) Census of September 1960

TOTAL POPULATION AND ITS GEOGRAPHICAL DISTRIBUTION

	Total (thousands)	Density (population per sq. kilometer)
Federal Capital	2,967	14,271·0
Buenos Aires	6,735	21·9
Catamarca	172	1·7
Córdoba	1,760	10·4
Corrientes	543	6·2
Chaco	535	5·4
Chubut	142	0·6
Entre Rios	804	10·5
Formosa	178	2·5
Jujuy	240	4·5
La Pampa	158	1·1
La Rioja	128	1·4
Mendoza	826	5·5
Misiones	391	13·1
Neuquén	111	1·2
Río Negro	193	0·9
Salta	413	2·7
San Juan	352	4·1
San Luís	174	2·3
Santa Cruz	53	0·2
Sante Fe	1,866	14·0
Santiago del Estero	477	3·5
Tucumán	780	34·6
Tierra del Fuego & Antarctica	10	0·3(1)
	20,009	7·2

SEX AND ORIGIN

('ooo)

Men	Women	Argentines	Foreigners
10,035	9,974	17,440	2,565

The census of 1960 showed an increase of 4,112,000 in the population since 1947, representing an annual increase of 1.8 per cent.

The 1960 census of the federal capital produced an unexpected result. 'The census takers necessarily based their reports on the information provided by the people who were actually present when they made their rounds—they were unable to take into account those who were

1 Tierra del Fuego density of population does not include Antarctica.

away from home at the time—and their summaries consequently represent the actual and temporary distribution of the population on 30 September 1960 and not its distribution by place of permanent residence. As the authorities had declared a holiday for the Friday on which the census was taken, and as the weather happened to be fine, a number of Buenos Aires residents were in the country or by the seaside and not at their homes in the city. Because of this the figures actually suggest that the population of the federal capital has fallen since 1947' (*R.R.P.*, 31 August 1961).

ECONOMICALLY ACTIVE POPULATION, BY ACTIVITY, 1947 AND 1960

Activity	1947	1960	% Diff. $\frac{1960}{1947}$
Agriculture, forestry, fishing	1,622,128	1,460,541	− 9·9
Mining and quarrying ...	32,152	43,315	+ 13·5
Manufacturing	1,426,484	1,915,726	+ 13·4
Electricity, gas, sanitation	30,743	87,389	+184·0
Construction	338,027	423,268	+ 25·0
Transport, storage and communications ...	387,280	477,222	+ 23·2
Commerce	854,966	904,289	+ 5·8
Other services	1,374,632	1,519,054	+ 10·6
Unspecified	200,901	768,267	+ —

(SOURCE: *R.R.P.*, 10 December 1963)

APPENDIX III

COST OF LIVING

The Buenos Aires working-class cost-of-living index was as follows for the month of December in the years 1955–61:

1955	105
1956	123
1957	156
1958	229
1959	438
1960	515
1961	607

(*R.R.P.*, 20 May 1960 and 20 February 1962)

The cost of living then rose by 31·7 per cent. in 1962 and a further 27·6 per cent. in 1963 (Bank of London & South America, *Fortnightly Review*, 25 January 1961).

APPENDIX IV

Agriculture and Livestock

AGRICULTURAL PRODUCTION

('ooo metric tons)

	Average 1934-8	Average 1948-52	1954-5	1955-6	1956-7	1957-8	1958-9	1959-60
Wheat	6,634	5,175	7,690	5,250	7,100	5,810	6,720	5,837
Linseed	1,702	513	405	238	620	630	620	825
Oats	748	743	890	723	1,140	995	850	983
Barley	503	656	1,112	951	1,364	1,010	1,050	1,116
Rye	254	526	844	654	880	630	817	1,060
Maize	7,892	2,509	2,546	3,870	2,698	4,806	4,932	3,980
Sunflower-seed	154	788	345	754	625	759	387	763

PATTERN OF CULTIVATION

For many years the area devoted to extensive farming (i.e. grains and forage) has remained practically constant, as these crops cannot be grown on a large scale outside the borders of the *pampa*, and virtually the whole of the *pampa* was brought under cultivation a quarter of a century ago. Within the *pampa*, however, in recent years the pattern of cultivation has changed. There has been a decline in the area planted with wheat and a corresponding increase in the area used for the cultivation of animal feeding-stuffs. This is mainly the result of government incentives to encourage cattle-raising. In 1959-60 38 per cent. of Argentina's cultivated land was devoted to grains, 51 per cent. to forage, this being a reversal of the previous ratio.

In recent years the area devoted to intensive farming has increased. The additional land brought under cultivation is mostly outside the *pampa*, sometimes in districts where irrigation is necessary. The crops include cotton, sugar, tobacco, tea, tung, grapes, *yerba*, rice, and hemp. The area under intensive farming only amounts to 11 per cent. of the cultivated land in the republic, but the market price of the crops is so high that in value the production of intensive farming almost equals that of extensive farming.

So the *pampa*, relatively, has been losing some of its importance. This should be a healthy sign of economic decentralization and of the development of new resources. (*R.R.P.*, 12 July 1960).

CATTLE STOCKS, AND MARKET DESTINATION OF BEEF

	Cattle Stocks mid-year estimates (thousand head)	*Market Destination of Beef*		
		Export	*Domestic Consumption*	*Domestic Consumption per capita (kilogrammes)*
		(thousand tons)		
1930	32,212	654	872	73
1937	33,207	677	1,066	79
1947	41,048	739	1,381	87
1952	41,910	301	1,513	87
1953	41,182	246	1,535	87
1954	43,596	241	1,583	88
1955	43,978	426	1,732	95
1956	46,940	636	1,873	100
1957	43,980	617	1,874	99
1958	41,327	665	1,894	99
1959	41,167	547	1,427	73
1960	43,398	425	1,514	76
1961	45,000	560	1,650	83

(*R.R.P.*, 20 February 1962)

Early in 1964 there was a recurrence of the problem—first experienced during the Perón régime[1]—of securing adequate supplies of cattle for Argentina's vitally important meat export trade. The meat-packing plants were hampered by the decline in the number of cattle offered for slaughter. An increasing proportion of meat went for local consumption, the suppliers for the domestic market offering higher prices than those obtainable abroad. (Bank of London & South America, *Fortnightly Review*, 7 March 1964).

LANDOWNING

The 1960 census revealed a notable increase in the number of agricultural landowners. The proportion of 38 per cent. of farms worked by owners in 1937 remained almost the same until 1952; in the next eight years it rose to 50 per cent.; the *area* of land worked by owners increased also; the number of tenants and share-croppers declined correspondingly (*R.R.P.*, 10 December 1963).

[1] See above, p. 147.

APPENDIX V

FOREIGN INVESTMENT

A Foreign Capital Investment Bill, drafted towards the end of 1958, was promulgated as Law No. 14780. The twofold purpose of this law was to attract foreign capital while ensuring that it served the national interest. Foreign capital invested in Argentina for the promotion of new industries or improving established industries necessary for the country's economic advancement would enjoy the same rights as capital of Argentine origin. Such investment would require the prior authorization of the Government, who would demand proof of technical efficiency and evidence that the investment would contribute to the substitution of imports or the expansion of exports, or that it would assist the balanced growth of the national economy. The investment might be in the form either of foreign exchange or of machinery and other supplies. Preference would be given to investments for the processing of Argentine industrial materials, and to those which were planned to share in the development of sound Argentine companies already existing or to be established. Preference would also be given to investors who undertook to reinvest their profits in Argentina. Net profits, however, would be eligible for remittance to the country of origin at the free market rate of exchange.[1]

The principal countries investing under this law during 1959 were the following:

Country	Investment in U.S. $ million
United States	95·3
Switzerland	35·0
Netherlands	26·2
Germany	15·0
Italy	8·4
United Kingdom	6·8
France	4·9

Of those approved investments, U.S. $67·9 million were placed in chemical and pharmaceutical projects, and U.S. $64·8 million in motor-vehicle and tractor industries.[2]

[1] Bank of London & South America, *Fortnightly Review*, 28 Feb. 1959.
[2] Bank of London & South America, *Quarterly Review*, July 1960.

Appendices

In December 1961 the Ministry of Economy published the following details of foreign capital investments which had been approved under Law No. 14780 since December 1958:

Country	Investment in U.S. $m.
U.S.A.	193·21
Switzerland	49·48
United Kingdom	31·75
Netherlands	26·25
Western Germany	25·11
Canada	22·10
Italy	18·15
France	11·18
Panama	3·56
Others	6·60
TOTAL	387·40

Purpose	U.S. $m.
Chemical products	118·04
Motor vehicles	96·73
Non-ferrous metals	44·37
Petroleum refining	28·93
Machinery (excluding electric machinery)	26·57
Sea transport (other than coastal)	10·25
Others	62·51
TOTAL	387·40

SOURCE: Bank of London & South America, *Fortnightly Review*, 30 December 1961.

APPENDIX VI

TERMS OF TRADE

1953 = 100

	1951	1953	1954	1955	1956	1957	1958	1959	1960	1961
Export prices	120	100	90	87	78	76	73	75	79	79
Import prices	108	100	93	94	97	102	90	85	87	92
Terms of trade	111	100	97	93	80	74	81	88	91	86

(SOURCE: Bank of London & South America)

APPENDIX VII

FOREIGN TRADE

(U.S. $ million)

TOTAL TRADE AND BALANCE

	1958	1959	1960	1961	1962	1963
Exports (f.o.b.)	994	1,009	1,079	964	1,216	1,366
Imports (c. & f.)	1,233	993	1,249	1,460	1,357	981
BALANCE with:	−239	+ 16	−170	−496	−140	+385
Venezuela ...	− 96	−102	− 85	− 61	...	...
U.S.A. ...	− 74	−84	−237	−299	−310	− 92
Brazil ...	− 52	+ 31	+ 19	− 51	+ 5	+ 20
United Kingdom ...	+135	+145	+108	+ 34	+ 84	+122
Netherlands ...	+ 81	+ 97	+112	+117	...	...
Italy ...	+ 6	+ 48	+ 41	+ 5	+ 19	+ 84
Germany (F.R.) ...	− 21	− 20	− 65	−135	− 65	− 12

... = not available

SOURCE: Bank of London & South America, *Fortnightly Review: Trade Statistics*, 22 September 1962; 16 May 1964.

EXPORTS

(U.S. $ million)

	1959	*1960*	*1961*	*1962*	*1963*
Destination					
United Kingdom ...	235	221	173	204	200
Netherlands	118	131	141	170	146
Italy	98	127	106	140	212
U.S.A.	107	91	84	89	150
Germany (F.R.) ...	92	87	76	121	94
Brazil	89	83	27	68	78
Chile	25	42	43	32	41
Japan	26	40	52	27	39
Belgium	32	37	41	58	59
France	36	37	35	59	59
U.S.S.R.	21	19	14	...*	...*
Others	130	165	172	248	288
Commodity Groups					
Cereals & linseed ...	293	324	195	345	282
Wheat, unmilled ...	135	143	...	...	...
Maize, unmilled ...	124	124	...	...	...
Meat	259	219	217	228	334
Wool	121	145	142	145	161
Vegetable oils & oilseeds	98	125	128	167	139
Hides	70	70	79	92	78
Dairy produce ...	43	48	32	28	30
Fruit, fresh	17	25	20	28	41
Quebracho extract & other forestal products	18	15	13	...	...
Others	90	107	138	183	301

* Soviet area, U.S. $ 79 m. in 1962 and 55 m. in 1963.
... = not available.

SOURCE: Bank of London & South America, *Fortnightly Review: Trade Statistics*, 22 September 1962; 16 May 1964.

IMPORTS

(U.S. $ million)

	1959	*1960*	*1961*	*1962*	*1963*
Sources					
U.S.A....	191	327	383	399	242
Germany (F.R.) ...	112	151	211	186	106
United Kingdom ...	90	113	140	120	78
Venezuela	108	90	66	48	21
Italy	49	86	101	121	128
Brazil	58	63	78	63	58
France...	34	60	79	69	39
Belgium	36	31	29	...	...
Japan	18	28	33	64	47
Sweden	23	22	34	29	23
Netherlands Antilles ...	31	21	25	...	...
Others...	243	255	281	258	239
Commodity Groups					
Machinery & vehicles	260	534	661	731	481
Iron & steel & mfrs	194	204	216	145	102
Fuels & lubricants ...	211	156	130	92	57
Chemicals & products	72	62	90	81	77
Non-ferrous metals & manufactures ...	51	59	81	60	56
Wood & manufactures	55	47	72	49	46
Rubber & manufactures	21	43	37	26	20
Textiles & manufactures	40	39	34	48	35
Food	33	36	43	40	35
Paper, paperboard, & manufactures ...	25	30	46	33	32
Others...	30	38	50	52	40

... = not available.

SOURCE: Bank of London & South America, *Fortnightly Review: Trade Statistics*, 22 September 1962; 16 May 1964.

BIBLIOGRAPHY

I. LATIN AMERICA: GENERAL

Benham, F. and Holley, H. A. *A Short Introduction to the Economy of Latin America*. London, O.U.P. for R.I.I.A., 1960.

Bernstein, Harry. *Modern and Contemporary Latin America*. New York, Lippincott, 1952.

De Conde, Alexander. *Herbert Hoover's Latin-American Policy*. California, Stanford University, 1951.

Davies, Howell, ed. *The South American Handbook*. London, Trade & Travel Publications. (Published annually. Contains useful information for travellers.)

Fitzgibbon, R. H., ed. *The Constitutions of the Americas*. Univ. of Chicago Press, 1948.

García Calderón, F. *Latin America: its Rise and Progress*, trans. by Bernard Miall. 7th ed. London, Fisher Unwin, 1924. (First published 1913.)

Gordon, Wendell G. *The Economy of Latin America*. New York, Columbia Univ. Press, 1950.

Great Britain, Ministry of Agriculture and Fisheries. *Report of the South American Agricultural Mission, 1947*. London, 1947, mimeo.

Hanke, Lewis. *South America*. New York, Van Nostrand (Anvil Books), 1959.

Hanson, Simon G. *Economic Development in Latin America*. Washington, Inter-American Affairs Press, 1951.

Haring, C. H. *South American Progress*. Harvard Univ. Press, 1934.

—— *The Spanish Empire in America*. New York, O.U.P., 1947.

Herring, Hubert. *A History of Latin America from the Beginnings to the Present*. London, Cape, 1956. (Probably the best general history. 822 pp.)

Hughlett, Lloyd J., ed. *Industrialization in Latin America*. New York, McGraw-Hill, 1946.

Humphreys, R. A. *British Consular Reports on the Trade and Politics of Latin America, 1824–26*. London, Royal Historical Society, 1940. (Camden 3rd Ser., vol. 63.)

—— *The Evolution of Modern Latin America*. Oxford, Clarendon Press, 1946.

—— 'Latin America: the Caudillo Tradition', in *Soldiers and Governments*. ed. Michael Howard. London, Eyre & Spottiswoode, 1957.

—— *Latin American History: A Guide to the Literature in English*. London, O.U.P. for R.I.I.A., 1958. (An outstanding bibliography, containing some 2,200 entries.)

Bibliography

Humphreys, R. A. *Liberation in South America, 1806–1827: the Career of James Paroissien.* Univ. of London, Athlone Press, 1952.

James, Preston E., *Latin America.* Rev. ed., London, Cassell, 1950; 3rd ed., New York, Odyssey Press, 1959. (The perfect geographical textbook.)

Johnson, John J. *Political Change in Latin America: The Emergence of the Middle Sectors.* Stanford Univ. Press, 1958.

Jorrín, Miguel. *Governments of Latin America.* New York, Van Nostrand, 1953.

Kaufmann, W. W. *British Policy and the Independence of Latin America, 1804–1828.* Yale Univ. Press, 1951.

Kirkpatrick, F. A. *Latin America: a Brief History.* Cambridge Univ. Press, 1938.

Macdonald, Austin F. *Latin American Politics and Government.* New York, Crowell, 1949.

Martin, Michael Rheta, and Lovett, Gabriel H. *An Encyclopaedia of Latin-American History.* New York, Abelard-Schuman, 1956.

Mulhall, Michael G. *The English in South America.* Buenos Aires, 'The Standard', 1878.

Pendle, George. *South America.* O.U.P. (The Oxford Visual Geographies), 1958.

Rich, John Lyon. *The Face of South America: an Aerial Traverse.* New York, American Geog. Soc., 1942 (Special Publications No. 26). (Aerial photographs and explanatory text.)

Rippy, J. Fred. *Historical Evolution of Latin America.* 3rd ed. New York, Crofts, 1945.

—— *Latin America and the Industrial Age.* New York, Putnam, 1944.

Robertson, William Spence. *France and Latin-American Independence.* Baltimore, Johns Hopkins Press, 1939.

Sánchez, Luis Alberto. *Existe América Latina?* Mexico, Fondo de Cultura Económica, 1945.

Schurz, W. L. *This New World: The Civilization of Latin America.* London, Allen & Unwin, 1956. (Mainly concerned with the colonial period.)

Tannenbaum, Frank. 'The Political Dilemma in Latin America', *Foreign Affairs*, Apr. 1960, pp. 497–515.

Thomas, A. B. *Latin America: A History.* New York, Macmillan, 1956. (801 pp.)

United Nations:

Dept. of Economic Affairs. *Foreign Capital in Latin America.* New York, 1955.

—— *A Study of the Iron and Steel Industry in Latin America.* Vol. 1. New York, 1954.

—— *Study of Trade between Latin America and Europe.* Geneva, 1953. (Prepared by the Secretariat of the Economic Commission for Latin

Bibliography

America, the Economic Commission for Europe, and the Food and Agriculture Organization.)

E.C.L.A. *Economic Survey of Latin America.* New York, annually.

Food and Agriculture Organization. *Prospects for Agricultural Development in Latin America.* Rome, [1953].

Webster, C. K. *Britain and the Independence of Latin America, 1812–1830.* O.U.P., for the Ibero-American Inst. of Great Britain, 1938. 2 vols.

Who's Who in Latin America: Pt V. (Argentina, Paraguay, and Uruguay.) California, Stanford Univ. Press, 1950.

Wythe, George. *Industry in Latin America.* 2nd ed. New York, Columbia Univ. Press, 1949.

II. ARGENTINA: GENERAL

Amadeo, Santos P. *Argentine Constitutional Law: the judicial function in the maintenance of the federal system and the preservation of individual rights.* New York, Columbia Univ. Press, 1943. (Columbia Legal Series, No. IV.)

Barclay, W. S. *The Land of the Magellan.* London, Methuen, 1926.

Battolla, Octavio C. *Los Primeros Ingleses en Buenos Aires, 1780–1830.* Buenos Aires, Editorial Muro, 1928.

Box, Pelham Horton. *The Origins of the Paraguayan War.* Urbana, Illinois, 1929. 2 vols. (Univ. of Illinois, Studies in the Social Sciences, XV, nos. 3 and 4.)

Bunge, Alejandro E. *La Economía Argentina.* Buenos Aires, Agencia General de Librerías y Publicaciones, 1928–30. 4 vols.

—— *Una Nueva Argentina.* Buenos Aires, Kraft, 1940.

Bunge, Carlos Octavio. *Nuestra América: Ensayo de psicología social.* 6th ed. Buenos Aires, Casa Vaccaro ('La Cultura Argentina'), 1918.

Bunkley, Allison Williams. *The Life of Sarmiento.* Princeton Univ. Press, 1952.

Burgin, Miron. *The Economic Aspects of Argentine Federalism, 1820–1852.* Cambridge, Mass., Harvard Univ. Press, 1946.

Cady, John F. *Foreign Intervention in the Rio de la Plata, 1838–50.* Philadelphia, Univ. of Pennsylvania Press, 1929.

Dodds, James. *Records of the Scottish Settlers in the River Plate and their Churches.* Buenos Aires, Grant & Sylvester, 1897.

Farnworth, Constance H., and Kevorkian, Arthur G. *Argentina, Competitor of U.S. Agriculture in World Markets.* Washington, U.S. Dept. of Agriculture, 1957.

Ferns, H. S. 'Beginnings of British Investment in Argentina', *Economic History Review* (C.U.P.), 2nd ser. IV, no. 3, 1952, pp. 341–52. (Covers the years 1806–30.)

—— 'Investment and Trade between Britain and Argentina in the Nineteenth Century', *Economic History Review*, 2nd ser., III, no. 2, 1950, pp. 203–18.

Bibliography

Ferns, H. S. *Britain and Argentina in the Nineteenth Century.* Oxford, Clarendon Press, 1960.

Ford, A. G. 'Argentina and the Baring Crisis of 1890', *Oxford Economic Papers* (Clarendon Press), 1956, pp. 127–50.

Frondizi, Arturo. *Petróleo y Política.* Buenos Aires, Raigal, 1955. (Dr. Frondizi believed that Argentina did not need foreign assistance in the exploitation of local petroleum resources. When he became President of the Republic he changed his mind.)

Frondizi, Silvio. *La Realidad Argentina: Ensayo de Interpretación Sociológica.* Buenos Aires, Praxis, 1955–6. 2 vols. (A Marxist interpretation of Argentine history.)

García-Mata, Rafael and Llorens, Emilio. *Argentina Económica 1939.* Buenos Aires, Compañía Impresora Argentina, 1939.

Gibson, Herbert. *The History and Present State of the Sheep-breeding Industry in the Argentine Republic.* Buenos Aires, Ravenscroft & Mills, 1893.

Graham, R. B. Cunninghame. *The Conquest of the River Plate.* London, Heinemann, 1924.

—— *The Horses of the Conquest.* London, Heinemann, 1930.

Hanson, Simon G. *Argentine Meat and the British Market: Chapters in the History of the Argentine Meat Industry.* Stanford Univ. Press, 1938.

Haring, C. H. *Argentina and the United States.* Boston, World Peace Foundation, 1941.

Ingenieros, José. *La Evolución de las Ideas Argentinas,* ed. by Aníbal Ponce. Buenos Aires, Editorial Problemas, 1946. 4 vols.

—— *Sociología Argentina.* Buenos Aires, J. L. Rosso, 1915.

Jefferson, Mark. *Peopling the Argentine Pampa.* 2nd impression. New York American Geog. Soc., 1930. (Research Series No. 16.)

Jones, Wilbur Devereux. 'The Argentine British Colony in the Time of Rosas', *Hispanic American Historical Review,* Feb. 1960, pp. 90–97.

Kennedy, John J. *Catholicism, Nationalism, and Democracy in Argentina.* Univ. of Notre Dame Press, 1958.

Kirkpatrick, F. A. *A History of the Argentine Republic.* Cambridge Univ. Press, 1931.

Kroeber, Clifton B. *The Growth of the Shipping Industry in the Río de la Plata Region, 1794–1860.* Univ. of Wisconsin Press, 1957.

Kühn, Franz. *Geografía de la Argentina.* 2nd ed. Barcelona, Editorial Labor, 1941. (Colección Labor, Sección VII, Geografía, No. 271.) (An authoritative handbook.)

Legón, Faustino J. and Medrano, Samuel W. *Las Constituciones de la República Argentina.* Madrid, Ediciones Cultura Hispánica, 1953.

Levene, Ricardo. *A History of Argentina,* trans. and ed. by W. S. Robertson. Chapel Hill, Univ. of North Carolina Press, 1937.

Lynch, John. *Spanish Colonial Administration, 1782–1810: The Intendant System in the Viceroyalty of the Rio de la Plata.* Univ. of London, Athlone Press, 1958.

Bibliography

Macdonald, Austin F. *Government of the Argentine Republic*. New York, Thomas Y. Crowell, 1942.

McGann, Thomas F. *Argentina, the United States, and the Inter-American System, 1880–1914*, Harvard Univ. Press, 1957.

Mitre, Bartolomé. *Historia de Belgrano*. Buenos Aires, Imprenta de Mayo, 1859. 2 vols.

—— *Historia de San Martín y de la Emancipación Sud-Americana*. 2nd ed. Buenos Aires, Felix Lajouane, 1890. 4 vols.

Peters, H. E. *The Foreign Debt of the Argentine Republic*. Baltimore, Johns Hopkins Press, 1934.

Phelps, Vernon Lovell. *The International Economic Position of Argentina*. Philadelphia, Univ. of Pennsylvania Press, 1938.

Quien es Quien en la Argentina: Biografías Contemporáneas. 5th ed. Buenos Aires, Kraft, 1950.

Rennie, Ysabel F. *The Argentine Republic*. New York, Macmillan, 1945. (A comprehensive historical account.)

Robirosa, Lucio A. *Fronteras Democráticas*.... Buenos Aires, Gure, 1957. (The author, a highly-respected Argentine lawyer, suggests that since the death of Sáenz Peña in 1914 political decadence has continued almost without interruption in Argentina.)

Rowe, L. S. *The Federal System of the Argentine Republic*. Carnegie Inst. of Washington, 1921.

Scalabrini Ortiz, R. *Política Británica en el Río de la Plata*. Buenos Aires, 1940.

Schoo Lastra, Dionisio. *El Indio del Desierto, 1535–1879*. Buenos Aires, Agencia General de Librería y Publicaciones, 1928. (The indigenous Indians of Argentina.)

Schopflocher, Roberto. *Historia de la Colonización Agrícola en Argentina*. Buenos Aires, Raigal, 1955. (A monograph in Raigal's interesting series 'Colección Campo Argentino'.)

Smith, O. Edmund. *Yankee Diplomacy: U.S. Intervention in Argentina*. Dallas, Southern Methodist Univ. Press, 1953. (Arnold Foundation Studies, vol. 3, new series.)

Street, John. *Artigas and the Emancipation of Uruguay*. Cambridge Univ. Press, 1959. (The Uruguayan struggle for independence was a part of Argentina's history during the nineteenth century.)

Tandy, A. H. *Argentina: Economic and Commercial Conditions*.... London, H.M.S.O. (Overseas Economic Surveys), 1956. (The previous survey of Argentina in this Board of Trade series was by J. G. Lomax, 1948.)

Taullard, A. *Nuestro Antiguo Buenos Aires*.... Buenos Aires, Peuser, 1927. (Illus. with old photographs.)

Taylor, Carl C. *Rural Life in Argentina*. Baton Rouge, Louisiana State Univ. Press, 1948.

U.S. Tariff Commission. *Agricultural, Pastoral and Forest Industries in Argentina*. Washington, 1947.

Bibliography

U.S. Tariff Commission. *Economic Controls and Commercial Policy in Argentina.* Washington, 1945.

—— *Mining and Manufacturing Industries in Argentina.* Washington, 1945.

Wallace, Robert. *Argentine Shows and Live Stock.* Edinburgh, Oliver & Boyd, 1904.

Weil, Felix J. *Argentine Riddle.* New York, Day, 1944.

Whitaker, Arthur P. *The United States and Argentina.* Harvard Univ. Press, 1954.

White, John W. *Argentina; the Life Story of a Nation.* New York, Viking Press, 1942.

III. The Perón Era, and After

Alexander, Robert J. *The Perón Era.* London, Gollancz, 1952. (Particularly useful regarding labour, trade unions, etc.)

Argentina, Ministerio de Relaciones Exteriores y Culto. *Expresiones de una Política Continental: Argentina y Nicaragua Bajo el Signo de América.* Buenos Aires, 1953.

—— *Expresiones de una Política Continental: Discursos de los Presidentes Chaves y Perón.* Buenos Aires, 1953.

—— *Mensaje a los Pueblos de América de los Presidentes Perón e Ibañez: Afirmación de un Destino Común.* Buenos Aires, 1953.

—— *Unión Económica Argentina Ecuatoriana: Afirmación de un Destino Común.* Buenos Aires, 1953. (The texts of President Perón's pacts of economic union.)

— Presidencia, Subsecretaría de Informaciones. *Plan Quinquenal del Gobierno del Presidente Perón, 1947–1951.* Buenos Aires, 1947. (The text of President Perón's first Five Year Plan.)

—— *Segundo Plan Quinquenal.* Buenos Aires, 1953. (The text of President Perón's second Five Year Plan.)

—— *The Constitution of the Argentine Nation, approved by the National Constituent Assembly, March 11th, 1949.* Buenos Aires, 1949.

Barager, Joseph R. 'Historiography of the Río de la Plata since 1930', *Hispanic American Historical Review,* Nov. 1959. (Contains an interesting passage on historical study during the Perón régime.)

Blanksten, George I. *Perón's Argentina.* Univ. of Chicago Press, 1953. (An authoritative analysis of the Perón régime.)

Cowles, Fleur. *Bloody Precedent: the Perón Story.* London, Muller, 1952. (The author, who is not a historian, draws a parallel between the régimes of Rosas and Perón.)

Gómez Morales, Alfredo. *El Estado Económica del País y la Ejecución del Segundo Plan Quinquenal: Conferencia Pronunciada . . . en la Escuela Nacional de Guerra.* Buenos Aires, Presidencia de la Nación, Ministerio de Asuntos Económicos, 1953.

Greenup, Ruth and Leonard. *Revolution before Breakfast: Argentina, 1941–1946.* Univ. of North Carolina Press, 1947.

Bibliography

Hoffmann, Fritz L. 'Perón and After', pts I and II, in *Hispanic American Historical Review*, Nov. 1956, pp. 510–28, and May 1959, pp. 212–33. (Two review articles dealing with the flow of publications on the Perón régime which appeared after the revolution of September 1955.)

Horowitz, Irving L. 'Modern Argentina: the Politics of Power', *Political Quarterly* (London), Oct.–Dec. 1959, pp. 400–10.

Josephs, Ray. *Argentine Diary*. New York, Random House, 1944. (A journalist's impressions.)

—— *Latin America: Continent in Crisis*. New York, Random House, 1948. (Contains a chapter on Argentina in the same journalistic manner as *Argentine Diary*.)

Kennedy, John J. 'Accountable Government in Argentina', *Foreign Affairs*, Apr. 1959, pp. 453–62.

MacKenzie, Norman. *Argentina*. London, Gollancz, 1947. (A Socialist interpretation of the rise of Perón.)

Magnet, Alejandro. *Nuestros Vecinos Justicialistas*. Santiago de Chile, Editorial del Pacífico, 1953. (A Chilean study of President Perón's Argentina, with special reference to the Argentine-Chilean pact of 'economic union', 1953.)

Mende, Raúl A. *El Justicialismo: Doctrina y Realidad Peronista*. Buenos Aires, ALEA, 1950. (An English translation of extracts from this book was published with the title *Justicialism: the Peronist Doctrine and Reality*, Buenos Aires Imprenta López, 1952.)

Perón, Eva. *La Razón de mi Vida*. Buenos Aires, Peuser, 1951.

Perón, Juan D. *Conferencia pronunciada en el Acto de Clausura del Primer Congreso Nacional de Filosofía, Mendoza, 9 de Abril de 1949*. Buenos Aires, Presidencia, Subsecretaría de Informaciones, 1949.

[Perón, Juan D.] *Los Mensajes de Perón*. Buenos Aires, Ediciones Mundo Peronista, 1952. (President Perón's annual messages to Congress, 1946–1952.)

Potash, Robert A. 'Argentine Political Parties 1957–8' in *Journal of Inter-American Studies*, Oct. 1959, pp. 515–24.

Richmond, Leonardo T. *La Tercera Posición Argentina, y otros sistemas comparados*. Translated by Eustasio de Amilibia. Buenos Aires, Acme Agency, 1950.

U.S. Dept. of State. *Consultation among the American Republics with Respect to the Argentine Situation*. Washington, 1946. (The 'Blue Book' published two weeks before the Argentine elections of February 1946.)

Whitaker, Arthur P. *Argentine Upheaval: Perón's Fall and the New Régime*. London, Atlantic Press, 1956. (In his previous book—see Section II above—the author had overestimated the stability of the Perón régime. In this volume he acknowledged his error and, although writing with journalistic haste, related Perón and his downfall to the past history of the country.)

Bibliography

NOTE: Interesting impressions of Perón will be found in the books by James Bruce, G. S. Fraser, and Sir David Kelly (Section V below).

IV. EARLY TRAVEL AND DESCRIPTION

Andrews, Captain. *Journey from Buenos Ayres*, &c. London, Murray, 1827. 2 vols.

'An Englishman'. *A Five Years' Residence in Buenos Aires during the years 1820 to 1825*. London, G. Herbert, 1825. (The author was probably Thomas George Love, founder of the English newspaper *The British Packet*, Buenos Aires.)

Anonymous. *A Relation of R.M.'s Voyage to Buenos-Ayres, and from thence by land to Potosí*. London, John Darby, 1716.

Azara, Felix de. *Voyages dans l'Amérique Méridionale*, &c. Paris, 1809. 4 vols.

Baudizzone, Luis M., ed. *Buenos Aires visto por los viajeros ingleses, 1800-1825*. Emecé (Colección Buen Aire), 1941. (An introduction to some of the early English travel books.)

Beaumont, J. A. B. *Travels in Buenos Ayres and the Adjacent Provinces of the Rio de la Plata*. London, James Ridgway, 1828.

Bourne, Benjamin Franklin. *The Captive in Patagonia* ... Boston, Gould & Lincoln, 1853.

Brackenridge, H. M. *Voyage to South America*, &c. London, Allman, 1820, 2 vols.

Brand, Lieut. Chas. *Journal of a Voyage to Peru*, &c. London, Henry Colburn, 1828.

Caldcleugh, Alexander. *Travels in South America*, &c. London, Murray, 1825. 2 vols.

Darwin, Charles. *Charles Darwin's Diary of the Voyage of H.M.S. 'Beagle'*, ed. by Nora Barlow. Cambridge University Press, 1933. (The complete text of Darwin's manuscript diary.)

Davie, John Constanse. *Letters from Paraguay*. London, Robinson, 1805.

Haigh, Samuel. *Sketches of Buenos Ayres, Chile and Peru*. London, Effingham Wilson, 1831.

Head, Captain F. B. *Rough Notes taken during some Rapid Journeys across the Pampas and among the Andes*. London, Murray, 1826.

Helms, Anthony Zachariah. *Travels from Buenos Aires by Potosí to Lima*. 2nd ed. London, Richard Phillips, 1807.

Hutchinson, Thomas J. *Buenos Ayres and Argentine Gleanings*. London, Edward Stanford, 1865.

—— *The Paraná . . . and South American Recollections*. London, Edward Stanford, 1868.

Isabelle, Arsène. *Voyage a Buenos-Ayres*, &c. Havre, J. Morlent, 1835.

Jackman, Sydney. *Galloping Head*. London, Phoenix, 1958. (The life of Sir Francis Bond Head.)

Bibliography

Jones, Tom B. *South America Rediscovered*. Univ. of Minnesota Press, 1949. (The best book about the early travellers.)

King, Col. J. Anthony. *Twenty-four Years in the Argentine Republic*, &c. London, Longman, 1846.

MacCann, William. *Two Thousand Miles' Ride through the Argentine Provinces*, &c. London, Smith, Elder, 1853. 2 vols.

Mackinnon, Commander. *Steam Warfare in the Parana* . . . London, Charles Ollier, 1848. 2 vols.

Miller, John. *Memoirs of General Miller*. 2nd ed. London, Longman, 1829. 2 vols.

Notes on the Viceroyalty of La Plata in South America, &c. London, J. J. Stockdale, 1808.

Page, Thomas Jefferson. *La Plata, the Argentine Confederation and Paraguay*. London, Trubner, 1859.

Pallière, Léon, *Diario de Viaje por la América del Sud*. Buenos Aires, Peuser, 1945. (A mid-nineteenth century diary, lavishly illustrated with reproductions of Pallière's water-colours and drawings.)

Parish, Sir Woodbine. *Buenos Aires and the Provinces of the Rio de la Plata*. London, Murray, 1838. (2nd ed., London, 1852.)

Proctor, Robert. *Narrative of a Journey across the Cordillera of the Andes*, &c. London, Constable, 1825.

Robertson, J. P. and W. P. *Letters on Paraguay*. London, Murray, 1838 and 1839. 3 vols.

—— *Letters on South America*, &c. London, Murray, 1843. 3 vols.

Rodney, C. A. and Graham, John. *The Reports on the Present State of the United Provinces of South America*. London, Baldwin, Cradock & Joy, 1819.

Scarlett, The Hon. P. Campbell. *South America and the Pacific*, &c. London, Henry Colburn, 1838. 2 vols.

Schmidl, Ulrich. *Derrotero y Viaje a España y las Indias*, trans. by Edmundo Wernicke. Buenos Aires, Aspasa-Calpe, 1944. (Colección Austral.) (A chronicle of the first founding of Buenos Aires.)

Schmidtmeyer, Peter. *Travels in Chile over the Andes in the years 1820 and 1821*. London, Longman, 1824.

Snow, W. Parker. *A Two Years' Cruise off Tierra del Fuego*, &c. London, Longman, 1857. 2 vols.

Temple, Edmond. *Travels in Various Parts of Peru*, &c. London, Colburn & Bentley, 1830. 2 vols.

Vidal, E. E. *Picturesque Illustrations of Buenos Aires and Monte Video*. London, Ackermann, 1820. (A beautifully illustrated volume.)

Wilcocke, Samuel Hull. *History of the Viceroyalty of Buenos Aires*, &c. London, H. D. Symonds, 1807.

Wilde, José Antonio. *Buenos Aires desde Setenta Anos Atrás*. Buenos Aires, Espasa-Calpe, 1944. (Colección Austral.) (Reminiscences of the early nineteenth century.)

Bibliography

V. Later Travel and Description

Bridges, E. Lucas, *Uttermost Part of the Earth*. London, Hodder & Stoughton, 1948. (Reminiscences of Tierra del Fuego.)

Bruce, James. *Those Perplexing Argentines*. London, Eyre & Spottiswoode, 1954. (The author was U.S. Ambassador to Argentina, 1947–8.)

Bryce, James. *South America: Observations and Impressions*. New York, Macmillan, 1920.

Burton, Richard F. *Letters from the Battle-Fields of Paraguay*. London, Tinsley, 1870.

Clark, Edwin. *A Visit to South America*. London, Dean, 1878.

Crawford, Robert. *Across the Pampas and the Andes*. London, Longmans, 1884.

Daireaux, Emile. *La Vie et les Moeurs à la Plata*. 2nd ed. Paris, Hachette, 1889. 2 vols.

Elliott, L. E. *The Argentina of Today*. London, Hurst & Blackett, [1925].

Frank, Waldo. *America Hispana*. New York, Scribner's, 1931. (Waldo Frank had a considerable influence on Argentine intellectuals in the uncertain 1930's.)

—— *South American Journey*. London, Gollancz, 1944.

Fraser, G. S. *News from South America*. London, Harvill Press, 1949. (A poet's impressions.)

Gibson, Sir Christopher. *Enchanted Trails*. London, Museum Press, 1948.

Graham, R. B. Cunninghame. *El Río de la Plata*. London, Hispania, 1914. (Articles reprinted from the magazine *Hispania*.)

Hinchliff, Thomas Woodbine. *South American Sketches*. London, Longman, 1863.

Hirst, W. A. *Argentina*. London, Fisher Unwin, 1910.

Holdich, Col. Sir Thomas Hungerford. *The Countries of the King's Award*. London, Hurst & Blackett, 1904.

Hudson, W. H. *Far Away and Long Ago*. London, Dent, 1918.

—— *Idle Days in Patagonia*. London, Chapman & Hall, 1893.

—— *The Naturalist in La Plata*. London, Chapman & Hall, 1892.

Isherwood, Christopher. *The Condor and the Cows*. London, Methuen, 1949. (A novelist's impressions.)

Johnson, H. C. Ross. *A Long Vacation in the Argentine Alps* . . . London, Richard Bentley, 1868.

Kelly, Sir David. *The Ruling Few*. London, Hollis & Carter, 1952. (The author was in Argentina during 1919–21 and, as H.M. Ambassador, 1942–6.)

Keyserling, Count Hermann. *South American Meditations: on Hell and Heaven in Man's Soul*, trans. by Therese Duerr, London, Cape, 1930. (Keyserling's opinions on Argentina aroused violent protest in the local press.)

Knight, E. F. *The Cruise of the 'Falcon'* . . . London, Sampson Low, 1884. 2 vols.

Koebel, W. H. *Argentina Past and Present.* London, Kegan Paul, 1910.

—— *The Great South Land: the River Plate and Southern Brazil Today.* London, Butterworth, 1919.

Larden, Walter. *Argentine Plains and Andine Glaciers.* London, Fisher Unwin, 1911.

Latham, Wilfrid. *The State of the River Plate,* &c. London, Longmans, 1866.

Morand, Paul. *Air Indien.* Paris, Grasset, 1932.

Mulhall, M. G. and E. T. *Handbook of the River Plate.* 6th ed. Buenos Aires, published by the authors, 1892.

Mulhall, Mrs M. G. *Between the Amazon and the Andes.* London, Edward Stanford, 1881.

Musters, George Chaworth. *At Home with the Patagonians* . . . 2nd ed. London, Murray, 1873.

Roberts, Morley. *W. H. Hudson: a Portrait.* London, Eveleigh Nash & Grayson, 1924.

Ross, Gordon. *Argentina and Uruguay.* London, Methuen, 1917.

Seymour, Richard Arthur. *Pioneering in the Pampas,* &c. 2nd ed. London, Longmans, 1870.

Simpson, George Gaylord. *Attending Marvels; a Patagonian Journal.* New York, Macmillan, 1934.

Thompson, R. W. *Voice from the Wilderness.* rev. ed. London, Macdonald, 1947. (Pt II of this book is devoted to the Argentine province of Misiones.)

[Todd, Aline.] *Journal of a Tour to and from South America.* Privately printed [?1892]. (Impressions of a well-to-do English lady.)

Tschiffely, A. F. *Don Roberto.* London, Heinemann, 1937. (The biography of R. B. Cunninghame Graham.)

—— *Southern Cross to Pole Star.* London, Heinemann, 1933. (The description of a famous ride on horseback from Argentina to Washington.)

Turner, Thomas A. *Argentina and the Argentines.* London, Sonnenschein, 1892.

VI. The English Invasions

Anon. *An Authentic Narrative of the Proceedings of the Expedition under the Command of Brigadier-Gen. Crauford,* &c. By an officer of the expedition. London, for the author, 1808.

Anon. *An authentic and interesting description of the city of Buenos Ayres and the adjacent country,* &c. London, John Fairburn, 1806.

Beverina, Juan. *Las invasiones inglesas al Río de la Plata.* Buenos Aires, 1939. 2 vols.

Bibliography

Costa, Ernestina (Baroness Peers de Nieuwburgh). *English Invasion of the River Plate*. Buenos Aires, Kraft, 1937.

Fortescue, The Hon. J. W. *The History of the British Army*. Vol. V, 1803–1807. London, Macmillan, 1910. (Contains the history of the British invasions of the River Plate, 1806–7. cf. also the histories of the regiments which took part in the invasions.)

Gillespie, Major Alexander. *Gleanings and Remarks collected during many months of residence at Buenos Ayres and within the upper country*. Leeds, the author, 1818.

[Gurney, W. B.] *The Proceedings of a General Court Martial . . . for the Trial of Lieut. Gen. Whitelocke*. Taken in shorthand by Mr Gurney. London, 1808. 2 vols.

[Hook, Theodore E.] The Life of General the Right Honourable Sir David Baird, Bart. London, R. Bentley, 1832. 2 vols.

Instituto de Estudios Históricos [various authors]. *La Reconquista y Defensa de Buenos Aires*. Buenos Aires, Peuser, 1947.

[Pococke, Captain.] *Journal of a soldier of the 71st or Glasgow Regiment*, &c. 2nd ed. Edinburgh, 1819.

Roberts, Carlos. *Las Invasiones Inglesas del Río de la Plata, 1806–1807*, &c. Buenos Aires, Peuser, 1938.

VII. The Welsh Colony

Baur, John E. 'The Welsh in Patagonia: an Example of Nationalistic Migration', *Hispanic American Historical Review*, Nov. 1954.

Beerbohm, Julius. *Wanderings in Patagonia* . . . London, Chatto & Windus, 1879.

Bertomeu, Carlos A. *El Valle de la Esperanza: una Historia de Gales y Chubut*. Buenos Aires, El Ateneo, 1943. (An historical novel about the Welsh colony in Chubut.)

Great Britain, Parliamentary Paper: *Correspondence Respecting the Establishment of a Welsh Colony on the River Chupat, in Patagonia*. London, 1867.

Jones, Idris. *Modern Welsh History; from 1485 to the Present Day*. London, Bell, 1934. (Ch. XV recounts the history of the Welsh colony in Patagonia.)

Matthews, Abraham. *Hanes y Wladfa Gymreig yn Patagonia*. Aberdare, 1894. (In Welsh. The reminiscences of one of the original colonists. cf. Spanish translation: Matthews, Reverendo A. *Crónica de la Colonia Galesa de la Patagonia*, trans. F. E. Roberts. Buenos Aires, Editorial Raigal, 1954.)

Pendle, George. 'The Welsh in Patagonia', *Wales* (London), Feb. 1959.

Prichard, H. Hesketh. *Through the Heart of Patagonia*. London, Heinemann, 1902.

Smith, W. G. Rae. 'A Visit to Patagonia', *Scottish Geographical Magazine*, XXVIII, 1912.

Bibliography

Tschiffely, A. F. *This way Southward* . . . London, Heinemann, 1940.

Williams, R. Bryn. *Cymry Patagonia*. Aberystwyth, 1945. (In Welsh.)

NOTE: For another traveller's impressions of the Colony see Holdich (Section V above).

VIII. RAILWAYS

Brady, George S. *The Railways of South America*, Pt II. Washington, U.S. Dept of Commerce, 1927.

Dirección de Informaciones y Publicaciones Ferroviarias. *Origen y Desarrollo de los Ferrocarriles Argentinos*. Buenos Aires, El Ateneo, 1946.

Halsey, Frederic M. *The Railways of South and Central America*. New York, F. E. Fitch, 1914.

Ortiz, Ricardo M. *El Ferrocarril en la Economía Argentina*. Buenos Aires, Editorial Problemas, 1946.

Pendle, George. 'Railways in Argentina', *History Today* (London), Feb. 1958, pp. 119–25.

Railway Gazette. London, Transport Ltd, 1910 and 1926. Special nos. devoted to South American railways.

Robins, Michael. 'The Balaklava Railway', *Journal of Transport History* (Univ. College of Leicester), May 1953, pp. 41–42.

Scalabrini Ortiz, Raúl. *Historia de los Ferrocarriles Argentinos*. Buenos Aires, Devenir, 1957. (A re-publication of essays in which, between 1935 and 1946, the author expressed his disgust at British 'conspiracy' to 'enslave' Argentina.)

IX. THE FALKLAND ISLANDS AND DEPENDENCIES

Arce, José. *Las Malvinas*. Madrid, Inst. de Cultura Hispánica, 1950.

Argentina, Ministerio de Relaciones Exteriores y Culto. *Soberanía Argentina en la Antártica*. Buenos Aires, 1948. (The official statement of Argentina's Antarctic claims.)

Asociación Integridad Argentina. *Son Argentinas las islas Malvinas?* Buenos Aires, 1918.

Bates, Mrs D. B. *Incidents on Land and Water* . . . 5th ed. Boston, E. O. Libby, 1858.

Beltrán, Juan G. *El Zarpazo Inglés a las Islas Malvinas*. Buenos Aires, Gleizer, 1934.

Boyson, V. F. *The Falkland Islands*. London, O.U.P., 1924.

Caillet-Bois, Ricardo R. *Una Terra Argentina: Las Islas Malvinas*. Buenos Aires, Peuser, 1948.

Christie, E. W. Hunter. *The Antarctic Problem*. London, Allen & Unwin, 1951.

The Falkland Islands Company Ltd, 1851–1951. London, Falkland Islands Company Ltd, 1951. (A brief historical record published on the occasion of the company's centenary.)

Bibliography

Frezier, Amédée François. *A voyage to the South Sea* . . . London, Jonah Bowyer, 1717. (Frezier was a navigator from St Malo, and his book contains one of the most valuable early records of the Falkland Islands.)

Goebel, Julius. *The Struggle for the Falkland Islands*. Yale Univ. Press, 1927. (The best book on the subject.)

Great Britain, Colonial Office. *Falkland Islands and Dependencies*. London, H.M.S.O. (A factual report, usually published biennially, with historical chapters and bibliography.)

Hernández, José. *Las Islas Malvinas; and a letter by Augusto Lasserre*, ed. by Joaquín Gil Guiñón. Buenos Aires, Joaquín Gil, 1952. (José Hernández, the author of *Martín Fierro*, published this newspaper article in 1869. Lasserre was the Commander of the Argentine navy at that time.)

Mackinnon, L. B. *Some Account of the Falkland Islands* . . . London, A. H. Baily, 1840.

McWhan, Forrest. *The Falkland Islands Today*. For the author, Stirling Tract Enterprise, Drummond Tract Depot, 1952.

Pernety, A. J. *The History of a Voyage to the Malouine (or Falkland) Islands* . . . trans. from the French. London, T. Jeffreys, 1771.

Pinochet de la Barra, Oscar. *La Antártica Chilena*. Santiago de Chile, Editorial del Pacífico, 1948. (An exposition of Chile's Antarctic claims.)

Pitt, Barrie. *Coronel & Falkland*. London, Cassell, 1960. (The story of the two naval battles, fought in 1914.)

Rodríguez, J. C. *La República Argentina y las Adquisiciones Territoriales en el Continente Antártico*. Buenos Aires, 1941.

Simpson, Frank A. *The Antarctic Today*. Wellington, N.Z., A. H. and A. W. Reed, in conjunction with the N.Z. Antarctic Soc., 1952.

Weddell, James. *A Voyage towards the South Pole* . . . London, Longmans, 1825.

X. CULTURE

Arciniegas, Germán, ed. *The Green Continent: Latin America by Leading Writers*, trans. by H. de Onís, &c. London, Editions Poetry, 1947. (An anthology in English of extracts from Latin American writers, including the Argentine authors Leopoldo Lugones, Victoria Ocampo, Julio Rinaldini, Ricardo Rojas, and Domingo Faustino Sarmiento.)

Arrietta, Rafael Alberto. *Historia de la Literatura Argentina*. Vol. I. Buenos Aires, Peuser, 1958. (Covering the period from the discovery to independence. Other volumes are to follow.)

Barager, Joseph R. 'The Historiography of the Río de la Plata Area since 1830', *Hispanic American Historical Review*, Nov. 1959, pp. 588–642.

Bibliography

Borges, Jorge Luis. *Aspectos de la Literatura Gauchesca.* Montevideo, Número, 1950. (An essay by a leading Argentine poet.)

Crawford, W. R. *A Century of Latin American Thought.* Harvard Univ. Press, 1945.

Espinoza, Enrique. *Tres Clásicos Ingleses de la Pampa.* Santiago de Chile, Babel, 1951. (Essays on F. B. Head, W. H. Hudson, and Cunninghame Graham.)

Fitts, Dudley, ed. *Anthology of Contemporary Latin-American Poetry.* Norfolk, Conn., 1942 and 1947. (Includes verses—with English translation on facing page—by several Argentine poets, among them Jorge Luis Borges, Luis Cane, Francisco López Merino, Conrado Nale Roxlo, Silvina Ocampo, and Pedro Juan Vignale.)

Furlong, Guillermo. *Nacimento y Desarrollo de la Filosofía en el Río de la Plata, 1536–1810.* Buenos Aires, Kraft, 1952. (Publicaciones de la Fundación Vitoria y Suárez.) (An encyclopaedic volume by a Jesuit.)

Ghiano, Juan Carlos. *Constantes de la Literatura Argentina.* Buenos Aires, Editorial Raigal, 1953.

González Garaño, Alejo B. *Iconografía Argentina anterior a 1820; con una noticia de la vida y obra de E. E. Vidal.* Buenos Aires, 1943. (An essay on the early prints of Argentine scenes; with a biography of Vidal.)

Güiraldes, Ricardo. *Don Segundo Sombra: Shadows on the Pampas,* trans. by Harriet de Onís. Penguin Books, 1948. (First published in Spanish in 1926. First English ed. published by Cassell in 1935.)

Henríquez-Ureña, Pedro. *Literary Currents in Hispanic America.* Harvard Univ. Press, 1949. (An excellent cultural history of Latin America.)

Hernández, José. *El Gaucho Martín Fierro.* Buenos Aires, Ateneo, 1950. (The famous epic poem, first published in two parts in 1872 and 1879.)

——— *The Gaucho Martín Fierro,* trans. into English verse by Walter Owen. Oxford, Blackwell, 1935.

Hespelt, E. Herman, ed. *An Outline History of Spanish American Literature.* 2nd ed. New York, Crofts, 1947.

Lloyd, A. L. *Dances of Argentina.* London, Max Parrish, 1954.

Mallea, Eduardo. *Conocimiento y Expresión de la Argentina.* Buenos Aires, Sur, 1935. (An essay by a distinguished novelist.)

——— *Historia de una Pasión Argentina.* 4th ed. Buenos Aires, Espasa-Calpe, 1945. (Colección Austral.)

Martínez Estrada, Ezequiel. *Radiografía de la Pampa.* 2nd ed. Buenos Aires, Losada, 1942. 2 vols. (Biblioteca Contemporánea.) (An interpretation of Argentine history and character.)

Otero, Gustavo Adolfo. *La Cultura y el Periodismo en América.* 2nd ed. Quito (Ecuador), Liebmann, 1953.

Bibliography

[Pilling, W.] *Ponce de León, or The Rise of the Argentine Republic; a novel by an Estanciero.* London, Chapman & Hall, 1878.

Rodríguez Monegal, Emir. *El Juicio de los Parricidas: La Nueva Generación Argentina y sus Maestros.* Buenos Aires, Deucalión, 1956. (A study by an Uruguayan literary critic, of the young Argentine writers of the 1950's.)

Sarmiento, Domingo Faustino. *Life in the Argentine Republic in the Days of the Tyrants: or Civilization and Barbarism,* trans. by Mrs Horace Mann, New York, 1868. (This is an English translation of Sarmiento's famous *Facundo,* 1845.)

Scalabrini Ortiz, Raúl. *El Hombre que está solo y espera.* Buenos Aires, Gleizer, 1931. (Essays on Argentine life.)

Zea, Leopoldo. *Dos Etapas del Pensamiento en Hispanoamérica: del romanticismo al positivismo.* México, Colegio de México, 1949.

XI. PERIODICALS

Atlante. London, The Hispanic and Luso-Brazilian Councils. (Published quarterly, 1953–5.)

Boletín Mensual de Estadística. Buenos Aires, Secretaría de Estado de Hacienda, Dirección Nacional de Estadística y Censos. (A monthly collection of official statistics.)

Business Conditions in Argentina. Buenos Aires, Ernesto Tornquist. (Quarterly.)

Fortnightly Review. London, Bank of London & South America.

Hispanic American Historical Review. Durham (N.C.), Duke Univ. Press. (Quarterly.)

Hispanic American Report. California, Stanford Univ. (A monthly review of current affairs.)

Inter-American Economic Affairs. Washington, Inst. of Inter-American Studies. (Quarterly.)

Journal of Inter-American Studies. Univ. of Florida. (Quarterly.)

Latin-American Business Highlights. New York, Chase Manhattan Bank. (Quarterly.)

Marcha, Montevideo (Uruguay). (A weekly which frequently publishes commentaries on Argentine political affairs.)

Quarterly Review, Bank of London & South America. (The first no. was published in July 1960.)

Realidad. Vols. I–VI. Buenos Aires, 1947–1949. (Directed by Francisco Romero and a distinguished editorial board, this cultural review ceased publication in 1949.)

Review of the River Plate. Buenos Aires. (Published at ten-day intervals.)

South American Journal, London. (Contained useful information on economic and financial matters until the ownership of the review changed in 1951.)

Sur. Buenos Aires. (The leading Argentine literary review since its

Bibliography

foundation by Victoria Ocampo in the summer of 1930-1931. Usually published monthly.)

U.N., Economic Commission for Latin America. *Economic Bulletin for Latin America*. Published twice a year. cf. 'The Problem of the Economic Development of Argentina' in vol. IV, no. 1, Mar. 1959.

INDEX

Index

Economic nationalism, 70–80, 83 f., 103–8, 128–30, 140, 148, 151
Ecuador, economic union with, 157
Education, 45, 47–48, 51, 109, 116–18, 119, 120 f., 177
Electric power, 107–8, 178
Employers' federation, 126

Falkland Islands, 8, 155, 162; Dependencies, 165–9, 179
Fárrell, Gen., 92, 101
Fascism and Nazism, 81, 84, 112
Five Year Plans, 107–8, 128–31, 149
Foreign capital, 45, 104, 130, 148, 150 f., 171, 185–6
Foreign relations, 82 f., 86, 99, 161; inter-Latin American, 155–62; see also under countries
Foreign trade, 70, 104, 125 f., 131 n. 70, 153, 187–9; inter-Latin American, 155–7, 161–2; see also I.A.P.I.
Frondizi, Dr Arturo, 138, 144–5
Fruit-farming, 5, 8, 9

Gauchos, 32–34, 37, 51–52, 56, 170 f., 173–5
Germany, relations with, 83 f., 89 f.; see also Fascism and Nazism
Great Britain: and war of independence, 18; invasions, 19–26; diplomatic representation, 35; economic relations with, 55–57, 78–80, 83 f., 154 f.; investments (1939), 83; cultural and social influences, 83 f.; denunciations of colonialism of, 155; see also Antarctic; Falkland Islands; Meat trade
Grupo de Officiales Unidos (G.O.U.), 89, 92, 99, 118
Güiraldes, Ricardo, 173

Hernández, José, 33
Horses, 12 f., 16

I.A.P.I. (Instituto Argentino de Promoción del Intercambio), 105–6, 132, 134, 140, 142
Iguazú Falls, 10
Immigration, 35 f., 44, 51, 54, 58–62, 67, 76, 107, 180
Independence, War of, 18, 24–31
Indians, wars against, 38, 50, 54; help Welsh settlers, 58–59

Industry, 70, 75, 88–89, 104 f., 128–9, 146, 148, 154
Ingenieros, José, 178
Invasions, British, see under Great Britain
Irigoyen, Hipólito, 66, 69–71, 74–75, 88 n. 23, 101, 116–17

Japan, diplomatic relations with, 94
Jones, Michael D., 58–59
Juárez Celman, Miguel, 63 f.
Justicialismo, 127–8, 131, 155, 159
Justo, Gen. Augustín P., 73–74, 80–81
Justo, Juan B., 67

Labour, 70 f., 75–77; see also C.G.T. and under Perón, J. D.
Liniers, Santiago, 21, 25, 27
Livestock, see Cattle
Lonardi, Eduardo, 140, 141–2
Lucero, Gen. Franklin, 135
Lugones, Leopoldo, 173

Mallea, Eduardo, 172–3, 176
Martínez Estrada, Ezequiel, 171, 176
Meat trade, 37, 55–57, 78–79, 86, 105, 147 n. 12, 154
Mende, Raúl, 127
Méndez San Martín, Armando, 137
Mendoza, 6–7, 11
Mendoza, Pedro de, 12
Merchant navy, 108
Mexico, relations with, 159
Miranda, Miguel, 106
Mitre, Gen. Bartolomé, 44–45, 49, 53, 65 f., 84

National Democrat Party, founding of, 74
National Economic Council, 106–7
Nationalization, 101, 103–4, 107 f., 130 f.
Navy, 135–7
Nicaragua, relations with, 157, 159

Ocampo, Victoria, 114, 169
Oil, 1, 8, 129–30, 151, 153
Organización Regional Interamericano de Trabajadores (O.R.I.T.), 158
Ortiz, Roberto M., 81 f., 87

Index

Index

SET IN GREAT BRITAIN AT THE
BROADWATER PRESS, WELWYN GARDEN CITY,
HERTFORDSHIRE, AND REPRINTED
LITHOGRAPHICALLY BY FLETCHER AND SON, LTD.,
NORWICH